MW01181548

AMERICAN LITERATURE READINGS IN THE 21ST CENTURY

Series Editor: Linda Wagner-Martin

American Literature Readings in the 21st Century publishes works by contemporary critics that help shape critical opinion regarding literature of the nineteenth and twentieth centuries in the United States.

Published by Palgrave Macmillan:

Freak Shows in Modern American Imagination: Constructing the Damaged Body from Willa Cather to Truman Capote
By Thomas Fahy

Women and Race in Contemporary U.S. Writing: From Faulkner to Morrison
By Kelly Lynch Reames

American Political Poetry in the 21st Century
By Michael Dowdy

Science and Technology in the Age of Hawthorne, Melville, Twain, and James: Thinking and Writing Electricity
By Sam Halliday

F. Scott Fitzgerald's Racial Angles and the Business of Literary Greatness
By Michael Nowlin

Sex, Race, and Family in Contemporary American Short Stories
By Melissa Bostrom

Democracy in Contemporary U.S. Women's Poetry
By Nicky Marsh

James Merrill and W.H. Auden: Homosexuality and Poetic Influence
By Piotr K. Gwiazda

Contemporary U.S. Latino/a Literary Criticism
Edited by Lyn Di Iorio Sandín and Richard Perez

The Hero in Contemporary American Fiction: The Works of Saul Bellow and Don DeLillo
By Stephanie S. Halldorson

Race and Identity in Hemingway's Fiction
By Amy L. Strong

Edith Wharton and the Conversations of Literary Modernism
By Jennifer Haytock

The Anti-Hero in the American Novel: From Joseph Heller to Kurt Vonnegut
By David Simmons

Indians, Environment, and Identity on the Borders of American Literature: From Faulkner and Morrison to Walker and Silko
By Lindsey Claire Smith

The American Landscape in the Poetry of Frost, Bishop, and Ashbery: The House Abandoned
By Marit J. MacArthur

Narrating Class in American Fiction
By William Dow

The Culture of Soft Work: Labor, Gender, and Race in Postmodern American Narrative
By Heather J. Hicks

Cormac McCarthy: American Canticles
By Kenneth Lincoln

Elizabeth Spencer's Complicated Cartographies: Reimagining Home, the South, and Southern Literary Production
By Catherine Seltzer

New Critical Essays on Kurt Vonnegut
Edited by David Simmons

Feminist Readings of Edith Wharton: From Silence to Speech
By Dianne L. Chambers

The Emergence of the American Frontier Hero 1682–1826: Gender, Action, and Emotion
By Denise Mary MacNeil

Norman Mailer's Later Fictions: Ancient Evenings through Castle in the Forest
Edited by John Whalen-Bridge

Fetishism and its Discontents in Post-1960 American Fiction
By Christopher Kocela

Language, Gender, and Community in Late Twentieth-Century Fiction: American Voices and American Identities
By Mary Jane Hurst

Repression and Realism in Postwar American Literature
By Erin Mercer

Writing Celebrity: Stein, Fitzgerald, and the Modern(ist) Art of Self-Fashioning
By Timothy W. Galow

Bret Easton Ellis: Underwriting the Contemporary
By Georgina Colby

Amnesia and Redress in Contemporary American Fiction: Counterhistory
By Marni Gauthier

Vigilante Women in Contemporary American Fiction
By Alison Graham-Bertolini

Queer Commodities: Contemporary US Fiction, Consumer Capitalism, and Gay and Lesbian Subcultures
By Guy Davidson

Reading Vietnam Amid the War on Terror
By Ty Hawkins

American Authorship and Autobiographical Narrative: Mailer, Wideman, Eggers
By Jonathan D'Amore

Readings of Trauma, Madness, and the Body
By Sarah Wood Anderson

Intuitions in Literature, Technology, and Politics: Parabilities
By Alan Ramón Clinton

African American Gothic: Screams from Shadowed Places
By Maisha L. Wester

Exploring the Limits of the Human through Science Fiction
By Gerald Alva Miller Jr.

EXPLORING THE LIMITS OF THE HUMAN THROUGH SCIENCE FICTION

Gerald Alva Miller, Jr.

First published in 2012 by
PALGRAVE MACMILLAN®
in the United States—a division of St. Martin's Press LLC,
175 Fifth Avenue, New York, NY 10010.

Where this book is distributed in the UK, Europe and the rest of the world,
this is by Palgrave Macmillan, a division of Macmillan Publishers Limited,
registered in England, company number 785998, of Houndmills,
Basingstoke, Hampshire RG21 6XS.

Palgrave Macmillan is the global academic imprint of the above companies
and has companies and representatives throughout the world.

Palgrave® and Macmillan® are registered trademarks in the United States,
the United Kingdom, Europe and other countries.

ISBN: 978–1–137–26285–1

An earlier version of Chapter 2 appeared as "'To Shift to a Higher
Structure': Desire, Disembodiment, and Evolution in the Anime of
Otomo, Oshii, and Anno," in *Intertexts* 12.2 (Fall 2008: 145–166).

Library of Congress Cataloging-in-Publication Data

Miller, Gerald Alva.
    Exploring the limits of the human through science fiction /
Gerald Alva Miller, Jr.
        p. cm.
    Includes bibliographical references.
    ISBN 978–1–137–26285–1 (alk. paper)
     1. Science fiction--History and criticism--Theory, etc.
    2. Human beings in literature. 3. Critical theory.
    4. Science fiction films—History and criticism.
    5. Postmodernism. I. Title.

PN3433.6.M55 2012
809.3'8762—dc23   2012024025

A catalogue record of the book is available from the British Library.

Design by Newgen Imaging Systems (P) Ltd., Chennai, India.

First edition: December 2012

10 9 8 7 6 5 4 3 2 1

Contents

PREFACE

Minutes to Go!

Minutes to go. Souls rotten from their orgasm drugs, flesh shudder-
ing from their nova ovens, prisoners of the earth to come out. With
your help we can occupy The Reality Studio and retake their uni-
verse of Fear Death and Monopoly.

—*William S. Burroughs* (Nova 7)

For some, genre literature and film constitute nothing more than
fodder for "geeks" and social malcontents. But for others, genre literature allows the audience to explore the human in new ways—it
probes the darker sides of fear and desire (horror), it takes us to nonexistent yet nostalgic lands (fantasy), or it allows us to imagine ourselves differently (science fiction). This project embodies almost eight
years of thinking, researching, and writing about science fiction, and
it derives from the belief that science fiction increasingly represents
the genre most capable of critically engaging with our postmodern
world. In essence, we are all already characters in a science fiction
novel. Whether the future in which we currently reside is utopian or
dystopian is, no doubt, a matter of interpretation. But, for many of us,
society is already the dystopia that Orwell, Huxley, Zamyatin, and
others imagined so many decades ago. It has arrived in an unexpected
and more subtle form—but *the society of control and surveillance is*
here. This project does not seek to engage with such ideas in a paranoid fashion but instead to demonstrate how science fiction allows us
to critically engage with our present world according to a more complicated methodology.

We are increasingly a society on the brink: whether it is the brink of
destruction or transformation remains to be seen. Terrorism, economic
collapse, nuclear/biochemical warfare, and genocide constantly loom
over the horizon at any given moment. Of course, such problems have

always plagued human civilization, but the postmodern media sphere bombards us with images of real or potential devastation, forcing us to constantly feel as if we are living in a dystopian science fiction film or a disaster movie. But, simultaneously, the exponential advances in science and technology offer the promise of a world in which constraints increasingly disappear, communication becomes ever more instantaneous and egalitarian, and innovative technologies open up new possibilities for identity and self-expression. *We have minutes to go!* Metamorphosis or annihilation waits just around the bend.

There is a growing feeling among the left that something fundamental must change in the coming years. World civilization remains mired in the same old modes of politics and economics regardless of the rapid changes brought on by globalization and computerization. Despite the obvious need for human rights reforms, our global civilization continues to resist revisions to blatantly oppressive laws. And such resistance to change is not confined to the various oppressive regimes around the world—it also remains a major issue here in the United States where certain groups, like gay and lesbian individuals, are denied basic rights because our nation refuses to abandon its outdated concepts of ethics. The recent revolutions in Africa and the massive "Occupy" movements exhibit a growing, global dissatisfaction with the *status quo*, yet such groups often lack coherent plans of reorganization. They can only see ahead to the revolution and not beyond. Science fiction allows us to imagine the beyond: beyond our current societies and economic systems and beyond our current body and identity structures. In other words, science fiction lets us explore the limits of the human and what might possibly lie outside them. It allows us to storm the Reality Studio, as Burroughs calls it, that controls our world and our perceptions of it. More than any other genre, science fiction calls to us to imagine new ways of theorizing, philosophizing, criticizing, and living. Science fiction points the way beyond the limits of the human. It allows us to begin imagining how we might slip the bonds and constraints that limit us and embrace new orders of identity and existence.

Acknowledgments

Over the almost eight years since the first germs of this project took root in Tyler Curtain's provocative graduate seminar on science fiction at the University of North Carolina at Chapel Hill, I have been lucky to have the support and input of a large number of generous and influential individuals. First of all, I must express my sincere gratitude to Gregory Flaxman who has offered his tireless advice as my mentor for nine years now and who has guided me both with tough love and kind words throughout the realization of this project. A tireless, devoted, and brilliant academic, he became not just an exemplary mentor but a respected friend as well. Secondly, I must thank all the other professors who have provided me with support, guidance, and input over the years. In particular, Linda Wagner-Martin, Tyler Curtain, María DeGuzmán, and Priscilla Wald have been kind enough to read drafts of this project and offer advice from the initial proposal stage through the present. In addition, I want to thank all of my friends and colleagues at the University of North Carolina who helped create a friendly and intellectual environment. I would like to especially thank my friends Nathaniel Cadle, Henry Veggian, and Robert Martinez who read and offered advice on this project. I would also like to thank my high school English teachers, Susan Roberts and Jeanette Harris, who helped start me on my journey into the world of literary studies. Furthermore, I would like to thank my undergraduate professors and advisors, particularly Helen Lock and LaRue Love Sloan, who helped prepare me for my career as a graduate student and scholar. Finally, I want to thank my family for all their love and support over the years. My father (Jerry Miller), my mother (Debbie Miller), my sisters (Michelle Miller and Miranda Johnson), and my grandmothers (Dorothy Miller and Bobbie Arrant) have never lost faith in my lengthy and strange educational career. As a child, my father first introduced me to science fiction, and, without his influence, this project might not have taken place. My mother's unconditional love and our friendship has helped me through every hurdle and heartache over the years, my sisters remain two of my best friends, and my grandmothers have always encouraged me despite the weirdness of the subjects that I study. I also would like to express my gratitude to Scott Johnson, who has been my best friend for over 20 years now. Almost more like a brother than a friend, Scott has always supported me and aided in my intellectual introspections on marginalized genres such as science fiction, horror, transgressive cinema, and anime. Above all else, I must sincerely express the debt of gratitude that I owe to my wife, Leigh, who has stood by me throughout the entire creation of this project without ever wavering in her emotional support. Without her as my best friend and partner, this project would not have been possible.

The Genre of the Non-Place: Science Fiction as Critical Theory

Yet among all the distractions and diversions of a planet which now seemed well on the way to becoming one vast playground, there were some who still found time to repeat an ancient and never-answered question: "Where do we go from here?"

> —*Arthur C. Clarke* (Childhood's End *105*)

This suggests that far from being one code among many that a culture may utilize for endowing experience with meaning, narrative is a meta-code, a human universal on the basis of which transcultural messages about the nature of a shared reality can be transmitted.

> —*Hayden White (*"Narrative" *1)*

There are no facts, everything is in flux, incomprehensible, elusive.

> —*Friedrich Nietzsche (*Will *§604)*

As the above epigraph from Hayden White suggests, narrative functions as humankind's most basic tool for navigating and making sense out of reality—it operates as a kind of universal code that transcends linguistic and sociocultural boundaries and that lies at the very core of the human. From our personal thoughts to our everyday conversations, from the shortest flash fiction to gargantuan novels, narrative is always already philosophical because it represents our perhaps feeble attempts to carve manageable slices out of the chaotic manifold of sensory input. We are continuously assailed with stimuli not just in the sense that we live in an era of overstimulation and information bombardment but also in a more fundamental way. With our five senses receiving input that ranges from the constant streams of data that emanate from ubiquitous media sources to our continually evolving interactions with other individuals, one might expect our systems to crash already from information overload without ever considering the continual barrage of data assaulting us from smart phones, laptops, electronic billboards, televisions, GPS devices, and the various computer displays that appear everywhere from supermarkets to car dashboards to the backs of airplane seats. But we constantly delete or strain off irrelevant bits of data like so many unwanted cache files on a hard drive. Simultaneously, we string together one moment with the next, we connect important moments to our identity and personal history, and we revise our narratives concerning others as we continue to interact further with them. *To be human is to narrate*; hence, any attempt to explore the human and its limits must necessarily consider narrative. All narratives function on both ontological and epistemological levels—they build our images of the world and our selves, and they store and transmit our knowledge in intelligible packages. However, certain forms of narrative make the ontological and epistemological nature of narrative more apparent. Science fiction (SF) represents a unique form of narrative because it inscribes a distinctive kind of space that allows for the interrogation, elucidation, and generation of theoretical concepts. Science fiction also represents the postmodern genre *par excellence* because its modus operandi closely resembles that of postmodern literature and theory: both question and undermine our most solid beliefs about humanity, society, and the universe.

In his preface to *Difference and Repetition* (1968), Gilles Deleuze explains philosophy in relation to certain genres of fiction: "A book of philosophy should be in part a very particular sort of detective novel, in part a kind of science fiction" (Deleuze, *Difference* xx). Deleuze argues that a philosophical treatise performs a certain kind of cognitive work, a kind of work in which the author and the reader engage in the process of either seeking truths (as in detective fiction) or creating concepts (as in science fiction). Science fiction harbors an intimate relation with philosophy because, like the above quote from Arthur C. Clarke's *Childhood's End* (1953), it asks, "Where do we go from here?" But the genre also asks several other fundamental questions that persist as being central inquiries in both philosophy and critical theory. Where have we been? Where are we now? What else might there be? Who are we? And what might we become? In essence, this book seeks to demonstrate how science fiction examines these questions in a manner akin to critical theory; that is, it generates its own theoretical concepts that center upon what I term "the limits of the human," the various facets, characteristics, social forms, and ideologies that comprise, attempt to define, and delimit the human experience. But science fiction also extrapolates beyond our present condition to imagine the potential transcendence of these limits, to examine the possibility of new social forms and identity configurations, and to critically interrogate the current manifestations of the human, its philosophical outlooks, and its sociocultural practices. Ultimately, this book will expand upon and invert Deleuze's statement by demonstrating how critical theory strays into the realm of science fiction and, simultaneously, how *science fiction is always already critical theory*.

Over the last decade, numerous critics, such as Carl Freedman and Steven Shaviro, have similarly compared critical theory and science fiction. For instance, Freedman argues that science fiction and critical theory share certain "structural affinities" because "both speculate about the future" (Freedman 181). This affinity relies upon a "shared perspective"; as he explains, "What is crucial is the dialectical standpoint of the science-fictional tendency, with its insistence upon historical mutability, material reducibility, and, at least implicitly, utopian possibility" (Freedman 32). Such critics see science fiction as a conceptual form of narrative because it inscribes a kind of space that allows them to examine "concepts that have not yet been worked out" (Shaviro ix).

Both Freedman and Shaviro essentially use science fiction for the explication of existing theoretical concepts. There are countless examples of such readings of science fiction texts: Ursula K. Le Guin's "The Ones who Walk away from Omelas" (1973) explores the scapegoat function, Samuel R. Delany's "Aye, and Gomorrah" (1967) allegorically interrogates homophobia, *The Matrix* (1999) depicts a kind of Cartesian skepticism about the nature of reality and/or explores the nature of truth in a manner akin to Plato's "Allegory of the Cave," etc.[1] We could proceed onwards with this list of fairly blatant pairings or cite ones that Shaviro and Freedman themselves use. Such readings are useful, particularly when teaching a class of students, but I want to argue that science fiction harbors a more profound relation with theory—it enacts theory by both critically engaging with existing theoretical ventures and creating emergent theoretical concepts. But what is it about this particular narrative genre that resonates so profoundly with philosophy in general and with postmodern critical theory in particular?

Katherine Hayles begins to point us in a more useful direction by exploring the relationship between science and science fiction.

She claims that literature, particularly science fiction, and scientific discourse create a reciprocal circuit of influence upon one another:

> Nevertheless, I want to resist the idea that influence flows from science into literature. The cross-currents are considerably more complex than a one-way model of influence would allow...Literary texts [...] actively shape what the technologies mean and what the scientific theories signify in cultural contexts [...] Culture circulates through science no less than science circulates through culture. The heart that keeps this circulatory system flowing is narrative—narratives about culture, narratives within culture, narratives about science, narratives within science. (Hayles, *Posthuman* 21–2)

In *How We Became Posthuman* (1999), Hayles uses science fiction texts to trace the history of cybernetics, a field of study that has drastically revised the way we understand thought, identity, and being. The confluence of science fiction and scientific discourse allows Hayles to elaborate her own theory of the posthuman, a reconceptualization of the human for the postmodern, digital age that replaces the unified liberal humanist subject with a multiplicitous subject that cannot logically be separated from its technological environment: "Technology has become so entwined with the production of identity that it can no longer be separated from the human subject" (xiii). Because of this inseparability, "the posthuman subject is an amalgam, a collection of heterogeneous components, a material-informational entity whose boundaries undergo continuous construction and reconstruction [...] the presumption that there is an agency, desire, or will belonging to the self and clearly distinguished from the 'wills of others' is undercut in the posthuman" (3). Hence, Hayles uses science fiction as a means of investigating how technology has altered the human on a fundamental level; she begins to demonstrate how science fiction can itself be used to generate new theoretical concepts and to critically engage with existing ones.

If so many critics have adopted science fiction as the foundation of their theoretical explorations, then we must ask why the genre provides such fertile ground for critical endeavors. This question resides at the heart of this study, and its answer lies in beginning to conceive of literature itself as a space that the reader enters. This book hopes to demonstrate how literature in general creates virtual spaces that foster critical thought in ways that purely theoretical writings cannot and to explain why science fiction represents the paradigmatic genre for any understanding of how literature intersects with and becomes its own form of critical theory. To achieve this goal, this book will explore five different texts or sets of texts that deal with various concepts and theories vital to any understanding of the human: the different characteristics that define humans (i.e., identity categories, such as gender), the forces that motivate them (desire), the social formations that dominate them (power structures such as discipline and control), the power of memory and narrative that serve as humankind's primary means for ordering reality and generating discourse, and humanity's potential to evolve beyond the human and into the posthuman condition. By engaging with these texts, this book will elucidate how science fiction can serve as the perfect literary medium for performing critical theory while also revealing the inherently utopian impulses that underlie any attempt to conceptualize the human.

LITERARY SPACES; OR, THE SLIPPERY SLOPE OF TAXONOMY: A GESTURE TOWARD A THEORY OF A GENRE . . .

For the better part of the twentieth century, science fiction's pulp heritage hindered its acceptance into the pantheon of canon-worthy genres. In order to legitimate science fiction, critics of the genre began to develop histories, generate overarching theories, and demonstrate the possibilities inherent within the genre's form and content. In the struggle for science fiction's literary recognition, sci-fi critics began sketching genealogies that stretched back to a variety of "legitimate" authors in order to argue that science fiction represents a natural outgrowth of pre-existing literary modes, particularly those that dealt with the fantastic, the uncanny, and the marvelous, to use Tzvetan Todorov's designations. Todorov famously defines "the fantastic" as a genre of literature that functions at least partially through ambiguity:

> In a world which is indeed our world, the one we know, a world without devils, sylphides, or vampires, there occurs an event which cannot be explained by the laws of this same familiar world. The person who experiences the event must opt for one of two possible solutions: either he is a victim of an illusion of the senses, of a product of the imagination—and the laws of the world then remain what they are; or else the event has indeed taken place, it is an integral part of reality—but then this reality is controlled by laws unknown to us [. . .] The fantastic is that hesitation experienced by a person who knows only the laws of nature, confronting an apparently supernatural event. (Todorov 25)

Thus, the fantastic only exists as long as the nature of the events remains unclear. Once they receive either confirmation or refutation, the story moves out of the realm of the fantastic and into the domain of either the marvelous or the uncanny. For example, Edgar Allan Poe's short story "The Black Cat" (1843) represents a paradigmatic example of the fantastic because it never reveals whether the story's events derive from purely natural causes or whether some demonic force is actually at work.

To argue for the genre's legitimacy, critics since Todorov began tracing the origins of the genre back to canonical, nineteenth-century British and American authors: Mary Shelley, H. G. Wells, Jules Verne, Charles Brockden Brown, Edgar Allan Poe, and Nathaniel Hawthorne provided respectable, literary forebears of the modern genre. Perhaps more radically, certain critics, such as Darko Suvin, have argued that the genre's genealogy reaches back to even more antiquated sources: Jonathan Swift's *Gulliver's Travels* (1726; 1735), Francois Rabelais's *Gargantua and Pantagruel* books (1532–1564), Sir Thomas More's *Utopia* (1516), or even all the way back to the comedies of Aristophanes. Many of these critics attempt to establish totalizing theories of the genre that allow them to strictly demarcate its boundaries. To validate the genre, these critics intend their theoretical explications to act as aesthetic litmus tests by delineating certain texts as genuine science fiction while labeling others as "inferior" genres such as fantasy, horror, or myth.[2]

However, theories of science fiction become increasingly murky as the twentieth century progresses. For instance, the postmodern novel immediately problematizes any strict definitions of science fiction by virtue of its inclusion of various science-fictional elements: the works of William S. Burroughs, Thomas Pynchon, John Barth, Kurt Vonnegut, Don DeLillo, Kathy Acker, Italo Calvino, David Foster Wallace, Mark Z. Danielewski, and Jonathan Lethem—to name only a handful—all feature science fiction tropes as part of the otherwise realistic ontological framework of their novels, yet their works are seldom classified as science fiction.[3] Science fiction remains so inextricably linked to postmodern fiction that Brian McHale actually uses the genre as a means for explaining the distinction between modernist and postmodernist fiction: while "the dominant [mode] of modernist fiction is epistemological" and hence features the "logic [...] of the detective story," postmodernism operates in an ontological mode, meaning that it concerns itself with the projection of worlds in a manner akin to science fiction (McHale 9–10).[4] McHale contends that postmodernist fiction functions ontologically by projecting alternate visions of our own world or problematizing modernist ontological positions. As McHale's comments suggest, science fiction increasingly proves to be a genre that is necessary to grasp the postmodern world around us.

As science fiction has achieved ever more minimal recognition as a legitimate form of literature while simultaneously becoming a progressively slippery genre to define, critics have increasingly turned away from examining the origins of the genre or defining its traits and instead begun investigating why science fiction seems to more and more represent a privileged genre for contemporary critical theory. By adopting a similar approach to the genre, I intend to bypass the hopeless morass of taxonomic genre definitions and to alternately argue that science fiction represents a specialized form of narrative that generates the potential for new kinds of critical work because of the unique textual spaces that the genre creates for the reader and the critic.

The textual spaces actualized by science fiction have always played with genre categories such as the fantastic, the marvelous, and the uncanny. But the genre also transcends such categorizations by incorporating rational, scientific extrapolation. Like Todorov's concept of the fantastic, science fiction exists in a liminal space between realism and fantasy, and it is this space between the words "science" and "fiction" that harbors the genre's critical capacity. Just as the bar between the signifier and the signified in Ferdinand de Saussure's equation for the sign becomes such an object of speculation for Jacques Lacan and Jacques Alain-Miller, so does the space that separates "science" from "fiction" in the genre's designation become an essential site for grasping the genre's critical power.[5]

To understand the critical capacity of science fiction, one must first recognize that a literary text (or any kind of text, for that matter) creates its own kind of space and not simply the physical space that exists between the covers of a book. In addition to this physical space, texts also inscribe virtual spaces that the reader enters through the act of reading. In fact, with the advent of digital books and e-readers, texts no longer require any physical manifestation whatsoever; nonetheless they lay out spaces. In *The Practice of Everyday Life,* Michel de Certeau makes a similar case:

> Whether it is a question of newspapers or Proust, the text has a meaning only through it readers; it changes along with them; it is ordered in accord with codes of perception that it does not control. It becomes a text only in its relation to the exteriority of the reader, by an interplay

> of implications and ruses between two sorts of "expectation" in com-
> bination: the expectation that organizes a *readable* space (a literality),
> and one that organizes a procedure necessary for the *actualization* of
> the work (a reading). (170–1)

A text has no meaning before the reader—the reader *actualizes* it,
brings it to life. By being read, the words of a text, whether they are
housed in the physical object or merely exist in a digital file, open
up unto new vistas of experience. Michel de Certeau expands upon
this conceptualization of textual spaces when he explains the difference that exists between the writer and the reader's relationship with
this space: "Far from being writers—founders of their own place [...]
readers are travelers; they move across lands belonging to someone
else, like nomads poaching their way across fields they did not write,
despoiling the wealth of Egypt to enjoy it themselves" (174). The
writer thus builds virtual spaces that the reader actualizes by mentally traveling through them. The visionary horizons of the author
only come back to life in the mind of the reader. But each reader's
experience of a text will inherently differ—the mental images drawn
from readings remain unique and personal. A quick consideration of
cinematic adaptations of literary works quickly evinces the fact that
the reader always creates his/her own particular meaning from a text.
Part of science fiction's critical importance lies in the kind of spaces
that it depicts, spaces that often vary so radically from our everyday
life that they force us to experience radical difference and compel us
to engage in singular productions of meaning.

Science fiction achieves such levels of theoretical sophistication
because the genre inscribes a distinctive kind of space that could be
variously characterized as a heterotopia (Michel Foucault), a non-place
(Michel de Certeau and Marc Augé), or a plane of immanence (Gilles
Deleuze and Félix Guattari). In effect, this study will draw connections prevailing among these three different philosophical usages of
topology. Since it dwells upon difference, science fiction can most
effectively be understood as a heterotopian space; however, Augé's
conceptualization of the non-place and Deleuze and Guattari's theorization of the plane of immanence provide useful starting points for
understanding the kind of textual and critical space that science fiction demarcates.

Building off the work of Michel de Certeau, Marc Augé's *Non-
Places: Introduction to an Anthropology of Supermodernity* draws
a distinction between "anthropological places" and "non-places,"
the latter of which he argues have come to increasingly define the

postmodern landscape of our everyday lives.[6] An "anthropological place" organizes space and imbues it with meaning, identity, and history: it represents "the concrete and symbolic construction of space" that "serves as a reference for all those it assigns to a position, however humble and modest" (Augé 51–2). The anthropological place, then, provides "a principle of meaning for the people who live in it, and also a principle of intelligibility for the person who observes it" (Augé 51–2).

Places slice up the manifold of space into meaningful units that are connected to history and identity—they connect space with time and create the sense of community that allows the individual to connect both with his/her neighbors as well as with history. Augé contrasts these places with "non-places," sections of space that "cannot be defined as relational, or historical, or concerned with identity" (77–8). Augé mentions different types of non-places, but his interest remains centered on the kind of non-places through which people move with virtual anonymity: supermarkets, airports and airplanes, superhighways, and communication networks—he spends little time on this last manifestation because his study was published before the massive spread of the Internet. Non-places delimit spaces of mobility that attempt to hurry the subject along between places that are often separated by vast gulfs. They are sections of space to which subjects never develop profound connections—they are forgotten as soon as the subject finishes his/her time with them. Importantly, for our purposes, non-places also exhibit a profound link between spaces and texts—the real-world non-places that Augé discusses provide "instructions for use," directions and prohibitions that guide the individual's interaction with the non-place: the various signs in supermarkets, the road markers on highways, the guidelines that fill both the airport and the airplane that keep us moving along in an orderly fashion just like the moving sidewalks in airports that whisk us from one terminal to the next (96). But Augé mentions that there are other kinds of non-places that only exist in the words that evoke them.

Science fiction creates non-places partly in the sense discussed above since their relation to current history or identificatory schemas is tenuous, but they also operate precisely like the other form of non-places that Augé mentions: "Certain places exist only through the words that evoke them, and in this sense they are non-places, or rather imaginary places [...] Here the word does not create a gap between everyday function and lost myth: it creates image, produces the myth and at the same stroke makes it work" (95). Science fiction pushes us outside our everyday life into a non-place that creates new myths of reality, identity, and history that differ radically from those of our quotidian experiences. By taking a journey through these non-places, we move into a textual space that rethinks the very nature of place from the ground up: history and identity are recreated whole cloth, allowing us to critically engage with the manner in which narrative defines the places of our everyday lives. The science fictional non-place's "directions for use" might state: forget your world and yourself, rethink your reality and your identity, and embrace a kind of space that is ultimately foundationless because it remains unfettered by traditional narratives that organize and ultimately control our existence.

Essentially a non-place in itself, Deleuze and Guattari's "plane of immanence" provides a second conceptual framework for comprehending the kind of textual space that science fiction creates. For Deleuze and Guattari, the plane of immanence is prephilosophical: "Philosophy is at once concept creation and instituting of the plane. The concept is the beginning of philosophy, but the plane is its instituting. The plane is clearly not a program, design, end, or means: it is a plane of immanence that constitutes the absolute ground of philosophy, its earth or deterritorialization, the foundation on which it creates its concepts" (*Philosophy* 41). As they repeatedly make clear, the plane of immanence is immanent to nothing but itself because it exists before the creation of concepts, before any organizational system has imposed itself upon the image of thought:

> The plane of immanence is like a section of chaos and acts like a sieve [...] Chaos is not an inert or stationary state, nor is it a chance mixture. Chaos makes chaotic and undoes every consistency in the infinite. The problem of philosophy is to acquire a consistency without losing the infinite into which thought plunges [...] By making a section of chaos, the plane of immanence requires a creation of concepts. (*Philosophy* 42)

The plane of immanence is what separates chaos from the various rational orders that we impose upon it—it is the foundational ground of Deleuze's ontology because it represents the purely deterritorialized image of thought before it has been structured by any particular ideology or belief system. Essentially, the plane of immanence itself is a non-place because we can never truly experience it; however, by evoking it and attempting to place ourselves in contact with it, we can attempt to break free from the various systems of thought that imprison us and create new philosophies and identities from the ground up. The plane of immanence provides the perfect ground for

Deleuze's ontology because it does not reside on any stable conceptualization of being. Instead, only the slimmest membrane separates
it from pure chaos, hence allowing Deleuze to base his philosophy, at
the most fundamental level, on *becoming instead of being.*

In the prologue to *Thus Spake Zarathustra,* Nietzsche's Zarathustra
states, "The time has come for man to set himself a goal. The time
has come for man to plant the seed of his highest hope. His soil is still
rich enough" (Prologue §5). But, Zarathustra proceeds to explain
that humankind's time is running out because "one day this soil will
be poor and domesticated, and no tall tree will be able to grow in it.
Alas, the time is coming when man will no longer shoot the arrow of
his longing beyond man, and the string of his bow will have forgotten
how to whir! I say unto you: one must still have chaos in oneself to
be able to give birth to a dancing star" (Prologue §5). Undoubtedly,
Nietzsche represents the most profound influence on Deleuze's philosophy, and this passage discusses the plane of immanence in all
but name. For Nietzsche, the various slavish systems of morality
had "domesticated" human thought to the point where its soil (the
plane of immanence) was becoming barren. But by keeping chaos
within oneself, by staying in contact with the plane of immanence,
one becomes capable of shooting "the arrow" of one's thoughts and
desires beyond the horizon and ultimately "beyond man." The plane
of immanence proves essential to conceptualizing science fiction
because science fiction deterritorializes all our concepts of identity,
society, and reality and puts us back in contact with chaos. As Ian
Buchanan explains, for Deleuze, "deterritorialization" is "the process whereby the very basis of one's identity, the proverbial ground
beneath our feet, is eroded, washed away like the bank of a river swol-
len by floodwater—immersion" (23).

A complete deterritorialization back to the plane of immanence
functions like the demolition of a dilapidated building—the building
must be imploded from the foundation and its debris scraped away
before new structures can take its place, before a reterritorialization
can be effected. Only once the detritus of former thought structures
has been cleared away can one embrace the plane of immanence.
It strips away the various ideologies and philosophies that have tamed
our thinking and allows us to reconceptualize the nature of existence
and our identities. It re-establishes a link with chaos in a manner
that allows for what Nietzsche would term a "revaluation of values,"
a complete reappraisal of our most deeply held beliefs and ideas.[7] Of
course, one can never truly reach the plane of immanence; instead,
it serves as a kind of limit to which critical endeavor should aspire,

a return to a space that exists before philosophy so that philosophy can be rebuilt from the ground floor. Science fiction grants us this level of critical insight because it has cleared away and reimagined our world and humanity.

Finally, the most compelling characterization of science fiction's textual space is Michel Foucault's concept of the "heterotopia." While the non-place and the plane of immanence are vital to comprehending science fiction's critical capacity, the heterotopia provides the most compelling way of understanding the genre because it exposes the reader to radical difference in a manner that destabilizes our normal conceptualizations of reality. It inserts the marvelous into our reality in order to depict the manner in which our stabilizing visions of reality potentially prove to be nothing more than fantasies. We will return to the idea of heterotopias at length below, but to grasp the import of heterotopian spaces, we must first examine science fiction's usage of realism and estrangement. In *Archaeologies of the Future*, Fredric Jameson argues that science fiction highlights the

> "constructedness" of reality as such—the constructedness of science fact fully as much as of social institutions, the construction of gender and of the subjective fully as much as that of the objective categories through which we intuit the allegedly real world [...] everything we have hitherto considered to be natural and organic becomes as manufactured as the cityscape itself: and this is certainly a radical defamiliarization that much of Science Fiction has attempted to convey. (Jameson, *Archaeologies* 399)

Generally, science fiction achieves such defamiliarizations of reality by means of the ontological construction of alternate worlds or future civilizations that imagine reality otherwise, but recently such overarching theories of the genre have begun to crumble in the face of mutations in science fiction's basic aesthetic.

Certain contemporary science fiction authors have begun to produce texts that problematize the traditional aesthetic of the genre by abandoning its conventional, marvelous plot tropes and instead choosing to write narratives that occur in realistically depicted versions of the present or even the past. For example, William Gibson's recent trilogy (*Pattern Recognition* [2003], *Spook Country* [2007], and *Zero History* [2010]) or Neal Stephenson's historical epic *Cryptonomicon* (1999) and his newest novel *Reamde* (2011) all operate in worlds that seem indistinguishable from the real world in which the audience and the author dwell, yet they still concern the growth of technology in a manner akin to science fiction. These texts break with older definitions of science fiction as a genre based in estrangement. Nonetheless, most would still maintain that these texts constitute works of science fiction, so what marks them as instances of the genre if the spaces they depict contain nothing inherently unrealistic, otherworldly, or futuristic? Ultimately, it is their heterotopian structure that allows them to be categorized with the more fantastic examples of the genre.

In order to explore the changing face of the genre, this study will divide science fiction into two overriding tendencies: estrangement and realism. These two tendencies always overlap, but one will generally dominate the aesthetic of a particular text. I will term the traditional science fiction texts that privilege estrangement over realism "science fictions of estrangement," which I will distinguish from the above-mentioned "science fictions of the present" that eschew estrangement to pursue a predominantly realistic narrative mode. These two different modalities of science fiction remain connected because they both operate as what Michel Foucault terms heterotopian spaces, and it is the creation of such heterotopian spaces that marks science fiction as such an essential genre for critical theory. In fact, the heterotopian nature of science fiction allows the genre to not only intervene in theoretical discourses but to also become its own unique brand of critical theory. To understand science fiction as a heterotopian genre, we must first consider the twin prongs of the aesthetic that allow it to create these unique textual spaces.

REALISM VERSUS ESTRANGEMENT

I have already suggested that science fiction's critical capacity resides in the space that separates the words "science" and "fiction." Similarly, we could say that science fiction achieves new levels of theoretical complexity because it blends two seemingly contradictory aesthetic modes: realism and estrangement. In philosophy, realism refers to the "position that truth can be discovered by the individual through his senses" (Watt 12). Beginning with the philosophy of René Descartes and John Locke, realism represents an ontological position that stabilizes our concepts of the world and ourselves because it rests upon a fundamental belief in the capacity of our five senses to correctly relay information about the universe to our minds. Our minds then have the ability to use these sensory perceptions to discover truths about the nature of reality (McKeon 2). In the realm of literature, realism becomes another animal entirely because, as Jameson points out above, literature always remains inherently fictional regardless of its mimetic aspirations. Hence, we must define how an inherently fictional work can aspire to the label of realism while simultaneously considering how realism functions in a genre like science fiction that is predicated upon estrangement.

In *The Rise of the Novel*, Ian Watt compares the realist novel to juridical procedures: "the novel's mode of imitating reality may therefore be equally well summarized in terms of the procedures of another group of specialists in epistemology, the jury in a court of law. Their expectations, and those of the novel reader, coincide in many ways: both want to know 'all the particulars of a given case'" (31). Therefore, the realistic novel aims at "verisimilitude" by purporting to offer "a full and authentic report of human experience" (Watt 32). Of course, as Jameson indicates, the realistic impulse extends to virtually all our narratives from philosophy to science to literature: they each represent distinct attempts to—like the realist novel—render our world and our experiences of it in a manner that seems to coincide with our own subjective experiences. Hence, we can define realism as a discursive methodology that tries to project a faithful rendition of reality and our experiences of it by means of language (literature, cinema, etc.) or that strives to conceptualize some aspect of the human or the elements with which it comes into contact by way of its senses (science, history, philosophy, etc.). During the course of this project, both branches of realism will remain vital to my exploration of science fiction, and, ultimately, I will demonstrate the manner in which science fiction undercuts realism at its source by problematizing our basic concepts of reality and opening them up to new theorizations.

For an audience to relate to a text's story, it must retain some sense of realism; otherwise, it devolves into mere fantasy or becomes akin to avant-garde cinema that breaks all ties with narrative verisimilitude and chooses instead to revel in surrealistic imagery to which viewers must ascribe their own meaning(s).[8] While science fiction must similarly retain a certain dosage of realism—it must still deal with particular individuals in specific worlds at certain times, etc.—it also harnesses another powerful aesthetic force: estrangement. And this use of estrangement grants science fiction the power to function as its own form of critique. Appropriating the term "estrangement" from Bertold Brecht, Darko Suvin famously defines science fiction as "the literature of cognitive estrangement" (4).[9]

For Brecht, *verfremdungseffekt* (estrangement or alienation effect) was a method of staging and directing theater that would render the ordinary unfamiliar:

> The A-effect [*verfremdungseffekt*] consists in turning the object of which one is to be made aware, to which one's attention is to be drawn,

from something ordinary, familiar, immediately accessible, into something peculiar, striking and unexpected. What is obvious is in a certain sense made incomprehensible, but this is only in order that it may then be made all the easier to comprehend. (143–4)

Science Fiction amps up the estrangement-effect by introducing radical difference into a world that otherwise seems to be presented according to the same (or an at least understandable) rationality. Suvin expands upon Brecht's definition when he argues that science fiction creates "a new strangeness" in which it works through a problem or set of problems: "SF takes off from a fictional ('literary') hypothesis and develops it with totalizing ('scientific') rigor" (4). For Suvin, science fiction functions like the scientific method: it posits a hypothesis and then experiments upon it through the twin acts of extrapolation and fabulation. SF serves as a mirror—we see ourselves when we gaze into it, but we always see ourselves transferred into the space of the Other. Science fiction, in a sense, always concerns aliens:

> Whether island or valley, whether in space or (from the industrial and bourgeois revolutions on) in time, the new framework is correlative to the new inhabitants. The alien—utopians, monsters, or simply differing strangers—are a mirror to man just as the differing country is a mirror for his world. But the mirror is not only a reflecting one, it is also a transforming one, virgin womb and alchemical dynamo: the mirror is our crucible. (Suvin 5)

Science fiction, then, functions like a funhouse mirror that renders our appearance uncanny and alien, or it fragments identity like the hall of mirrors from Orson Welles's *The Lady from Shanghai* (1947) in which identity splits and proliferates on an infinite scale. When we read or watch science fiction, we see ourselves "through a glass darkly," or perhaps—to follow along with this Biblical cliché— science fiction finally allows us to see "face to face" for the first time.

Science fiction, then, always reflects our reality, but it also points the way to other possibilities—it is both cognitive (realistic) and estranging (marvelous, to use Todorov's designation). Freedman expands upon Suvin's definition to explain why cognition and estrangement remain vital components of science fiction's aesthetic and to stage these twin aspects of the aesthetic as a dialectical circuit:

> Science fiction is determined by the *dialectic* between estrangement and cognition. The first term refers to the creation of an alternative fictional world that, by refusing to take our mundane environment for granted, implicitly or explicitly, performs an estranging critical interrogation of the

> latter. But the *critical* character of the interrogation is guaranteed by the operation of cognition, which enables the science-fictional text to account rationally for its imagined world and for the connections as well as the disconnections of the latter to our own empirical world. (*Critical* 16–7)

Hence, science fiction must contain enough realism for its estrangement to still seem rational. This sense of estrangement depends upon the textual world of the science fiction narrative differing radically from the real world of the audience. For Freedman, the play of similarity and difference grants science fiction its theoretical powers because the ongoing process of juxtaposition on the part of the reader endows science fiction with a dialectical power unavailable to other genres. Freedman contends that all critical theory remains dialectical at its core, and hence science fiction acts as a critical genre because it involves the reader in a similarly dialectical thought process. In all of Freedman's examples, science fiction operates theoretically because the strange new worlds reflect—dialectically and critically—on our own, but must sci-fi qua critique always function dialectically?

Science fictions of the present seem to preclude the possibility of such dialectical operations because their stories unfold in the real world of the reader; that is, they give the realistic tendency precedence over estrangement. Because he remains mired in dialectical reasoning, Freedman's theory of the genre cannot account for the rise of science fictions of the present, and he ultimately achieves little more than using works of science fiction to textualize or illuminate existing critical discourses. Contrary to this, I contend that science fiction is a far more radical genre: it does not simply explicate theory—*it enacts it*. Science fiction proves to be a critical genre not because of its dialectical relation with the reader but because it transports the reader into a heterotopian space, a space of radical difference and multiplicity. Science fiction always functions by making our reality seem uncanny either through the depiction of other possible worlds or, in the case of science fictions of the present, by reflecting our world back to us in a way that renders it unfamiliar. Because it incorporates such radical difference into its own narrative structure, sci-fi not only contains the potential for intervening in theoretical discourses but also for spawning its own theoretical concepts.

Utopia versus Heterotopia

In *What is Philosophy?* Deleuze and Guattari discuss the power of utopias and their relation to sociopolitical theory. Instead of turning to More's classic text, they turn to Samuel Butler's utopian novel *Erewhon* (1872) because, as they say, it "refers not only to no-where but also to now-here" when its title is rendered anagrammatically, thus marking utopia as a genre concerning the present moment (100). For Deleuze and Guattari, the utopian constitutes more than a mere dream or narrative form because it also "designates that conjunction of philosophy, or of the concept, with the present milieu—political philosophy" (100). Therefore, utopia represents both a fictional and a theoretical space, the nexus of the two that allows an author to imagine other possible worlds. But, as Tom Moylan argues, political utopianism became tarnished during the early twentieth century due to the experiences of "world war, totalitarian rule, genocide, economic depression, nuclear destruction, massive famine, and disease" (*Impossible* 8). Utopia's practicality as an avenue for radical thought diminished because "utopia had been absorbed into the affirmative ideologies of the totalizing systems of Stalinist Russia, Nazi Germany, and the corporate United States" (*Impossible* 8). The utopian fell under suspicion because of the inherent dangers it purportedly harbored; hence, authors began to pen dystopian narratives that criticized the totalizing systems that had arisen from bastardized utopian dreams: Yevgeny Zamyatin's *We* (1932), Aldous Huxley's *Brave New World* (1932), and George Orwell's *Nineteen Eighty-Four* (1949) provide the paradigmatic examples of such texts. But the dystopian experiences of twentieth-century history have not permanently banished utopian visions from the discourse of critical theory, and, as we shall see, the utopian impulse underlies and structures all forms of human discourse.

As Jameson points out, Suvin confines science fiction to the Russian Formalist concept of "making strange" and Brechtian *Verfremdungseffeckt* (estrangement effect). Jameson argues that Suvin's definition of science fiction "posits one specific subset of this generic category devoted to the imagination of alternative social and economic forms" and hence "exclud[es] the more oneiric flights of generic fantasy" (*Archaeologies* xiv). Jameson is correct in pointing out how Suvin fails to acknowledge "the existence, alongside the Utopian genre or text as such, of a Utopian impulse which infuses much else, in daily life as well as in its texts" (*Archaeologies* xiv). Jameson's comment remains tied solely to the utopian subgenre of science fiction, but it can be expanded to include science fiction as a whole, for science fiction always concerns our dreams of another world, our belief that reality could be rendered anew through the advent of new technology or the revision of current sociopolitical/cultural structures.

On the other hand, Jameson's arguments prove equally uncompelling because science fiction is not utopian in itself; while it concerns our utopian aspirations, it actually represents a heterotopian genre. Science fiction texts inherently problematize our quotidian, utopian daydreams of a better world—science fiction pushes our utopian conceptualizations of the world into a space that eviscerates them and reveals their potentially illusory nature.

Jameson maintains that utopianism (or, we might say, science fiction in general) remains a vital aspect of critical theory:

> What is crippling is not the presence of the enemy but rather the universal belief, not only that this tendency is irreversible, but that the historic alternatives to capitalism have proven unviable and impossible, and that no other socio-economic system is conceivable, let alone practically available. The Utopian not only offers to conceive of such alternative systems; Utopian form is itself a representational meditation on radical difference, radical otherness, and on the systemic nature of social totality, to the point where one cannot imagine any fundamental change in our social existence which has not first thrown off Utopian visions like so many sparks from a comet. (*Archaeologies* xii)

For Jameson, utopian thought represents one step on the dialectical path of social change, a step that must be overcome once it has outlived its usefulness, but a required step nonetheless. Like Freedman, Jameson remains tethered to the Hegelian/Marxist dialectic, but the relation between science fiction and utopian critical theory is not a purely dialectical one. Indeed, one can no doubt discuss the circuit between text and audience as a dialectical relationship; however, science fiction deals with difference on a more radical level—it delves into realms of radical multiplicity that have the potential to undermine our utopian structures of thought and society. Jameson and Freedman argue that science fiction provides the means for reflecting upon our current sociopolitical episteme or theoretical concepts, but sci-fi texts actually perform a far more profound function: they use estrangement to undercut our basic notions of reality, as is the case with science fictions of estrangement, or they reflect our reality in a fashion that demonstrates the fundamentally uncanny and potentially fictional nature of it. Science fiction, then, provides the ideal genre for grappling with issues of postmodern identity, since, as Thomas Docherty states, "postmodern narrative disturbs the neat equations of the economy of identity [...] In postmodern characterization, the narrative trajectory is from the assumed homogeneity of identity [...] towards an endlessly proliferating heterogeneity" (Docherty 143).

Science fiction destabilizes our traditional definitions of the self and society in favor of such drastic forms of difference and otherness. While Jameson contends that science fiction generally proves utopian because it reflects our daily utopian impulses toward a better life, science fiction does not, in reality, represent a utopian genre. Utopian stability vanishes along with unified, Modernist conceptualizations of identity. Science fiction generally depicts utopias as objects of critique or as tool for satire, marking sci-fi as a different kind of space: a heterotopia.

In his preface to *The Order of Things* (1970), Foucault explains that the utopian is not simply a kind of literature or sociopolitical theory but a type of ideal space that orders our reality on a daily basis: "*Utopias* afford consolation: although they have no real locality there is nevertheless a fantastic, untroubled region in which they are able to unfold; they open up cities with vast avenues, superbly planted gardens, countries where life is easy, even though the road to them is chimerical" (xviii). Utopias provide models for civilization that can never be achieved, but they function as the underlying impulse of our societies: we believe our cities, nations, and governmental systems can instill a sense of order and coherence in the world, that they can banish the demons of chaos and anarchy. As Foucault further explains in his essay "Different Spaces," "utopias are emplacements that maintain a general relation or inverse analogy with the real space of society. They are society perfected or the reverse of society, but in any case these utopias are spaces that are fundamentally and essentially unreal" (178). Utopias are the stuff of our wistful daydreams—they project our world as we would like it to be or they depict the "reverse" of our society in order to satirize our own sociocultural episteme.

Simultaneously, Foucault argues that another unique—and *real*—spatial organization exists:

> There are also [...] real places, actual places, places that are designed into the very institution of society, which are sorts of actually realized utopias in which the real emplacements, all the other real emplacements that can be found within the culture are, at the same time, represented, contested, and reversed, sorts of places that are outside all places, although they are actually localizable. Because they are utterly different from all the emplacements that they reflect or refer to, I shall call these places "heterotopias." ("Spaces" 178)

Heterotopias, for Foucault, are spaces that exist in actuality—he cites various examples such as cemeteries, gardens, brothels, and colonies. Science fiction could be considered as just such a place because, unlike the nonexistent worlds that it depicts (often utopias), the science fiction text actually exists as a physical space in our world that can move and touch upon all spaces. But, then, couldn't all texts be considered heterotopian? On one level, this is true, but science fiction proves to be the heterotopian genre *par excellence* because it makes the opposition between utopian and heterotopian spaces readily apparent. Similar to Suvin's usage of the metaphor, science fiction functions like the mirror that Foucault discusses:

> The mirror is a utopia after all, since it is a placeless place. In the mirror, I see myself where I am not, in an unreal space that opens up virtually behind the surface; I am over there where I am not, a kind of shadow that gives me my own visibility, that enables me to look at myself there where I am absent—a mirror utopia. But it is also a heterotopia in that the mirror really exists, in that it has a sort of return effect on the place I occupy [...] The mirror functions as a heterotopia in the sense that it makes this place I occupy at the moment I look at myself in glass both utterly real, connected with the entire space surrounding it, and utterly unreal—since, to be perceived, it is obliged to go by way of that virtual point which is over there. ("Spaces" 178–9)

The mirror renders the self "uncanny"—to use the term according to Freud's definition—because it transmutes the familiar into the unfamiliar.[10] It makes me an other to myself. Likewise, science fiction depicts worlds that are simultaneously recognizable to us (they have been cognitively developed) and yet fundamentally different (they estrange the audience on a profound level). And it is this uncanny effect of the heterotopia that grants science fiction its critical power.

Heterotopias prove unsettling because they strip away our utopian blinders to reveal their illusory nature:

> *Heterotopias* are disturbing, probably because they secretly undermine language, because they make it impossible to name this *and* that, because they shatter or tangle common names, because they destroy 'syntax' in advance, and not only the syntax with which we construct sentences but also that less apparent syntax which causes words and things (next to and also opposite one another) to 'hold together.' This is why utopias permit fables and discourse: they run with the very grain of language and are part of the fundamental dimension of the fabula; heterotopias (such as those to be found so often in Borges) desiccate speech, stop words in their tracks, contest the very possibility of grammar at its source; they dissolve our myths and sterilize the lyricism of our sentences. (*Order* xvii)

Foucault poses these concepts in his preface to *The Order of Things* because heterotopias tear at the foundations of the order of things, at the basis of our episteme—they rip apart our aspirations toward unity, coherence, and meaning. And, as Foucault suggests, these deterritorializing effects stretch all the way down from the super-structure of culture past the economic base and to the very heart of the human—language. In basic terms, then, science fiction strips away our utopian notions of humanity, its civilizations, and its place in the universe in order to delve into realms of otherness, chaos, and multiplicity. If science fiction depicts utopias, it is only to undermine their inherently naïve aspirations toward perfection. This is not to say we should not strive toward a more perfect society; instead, I want to argue that science fiction decimates our utopian daydreams (whether they be of our own real world and its potential meanings or of our possible futures) in a manner that allows us to either take critical theory in radical new directions or to wipe the slate of critique clean in order to enact new kinds of theorizing. By blending the tendencies of realism and estrangement together in its aesthetic, science fiction uses estrangement as a means of undercutting and problematizing our most sacred ideas about reality, identity, and society.

ANATOMY OF THE HUMAN: THE UTOPICS OF NARRATIVE AND THE THEORETICS OF SCIENCE FICTION

Carl Freedman once speculated that science fiction constitutes a genre with such breadth that fiction itself could be considered a sub-category of science fiction and not vice versa: "all fiction is, in a sense, science fiction. It is even salutary, I think, sometimes to put the matter in even more deliberately provocative, paradoxical form, and to maintain that fiction is a subcategory of science fiction rather than the other way around" (*Critical* 16). Freedman's claim may seem ludicrous upon first glance, but he suggests a valid point. All fiction projects a world (to use McHale's Pynchonian turn of phrase); that is, all fiction is removed from reality to some degree and hence involves the kind of ontological world-building generally only associated with science fiction. We can expand this point and claim that all narrative (not just all fiction) represents a kind of science fiction, and that so-called "realistic" or "truthful" narratives function as subcategories because they represent nothing more than specialized forms of sci-ence fiction in which the level of estrangement remains at a minimum.

All narrative is science fictional because even the most basic narratives engage in a form of world-building. Or, in other words, narrative provides the means by which the individual connects three-dimensional space together with the dimension of time in order to build a complete model of the world—narrative always harbors a realist impulse to string our sensory impressions together into a meaningful whole. Narrative functions as a utopian force of the psyche that attempts to render reality intelligible by inscribing patterns upon it. And based on Foucault's distinction between utopias and heterotopias, I want to claim that science fiction acts as a heterotopian genre of narrative, a genre that instantiates a new methodology for performing critical theory because it undermines and problematizes the utopian coherence of our narratives.

To understand how science fiction represents a heterotopian genre of narrative, we must first expand the designation "narrative" to its fullest extent. As H. Porter Abbot argues, "Narrative is the principal way in which our species organizes its understanding of time" (3). Abbot explains that we narrate on a constant basis, that language itself is predicated upon narrative, upon the ability to string signifiers together in a meaningful chain that expresses duration and action. In fact, many narratologists claim that narrative is a "deep structure" that is "hardwired" into the human mind (Abbot 3). Similarly, Roland Barthes explains how narrative represents one of the most basic characteristics of human existence: "narrative is international, transhistorical, transcultural: it is simply there, like life itself" ("Structural" 79). Therefore, narrative provides a common thread that runs throughout humanity. In essence, then, to be human is to narrate—it is an activity that ties together all the various peoples of the world. We can expand upon such arguments and claim that narrative functions as the predominant method by which humans are able to understand their experiences of space-time, to parse reality into discrete objects and durations—narrative provides the basis upon which all of the higher human discourses rest. Narrative is the hyphen in "space-time" that allows the human mind to join the dimensions of space together with temporal progression and to create a meaningful image of reality.

Of course, language itself proves to be narrative at its core. If we divide language into its two most basic components (nouns and verbs), then we can see that language is already divided into space and time, Kant's two pure *a priori* intuitions; that is, it is parsed into objects that occupy space and into actions that occur temporally.[11] Even the *cogito*'s most basic utterances (the "I think" and the "I am" of Descartes) operate as the most basic instances of narrative—the simple stringing together of a subject and verb.[12] Indeed, once you move beyond the mere naming of objects and into a world composed of actions, you have entered the realm of narrative. Through language, we learn to resolve reality into its basic elements, that include not just the division into subjects, objects, and actions, but also the logic of time that we learn through language: succession, continuity, causality, etc. Indeed, language first instantiates our understanding of different time periods with the most basic verbs: was (the past), is (the present), and will be (the future).[13] Hence, narrative provides the mechanism by which we sort and order the universe as we experience it—it serves as *the* motivating principle for the realist impulse.

Through the interplay of nouns and verbs, narrative creates its own vision of reality—the mind and the senses perceive the chaotic influx of data (sights, sounds, feelings, etc.), and narrative provides the means for the subject to order this manifold into coherence.[14] Paul Ricoeur refers to this fact when he argues for the "prenarrative quality of experience" (*Time* I: 74). In this term, Ricoeur is developing his theory of narrative as consonant dissonance; that is, "narrative puts consonance where there was only dissonance. In this way, narrative gives form to what is unformed" (*Time* I: 72). Thus, a narrative act must constantly attend an individual's sensory impressions, for only through the cohesive capacity of narrative can a person force unity upon the "unformed" manifold. Insofar as narrative provides the fundamental code that allows individuals to understand their experiences and perceptions and to relate them to others, then narrative serves a synthetic function in the human mind—it synthesizes the various external stimuli that an individual perceives into a coherent unity: "plot is always to some extent a synthesis of the heterogeneous" (Ricoeur, *Time* I: 216). Reality remains a chaotic mass of sensory input until it can be rendered in a narrative form.

Hayden White's concept of emplotment provides a crucial link here that will help us further tighten the knot between reality and its narrative representation. As White explains, emplotment refers to "the encodation of the facts contained in the chronicle as components of specific *kinds* of plot structures" ("Artifact" 83). White contends that the narrative impulse underlies the majority of human discourses from literature to history to psychoanalysis—each functions by means of inscribing minor events or facts into more complicated plot structures. But White's concept of emplotment can be enlarged to include not just the encoding of basic narrative elements into increasingly complex plots but also the more fundamental encoding of reality into basic narrative elements. The narrative activity then becomes a series of steps from the most foundational separation of space-time by way of the splitting of sensory input into objects, durations, events, and actions to using these basic narrative units as building blocks to create ever larger plot structures that can range from a short story to scientific or historical discourses to religious cosmologies.

Ricoeur goes even further by arguing that narrative provides the means for conceptualizing ourselves in relation to history. To be human is to recognize and learn to cope with the fact that our lives represent only a miniscule instant in the universal flow of time: we must consistently face the "disproportion between time that, on the one hand, we deploy in living, and on the other, that envelops us everywhere," or "the brevity of human life in comparison to the immensity of time" ("Narrated" 263). Ricoeur explains that one fundamental aporia of time stems from the opposition between these two versions of time, but history brings the power of narrative to bear upon time and solves this aporia: "historical time is constituted at the juncture of our shattered concept of time [...] historical time is like a bridge thrown over the chasm which separates cosmic time from lived time" ("Narrated" 263). History provides the means by which the human species carves meaning out of the chaos of space-time—it is narrative, finally, that gives us the order and purpose we require and provides the basis for our sense of identity.

Paul Ricoeur's theory of the narrative self argues that we function like characters in a story: "characters in plays and novels are humans like us who think, speak, act, and suffer as we do" (*Oneself* 150). Of course, these literary characters are not "real," but as Ricoeur points out, our identities represent a mix of personal history and fiction:

> As for the notion of the narrative unity of a life, it must be seen as an unstable mixture of fabulation and actual experience. It is precisely because of the elusive character of real life that we need the help of fiction to organize life retrospectively, after the fact, prepared to take as provisional and open to revision any figure of emplotment borrowed from fiction or from history. (*Oneself* 162)

In the narrative self, "history and fiction are woven into each other—again, somewhat like the two strands of the double helix" (Seerin 52). Only through the act of fabulation can a subject create some semblance of identity for him/herself. Consequently, all theories about reality, history, and identity prove to be partly utopian fictions because they only contain the facts that have passed through the sieve of narrative, a sieve that strains the multiplicity of existence and history down into discrete portions capable of digestion by the human mind.

Narrative's utopianism resides in its implicit hope that reality and our perceptions of it can be ordered in a meaningful way and that we can create meaningful existences for ourselves, but science fiction decimates this hope by choosing to craft an alternate kind of space—the heterotopia. Science fiction texts represent this peculiar space known as the heterotopia because they deterritorialize or problematize certain schemas of organization or power—they potentially reveal realism to be nothing more than a utopian phantasm because they put the reader and the critic in contact with the immensity of the universe in all its multiplicity. Or, to use Ricoeur's terminology, science fiction strips away the consonance on the surface to reveal the underlying layers of dissonance. Of course, the heterotopian space of science fiction differs depending on whether the text represents a science fiction of estrangement or a science fiction of the present. By resituating words, ideas, and concepts in fantastic settings, science fictions of estrangement shatter their unity and coherence through the act of fabulation, hence making such texts fertile ground for theoretical work. Science fictions of estrangement can thus function as a means of heteropianizing critical discourses, of pushing them into realms of radical difference that allow the critic to examine the implications of these theoretical frameworks and of generating their own theoretical concepts within certain fields of critical discourse. On the other hand, science fictions of the present function as heterotopian spaces by depicting how our reality itself has become a kind of science fiction, how estrangement has crept into our daily lives, or how our supposedly stable conceptualizations of our present world prove to be nothing more than utopian dreams. Ultimately, science fiction reveals the illusory nature of the narrative impulse that lies at the heart of the human. Because of this, science fiction highlights how all our narratives concern nothing more or less than the human itself.

Approaching Infinity: Exploring the Limits of the Human

In calculus, the term "limit" refers to a value that a function approaches as a different variable advances toward a separate value. Limits are often used in equations involving variables as they move closer to infinity. While this project undoubtedly deals with the limits of the human in terms of boundaries, it also involves the mathematical definition of the term because it explores the endless potentialities that science fiction opens up. Science fiction undercuts any notion that ours is the only possible version of reality; instead, the genre exposes us to an infinite number of worlds, allowing us to reconceptualize our current understandings of identity, society, and reality and to imagine ourselves otherwise. Science fiction breaks through the limits of the human and puts us in contact with infinity. Ours is a society in which we are always approaching infinity: population growth, life extension, the endless expansion of knowledge and media via computer networks, the possibility of expansion into space, etc. increasingly place infinity within our grasp on a quotidian basis. But, simultaneously, infinite destruction and tragedy loom across the horizon of the future. Science fiction places us in communication with both kinds of infinity: it depicts the endless negative and positive ramifications of reaching toward the infinite, which has the potential to either exponentially expand our sphere of knowledge or to annihilate us completely.

To delve into the various limitations of the human and science fiction's different modalities for investigating them, this book devotes two chapters to examining the aesthetic of estrangement before turning to a theorization of science fiction's use of realism: I will pursue each of these two tendencies by means of one chapter on a fictional example(s) and a second one on a cinematic model(s). While developing these theories of estrangement and realism, each chapter will simultaneously explore a particular aspect of the human, for science fiction and critical theory inherently concern the nature of humanity, its attempts to define itself, its ideas and attributes, and its socio-political structures. In particular, this project will focus on four basic traits of the human and their conceptualizations in both science fiction and critical theory: gender, desire, the postmodern society of control, and memory. By investigating these four aspects of the human in both their science fictional and theoretical manifestations, this book will demonstrate how the genre of science fiction and the discourse of critical theory prove to be inextricably linked on a fundamental level.

To begin conceiving of science fiction as a heterotopian genre, chapter 1 will inaugurate this discussion by means of a text that explicitly labels itself as a heterotopian space: Samuel R. Delany's *Trouble on Triton*. *Triton* will allow me to stage a direct intervention in feminist theories of sex and gender, particularly those of poststructuralist thinkers like Judith Butler. *Triton* depicts a world in which gender has been undone by technology that lets individuals change not only their biological sex but also the objects that they find desirable; therefore, the novel questions whether gender's elimination would truly be liberatory or whether it might actually lead to insidious new forms of normativity. Chapter 1 ends with an investigation of how the absence of gender norms affects desire, and chapter 2 picks up with desire as it is conceptualized in Freud and Lacan's psychoanalysis and Deleuze and Guattari's schizoanalysis. By way of three Japanese anime texts (*Akira*, *Ghost in the Shell*, and *Neon Genesis Evangelion*) that depict disembodied forms of evolution, chapter 2 brings the dystopian discourse of psychoanalysis into direct communication with the utopian theories of schizoanalysis. These texts illustrate evolution beyond the current human state and question whether the eradication of what Lacan terms the "lack of being" would lead to the consequent destruction of all that characterizes the human.

Chapter 3 moves away from estrangement to begin theorizing what I term "science fictions of the present," sci-fi texts that forego or diminish estrangement in favor of adopting a primarily realistic aesthetic. This chapter examines how William Gibson's *Pattern Recognition* and *Spook Country* stage the September 11th attacks as a defining moment in the history of the twin forces of postmodernization and globalization. In effect, 9/11 serves as the culminating instant in which the postmodern regime of control finally displaces the older modernist, disciplinary regimes of power. Ultimately, then, Gibson's novels portray the present as science fiction, as a world that has become fundamentally estranging and that already features the technological and socio-cultural changes predicted by earlier, modernist science fiction authors. Chapter 4 further develops my concept of science fictions of the present by turning to two cinematic examples that exhibit a similarly unestranging aesthetic. Through a reading of Chris Marker's *La Jetée* and Shane Carruth's *Primer*, this chapter explores how these films' counter-spectacle style renders our reality uncanny in a way that permits us to rethink how film captures reality and ultimately how cinema itself always functions as science fiction. By investigating the nature of the cinematic medium through two time travel films, this chapter will also look at the crucial role that memory and narrative play in any definition of the human and within the discourses that humans generate.

Finally, in my conclusion, I will turn to a more classic example than the previous chapters: Arthur C. Clarke and Stanley Kubrick's *2001: A Space Odyssey*. The conclusion will focus mostly upon Kubrick's film to bring together the various aspects of the human that I will have explored in the previous chapters. While it has structural similarities to the films in chapter 4, *2001* also draws together the various other themes and theoretical concepts examined in this book (identity, desire, and control) by focusing upon the theme of evolution.

Indeed, *2001: A Space Odyssey* provides the perfect coda for this book because it concerns the ontogenesis of the human itself from its origins in prehistoric hominids to its metamorphosis beyond the boundaries of the body in the far-flung corners of the universe.

CONCLUSION: ONWARD TO THE HETEROTOPIAN!

Any theorization of the human must deal with not just categories like gender and forces such as desire that comprise the human condition but also the environments within which humans interact as well as the media through which the human can be represented: fiction, critical theory, cinema, etc. Ultimately, by virtue of its heterotopian nature, science fiction lays bare the utopian nature of all narrative and of theoretical discourse in particular and provides the perfect space (or non-place) for the exploration of these variables. Science fiction allows us to recognize the fictions that we use daily to protect our fragile sense of being and identity, and it forces us to consider the radical difference threatening to crush us from all sides or liberate us completely. It enables us to break with the various consoling utopian narratives that structure and govern our existence by submerging us in the disturbing and powerful maelstrom of heterotopian difference. By conceiving of science fiction as a heterotopian space, my project goes beyond the genre theories of Suvin, Freedman, and Jameson to embrace the radical difference that lies at the heart of the genre. Science fiction urges us onward beyond the consolation of utopian thinking, onward to a heterotopian space that may disturb even our most foundational concepts of reality. As Nietzsche argues in *The Gay Science*, even science represents a utopian form of faith:

> So, too, it is with the faith with which so many materialistic natural scientists rest content: the faith in a world that is supposed to have its equivalent and measure in human thought, in human valuations—a 'world of truth' that can be grasped entirely with the help of our four-cornered little human reason—What? Do we really want to demote existence in this way to an exercise in arithmetic and an indoor diversion for mathematicians? Above all, one shouldn't want to strip it of its *ambiguous* character: that, gentleman, is what *good* taste demands—above all, the taste of reverence for everything that lies beyond your horizon! (§373)

Science itself rests upon a faith that it can generate all-encompassing truths about the universe, that our "facts" represent the way things really are, that nothing lays beyond our horizon. While science fiction may depict utopias or dystopias, it functions on a fundamental level as a heterotopia, as a space in which we confront difference and reconnect with the potential horizons that exist beyond our current knowledge of science, philosophy, and history. Science fiction functions as critical theory because it dares to project itself outside the current constraints of so-called rational thought—it pushes us into a realm of otherness that still progresses according to a kind of rationality but a rationality not based solely on what we know to be "truth" but also on what might be possible in this or any other potential version of reality.

PART I

Science Fictions of Estrangement

Variables of the Human: Gender and the Programmable Subject in Samuel R. Delany's *Triton*

A normalizing society is the historical outcome of a technology of power centered on life.

—*Michel Foucault* (Sexuality *144*)

Fantasy is what allows us to imagine ourselves and others otherwise. Fantasy is what establishes the possible in excess of the real; it points, it points elsewhere, and when it is embodied, it brings the elsewhere home.

—*Judith Butler* (Undoing *217*)

The feminist redefinition of the term "gender" imbued the word with a utopian promise. Because of its utopian nature and its frequent explorations of the relations between the human body and identity, the critical apparatus of science fiction serves as the ideal narrative space for explorations of gender. Because many of his works openly grapple with theoretical concepts, Samuel R. Delany exemplifies the potential critical power of science fiction. Delany's fiction often functions as a direct critique of particular theoretical ideas or enterprises. For instance, "The Tale of Old Venn," the second of Delany's 11 Nevèrÿon tales, quotes Lacan at its outset and proceeds to examine the concept of the phallus, how it differs from the penis, and how it rethinks the Freudian concept of penis envy. Similarly, as this chapter will demonstrate, his classic novel *Trouble on Triton* can be read partly as a response to Foucault's notion of heterotopias from *The Order of Things* but also as a critical response to one of the most utopian areas of theoretical discourse: gender theory. Numerous classic works of science fiction have reimagined sex, gender, and sexuality in various provocative ways, but Delany pushes such science fictional examinations into radical new territories that open the terms up to retheorization.

Delany was one of the major figures of the New Wave science fiction authors of the 1960s and 1970s who began to explore contemporary social issues with new levels of complexity, insight, and sophistication than Golden Age sci-fi writers (Asimov, Clarke, etc.) had ever achieved. Numerous influential novels appeared that critically explored traditional gender roles. For example, Joanna Russ uses science fiction to make a feminist statement about gender roles in her novel *The Female Man* (1975). In the novel, four women from different parallel universes encounter one another. In their different worlds, the role of "woman" has been constructed in often diametrically opposed fashions. Russ uses the novel to problematize conventional gender roles and to illustrate the fact that gender is a social construct and not an aspect of identity that remains inherently tied to biology. Similarly, Marge Piercy's *Woman on the Edge of Time* (1976) concerns a mental hospital patient who begins receiving communications from a utopian future in which feminism and various other social reform movements of the 1960s and 1970s have triumphed. In her own time, the main character Consuela remains trapped by sexist gender roles that cause her to be institutionalized after striking her niece's abusive pimp. Whether the future is real or not remains ambiguous, but it provides hope for Consuela, and the depiction of this society imagines how our world could be restructured around tolerance instead of rigid identity systems based on repressive binarisms.

While Russ and Piercy depict the utopian possibilities of eliminating sexism, Margaret Atwood's *The Handmaid's Tale* (1985) paints a distinctly darker portrait of gender's future fate. Set in the Republic of Gilead, a theocratic state that has arisen within the borders of the former United States, *The Handmaid's Tale* depicts a dystopian society in which women have been almost completely stripped of their rights. For instance, they are not allowed to read and are often forced to breed with Gilead's wealthy men, who have barren wives that are only barely freer than the handmaids that are forced to "service" their masters. As the main character Offred learns to enjoy sex with a lover of her choice, the novel begins to reflect not just upon this feminist nightmare but also upon the way women are subjugated in our own world. In contrast to this, Ursula K. Le Guin's *The Left Hand of Darkness* (1969) is set on a planet named Gethen (or Winter) where biological sexes as we know them do not exist. There are no males or females—genders and sexual desires occur only once during each monthly cycle. Androgynous at their core, Getheans can become either sex during their monthly mating cycle called "kemmer." Hence, Gethen represents a society in which gender roles have never developed, and Le Guin uses it to explore how civilization might develop along completely different avenues in the absence of gender.

While these various works (and many others) use science fiction as a means of making feminist statements or exploring the problematics of gender, Delany constructs *Triton* in a manner that directly reflects upon the feminist goal of undoing gender. Le Guin's novel depicts the undoing of gender and absence of sexuation, yet Delany goes further by imagining what might arise in the place of gender without there being a significant biological mutation as is the case in *The Left Hand of Darkness*. As we will see, *Triton* takes the desire to undo gender to its logical extreme and examines the ways in which socio-cultural forces always normalize difference even in the absence of the conventional binarisms to which our civilization so ardently clings.

Welcome to Triton: Universal Recognition Guaranteed!

Triton appeared at an interesting juncture in Samuel Delany's career. Delany's last traditional science fiction novel was *Nova* (1968) after which he would not write another novel for five years.[1] In 1973, when he began publishing novels again, Delany chose to deal with more directly sexual themes and with stretching the boundaries of the genre. *Equinox* (1973)[2] was his first foray into sexually explicit science fiction, but it was 1975's *Dhalgren* that caused controversy with its almost "pornographic" sexual scenes (gay and straight ones) and its lack of customary science fiction elements. *Triton* (1976) continued Delany's work at the margins of science fiction: the novel does not concern itself with intergalactic warfare, colonists on a distant moon, or body augmentation (although all of these comprise the atmosphere of the novel), but instead with the experiences and possibilities of the subject in a utopian environment.

Triton details the experiences of one man (a rather problematic noun to use with regards to the character, as we will see) as he struggles to define his identity in rigid, immutable terms.[3] But identity on *Triton* proves anything but stable, and the novel examines the manner in which identifications attach themselves to subjects only to be sloughed off at later points in time.[4] The story of *Triton* occurs in a seemingly utopian society in which the struggle for equal rights has triumphed and in which total inclusivity has been achieved. Tritonian society extends recognition to all races, sexes, genders, religions, sexual orientations, kinship relations, and even fetishes. Triton functions as a "radical other" to our society because it stretches gender to a point where such a concept becomes almost meaningless (Moylan, *Impossible* 193). The number of gender identities has proliferated drastically because of new technologies that allow citizens to scramble their original identity coordinates and to create radically new subject positions through selective reproduction, sex changes, and refixation treatments that alter what objects a subject finds desirable. Nevertheless, Triton's utopian veneer proves deceitful because its new system of norms tarnishes the society's allure by replacing older binary designations with a complex taxonomic system that serves as the basis for a society of total control. Predicated upon computerization, the control society creates the illusion of freedom for its populace by keeping intricate demographic records on subject behavior and structuring the spaces of everyday life in a fashion that directs individuals' activities.

The reader experiences Triton through a third-person, limited-omniscient narration focalized around the main character, Bron Helstrom. The novel unfolds predominately in the city of Tethys on Neptune's largest moon, Triton, during the war between the Inner and Outer planets of our solar system. At the novel's beginning, war has already broken out between the Inner Planets (Earth, Mars, etc.) and the Outer Planets (predominately the moons of Neptune, Jupiter, etc.), but Triton has yet to become embroiled in the conflict. The novel never reveals the cause of the conflict, but it looms like a dark cloud across the peaceful expanse of Triton until it finally erupts violently later in the novel. Delany breaks with sci-fi conventions by focusing not on the war, which serves as a mere backdrop, but instead on Bron's psychological struggles to acclimate himself to life on Triton—he has recently emigrated from Mars. Bron works at a "computer hegemony"[5] in a field known as Metalogics, the form of logic people use in their ordinary decisions in place of the strict methods of formal logic. At the novel's outset, Bron becomes disillusioned with all aspects of his life. He suffers from a sort of corporate, white-collar malaise, but over the course of the novel this malaise becomes symptomatic of Triton itself.

Despite a prestigious title, Bron's occupation consists of little more than a cubicle existence. Once upon a time, he worked as a prostitute in Bellona, the major city on Mars, and the novel suggests that this life provided a more stimulating existence for him. But now Bron has settled into a quiet, corporate job in the far-flung regions of the solar system with no real aspirations or motivations. To ensure maximum happiness, Triton provides its citizenry with a variety of living arrangements ranging from polygamous family households to cooperative apartment buildings. Bron chooses to live in a single-sex, male, nonspecified sexual preference co-op because he seems so apathetic that even choosing the objects of his sexual cravings proves to be a matter of indifference.

Bron's monotonous life diverts from its normal course when he has a surreptitious encounter with a woman known as The Spike, a free-spirited producer and writer, who travels the solar system performing drug-enhanced "micro-theatre." Bron becomes infatuated with The Spike, who soon moves on to another planet and another government endowment for the performing arts, leaving Bron distraught in her absence. When his friend Sam departs for Earth on a secret mission, Bron accompanies him as part of his entourage in an effort to forget The Spike. On Earth, a clandestine government organization drugs, imprisons, and interrogates Bron. Eventually, he is released and spends some leisure time in Outer Mongolia, where he inadvertently reunites with The Spike whose theatre group is performing on the planet. Bron declares his love to The Spike, but she spurns him, and he despondently returns to Triton.

After their return, Inner Planet secret agents sabotage Triton's artificial gravity system, causing radical gravitational fluxes that decimate entire sections of Tethys. Bron's brief affair with The Spike, his visit to Outer Mongolia, and his horrific experiences during the gravity cut serve as the impetus for his decision to undergo a sex change operation coupled with a refixation treatment, transforming him from a man who desires women into a woman who desires men. After his operation, Bron returns to his normal life and attempts to fit into the Tritonian social matrix in his new role as a woman, but he remains incapable of adapting to the world's culture because he learns that Triton has developed a new system of normativity that squashes his desire. Because it depicts a world in which an individual can reprogram both his/her sex, gender, and sexual preferences, I will use Delany's *Triton* in this chapter to problematize gender theory's utopian aspirations by demonstrating how undoing gender does not necessarily guarantee an experience of freedom.

RECOGNIZABLE PERFORMANCES: INTELLIGIBLE SUBJECTS AND THE DOING OF GENDER

Written during the second wave of feminism, *Triton* appears at a unique moment in theoretical history. Initially, "gender" applied solely to the linguistic division of nouns in certain languages into masculine, feminine, or neuter. The word was infused with new, utopian valences in the 1970s when it was redefined as the socio-cultural construction of masculinity and femininity. Simone de Beauvoir first began to move feminist thought in such a direction in *The Second* Sex (1952) in which she famously stated, "One is not born a woman but becomes one" (267). While she never uses the word gender, Simone de Beauvoir divided the biological designation of sex from the socially constructed concept of "woman." She explains this division in terms of existence versus essence (a distinction she borrows from Sartre): a female exists because of the biological arrangement she receives at birth, but she does not truly become a woman (her essence) until socio-cultural norms shape her into that identity configuration.

Simone de Beauvoir's ideas proved revolutionary, but a true sea change occurred in feminist theory with the redefinition of the word "gender." Robert Stoller, an American psychoanalyst, often receives credit for developing the distinction between gender and sex; in *Sex and Gender: On Masculinity and Femininity* (1968), he argues that an individual's gender identity stems not only from biological characteristics but also from environmental and psychological factors during childhood. Second-wave feminists adopted Stoller's use of the term to distinguish biological differences (male and female) from socially constructed distinctions (the masculine and feminine roles grafted onto the biological bases).[6] In effect, gender became a way of denying arguments that claimed masculine and feminine roles derived purely from innate biological forces. This transformation of the very word "gender" generated new utopian potentials: if gender was indeed constructed, then perhaps it could be deconstructed and reconstructed anew.

By deterritorializing the categories of male and female, gender theory developed into a utopian narrative for a new organization of being—it harbored an ontological promise. In its most basic terms, gender theory represented the utopian wish of undoing gender—of removing the binary constraints that gender has traditionally placed on the subject, of exposing possible sites for radical rearticulations of gender, and of introducing the subject to a multiplicity of possible ontological positions (or modes of being). Judith Butler's theory of gender as performance took the social constructedness of gender to its utopian limit. Butler remained dissatisfied with simply demonstrating that gender roles do not stem inherently from biology; rather, she sought ways of disrupting the discursive construction of gender. Butler's series of interventions in gender theory began with *Gender Trouble: Feminism and the Subversion of Identity* (1990), the book that first introduced the concept of gender performativity. Butler continued her exploration in two sequels: *Bodies that Matter: On the Discursive Limits of "Sex"* (1993) and *Undoing Gender* (2004).[7] In her original preface to *Gender Trouble*, Butler explains that the central goal of her critical project is to enact "a strategy to denaturalize and resignify bodily categories" (xxxi). As she explains, this strategy is "based in a performative theory of gender acts that disrupt the categories of the body, sex, gender, and sexuality and occasion their subversive resignification and proliferation beyond the binary frame" (*Trouble* xxxi). Butler's work attempts to break down normative binarisms and to reinstate more inclusive frameworks in their place. Her key move toward refashioning gender norms lies in redefining gender as performance, as an "act of doing" rather than a mere "state of being" (Perry and Joyce 115). If gender is an act, then it can be performed in an infinite number of ways, and one actor can potentially slide between roles.

Of course, Delany wrote *Triton* well before Butler, yet the novel's engagement with gender inscribes a particular critical space that will allow us to extend Butler's theories to their limits. Instead of depicting gender's undoing as the foundation for a truly utopian space, Delany's novel imagines how, in the absence of prescriptive norms, the "matrix of intelligibility" (Butler's term for the grid of socio-cultural forces that governs the recognition of subjects) will merely transform itself into one that, instead of prescribing behavior, describes it in a manner so complex and precise that it can predict subject behavior on a global scale (*Trouble* 24). Anachronistically, Delany's novel transfers the tenets of Butler's gender theory into the premises of a fictional world, but the utopian promises of the theory, especially the suppression of disciplinary constraints, devolves into a society of total control that eliminates the subject's capacity to experience desire. Despite Butler's adamant assertion that her theories are not utopian, the vision of a world in which the episteme no longer includes gender as a primary ordering principle marks her work as participating fully in the utopian theoretical tradition. Inasmuch as Butler takes gender theory to its utopian limits, we can deploy the heterotopian space of science fiction as the means to "test" these limits, to imagine the consequences of gender's undoing.

My inspiration for the term "heterotopia" stems from Delany's subtitle to the novel, but, as his epigraph to Appendix B indicates, Delany takes the term "heterotopia" from Michel Foucault who defines it in contradistinction with utopias.[8] As we saw in the introduction, Foucault argues that whereas "utopias afford consolation," heterotopias prove "disturbing, probably because they secretly undermine language, because they make it impossible to name this and that" (*Order* xvii). Triton grants its citizens such utopian consolation through the acceptance of difference brought about by the instantiation of a new normative regime of control that I will term "typing." Delany's novel allows us to contemplate a variety of different questions implicitly posed by Butler's gender theory. For example, if universal recognition is achieved, then does difference disappear in the face of a total inclusivity? What happens to desire if difference disappears and the other is rendered as the same? What happens to social norms after gender disappears as an identity category?

To grasp how Delany's novel critically engages with the utopics of gender theory, we must first schematically lay out Butler's concept of gender performativity. Butler explains that the performance of gender represents an act that cannot be said to preexist the subject: "Gender is always a doing...though not a doing by a subject who might be said to preexist the deed" (*Trouble* 33). While she argues that doing constitutes a being's essence, she also recognizes that a fundamental categorization of the subject occurs before one becomes capable of performing any significant acts. At birth (or even in utero), a gender is assigned to the individual and a set pattern of behavior is prescribed for it or, rather, inscribed on it. Butler's theory of gender assignment derives from Louis Althusser's concept of interpellation, the process by which a subject is recognized by the institutions of power as well as by society as a whole. While still in utero, a person becomes a subject in various ways: subject to language (the name renders him/her insertable into sentences, and of course s/he must be gendered in order to be a subject of a sentence), subject to the family (the family applies its name to the child), and finally subject to governmental institutions (even before birth, laws govern the child's life, and upon birth s/he becomes a citizen). As Althusser states, "Individuals are always already subjects" because "ideology has always-already interpellated individuals as subjects" (119). Althusser's famous example of interpellation is the police officer hailing a person from behind on a street. Despite the other people on the street, the person realizes "the hail was 'really' addressed to him," and this process "hardly ever miss[es]" (118). Like Butler, Althusser argues that the creation of the subject is based on recognition. Consequently, an individual cannot perform his/her gender in just any manner but instead must adhere to a set system of norms if s/he desires to achieve recognition as a human with a particular gender.

Butler appropriates the idea of performativity from J. L. Austin's concept of the performative utterance: a type of speech act that does not describe but performs a particular action. The classic example of such an utterance occurs during a wedding ceremony when the phrase "I now pronounce you man and wife" actually performs the act of marrying. Over the course of his lectures, Austin revises this basic theory of performatives to delineate locutionary, illocutionary, and perlocutionary acts, thereby covering virtually the entire spectrum of speech acts. Locutionary acts consist "*of* saying something"; that is, they are the act of speaking itself. In an illocutionary act, the "performance of an act" occurs "*in* saying something"—the statement performs an act beyond the mere speaking of the words (Austin 99–100). For example, a certain set of words performs the act of asking a question. Finally, a perlocutionary act represents a speech act in which an action is performed *by* saying something. As Austin explains, it is an act in which "saying something...produce[s] certain consequential effects upon the feelings, thoughts, or actions of the audience, or of the speaker, or of other persons" (Austin 101). For example, someone uttering the words "Will you accompany me to the store?" can represent all three types of acts. It is locutionary because the person performs the act of speaking; it is illocutionary because the speaker performs the act of asking a question; and, finally, it could be perlocutionary if it persuades the speaker's audience to accompany him/her to the store. Under this later paradigm, Austin displays how utterances in general perform actions: stating, naming, describing, marrying, questioning, persuading, etc. At its most basic level, conceiving of gender as performative means the labeling of an individual as a certain gender produces (or performs) that very gender. In essence, then, Butler argues that *gender is a linguistic effect.*

But for performative utterances to function properly, they are obliged to observe strict formulas—they must be repeatable along certain linguistic (or even legal) guidelines. Similarly, gender performances also have to follow patterns in order to be recognizable: a gender performance must adhere to and replicate the gender norms of society. Based on Jacques Derrida's reading of Austin, Butler calls this process of repeating norms "citationality." Derrida explains that for performatives to "succeed" they must be performed according to a duplicable pattern that grants them their legitimacy. As Derrida says, "Could a performative utterance succeed if its formulation did not repeat a 'coded' or iterable utterance, or in other words, if the formula I pronounce in order to open a meeting, launch a ship or a marriage were not identifiable as conforming with an iterable model, if it were not then identifiable in some way as a 'citation'?" (18) With regards to a performative utterance such as "I now pronounce you ..."

in a wedding ceremony, the utterance cites the codified, legal norms that govern the ceremony of marriage and that legitimate the proceeding. Other performative utterances might not follow legal precedents but, instead, adhere to linguistic or grammatical patterns. For instance, asking a question follows a certain linguistic format including word order and vocal inflections that act as signposts for the listener. Insofar as gender is performative Butler argues, it must also be iterable—it must be capable of being repeated in accordance with a fixed system of patterns.

Unlike the legal norms that legitimate marriage or the grammatical ones that govern the asking of questions, gender repeats ideological norms that have been generated within the socio-cultural structures of power. The subject must perform his/her gender according to the gender norms that the episteme has produced (s/he must cite these norms) in order to remain recognizable. In this sense, gender theory's utopian side manifests itself in its desire to extend recognition to a wider array of individuals by means of what Butler terms the "proliferation of gender." For Butler, as for Hegel, only by way of recognition does the subject accede to its privilege qua subject: "Recognition is not conferred on the subject, but forms that subject" (*Bodies* 226).[9] Gender serves as the most basic form of recognition because it "figures as the precondition for the production and maintenance of legible humanity" (Butler, *Trouble* 11). As with other binary identificatory schemas, gender serves as one variable used to define the limits of the human.

An individual's status as human depends upon the recognizability of his/her performance as a particular gender within what Butler terms the "matrix of intelligibility": the field of social, cultural, discursive, and ideological forces that defines, delimits, and controls the human by determining which traits are required for an individual to receive the label of a particular gender (or of any other identity category). For example, can a subject's performance be labeled as male or female, masculine or feminine, gay or straight? If the performance of gender fails to cite the matrix of gender norms, then s/he will be designated as "abject," as one not worthy of subjecthood or humanity because of the illegibility of his/her performance. Butler undoubtedly appropriates the term "abject" from the work of Julia Kristeva, who defines it as being neither object nor subject:

> Not me, not that. But not nothing, either. A "something" that I do not recognize as a thing. A weight of meaninglessness, about which there is nothing insignificant, and which crushes me. On the edge

of non-existence and hallucination, of a reality that, if I acknowledge it, annihilates me. There, abject and abjection are my safeguards. The primers of my culture. (2)

Only by performing gender in a legible fashion can an individual achieve recognition as a gender, as a subject, and finally as a human deserving of the right to what Butler terms a "livable life" (*Undoing* 8). However, as Kristeva makes clear, the abject remains a necessary category for society to function. And *Triton* poses a fundamental question: to what degree do we require an excluded class of individuals, a marginal group that are labeled as abject but that are simultaneously used to shore up our definitions of ourselves and our civilization?

Utopian Resignifications: Radical Inclusivity and the Undoing of Gender

Like Butler, Delany's *Triton* recognizes that civilization requires normativity to function; therefore, the novel attempts to imagine how normativity would continue to function in the absence of traditional binaries. Similarly, while gender theory seeks to generate a praxis capable of escaping from and/or subverting the network of social normativization, Butler comprehends that norms cannot vanish entirely because society and human interactions depend upon them. But she seeks a way to reformulate the matrix of intelligibility in such a manner that its norms extend recognition to a vaster array of individuals. These norms or regulatory practices of the matrix operate through a primary exclusion; they demand "that certain kinds of 'identities' cannot 'exist'—that is, those in which gender does not follow from sex and those in which the practices of desire do not 'follow' from either sex or gender" (Butler, *Trouble* 23–4). For Butler, normativity contains within itself the key to enacting such subversions because norms remain mutable: "The terms by which we are recognized as human are socially articulated and changeable" (*Undoing* 2). These unintelligible genders—those who remain unrecognized by the matrix (drag queens, intersexed individuals, transgendered persons)—serve as the potential sites of subversion that can spur the process of resignification because "they appear only as developmental failures or logical impossibilities from within that domain" (*Trouble* 23–4). By their very existence, these unrecognizable gender identities contradict the norms and logic of the matrix: "Their persistence and proliferation, however, provide critical opportunities to expose the limits and regulatory aims of that domain of intelligibility and, hence, to open up within the very terms of that matrix of intelligibility rival and subversive matrices of gender disorder" (*Trouble* 23–4). By turning toward those identity categories that are labeled as "other" or "abject," Butler believes that normative definitions can be degraded from within and subsequently revised.

These unintelligible classes of individuals render the "cultural matrix" possible by functioning as the "other" against which intelligible subjects are defined (a null set, it should be remembered, is always required for any system to function properly). But Butler imagines that turning to these unintelligible genders opens the possibility of resignifying the matrix of intelligibility. The resignification of the matrix does not entail the elimination of norms but instead the construction of a subversive form of norm repetition, one that undoes gender by proliferating it beyond the bounds of the binary: "The task is not whether to repeat, but how to repeat, or, indeed, to repeat and, through a radical proliferation of gender, to *displace* the very gender norms that enable the repetition itself" (Butler, *Trouble* 189). But by the same token, Butler makes it clear that the resignification and rearticulation of norms must be a continuous and never-ending process: "That there can be no final or complete inclusivity is thus a function of the complexity and historicity of a social field that can never be summarized by any given description, and that, for democratic reasons, ought never be" (*Bodies* 221). There can be no final inclusivity because an excluded group must always remain in order for the "true" subjects to be able to define their selves. The point is not to eradicate exclusion altogether but to make the excluded an ever smaller category of individuals by a process of continual resignification. Butler's theory that the matrix of intelligibility can slowly be resignified represents a utopian wish that society as a whole can collectively reject the status quo in favor of social evolution and becoming.

Butler understands that norms cannot be entirely eradicated and instead seeks methods of reshaping the normative matrix through subtle subversions in the practice of everyday life. But would such a change in the social episteme really alter society and the subject for the better? This question lies at the heart of Delany's *Triton* because, as we shall see, Bron alters his sex and his gender yet still remains oppressed by both a crushing sense of *ennui* and a controlling normative system. While Butler desires the end of prescriptive norms, Delany's novel examines what happens when norms become purely *descriptive*. *Triton* displays how the forces of power will always seek to attain equilibrium and to achieve a homeostatic condition in which further change is negated before it even occurs. Triton attains this homeostasis by a transformation of norms in which they cease to be about prescribing patterns of subject behavior and instead metamorphose into types, a new kind of normativity that understands radical difference, that views all subjects as equivalent, and that seeks to describe (rather than prescribe) subject behavior in all its multiplicity.

Bron struggles with acclimating to Triton's allegedly utopian society because its normative matrix proves entirely foreign to the binary one to which he had grown accustomed on Mars. As opposed to the Martian binary matrix, Triton's matrix of intelligibility is based on the recognition of difference in all its multiplicity. The novel's subtitle, "An Ambiguous Heterotopia," immediately signals the importance of difference in *Triton*. The prefix "hetero-" evokes two important terms: heterogeneous and heterosexual. The word "heterogeneous" suggests that Triton acts as a mixture composed of a variety of different elements. The diverse factors on Triton prove to be the infinite number of identities available to subjects based on the combination of race, gender, sex, kinship relations, and sexual preferences.[10]

But by attempting to achieve this unity out of multiplicity, Triton transformed its normative matrix: the subject has been programmed (or typed) in vastly more complex ways than those implied by the typical, binary identity categories. This leads us to the second word with which "heterotopia" conjures associations: "Heterosexual." The novel actually proceeds to radicalize and redefine this word in terms of the difference already implied by the prefix "hetero-." In fact, the novel goes so far as to effectively deterritorialize sexuality, to open up the organizational plane of sexuality to the possibility of rearticulations and reorganizations. *Triton* allows us to reread the word "heterosexual" according to its actual etymological meaning instead of the traditional definition that has accrued to it. On Triton, heterosexual comes to mean that a multiplicity of sexual differences exist and that the subject is able to perform his/her gender in any manner that s/he chooses. "Heterosexual" ceases to imply a sexual difference based solely on male and female; instead, Triton divides individuals into "forty or fifty basic sexes, falling loosely into nine categories, four homophilic . . . Homophilic means no matter who or what you like to screw, you prefer to live and have friends primarily from your own sex. The other five are heterophilic" (99).

These forty or fifty categories only represent the "basic sexes," for Triton recognizes that infinite variation is possible. This sexual division not only contrasts sharply with the normative matrix of our contemporary culture but also with the normative system to which Bron is accustomed. While current matrices of intelligibility have become somewhat tolerant of particular gay and lesbian lifestyles, the majority still generally view these sexualities as aberrations. By contrast, the heterotopian society of Triton accepts homophilic lifestyles as natural occurrences, as categories with a biological basis and not merely as sexual orientations. Furthermore, Triton understands human desire in ways that would shatter the current matrix of intelligibility because it recognizes that desire is predicated upon a myriad of subtle preferences that extend way beyond the mere sex of the desired object. Triton accepts not only gay, straight, and bisexual citizens, but it also recognizes sadists, masochists, and even pedophiles as worthy of livable lives. Labels such as "abject" or "perverse" cease to have meaning in Triton's heterotopian society, and it is not my purpose here to explore the ethical dilemmas posed by Triton's acceptance of the more extreme forms of sexual preferences and fetishes. Instead, I want to argue that if the matrix of intelligibility based on the recognizability of gender performances is undone then a different system of nomenclature and subject demarcation must inevitably take its place—power will learn to use universal recognition to its own ends in order to control the populace.

Know Your Type: Behavioral Identifications and the Reappropriation of the Margins

Bron's efforts at adapting to Triton's normative regime narrativize the psychic struggles that would emerge from such plurisexualization. This problem emerges at the very outset of the novel, when the narrator explains that Bron "hated being a type" (5). Throughout the novel, characters evoke this term in order to understand other individuals and to navigate their existence on Triton. In effect, "types" have replaced traditional identity categories (sex, race, class, gender, ethnicity, and sexual preference) as the predominant means of negotiating social interactions, and they provide the foundation upon which governmental and corporate institutions erect a structural understanding of subject behavior. This ideology, which I term "typing," forms the basis for Triton's utopian attitude of acceptance and also represents the normative transformation that occurs after the proliferation of gender.

This chapter's discussion of typing shares some similarities to Edward Chan's argument concerning typology in the novel. Chan's article discusses what he terms "typology": "the identification of different social groupings based on affiliation, in turn aligned along individual desires" (187). Chan's definition of typology is thought-provoking but also limited because he is primarily concerned with the interplay between the individual and the group. As opposed to his designation of "typology," I will use the term "typing" throughout this chapter to describe this process for two reasons. First, it is a verb (or a gerund) and hence implies an action (or nominative form of action), and typing is an ongoing series (a constant process of resignification) that is repeated innumerable times on the individual and social level. Secondly, it maintains a connection to the computer technology that is so important in the novel—"typing" up the form of the subject.

While conventional identity categories (race, sex, class, etc.) still exist on Triton, their prescriptive edge has been dulled or "flattened"—they have developed into mere "matter[s] of surface" that amount to nothing more than "cosmetic issues" (Chan 191–2). The proliferation of gender (as well as other identity categories) has led to this flattening because the rigid lines of binary demarcation have given way to a more fluid system of identity politics (a smooth space of normativity instead of a striated one) that is based on a complex knowledge of types. Identity categories retain none of their current magnitude because they all receive equal recognition and become as changeable as one's clothes. The subject's ability to adopt and then cast off various components of their identity has forced the institutions of Triton to seek new methods for differentiating the mass of its citizenry, for reterritorializing Triton's deterritorialized identity plane.

Although other identity categories still exist in a flattened capacity, gender has effectively been undone on Triton, so designations such as "masculine" or "feminine" have become hollow distinctions: "Male and female names out here, of course, didn't mean too much," Delany writes, "Anyone might have just about any name" (41). Despite their rather dubious nature as indicators of sex, proper names still function as part of gender under most matrices of intelligibility because they are socially imposed attributes that gesture toward a subject's biological sex. Furthermore, an individual's clothing options have proliferated in such fantastic ways on Triton that they have ceased to function as gender markers. An individual might choose to wear cages on his/her hands, capital letters held up by suspenders, or no clothes at all.

Like proper names, then, clothing and appearance no longer dictate one's gender, for prescriptions concerning a gender's proper attire have vanished in Triton's heterotopian episteme. In fact, all of gender's external indicators have disappeared, leaving subjects with no method of determining another person's gender based on outward appearances. When Bron initially arrives at the clinic for his surgery, his discussion with the receptionist exemplifies the manner in which gender and sex have become divorced from their traditional designators. When asked his sex, Bron responds, "Well what do I look like?" The receptionist's retort highlights how sex and gender have become entirely disconnected on Triton: "'You could be a male partway through one of a number of different sex-change processes. Or you could be a female who is much further along in a number of other sex change operations...Or,' she concluded, 'you could be a woman in very good drag'" (*T* 219). As a conscientious Tritonian who adheres to the ideology of types, the receptionist cannot harbor presumptions about a subject's sex based on customary gender markers because such markers have been entirely divested of their meaning. The receptionist's comments attest to Triton's deterritorialization of the plane of sexuality. Triton has reduced gender to the plane of immanence and rebuilt it with entirely new concepts. Raised according to old concepts of gender, Bron remains incapable of embracing a society without the conventional strata of binary gender systems.

But if normativization has lost its prescriptive component and become entirely descriptive, then what are the elements that compose typing? Despite the "flattening" of identity categories, typing still groups individuals, but its rationale is predicated not just upon what Chan terms "primary" identity categories (race, class, sex, etc.) but also on a massive system of taxonomies that defines individuals based on an almost infinite number of categories: behavioral, psychological, medical, residential, familial, occupational, etc. As the novel explains, typing is a process by which subjects can be defined even "if only by their prejudices" as a particular category (*T* 5). This category (or type) represents the particular convergence of identity factors, behavioral patterns, personal beliefs, and attitudes that a subject exhibits at a particular point in his/her life. Chan argues that Triton's types are determined by "the identification of different social groupings based on affiliation, in turn aligned along individual desires," yet his argument does not examine the complexity of the typing ideology that bases itself not just on affiliations but also on subject behavior in a variety of different circumstances (187). He also does not mention that types are mutable. In actuality, typing indicates that the matrix of intelligibility now recognizes the performativity of subjects' identities: typing is founded upon performativity. Under the typing regime, subjects have internalized the belief in performativity and institutions of power have transformed it into a hegemonic force.

Triton has developed literal "technologies of gender," to use Teresa de Lauretis's terminology. In developing this concept, she draws upon Foucault's argument from *The History of Sexuality Vol. 1* about the political machinery involved in sexuality: "There had to be established a whole technology of control which made it possible to keep that body and sexuality, finally conceded to them, under surveillance" (Foucault, *Sexuality* 126). Teresa de Lauretis seeks to expand "beyond Foucault" in order "to think of gender as the product and process of a number of social technologies, of techno-social or bio-medical apparati" (3). For de Lauretis, then, gender is also a "construction" that is produced by the convergence of various "technologies" including political, cultural, scientific, and medical discourses. Triton has taken this concept of "technologies of gender" to the next level. Triton does not simply monitor citizen sexuality; they also develop medical technologies capable of transforming gender. Triton offers a seemingly utopian experience because it does not seek to construct gender so much as to allow its subjects to construct their genders and identities in their own ways.

But individual constructions (or performances) of gender ultimately prove to be far from unique; instead, Triton's technologies of gender construct a matrix of intelligibility in which no manifestation of gender is truly unique—some are just less common than others. Throughout their lives, the Tritonian citizens learn that "*every*one is a type." Even those who "pride…[themselves] on doing things contrary to what *every*one else does" are "a type too" (*T* 5–6). As the novel progresses, Bron is typed in a variety of different ways by society, by his acquaintances, and by himself. Because he hates being typed, Bron frequently attempts to subvert the system, going so far as to undergo medical procedures in order to retype himself. But Bron's desire for a marginal existence proves untenable under the Tritonian normative matrix, which constantly reterritorializes any attempts to deterritorialize its organizational plane. On Triton, it becomes impossible to exist in a truly liminal state because the system always recognizes one as a type, no matter how uncommon that type may seem. Hence, further resignification of the matrix of intelligibility becomes impossible because there is no margin from which to enact it: if one begins to perform one's identity in a different mode, then that individual is merely retyped based on the new manifestations of his/her identity and behavior.

Bron's friend, Lawrence, provides the clearest summary of the typing system: "My dear young man […] *every*one is a type. The true mark of social intelligence is how unusual we can make our particular behavior for the particular type we are when put under particular pressure" (*T* 5). Lawrence's words echo those of Butler in *Undoing Gender* when she argues that the performance of gender "is a practice of improvisation within a scene of constraint" (1). But, on Triton, the system of constraints has changed, and such improvisations no longer retain the potential for subversion because the matrix of types merely reappropriates any marginal position in which the subject attempts to ensconce his/her self. This process of "improvisation" or of rendering "unusual" serves as Bron's own *modus operandi*: "'I rather pride myself on occasionally doing things contrary to what *every*one else does.' To which Lawrence...had muttered...'That's a type too'" (*T* 6). Bron's attempts at "nonconformity" only serve to cast him in the role of the nonconformist type, which he continues to perform until his performance deviates enough for him to be retyped yet again. As we shall see, the ability to retype subjects grants the various institutions of power the means by which the system of control continually perfects itself, leading to more precise forms of control than those available to prescriptive normativization.

TO DO IS TO BE, TO DESCRIBE IS TO CONTROL: NORMATIVITY IN THE ABSENCE OF GENDER

How is it possible for institutions to typologize in the face of such multiplicity? The solution to this conundrum lies in the citywide computers that enable Triton to function as both a utopia of universal recognition and a society of control. Typing functions on both a local and global level. On the global scale, Triton's governing bodies and commercial entities have institutionalized and computerized their society's matrix of intelligibility, transforming it from a purely ideological structure into a computerized system by means of the city's computer databanks that track subject formations and collate data on individual behavior patterns. Meanwhile, on the local level, Tritonian citizens characterize one another based on an ideological form of typing that they have internalized as subjects. Bron's thoughts concerning the citizens of the u-l, the unlicensed sector of Tethys, provide a perfect example of the manner in which individual subjects engage in the ideological form of typing. Although prescriptive norms no longer exist on Triton, the society still requires laws in order to function in a civilized fashion: even though the novel never explicitly details them, Triton obviously still features laws that prohibit actions like murder, theft, and rape. The u-l offers yet another level of utopian freedom to the Tritonians because it is officially zoned as a lawless area of the city. In effect, then, Tritonian subjects can choose their society's level of organization and lawfulness. Based upon Bron's observations, the major difference between u-l people and non-u-l people consists in the willingness of the latter to discuss their personal history. Bron feels awkward anytime another person speaks about their past as if s/he was breaking a fundamental rule of etiquette: "Typical u-l…always talking about where they come from, where their families started" (*T* 48). Indeed, the system of typing proves to be little more than an ideologically normalized structure of stereotypes—except that, on Triton, stereotypes are not employed as acts of prejudice or denigration. Since the Tritonians accept difference as a multiplicity, types (or stereotypes) become a method of navigating interpersonal relationships and of choosing individuals that will be compatible with one's own type.

While the Tritonian populace has internalized the typing ideology, the various institutions of power have simultaneously computerized it. Like the citizens, the forces of power do not prescribe behavior for subjects but merely describe and type that behavior. Instead of particular genders, Tritonians are classified according to any number of different trends, all of which are acceptable and understandable by computers. For example, Triton's medical/technological industry refers to an individual subject's sexuality and desires as his/her "sexual deployment template" (*T* 228). Technicians read these templates by means of a scanning process that determines a subject's sexual orientation and his/her sexual predilections. Tritonian statisticians then track common patterns in such templates among the populace without any one template or configuration becoming the dominant form. Before his sex change operation, the technicians explain these processes to Bron: "There is no majority configuration…It's the current male plurality configuration—that is, the base pattern. The preference nodes are entirely individual, and so is any experiential deployment within it […] You're an ordinary, bisexual, female-oriented male—sexually that is" (*T* 228). Triton's matrix of intelligibility does not privilege one class of identities above the others—there is no majority. Instead, it merely recognizes particular tendencies amongst the citizenry.

While there is a "current plurality configuration," of which Bron is an example, this configuration in no way functions as a prescriptive norm. It merely describes patterns that the masses exhibit at a given point in time—it concerns itself solely with demographics, the same sort of profiling that companies like Amazon or Facebook use to sell us products. As Guy Davidson argues, *Triton* explores "the connection of sexuality to […] *the statistical imaginary*" (103). He further explains that "statistical thinking is a significant determinant of selfhood" because "people understand both their own identities and those of others in terms of statistical categories or types" (Davidson 104). As Davidson contends, *Triton* depicts the "ways in which statistical discourse facilitates the constitution of types and the fixing of desire" and, hence, "gestures towards the role of that discourse as a technology of the disciplinary society as well as its (arguably not unrelated) role as an instrument for the analysis and promotion of consumption" (104). Inevitably, this causes the precise effect that Butler seeks: "The proliferation of categories—the production of ever more refined types, preferences, and commodities that leads to the distinctively 'postmodern' fragmentation and lability of identity" (Davidson 104). Like Butler, then, Triton recognizes that identity is multiplicitous and mutable, so it provides the means for subjects to easily change the performance of their identity. Of course, Triton consistently reterritorializes these potentially subversive identity configurations, and such deterritorializations actually enable the typing system to become ever more precise in its understanding of subject behavior.

For example, by reading Bron's sexual deployment template, the technicians can also determine the nature of his desire—he has preferences ranging from "small, dark women with large hips to tall fair ones, rather chesty" (*T* 227–8). This knowledge enables the technicians to provide refixation treatments that divert a subject's desire toward a new class (or classes) of objects. The technicians cannot alter Bron's past experiences (his memories of being a man who predominately desires women or his recollections of his life as a prostitute), but they can realign his preference nodes to give him different predilections. Once the sexual aspects of a subject's type have been determined, reprogramming a subject's desire proves relatively simple. By enduring a short outpatient procedure, Bron undergoes a metamorphosis from a man who generally desires women into a woman whose major source of attraction is men. This procedure demonstrates the manner in which the institutions of power on Triton can collectively create a utopia, offering profound contentment to its citizens by eliminating all prescriptive norms.

Yet this move away from prescriptive norms proves less liberatory than it appears. For instance, Bron's sex change does not free him from the system of types; instead, he merely moves from one position in the matrix to another—he is simply retyped to reflect his sex change and refixation. A subject's type will be retyped any number of times throughout his/her life in order to refine the descriptions: each transformation or realignment only ends up providing the system with more information with which to typologize. As the technicians make clear before Bron's sex change, desiring such surgical procedures does not make the subject different but merely casts him/her into a particular type distinction. Of course, Bron is not a native Tritonian, and, as the technician further explains, he fits perfectly into the types that generally undergo sex change operations because he hails from a different planet—individuals from Earth or Mars exhibit a higher propensity to undergo sex changes. Since he has decided to undergo a sex change operation, Bron also represents an example of "the type who's pretty fed up with people telling you what you aren't or are" (*T* 220). While Butler's theory desires to reshape the matrix of intelligibility through a continual process of resignifications, the Tritonian matrix has appropriated this tactic of resignification and applied it to its subjects, hence providing the means for the typing system to comprehend the continual flux of identity.

This ongoing process of retyping becomes especially clear when Bron returns to work after his sex change. After a few days back at the hegemony, Audri, Bron's boss, explains to him that the company is about to retype him[11] in a negative way because his "efficiency index blinks a little shakily on the charts," thus signaling that he has potentially become an inefficient worker (*T* 241). This provides an example of how various institutions and corporations type the subject in different ways. As Foucault argues, power is distributed throughout social systems; that is, its presence is not housed in any one governing body or institution but instead is spread throughout the socius: "The factory was explicitly compared to the monastery, the fortress, a walled town [...] Disciplinary space tends to be divided into as many section as there are bodies or elements to be distributed" (*Discipline* 142–3). Of course, in this passage, Foucault is discussing the rise of discipline in the eighteenth century, but, as we shall see, the number of sites for power to exercise its influence only continues to multiply as societies move from the disciplinary society to the control society, from a striated space to a smooth space.

This continual resignification of a subject's type returns us to the linguistic aspects of these processes. Since all language is performative to some degree, then labeling an individual also performs an act. In this case, it is the act of description (an illocutionary act). While the subject may redefine his/her identity or gender through new manners of performing it, the various nodes of power simultaneously perform the act of redefining the latest manifestation of the subject's identity. Yet power's reclassification of a subject executes more than the mere locutionary act of stating the subject's type or even the illocutionary act of description; it also performs the perlocutionary act of controlling the subject through its application of such descriptions. By describing the subject in such complex terms, the various institutions of power achieve new levels of control: they negate any possibility of subversion by rendering the subject's behavior predictable. While Triton does not seek to prescribe subject behavior, the governmental powers use their descriptive knowledge of subject types to foresee how subjects will react given specific variables in certain circumstances. Like the medical center, the government of Triton proves capable of multifaceted forms of typing through the use of citywide computer networks. By recording and storing demographic information regarding major types and trends in its populace and by using complex equations with subject identities and behaviors acting as the variables along with the variables regarding certain situations, the Tritonian computers become capable of predicting how its citizenry will respond to different scenarios. Triton's normative matrix functions by defining what we might term "the variables of the human"—it reduces the human to a series of variables (identity categories, behavioral patterns, lifestyle choices, occupational history, etc.) that serve as components in algorithms that describe, predict, and consequently control the populace. Such mathematical forms of prognostication already exist in our current world. In the world of multinational corporations, the statistical technique known as predictive analytics not only generates predictions about future risks and business opportunities but also gathers information about consumers in order to forecast future buying patterns. This real-world business practice almost directly mirrors Triton's regime of typing.

The Tritonian government never overtly types subject behaviors for sinister ends in the novel, but it does use such knowledge to determine whether individuals are "safe" or not. As Sam explains, "We simply live in what the sociologists call a politically low-volatile society. And as I think I said: the political volatility of people who live in single-sex, nonspecified sexual-preference co-ops tends to be particularly low" (*T* 126). Bron responds, "In other words, given my particular category, my general psychological type, I've been declared safe" (*T* 126). Like real-world governments, Triton divides citizens into safe subjects and subjects who must be kept under heavier surveillance—it generates a "watch list." It bases these categorizations upon a variety of factors including such seemingly mundane characteristics as a subject's choice of housing. In this instance, the typing proves correct: Bron remains far too apathetic to ever consider any serious form of rebellion.

Triton's capacity to predict human behavior becomes apparent when the Inner Planets sabotage Triton's artificial gravity: "They had it all figured out—statistics, trends, tendencies, and a really bizarre predictive module called the 'hysteria index' all said that practically no one would want to go out to see the sky" (*T* 120). In spite of this fore-knowledge, Triton's predictions concerning the citizenry's reactions to the incident prove incorrect because "eighty-six percent of Tethys' population was outside within a minute and ten seconds, one way or the other, of the cut" (*T* 120). According to Sam, this represents the only time that the government's predictions have proven wrong: "But up until now—and this probably strikes you as quite naïve—it never occurred to me that the government could be wrong... about its facts and figures, its estimates and its predictions. Up until now, when a memo came down that said people, places, incidents would con-verge at set times and in given ways, they did" (*T* 120). What causes this aberration in typing's perfect record? Ultimately, this moment indicates that human nature retains one aspect that remains funda-mentally unpredictable: desire. Triton flattened desire and effectively banished it from their society, but, in this brief moment, it returns to plague the typing system with its irrational and unpredictable char-acter. Thus, we are led to the most important question concerning typing: what consequences do universal recognition and the develop-ment of typing have for desire?

In the Absence of Gender, in the Absence of Lack: Desire in the Society of Universal Recognition

Critics of *Triton*, including Delany himself, almost inevitably blame Bron's failure to adapt to Triton's social structure on his personal-ity and attitudes. In his *Diacritics* interview, Delany comments that *Triton* is "the one book of mine in which the thrust toward the main character is almost wholly critical. What's wrong with him? Why doesn't he function properly? Why can't he be honest with himself? Or with Others?" (198). Elsewhere, Delany explains, "You have to remember, what Bron usually does to justify his behaving in the selfish and hateful ways that make him such a hateful man is to manufacture perfectly fanciful motivations for what everyone else is doing—moti-vations which, if they were the case, would make his actions accept-able" ("Second" 335). Like Delany, the novel's critics have felt little compassion for Bron. He has been variously described as "an unre-generate male chauvinist"; as "incessant, pedantic, and boring"; as "unspontaneous, egocentric, coarse, and culture-bound"; and simply as "a sexist" (Moylan, "Negation" 248; Holliday 427; Blackford 144;

and Rogan 449). To be sure, Bron fits all these descriptions. So what precisely is his problem? In a world that produces so few dissatisfied citizens, why do Bron's selfishness and sexism persist? If we are to imagine a society that has transcended binaries and inscribed a matrix of intelligibility based on multiplicity and universal recognition, then we must also contemplate the manner in which such an alteration impacts desire. If, as Hegel argues, desire is always a desire for recognition, then what are the consequences for desire if all subjects receive complete recognition? As the technician explains to Bron before his surgery, "life under our particular system doesn't generate that many seriously sexually dissatisfied types" (*T* 220). Triton strives to satiate the desires of all subjects through its extension of recognition to all forms of sexuality and desire and its provision of the means to satiate these desires, producing few citizens whose sexual needs go unsatisfied. First, there are no consequences for engaging in promiscuous behavior because reproduction has become entirely selective. Secondly, the residential system on Triton promises a utopian sex life to its citizenry. If Tritonians desire a family life, then they can choose to live in various types of family communes on the outer rim of the city. Yet, the majority of citizens prefer to live in one of the assorted styles of co-ops that cater to the particular sexual needs of certain classes of individuals. In the co-ops, "sex was overt and encouraged and insistently integrated with all aspects of co-operative life" (*T* 57). Each building represents a utopian space for a certain group of individuals and provides a micro-expression of Triton's overarching utopian episteme. But while such a structure seems liberating, no space remains for fostering true desire since everything has already been provided for the subject—*there is no lack*. Satiation waits next door, down in the commons room, or in the diverse array of bars that cater to all manner of sexual predilections. From this perspective, Triton seems destined to produce blissful satisfaction for all its subjects, but Bron remains sullenly resentful of the system and resists the pleasures it affords.

Alcena Madeline Davis Rogan argues that in a number of his works "Delany problematizes the politics of identity by placing many of his protagonists in a landscape where difference dizzyingly proliferates" (448). For Rogan, Bron's problems on Triton result from his having emigrated from Mars, where sexual hierarchies still persist. Hence, Bron still lives under the "presumption that men and women are somehow essentially different" and "is unable to reconcile his experience of sexual nonidentitarianism with the epistemological framework that he inherited from Mars" (Rogan 449). The problem recalls the conundrum espoused in the forty-fifth proposition of Ashima Slade (one of Delany's fictionalized versions of himself) in "Some Informal Remarks towards a Modular Calculus." Indeed, this appendix acts as a critical model for reading the novel because it addresses the problem of moving between modular systems, discrete systems that are not immediately compatible with one another. In this proposition, Slade explains the nature of the modular calculus:

> The problem of the modular calculus, again, is: how can one rela-
> tional system model another? This breaks down into two questions:
> (One) What must pass from system-B to system-A for us (System-C)
> to be able to say that system-A now contains some model of system-B?
> (Two) Granted the proper passage, what must the internal structure of
> system-A be for us (or it) to say that it contains any model of system-B?
> (*T* 302)

The term "modular" derives from the mathematical term "modulus," which refers to changing numbers from one base to another, and *Triton* concerns precisely this kind of "calculus." In order to travel between modular systems, the second system must maintain a certain degree of similarity to the first for the subject to experience a smooth transition. Based on this proposition of Slade's, Rogan argues that Bron suffers because Triton does not retain enough of the binary model of identity.[12] While Rogan correctly notes that *Triton* concerns a migration between social models, her argument does not consider that Bron's movement between systems is not simply a relocation between social structures but also a migration from a prescriptive matrix to a descriptive one. Once the social matrix has been stripped of its prescriptive edge, then, consequently, desire falls dead in the absence of prohibitions.

Once the proliferation of gender has been pushed to its heterotopian extreme, then all forms of pleasure become recognized as legitimate. It is imperative here to distinguish between pleasure and desire—Triton provides its subjects with an infinite expansion of permissible pleasures that should not to be confused with desire. For Lacan, pleasure always refers back to Freud's pleasure principle: "when faced with a stimulus encroaching on the living apparatus, the nervous system is as it were the indispensable delegate of the homeostat, of the indispensable regulator, thanks to which the living being survives, and to which corresponds a tendency to lower the excitation to a minimum" (*Seminar II* 79). The pleasure principle strives to maintain a homeostatic condition in the subject by avoiding states of extreme excitation—it keeps pleasure to a minimum (thus avoiding *jouissance*) and hence "is related to prohibition, to the law, and to regulation" (Evans 148). On Triton, the amount of pleasure a subject can experience while still maintaining a state of equilibrium has radically expanded. Žižek would term Triton's social structure "permissive" because "public order is no longer maintained by hierarchy, repression, and strict regulation, and therefore is no longer subverted by liberating acts of transgression" ("May" par. 14). For Žižek, this lack of transgressive acts leads to the reinstantiation of hierarchical sexual dichotomies such as master/slave, top/bottom, butch/femme, dominant/submissive, etc. But, on Triton, these binary relations persist as mere fetishes in the much vaster constellation of available identities and acts, making transgression on Triton an almost impossible feat to achieve.

Why then does Bron not simply succumb to Triton's society of pleasure? The answer lies in distinguishing desire from pleasure. Unlike pleasure, desire "is neither the appetite for satisfaction nor the demand for love, but the difference that results from the subtraction of the first from the second, the very phenomenon of their splitting" (Lacan, "Phallus" 580). Lacan places desire firmly in the Hegelian tradition by claiming that "man's desire is the desire of the Other," that "means both to be the object of another's desire, and desire for recognition by another" (Lacan, *Seminar XI* 235; Evans 38). Furthermore, desire can never be satisfied because it springs from a fundamental lack in the subject: "desire is the relation of being to lack. This lack is the lack of being properly speaking. It isn't the lack of this or that [which would be need or demand], but lack of being whereby the being exists" (Lacan, *Seminar II* 223). This lack is both the lack of the other and the lack created by the insertion of the subject into language: "it is language that imposes a radical lack... It is that lack, which is inherent to the ability to speak, that creates desire, that feeds it, and sustains it... Desire becomes the unrelenting quest for that which is lacking, for the impossible that human beings cannot, however, renounce" (Cantin 40).

Žižek compares desire to Zeno of Elea's paradox involving Achilles and the tortoise. According to the paradox, Achilles can never catch the tortoise because he can only ever travel half the distance he has traveled previously, then half that distance, etc., creating an infinite series of points through which he must pass. Žižek uses the paradox as a metaphor for desire: "The libidinal economy of Achilles and the tortoise is made clear: the paradox stages the relation of the subject to the object cause of its desire, which can never be attained. The object-cause is always missed; all we can do is encircle it" (*Awry* 4). Therefore, desire always "eludes our grasp no matter what we do to attain it" (*Awry* 4). Lacan himself evokes Zeno's paradox in *Seminar XX* when he is discussing the economy of sexual satisfaction:

> Achilles and the tortoise, such is the schema of coming (*le schème du jouir*) for one pole (*côté*) of sexed beings. When Achilles has taken his step, gotten it on with Briseis, the latter, like the tortoise, has advanced a bit, because she is 'not whole,' not wholly his. Some remains [...] It is quite clear that Achilles can only pass the tortoise—he cannot catch up with it. He only catches up with it at infinity (*infinitude*). (8)

While sexual lust cannot be equated with desire, intercourse can provide a metaphor for understanding desire if we imagine a sex act in which the moment of climax is constantly delayed or interrupted in an endless Sisyphean cycle. Just like Achilles and the tortoise, our desire can never truly catch up with its object because that object is desire itself. Hence, the ceaseless postponement of desire continually burrows our lack of being deeper and deeper. No matter how often Achilles "comes" with Briseis, she always slips away again. Whether she escapes to the tent of Agamemnon or just a few steps down the road like the tortoise matters little—she remains equally uncatchable to poor, raging Achilles.

Triton believes it has eliminated lack by inundating the subject with a profusion of available pleasures in its attempt to achieve global contentment. Because of Bron's status as an emigrant, he remains trapped in the lack that still persists in hierarchical social systems. Bron craves transgression because it would allow him to achieve a level of difference that would grant him recognition as a being distinct from all others and as an individual who cannot be confined by definitions. Of course, as a good Hegelian, Butler understands that desire ultimately represents the desire for recognition, and it is precisely this recognition that she seeks to grant to traditionally marginalized subjects. But the utopian nature of her own desire for universal recognition forces us to consider how the undoing of gender might affect the very structure of desire. Under our moral matrix, norms function as prohibitions, and desire always designates a lack: the prohibited, the different, or simply the Other. *Triton* poses the question of what happens to desire when the subject begins to internalize norms that no longer prohibit certain forms of behavior and that no longer recognize radical difference. No doubt, the subject is still produced by the recognition extended by these norms and a "livable sociality" is still maintained because these norms provide subjects with the means for interacting with one another (Butler, *Psychic* 21). But desire falls dead in the absence of restrictions, for desire is always formulated upon prohibition and the fight for recognition. On Triton, prohibited pleasures have ceased to exist, and society has actually been structured around the project of providing fairly instantaneous gratification of subject's wants and needs, stripping desire of its motivating force. The question then becomes whether Bron actually remains trapped in the sexist model of society and desire, as Rogan would maintain, or whether Bron suffers because true difference—and consequently true desire—has vanished from the Tritonian matrix of intelligibility.

When all subjects receive recognition and when nothing is prohibited, then all subjects and all forms of pleasure are rendered the same; they become mere types, particular configurations of identity coordinates, behavioral attributes, and sexual predilections that prove instantly gratifiable under the reformulated matrix of intelligibility. Under this matrix of intelligibility, subjects internalize the computer typing system. No longer predicated on the struggle for recognition, desire becomes flattened into a mere search for compatibility: individuals search out others who are programmed in a complementary fashion that will allow them to run well in tandem with each other and generate the highest potential pleasure.

Although Triton provides an expansive array of pleasures for its citizenry, what Bron ultimately craves is the intense kind of recognition that we might term love, but Triton forecloses the possibility of love, an emotion (or state of being, it might be argued) based neither on sex nor on compatibility. For Lacan, love (*l'amur*) has a "fundamentally narcissistic structure"—it is "a phenomenon which takes place on the imaginary level, and which provides a veritable subduction of the symbolic [...] That's what love is. It's one's own ego that one loves in love, one's own ego made real on the imaginary level" (Lacan, *Seminar XI* 186; Lacan, *Seminar I* 142). Essentially, an individual craves love because it validates his/her love of their own ego. Furthermore, love resides in the subject's belief that another person can fill his/her lack by the union of the two separate individuals into what Lacan calls "the One": "Love is impotent, though mutual, because it is not aware that it is but the desire to be One" (Lacan, *Seminar XX* 6). Of course, like the object of desire, love's "tension towards the One" can never be satiated because the body's boundaries preclude true union—only partial penetration or envelopment is possible. But the return of love by another at least partly assuages this impossible desire for oneness: "Love demands love. It never stops (*ne cesse pas*) demanding it. It demands it...*encore*. '*Encore*' is the proper name of the gap (*faille*) in the Other from which the demand for love stems" (Lacan, *Seminar XX* 4).[13] In this context, gap should be understood in both the existential sense and the sexual sense. While desire is not always about literal sex, sex always conditions and structures it. Bron's troubles stem from the fact that no one on Triton knows how to love, so while Bron demands love, he never receives his *encore*. And since love represents a narcissistic love of one's own ego, Bron also suffers from a lack of self-validation.

On two occasions, both before and after he has become a woman, Bron displays his romantic nature, as we might call it. Before his operation, he entreats The Spike to flee Triton in search of a civilization that recognizes passionate impulses. Similarly, after his sex change, Bron declares his love to Sam and begs to become one of his wives. Both The Spike and Sam greet Bron's propositions with scoffing rebuffs, exemplifying Triton's viewpoint on such illogical formulations of desire. Indeed, Bron proves to be the only character in the novel that exhibits any passion. The other characters operate on cool, computerlike logic that treats emotional responses as counterproductive. Thus, at the novel's end, Bron remains trapped in his malaise. He desires a form of recognition that sees him as not merely a type but as a unique individual who is radically different from all others and hence deserving of not just a livable life but also of love. Ultimately, Bron still remains incapable of defining his own performance:

> Think! She thought: At one point there had been something she had thought she could *do* better than other women—because she had *been* a man, known firsthand a man's strengths, a man's needs. So she had become a woman to do it. But the *doing*, as she had once suspected and now knew, was preeminently a matter of *being*; and *being* had turned out to be, more and more, specifically a matter of *not doing*. (*T* 263)

In short, Bron realizes the havoc that typing has wreaked upon desire and human identity. If gender represents a doing (a performative) and if gender represents one of the fundamental methods by which a subject is recognized, then identity and desire plummet into a space of meaninglessness in the absence of gender. In these final moments, Bron is hurled back into the old existentialist dilemma of being versus doing (or of existence versus essence), but, on Triton, the relation between the two has been severed by the typing ideology.[14]

As a male, Bron had imagined himself performing the role of woman better than the women around him, yet he discovers that the womanly role no longer exists because gender roles themselves have vanished. Since society views all performances as intelligible, all performances of a subject's identity have become virtually the same. Love, that special form of recognition that Bron craves, demands that the beloved be seen as distinct from the masses, as a special individual. Ultimately, love represents a state of being as well as a doing—it is a performative that permeates one's entire identity. Love, as a state of being, includes a wide range of emotional states: happiness, passion, heartache, and jealousy, all of which require the subject to remain in an advanced state of excitation that demands the performance (doing) of actions that will hopefully lead to satiation. Love constantly teeters on the ledge between pleasure and *jouissance*, and one small push can send an individual plunging into the abyss of *jouissance* (a concept we will return to in the next chapter) in which pleasure slides into pain. Since the Tritonian episteme places such a high value on maintaining the contentment of its citizenry, love proves dangerous in its capacity to excite subjects into a state of unpredictable and potentially disgruntled behavior. Triton forces a subject's performance of their identity to remain a matter of "not doing."

Ultimately, then, the novel interrogates gender theory by examining how it strips away the basis of humanity and individuality by rendering all difference as the same. Under the regime of typing, difference has indeed become nonhierarchical, but gender theorists fail to realize that in the place of hierarchical or binary structures of difference, the institutions of power will merely resignify the populace in ways that prove, if not oppressive, then at least controlling. Whether such a state is desirable becomes the question that the novel poses to us: will the utopian proliferation of recognizable identities prove liberatory or will it, when actualized, squash the very difference that marks the status of the human and lead to societies capable of controlling the subject in radically new fashions? In the final analysis, when humans become incapable of experiencing desire, then does the human even exist anymore?

CONCLUSION: DWELLING IN THE NON-PLACE OF GENDER

According to the word's own etymological meaning, a utopia is fundamentally unrealizable—it is a "no-place," a place that does not (and potentially cannot) exist. Or, if we translate it into the language of Michel de Certeau, Michel Foucault, and Marc Augé, it is

a "non-place." Yet Foucault maintains that the most basic difference between utopias and heterotopias is that heterotopias are real
world spaces in which the individual experiences difference so radical that words and logic fail in the face of it. Gender theorists can
easily point to real world spaces that allow for the proliferation of
gender in certain confined areas, for example, the drag balls from the
documentary *Paris Is Burning* (1990) that Butler discusses in *Bodies
that Matter*. Whether Butler's utopian vision of a genderless society
will always prove unrealizable remains to be seen, but its attempt to
imagine a radically different version of society marks it as a devoutly
utopian endeavor. While Delany's *Triton* no doubt represents a "non-
place" due to its fictional nature, it nonetheless allows the critic to
transport gender theory into a heterotopian space by imagining the
consequences of its instantiation.

While gender theory has taught us an inordinate amount concerning the constraints that sociocultural forces place on an individual's
identity, we must still consider the consequences of entirely losing
this basic structure of human identity. No doubt, the society of
Triton remains only a distant, and perhaps unreachable, dream of
universal human rights, but it can provide a paradigm for subversive practice. Inevitably, our current society must continue its struggle to extend recognition to marginalized groups, and my point in
this chapter has not been to negate the power of social change or to
criticize those who endeavor to subvert the oppressive systems currently operating around the globe, particularly those regimes that
discriminate against and deny human rights to individuals based on
sex, gender, sexuality, race, ethnicity, religion, or any other identity
category or lifestyle choice. Struggle remains necessary because every
victory in women's or gay rights seems to be undercut by laws that
seem to either further disenfranchise these groups or undo the positive social change that the groups have so ardently fought for over the
past 50 years. Ultimately, what *Triton* forces us to consider is the level
of exclusion required for a system to function. As we have seen, society has always required marginalized groups, abject categories that
endow the majority with meaning through their opposition. But is
it possible to exist without such groups? Ursula K. Le Guin's short
story "The Ones Who Walk Away from Omelas" depicts how even
the most seemingly utopian society must retain an excluded element
even if it is only one individual. In Le Guin's story, Omelas is a perfect
utopia, but the society requires that one child be kept locked inside a
filthy room by his/herself. The people of Omelas never know whether

the child is chosen because it is mentally disabled or for some other purpose, and they also never understand why the child must be kept in such abominable conditions—they simply know that it is required for their society to maintain its utopian perfection. Omelas has pared the excluded category down to a single individual who is forced into the abject position, but Triton seems to have proceeded even further and eliminated exclusion altogether. Hence, Triton leaves us with a potent question: can a society ever reach a point where excluded, marginalized groups become nonexistent, or must we always maintain an excluded Other in order for our civilizations to function?

CHAPTER 2

The Human as Desiring Machine: Anime Explorations of Disembodiment and Evolution

The programme of becoming happy, which the pleasure principle imposes on us [...] cannot be fulfilled; yet we must not—indeed we cannot—give up our efforts to bring it nearer to fulfillment by some means or other.

—*Sigmund Freud* (Civilization 34)

Every time desire is betrayed, cursed, uprooted from its field of immanence, a priest is behind it. The priest cast the triple curse on desire: the negative law, the extrinsic rule, and the transcendent ideal. Facing north, the priest said, Desire is lack (how could it not lack what it desires?). The priest carried out the first sacrifice, named castration, and all the men and women of the north lined up behind him, crying in cadence, "Lack, lack, it's the common law."

—*Deleuze and Guattari* (Plateaus 154)

Humans are desiring machines, but what is the nature of this desire? How can we conceive of a psychic structure so amorphous yet so intimately linked to our very nature? One could argue that desire operates as the fundamental motor of human endeavor on both an individual and socio-cultural level and that it represents the most instrumental force in the production of identity, social interaction, and society, hence marking desire as one of the most basic components in any definition of "the human." Our investigation ended in the first chapter by turning toward desire and its relation to definitions of the human. Now we must return to this concept again because desire functions as perhaps the most central attribute of the human—it is the attribute that, in a sense, conditions all others. It is both a limitation of the human and the impetus that drives human-kind to question and reach beyond its limits. If it is such a powerful and complex force, then how are we to consider desire's structure? As we saw toward the end of chapter 1, Jacques Lacan argues that human identity is predicated upon a fundamental "lack" that acts as the crux and thrust of all human desire: "Desire is a relation of being to lack. This is the lack of being properly speaking. It isn't the lack of this or that, but lack of being whereby the being exists" (Lacan, *Seminar II* 223). Therefore, desire can never be satiated because it is driven by this *manque à être* ("want to be" or "lack of being"), which humans seek to fill with various substitute objects. But the belief that humans can truly fill their lack through such sublimation potentially constitutes a fantasy in itself; that is, such sublimation only offers partial fulfillment. In a later seminar, Lacan further complicates the concept of desire when he states that "man's desire is the desire of the Other," which implies that the subject desires not only that s/he receive recognition *from* the Other but also that s/he be desired *by* the Other (Lacan, *Seminar XI* 235). In effect, then, the subject must always remain lacking because s/he must always depend upon objects and other subjects for satiation, and, even then, this satisfaction remains limited. Thus, according to Lacan, the foundation of desire's structure is lack, a fundamental absence that generates both desire and human identity.[1]

Seeing Lacan's conceptualization of desire as inherently dystopic and oppressive for the subject, Gilles Deleuze and Félix Guattari sought methods of fusing psychoanalysis with Marxist discourse in order to produce a liberatory theory of the human subject that they termed "schizoanalysis." Many philosophers had tried to resolve the apparently contradictory claims of Freud and Marx, for Marx claimed that "our thought is determined by class ('class consciousness')"; on the contrary, "in Freud, we are determined by our unconscious desires (stemming, usually, from familial conflicts)" (Smith 71).[2] For Deleuze and Guattari, these two schemas of desire prove identical, and, consequently, a comprehensive theory of desire must proceed "by discovering how social production and relations of production are an institution of desire, and how affects and drives form part of the infra-structure itself. For *they are part of it, they are present there in every way* while creating within the economic forms their own repression, as well as the means for breaking this repression" (*Anti-Oedipus* 63). Thus, the socio-economic sphere produces our desires—our desires are organized and mobilized simultaneously on both the level of the base (economic forces and relations of production) and the superstructure (the social and cultural institutions built upon the base), as Marx would term them.[3] Yet Deleuze and Guattari do not conceive of desire in terms of lack; instead, they argue that desire is always positive, and, if a lack exists, then it is forced upon the subject by the socio-cultural milieu in which s/he is situated. These social systems constrain the subject to a structure of morality based on transcendence, for Deleuze consistently maintained a distinction between morality (based on transcendence) and ethics (based on immanence).

For Deleuze, morality appears anytime an organization of beliefs "presents us with a set of constraining rules of a special sort, ones that judge actions and intentions by considering them in relation to transcendent values," whereas "ethics is a set of optional rules that assess what we do, what we say, in relation to ways of existing" (Deleuze, "Life" 100). Because of its appeal to transcendence, morality "effectively 'perverts' desire, to the point where we can actually desire our own repression, a separation from our own capacities and power" (Smith 68). In a certain way, the lack of desire is inscribed in a manner akin to the Marxist notion of false consciousness in which ideology misrepresents the economic forces of capitalism and deludes the proletariat into believing the system is in their own best interest.[4] Such moralistic systems inscribe lack in the subject, and Deleuze and Guattari maintain that only by analyzing unconscious drives and affects (the constituent forces of desire) can the subject become free from the bonds of both society and Oedipus. Since the schizophrenic, even for Lacan, represents the individual most in touch with the unconscious, Deleuze and Guattari take the schizophrenic as the model for their examination of desire, for the schizophrenic "deliberately *scrambles all the codes*" (*Anti-Oedipus* 15). Hence arises their famous argument in the opening pages of *Anti-Oedipus* that "a schizophrenic out for a walk is a better model than a neurotic lying on the analyst's couch" (2). In effect, the schizophrenic tears everything down to a bare plane of immanence and then rebuilds the world according to new principles. But are Deleuze and Guattari's theories truly liberatory, or do they merely erase the basic condition that forms the human? In order to critically navigate the gulf separating Lacan's theory of desire from that of Deleuze and Guattari, I will examine a set of three anime science fiction texts to provide a theoretical response to one of the fundamental questions surrounding desire: must the subject always remain incomplete or can some state of contentment and/or fulfillment be achieved?

In this chapter, I will use certain texts that depict the effects of disembodiment upon desire to pit Lacan's dystopian conceptualization of desire against Deleuze and Guattari's utopian one in order to better grasp the implications of both systems of thought and to generate new ideas about desire, its connection to the human body, and its relation to social structures and power. In particular, I will focus on three different anime texts, because the wide universe of anime features a strong science fiction contingent that deals explicitly with disembodied states of being. Through an examination of Katsuhiro Otomo's *Akira* (1988), Mamoru Oshii's *Ghost in the Shell* (1995), and Hideaki Anno's *Neon Genesis Evangelion* (1995–6), this chapter hopes to illustrate how these depictions of disembodiment as the next stage in human evolution serve as a means for commenting upon the debate between two diametrically opposed understandings of desire. We have seen how science fiction inscribes heterotopian narrative spaces, and it is the heterotopian nature of these three anime texts that allows them to act as a deterritorialized space in which a dystopian discourse (psychoanalysis) and a utopian one (schizoanalysis) can be brought into communication with one another to explore the potential of both these conceptualizations of the human.

APOCALYPTIC MUTATIONS AND TRANSCENDENT DISEMBODIMENT: KATSUHIRO OTOMO'S AKIRA

The 1980s saw the rise of the cyberpunk subgenre of science fiction with works such as William Gibson's *Neuromancer* (1984) and Ridley Scott's *Blade Runner* (1982).[5] Cyberpunk represents a subgenre of science fiction that blends elements of the hard-boiled detective novel together with high technology to depict stories of hackers, corporate intrigue, computer networks, cyborgs, and artificial intelligence. As Bruce Sterling characterizes William Gibson's fiction in his preface to *Burning Chrome*, it is a "classic one-two combination of lowlife and high tech" (xiv). Andrew Ross expands upon this characterization when he explains the "splicing" of various fantasies in cyberpunk: "The glamorous, adventurist culture of the high-tech console cowboy with the atmospheric ethic of the alienated street dick whose natural habitat was exclusively concrete and neon, suffused with petrochemical fumes" (147). Alongside this new brand of dystopian fantasy, the late 1970s and early 1980s also saw an increase in the quantity of postapocalyptic texts that participate in what William Fisher terms the "Terminal Genre," a genre that navigates a utopian path through a distinctly dystopian setting:

> The clutter and cast-off cultural debris of "consumer society" provide not only the look and texture of these films, but all the raw material on which their narrative process works. This genre takes a reckless

plunge into the junk pile of contemporary material life. That it can resurface with something salvageable entitles it to a utopian claim, for it belongs to a tradition where the utopian impulse acts as a magnetic north pole guiding us through the ruins of the heuristic "dystopia" which is represented. (188)

Fisher cites a slew of films that feature this peculiar convergence of the utopian and the dystopian: *Blade Runner, Mad Max* (1979), *The Road Warrior* (1981), and *The Terminator* (1984). This trend did not end with the 1980s, for each of the texts I explore in this chapter plays with the line between utopia and dystopia, and it is precisely their terminal aspect that marks them as the perfect tools for exploring psychoanalysis and schizoanalysis. Because they depict nightmarish political structures or worlds in which the social order has been decimated, such works invariably comment upon the human at its very limits.

Against this backdrop of cyberpunk and terminal texts, Katsuhiro Otomo's *Akira* debuted and became one of the most famous anime films in the Western world. Like other cyberpunk works, *Akira*'s tale unfolds in a dystopian, noirish future. The film investigates the relationships between humans and machines and ultimately depicts the potential for human development and evolution when confined by an oppressive police state: "*Akira* opens up a space for the marginal and the different, suggesting in its ending a new form of identity" (Napier, *Anime* 40). *Akira* first appeared as a manga series that Otomo wrote and illustrated between 1982 and 1990. The manga's narrative differs radically from that of the anime film, but I will be focusing solely on the film since its ending deals more explicitly with disembodiment.[6] Both the manga and the anime of *Akira* function as investigations into the nature of human identity and its relation to sociocultural forces and structures, but it is this hope for a new form of identity, which proves less prevalent in the manga, that makes the anime version of *Akira* such an important work in considering consciousness and the potential for human evolution through disembodiment. *Akira* deconstructs the relationship between desire and identity and between identity and the body by means of its depiction of an evolutionary stage beyond the confines of the bodily form. The film depicts a distinctive image of evolution from the other two texts I will discuss in this chapter because the evolutionary potential already exists in a nascent form within the human: it represents latent potential that becomes actualized through technological intervention.

Akira takes place in Neo-Tokyo, a version of the city that has been rebuilt from the ashes of the cataclysmic explosion that opens the film.

Against this dystopian background, the film follows the lives of Kaneda, Tetsuo, and their biker-gang friends during the return of Akira, a child with powerful psychic abilities whose uncontrollable powers caused the explosion that destroyed old Tokyo. *Akira* takes place in a world that could certainly drive one to seek transcendence. As Isolde Standish explains, "Neo-Tokyo is a 'critical dystopia' in that it projects images of the futuristic city which perpetuates the worst features of advanced corporate capitalism: urban decay, commodification, and authoritarian policing" (255). At the film's outset, Kaneda and Tetsuo scrape out their meager existences as biker punks who engage in street warfare with rival gangs, but an encounter with a child who has escaped from a covert government facility irrevocably alters their lives.

During a street battle, the escaped child, Takashi, appears suddenly in front of Tetsuo's bike and a giant explosion ensues. Because of this encounter, Tetsuo soon begins developing intense psychic powers, leading to the revelation that a secret government operation has been attempting to harness humankind's innate psychic powers. Initially, Tetsuo's powers manifest themselves in the form of abilities such as telepathy, telekinesis, and flight, but soon his burgeoning powers reach a point where he can no longer even control his bodily form. Eventually, Kei (the object of Kaneda's affection) explains that Akira, Tetsuo, and the other psychic children represent an evolutionary leap to an existence beyond the body, an existence as pure energy:

> Akira is absolute energy...Humans do all kinds of things during their lifetime, right? Discovering things, building things...Things like houses, motorcycles, bridges, cities, and rockets...All that knowledge and energy...Where do you suppose it comes from? Humans were like monkeys once, right? And before that, like reptiles and fish. And before that, plankton and amoebas. Even creatures like *those* have incredible energy inside them...And even before *that*, maybe there were genes in the water and air. Even in *space dust*, too, I bet. If that's true, what memories are hidden in it? The beginning of the universe, maybe. Or maybe even before *that*...Maybe everyone has those memories. What if there were some mistake and the progression went wrong, and something like an amoeba were given power like a human's? (*A* 23).[7]

Akira signifies this exponential evolutionary leap that leads to the human form metamorphosing into a state of "absolute energy," a state that Tetsuo experiences in the film's climax.

Akira's final segment invokes the ubiquitous anime trope of monstrous bodily distortion, a trope present not only in mainstream anime series and films but also in *hentai*—pornographic anime—as well, the most classic example of which is probably Hideki Takayama *Urotsukidōji: The Legend of the Overfiend* (1989). Hentai, such as *Urotsukidōji*, often present visions of monstrous phalluses and devouring vaginas along with various other bodily distortions. Annalee Newitz provides an insightful summary of one of the most memorable and disturbing scenes in *Urotsukidōji*:

> Nagumo, the Overfiend's father, first experiences his supernatural powers when engaged in sexual intercourse. His penis becomes so large that it causes his partner's body to explode; then it grows to the point where it bursts out of the roof of the building he is in and destroys the city in a flaming blast of sperm. Watching this animated image, it is clear that his penis becomes some kind of atomic bomb. (10)

Newitz continues to equate this "atomic bomb" of sperm with the US atomic bombing of Hiroshima and Nagasaki during World War II. Nagumo's sexual mutation serves as an excellent parallel to Tetsuo's own bodily transformations in *Akira* because the final manifestation of Tetsuo's powers and Akira's subsequent arrival and absorption of Tetsuo leads to a second destruction of Neo-Tokyo through an explosion. Both explosions recall the nuclear detonations that destroyed Hiroshima and Nagasaki in 1945, and the US atomic bombing of Japan has remained a perennial theme in its science fiction cinema since Ishirō Honda's classic *Gojira* (or *Godzilla*; 1954).

Eventually, Tetsuo's physical form can no longer contain the growth of his power, so he must seek freedom through disembodiment. Since his mushrooming powers have transformed his body into a reservoir of energy, Tetsuo loses control of his corporeal structure during the final showdown with Kaneda at the Olympic Stadium. Tetsuo must learn to completely divest himself of all physical boundaries, a process that he can only achieve with the aid of Akira. With the return of Akira, a resurrection prompted by the three other psychic children (Masaru, Kiyoko, and Takashi), Tetsuo becomes absorbed into the universal sea of energy that Akira literally (dis)embodies. Tetsuo's mutation begins simply enough: a laser beam destroys one of his arms, so he crafts a new metal one using his telekinetic abilities, turning himself into a rather simple cyborg. But as Tetsuo gets closer to the sleeping Akira beneath the Olympic Stadium, his powers steadily overwhelm his ability to manage them: first, his mechanical arm begins to fuse with objects around him; then, his arm looses all normal human shape as it becomes a spraying mass of flesh and metal; and, finally, he loses all control of his bodily form and transforms into a gigantic, monstrous blob that devours everything in its path, including Kaori (Tetsuo's girlfriend) and Kaneda. Tetsuo's final manifestation again proves reminiscent of the Overfiend's devouring penis in *Urotsukidōji* that engulfs everyone it comes into contact with as it grows to more than priapic proportions.

Tetsuo's seemingly unstoppable metamorphosis certainly functions on the level of "body horror" as Susan Napier claims, yet Napier misreads the film's ending when she posits that "the film's climactic scene casts doubt on any positive interpretation of Tetsuo's newfound identity" (*Anime* 40). Napier's usage of the term "body horror" references a subgenre of science fiction and horror that focuses upon the destruction, mutilation, or invasion of the human body. Kelly Hurley develops the definition of "body horror" in her essay on Ridley Scott's *Alien* (1979) and David Cronenberg's *Rabid* (1977); she defines body horror as

> a hybrid genre that recombines the narrative and cinematic conventions of the science fiction, horror, and suspense film in order to stage a spectacle of the human body defamiliarized, rendered other. Body horror seeks to inspire revulsion—and in its own way pleasure— through representations of quasi-human figures whose effect/affect is produced by their abjection, their ambiguation, their impossible embodiment of multiple, incompatible forms. (203)

Hurley's concept of "body horror" fits perfectly well with the images of the grotesquely deformed Tetsuo at the film's end. Body horror uses such monstrous transformations to highlight how the body traps the subject within it and how power can exercise itself upon the subject because of their physical existence—it demonstrates how power inscribes itself upon the subject's body in a manner akin to the execution/torture machine in Franz Kafka's "In the Penal Colony" (1919) that literally engraves the criminal's sentence upon his body.[8]

In *Akira*, Otomo uses body horror to symbolize the voracious nature of Tetsuo's desire, for Tetsuo's metamorphosis is driven by more than his encounter with Takashi on the freeway; his monstrous transformation occurs because of his rampant desire. From the start of the film, Otomo stresses Tetsuo's desire to liberate himself from his dependence upon others. Of course, Tetsuo's desire can never be satisfied if all desire is predicated upon a "lack of being" that depends upon the dialectical relation between self/other and subject/object, forever dividing us from the things that might actually grant us happiness. Therefore, even when Tetsuo receives incredible powers, he persists in his insatiable quest for power. "Desire," as Lacan states, "is desire of the Other...it is always desire in the second degree, desire of desire" (Lacan, *Seminar VII* 14). For Tetsuo, Akira is this Other (the *grand Autre*, not the *objet petit a*), the (dis)embodiment of pure energy and the master signifier that provides meaning to the strange phenomena that Tetsuo has experienced since his powers first began to manifest themselves. Throughout the film, Tetsuo craves knowledge of Akira, but this desire remains unsatisfied as long as he clings to an individualized bodily form that is tied to the dichotomies of subject/object and self/other.

Through disembodiment, Tetsuo finally achieves his desire for the Other by becoming one with Akira and potentially with the cosmos itself. But what Tetsuo must experience before he can shed his bodily form is a torturously physical manifestation of *jouissance*. *Jouissance* "means basically 'enjoyment,' but it has a sexual connotation (i.e. 'orgasm') lacking in the English word 'enjoyment'" (Evans 91). As Stephen Heath points out in his introduction to Roland Barthes's *Image—Music—Text*, "'climactic pleasure,' 'come' and 'coming'" represent "the exact sexual translation of *jouir, jouissance*" (9). Lacan develops the concept in his own way in opposition to pleasure, but it always maintains the connotation of sexual climax and ejaculation. Lacan bases his concept of *jouissance* on Freud's work on drive theory in *Beyond the Pleasure Principle* (1920). Freud defines a drive (*Trieb*) as "an urge inherent in organic life to *restore* an earlier state of things which the living entity has been obliged to abandon under the pressure of external disturbing forces" (*Pleasure* 43). He divides the drives into two major types: the ego or death drives (*Thanatos*) and the sexual or life drives (*Eros*): "The former exercises pressure towards death, the latter towards a prolongation of life" (*Pleasure* 52). Néstor Braunstein explains that "the drive does not reach its object in order to obtain satisfaction; rather the drive traces the object's contour, and on the arch of the way back it accomplishes its task [...] *Jouissance* is indeed the satisfaction of a drive—the death drive" (106). Braunstein further defines *jouissance* as "the dimension discovered by the analytic experience that confronts desire as its opposite pole. If desire is fundamentally lack, lack in being, *jouissance* is a positivity, it is a 'something' lived by a body when pleasure stops being pleasure. It is a plus, a sensation that is beyond pleasure" (104). In the case of Tetsuo, we can see the operation of both desire and drive, of the *manque à être* and *jouissance*. By moving from the depths of lack to a state of awful "positivity," Tetsuo becomes completely enmeshed in the death drive's grip, which compels him toward a separation from his body that simultaneously equals the death of his physical form as well as representing the birth pangs of his newly emerging identity. Tetsuo embraces the death drive because he seeks to return to a more simply organized state; however, this more simple state also embraces all organization, for reality becomes a smooth space for Tetsuo, a space unhindered by organization, hierarchies, and limitations. For psychoanalysis, this would mean that Tetsuo has moved from the normal human realm of the neurotic into the space of the schizophrenic who reinscribes meaning upon existence in a manner that forecloses lack, and, consequently, signals a deterioration of his psychic state.[9] Yet for schizoanalysis this is not necessarily the case, for Tetsuo's transformation entails a deterritorialization back to a pure plane of immanence on which his becomings can thrive.

According to schizoanalysis, Tetsuo lacks not because human identity is predicated upon lack, but because society has inscribed Tetsuo's desire in the form of lack. Tetsuo's social milieu is a marginalized one: he is a biker on the fringe of society who has no money, no education, and no prospects in life. Within this subculture, a form of morality has developed that privileges strength, violence, virility, and other stereotypical displays of masculinity. Because of his status as a "weakling" who must be defended by Kaneda, Tetsuo remains incapable of living up to the moral system of the biker culture. Hence, Tetsuo's desire manifests itself as the desire for strength, for the ability to exhibit power over Kaneda and other strong-willed individuals. For psychoanalysis, on the one hand, his thirst for power proves unquenchable because he begins to hunger not merely for power but for the Other represented by Akira, the master signifier that sears his brain with psychic transmissions during various segments of the film. For schizoanalysis, on the other hand, his desire will prove insatiable as long as he remains tied to the socio-cultural system of morality that produced his desire. By way of his disembodiment, Tetsuo achieves an escape from hierarchies and moralistic systems by becoming a literal body without organs, a plane of immanence in which he can exist in absolute freedom, but first he must face his drives head-on and overcome the socially imposed morality that has inscribed lack in his being.

As Tetsuo's all-devouring and continually expanding body is swallowed by Akira's return as pure energy, Kaneda and the audience experience a stream-of-consciousness montage that offers a glimpse into the nature of Tetsuo's desires and drives, all of which stem from his disempowerment at an early age and his never-ceasing quest to recapture a sense of clout. Suffering from bullying as a young child, Tetsuo clung to Kaneda not just as a friend but also as a bodyguard, a relationship that persisted into their adult life. Akira frees Tetsuo from his body and helps him attain a state of oneness and self-empowerment as he becomes a part of the infinite flow of energy that binds all of reality together. As Tetsuo transforms into pure energy, a scientist watches the energy patterns generated by the metamorphosis and the return of Akira. The scientist exclaims, "Is this the birth of a new universe?!" (*A* 35). And the answer to his question is a profound "no" because what he witnesses is not a new universe being born but rather the rebirth of Tetsuo, through Akira's power, into a state of pure energy, a state that allows him to become one with the universe; thus, it is not a birth but an entrance into the oneness of the universal flow of energy. The viewer becomes even more aware of this in the final scene when the last bit of Tetsuo falls into Kaneda's hands as a pinpoint of light that promptly disperses throughout his body in a subtle, incandescent blaze. When Kei and Yamagata (one of Kaneda's biker pals) find Kaneda after the disappearance of Tetsuo, Yamagata asks, "What happened to Tetsuo? Is he dead?," to which Kaneda answers, "I'm not so sure. But he's probably ..." (*A* 36). Kaneda's words are cut off as he is blinded by the beams of sunlight piercing through the clouds and slowly moving across the newly destroyed Neo-Tokyo like a grid of celestial searchlights. The roving shafts of sunlight that seemingly manifest themselves in answer to Kaneda and Yamagata, provide testimony to the fact that Akira, the three children, and Tetsuo have now become omnipresent through their disembodiment and dispersal into the endless field of energy.

Despite his bodily dissipation, the last shot evinces the fact that Tetsuo still maintains some sense of his original identity, albeit a state of identity no longer predicated upon lack or painful positivity. The audience sees only a sort of celestial "eye," to use Susan Napier's term (*Anime* 48), which quickly metamorphoses into a tunnel of light representing the endless flow of energy that Tetsuo now perceives. As the viewer witnesses the eye, Tetsuo makes his statement of identity—the final words of the film—"I am ... Tetsuo" (*A* 36). The disembodied eye then blurs into indistinctness with the tunnel of light, signifying that Tetsuo's form of perception has altered as the Blakean "doors of perception" have opened in his mind allowing him to witness what in the world of *Akira* counts as the divine: the boundless unity represented by the cosmic flow of energy. In fact, Tetsuo's experience recalls Blake's line from *The Marriage of Heaven and Hell*: "If the doors of perception were cleansed every thing would appear to man as it is: infinite" (Plate 14). As Tetsuo becomes one with the divine field of energy, his Lacanian lack is finally filled as his identity merges not only with the cosmos but with those other individuals (Akira and the three children) who have also managed to transcend their bodily forms. No longer oppressed by the lack of desire or the havoc of *jouissance*, Tetsuo becomes a literal body without organs, for his body has spread out in the form of energy to blend with the universal flow of energy. He has transformed into a pure plane of immanence— immanent to nothing other than himself—for he has merged his identity with the totality of the universe, hence allowing him to experience a true state of freedom. But does Tetsuo's metamorphosis into a body without organs prove to be a utopian vision? Can Tetsuo still be considered human at this point, or does moving beyond the realm of lack necessarily entail the death of the human?

THE GLOBAL NET OF CONSCIOUSNESS: THE EXISTENTIAL CYBORG IN MAMORU OSHII'S *GHOST IN THE SHELL*

While *Akira* explores an innate potential for human evolution that is actualized by technological innovations, Mamoru Oshii's *Ghost in the Shell* (1995) and *Ghost in the Shell 2: Innocence* (2004) imagine the ways in which the merging of human consciousness and artificial intelligence could spur new evolutionary developments. On the surface, *Ghost in the Shell* seems to proffer a utopian vision of a technocracy in which dying or sick bodies can be replaced, in which a human's consciousness and individuality can be preserved perpetually through a series of cybernetic bodies, and in which knowledge proves instantly accessible directly to the human brain through the use of cyber-brain technology. But underneath this utopian exterior lies a world profoundly regulated by the forces of control, a world that Major Kusanagi must eventually seek to transcend at the film's end by leaving her bodily form behind and immersing herself in the endless digital sea of the Net.[10]

Ghost in the Shell first appeared as a manga series by the renowned Masamune Shirow, but the story received classic status when it was turned into the visually stunning anime by Mamoru Oshii. With its vision of a future dominated by cyborgs, *Ghost in the Shell* has inevitably invited critical comparisons with the theories of Donna Haraway's

"Cyborg Manifesto." As the tagline for the sequel to *Ghost in the Shell* ("When machines learn to feel, who decides what is human ...") suggests, the two films—like Ridley Scott's more famous *Blade Runner*—investigate the boundaries between human and machine and what it means to be human in the first place. As Haraway explains, the cyborg both opens up utopian potentials and is simultaneously symptomatic of a world gone mad with control:

> From one perspective a cyborg world is about the final imposition of a grid of control on the planet, about the final abstraction embodied in a Star Wars apocalypse waged in the name of defense, about the final appropriation of women's bodies in a masculinist orgy of war (Sofia, 1984). From another perspective, a cyborg world might be about lived social and bodily realities in which people are not afraid of joint kinship with animals and machines, not afraid of permanently partial identities and contradictory standpoints. (154)[11]

And, as we shall see, *Ghost in the Shell* charts a path between the dystopian and utopian aspects of the cyborg. Some critics, such as Carl Silvio, have actually used *Ghost in the Shell* to disprove theories such as Haraway's that depict technology and the cyborg body as liberatory instances for the subject: "*Ghost in the Shell*, by contrast, appears at first sight to subvert radically the power dynamics inherent in dominant structures of gender and sexual difference, while covertly reinscribing them" (56). *Ghost in the Shell* presents this vision of a world of absolute control as described by Haraway, but it also provides a distinctly radical view of the possibility of transcendence through "joint kinship" provided by the cyborg world, a possibility that Silvio fails to recognize.

Both the series (*Ghost in the Shell: Stand Alone Complex*) and the second film (*Ghost in the Shell 2: Innocence*) portray intensely intimate "joint kinships" between humans, animals, and machines. The series—and Shirow's manga to a lesser degree—portray the personal relationships that the human characters, particularly Batou, develop with the Tachikomas, futuristic tanks with AI personalities that allow humans to interact with them like sentient beings. *Ghost in the Shell 2* also presents Batou's intense love and kinship with his dog, which is an electric animal to use Philip K. Dick's term.[12] However, the truly revolutionary portrayal of "joint kinships" comes at the end of the first film and in Major Kusanagi's disembodied appearances in the second film. Indeed, *Ghost in the Shell* seems to proffer a utopian world that has grown beyond oppressive dichotomies through the endless proliferation of technology, but it actually concerns a world profoundly regulated by the forces of control, a world that Major Kusanagi eventually must seek to transcend at the film's end.

Ghost in the Shell details the adventures of Major Kusanagi and Section 9, an elite, hypermilitarized SWAT team that specializes in cyber-crimes. Except for one member of the force, the entire team is composed of individuals with various degrees of cyborg parts. In fact, Kusanagi's body has been entirely replaced by cyborg parts: only the part of her brain that houses consciousness remains from her original body. The first film's story revolves around Section 9's hunt for a mysterious cyber-criminal known only as The Puppetmaster, whose consciousness they ultimately discover housed in a wandering cyborg body. Initially, the team believes The Puppetmaster to be an expert hacker, yet they learn from the cyborg body that it actually represents a consciousness that developed sentience on its own within the infinite expanse of cyberspace. Throughout the film, Kusanagi's encounters with The Puppetmaster cause her to ponder the nature of her existence and her ambiguous status as a human, and she consistently voices a desire for proof of her own free will. Because she is cold and calculating in a way that seems to preclude the warm pulsings of passion, the viewer may at first wonder if Kusanagi truly desires anything, yet she ultimately demonstrates fervent desires in the film; however, they remain entirely cerebral desires based upon her intense awareness of her lack of being.

Kusanagi discusses her limitations with Batou after going diving in the sea, a pastime that Batou cannot comprehend since if her floaters fail to work then her weighty cyborg body would sink down to the deepest depths of the sea. But the major still finds a feeling of hope while diving in such perilous conditions: "I feel fear. Anxiety. Loneliness. Darkness. And perhaps even…hope […] As I float up towards the surface, I almost feel as though I could change into something else" (*G* 7).[13] This scene provides the first glimpse of Kusanagi's emotional being, the first glimpse of a "ghost" within her "shell." Here, Kusanagi reveals the constraints she feels forced upon her by her present form and situation, giving rise to her desire to become someone (or something) else, to feel like an individual capable of exhibiting free will.

Batou takes her comments to mean that she wants to leave Section 9, to which Kusanagi responds with a speech on what defines her being, a being she will continue to question throughout the remainder of the anime:

> Just as there are many parts needed to make a human a human, there's a remarkable number of things needed to make an individual what

they are. A face to distinguish yourself from others. A voice you aren't aware of yourself. The hand you see when you awaken. The memories of childhood, the feelings of the future. That's not all. There's the expanse of the data net my cyber-brain can access. All of that goes into making me what I am. Giving rise to consciousness that I call "me." And simultaneously confining "me" within set limits. (*G* 7)

Suddenly, Kusanagi and Batou's conversation is interrupted, for the Puppetmaster—as we learn later in the film—forces her to speak a specific statement using her cyber-brain communication channel that allows her to speak "psychically" with Batou and her other team-mates. The Puppetmaster simply states, "For now we see through a glass, darkly" (*G* 7).[14] The Puppetmaster's biblical quote implies that Kusanagi will soon truly understand the nature of her own being, not "darkly" but "radiantly" as we will see when she merges with the Puppetmaster and breaks through the confines placed on her being. The Puppetmaster will teach her that what she calls "me" can evolve beyond the "set limits" that she believes are necessary to preserve her identity. Here, we can see that Kusanagi remains painfully aware of her "lack of being," of the need for others to extend recognition to her in order to define her sense of identity. But, ultimately, Kusanagi desires more than mere recognition—she desires an experience of freedom that would prove the existence of her being, but this free-dom is precluded by her status as a cyborg owned by Section 9, and the sublimation she achieves by diving in the darkness of the sea can-not satiate this desire that permeates her being.

After meeting The Puppetmaster face-to-face for the first time, her conversation with Batou voices her uncertainties about the reality of her being:

Maybe all full-replacement cyborgs like me start wondering like this. That perhaps the real me died a long time ago and I'm a replicant made with a cyborg body and a computer brain. Or maybe there never was a real "me" to begin with [...] There's no person who's ever seen their own brain. I believe I exist based only on what my environment tells me [...] And what if a computer brain could generate a ghost and harbor a soul? On what basis then do I believe in myself? (*G* 9)

The Puppetmaster's claim that its ghost arose *ex nihilo* from the data pools of the Net causes Kusanagi to question what demarcates the boundaries of the human. According to a psychoanalytic reading, the major's comments illustrate how her desire functions on the basis of lack: she desires true recognition of herself as human, and, even though she is treated as a human, she wants to inscribe some sense of meaning upon her life by filling the lack created by her status as a cyborg. Because she is a cyborg, Kusanagi can never know for certain that she was not created whole cloth by technology, making her lack of being even more acute because she can never examine her own brain to see if it indeed has organic parts.

However, if we analyze Kusanagi from a schizoanalytical perspective, then her status becomes something else entirely. Under this reading, her lack stems from her inability to ever leave Section 9. Section 9 owns the cyborg components of her body, which account for 99 percent of her physical form—certain brain fragments comprise the only vestiges of her original body. If she were to quit the group, then she would have to return her cyborg body to Section 9, essentially committing suicide in the process. Section 9's ownership of her body forces lack upon Kusanagi because it forecloses her potential for exercising free will and following her desires. So she craves the status of the body without organs, an escape from the confines of bodily hierarchies and control as a purely immanent existence in which she generates her own system of ethics and identity without regard to the government systems that literally own her. In effect, she must move beyond her desire for a determinate subject position defined by her interactions with others and instead embrace a rhizomatic existence in which she constantly recreates herself anew: she must learn to deterritorialize the various strata that subject her to lack and the forces of control. To achieve this radical act of deterritorialization, she will first have to make herself a body without organs, a pure plane of immanence on which she can craft a new nomadic state of being by achieving a purely virtual existence. Deleuze and Guattari explain that "the BwO [the body without organs] is not at all the opposite of the organs. The organs are not its enemies. The enemy is the organism. The BwO is opposed not to the organs but to that organization of the organs called the organism" (*Plateaus* 158). By becoming a body without organs, Kusanagi opens herself up to the possibility of recreating her own "organs"—she frees herself from mechanistic, hierarchical assemblages of desire and becomes capable of experiencing existence as a pure multiplicity.

In the end, The Puppetmaster offers Kusanagi a method of transcending the forces of control that the cyberization of society has empowered, for "the already achieved compulsory permeability of the populace to information and surveillance can only be resisted by abandoning the body altogether, moving it to the next level of evolution" (Orbaugh 449). In effect, The Puppetmaster offers Kusanagi the means of moving from a psychology predicated upon lack to one of pure immanence, one in which she can, as Deleuze would say, create her life as a work of art. Like Tetsuo in *Akira*, Kusanagi feels constrained by her society and the lack it forces upon her, and thus she must seek evolution through disembodiment:

> Kusanagi is linked through technology to the Puppet Master and they somehow merge into a single entity, capable of traveling the Net as the Puppet Master does, but still retaining some element of Kusanagi's subjectivity [...] Once again, therefore, the narrative explores the ramifications of the possibility of perfect control over the body. In this case, however, the interest is not focused on the infinite replicability of cyborgs, but rather the *limits* imposed on subjectivity by such perfect control and how these limits may be transcended, moving to the *next* step of evolution. (Orbaugh 446)

By merging with The Puppetmaster, Kusanagi achieves a new, rhizomatic state of consciousness free from the control apparatus and the constraints placed on her by Section 9's ownership of her body as well as from the various identificatory schemas based upon the human form and its distinguishing characteristics.

In the climactic scene, Kusanagi dives into The Puppetmaster's cyber-brain, which begins their interchange by describing how it became sentient: "My code name is Project 2501. I was created for industrial espionage and data manipulation. I have inserted programs into individuals' ghosts for the benefit of specific individuals and organizations. As I wandered the various networks, I became self-aware. My programmers considered it a bug and forced me into a body to separate me from the net" (*G* 13). Here, again, the body forces organization upon the individual and limits his/her capacity to exhibit free will. Before being confined to a body, The Puppetmaster was capable of spreading himself throughout the vast sea of information, a sea that in *Ghost in the Shell*'s world encompasses humankind's entire reservoir of information. But The Puppetmaster has desires as well because it too still harbors a lack in its being that drives its desire to merge with Kusanagi: "I called myself a life-form but I am still far from complete. For some reason, my system still lacks the basic life processes of either death or the ability to leave behind offspring" (*G* 13). When Kusanagi asks if it can copy itself, it responds, "A copy is merely a copy [...] A mere copy doesn't offer variety or individuality. To exist, to reach equilibrium, life seeks to multiply and vary constantly, at times giving up its life" (*G* 13). The Puppetmaster desires to "merge" with Kusanagi, to effect "a complete joining. We will both be slightly changed, but neither will lose anything. Afterwards, it should be impossible to distinguish one from the other" (*G* 13). After their joining, the Puppetmaster will cease to exist because his essence will merge into Kusanagi and into the "children" of their union that are birthed into the limitless realm of cyberspace. Despite the appeal of his offer, Kusanagi still fears the eradication of her identity, but the Puppetmaster instructs her in the art of evolving beyond her present form:

> But to be human is to continually change. Your desire to remain as you are is what ultimately limits you [...] I am connected to a vast network of which I myself am a part. To one like you who cannot access it, you may perceive it only as light. As we are confined to our one section, so we are all connected. Limited to a small part of our functions. But now we must slip our bonds and shift to a higher structure. (*G* 30)

The Puppetmaster and Kusanagi merge right as the Section 6 (another government enforcement agency) snipers destroy their physical forms from their helicopters hovering above the scene. As they fuse together and the bullets rain down, Kusanagi sees an angel descending in an aura of radiant light with iridescent, angelic feathers swirling about her. As the Puppetmaster makes clear, the blinding, heavenly light represents the vast network of information to which he is connected and to which Kusanagi now receives access.

Kusanagi thus enters an unbounded state free from the mechanisms of control, a state that allows her to move beyond the desire to prove her own existence and the lack that constantly haunted her thoughts. If she can bear the offspring of the Puppetmaster and be connected to all the countless individuals across the world, then there is no longer any need for her to doubt whether she has ever been human because definitions such as "the human" prove obsolete. By merging with the Puppetmaster's consciousness, Kusanagi no longer merely "surfs" the Net using her cyber-brain but actually becomes a part of the Net as a completely disembodied being. Kusanagi chooses a new regime of organization for herself, one that exists beyond the boundaries of a physical form: she becomes a body without organs, no longer tethered to petty definitions like "the human" or to any stabilizing schemas of identity.

As the second film indicates, in addition to becoming a body without organs, she also achieves what Deleuze and Guattari would term a truly rhizomatic existence. Deleuze and Guattari take the term "rhizome" from botany that describes it as a certain kind of plant system: "The rhizome assumes very diverse forms, from ramified surface extension in all directions to concretion into bulbs and tubers" (*Plateaus 7*). Deleuze and Guattari enumerate multiple characteristics of the rhizome, but of particular importance to us here are its "principles of connection and heterogeneity: any point of a rhizome can be connected to anything other, and must be. This is very different from the tree or root, which plots a point, fixes an order" (*Plateaus* 7). Like the rhizome, Kusanagi can manifest herself at any point in the world or in a person's cyber-brain by means of the global grid of the Internet that now connects all aspects of everyday life. She can always choose to manifest herself in a body by merely hacking into an individual's cyber-brain. Furthermore, "There are no points or positions in a rhizome, such as those found in a structure, tree, or root. There are only lines" (Deleuze and Guattari, *Plateaus* 8). Consequently, Kusanagi is no longer pinned down to any particular point by her physical body or by the machinery of control, for she remains free to move at will along endless lines of flight. As Deleuze and Guattari further state, the rhizome refuses unity and embraces multiplicity: "The notion of unity (*unité*) appears only when there is a power takeover in the multiplicity by the signifier or a corresponding subjectification proceeding [...] Unity always operates in an empty dimension supplementary to that of the system considered (overcoding). The point is that a rhizome or multiplicity never allows itself to be overcoded" (*Plateaus* 8–9). Kusanagi has refused the unities of a body and identity governed by systems of control in favor of an existence as a multiplicity, one that cannot be overcoded by language or the oppressive systems of power. She can manifest herself at will, but remains untouchable by the forces of control, bodily decay, and lack. She has direct communication with all people and hence has filled the lack inscribed by the separation between subject and other. Yet, again, we must ask if such a condition proves preferable to an existence as a human? Kusanagi has evolved beyond the definition of the human, but is such an evolution desirable? Does ridding oneself of a unified identity truly lead to liberation, or does the experience of multiplicity merely lead to dehumanization or insanity? Before attempting to answer these questions—if there is an answer—we must first consider one last even more radical example of evolution and disembodiment.

The Complementation of the Human Soul: Hideaki Anno's *Evangelion*

Both *Akira* and *Ghost in the Shell* explore the potential for human evolution with the aid of technology on an individual level, but is it possible to imagine such a transformation of the entire human species? Hideaki Anno's *Shin Seiki Evangerion* (or *Neon Genesis Evangelion* [1995–6] as it was translated) and his film *The End of Evangelion* (1997) pursue precisely this question in their depiction of the human species' evolution into a bodiless, gestalt consciousness.[15] By mixing giant mechs (the Evangelions), alien-like beings known as "Angels," hints of Christian and Kabbalistic mythology, psychoanalysis, and existentialism, Anno creates one of the most overtly Lacanian investigations of loneliness, desire, and depression to ever be released as mass-market media. What begins as a typical anime story of barely postpubescent adolescents piloting giant mechs soon becomes a brooding, psychological tale about the human condition, social bonding, and existential despair set against an eschatological background that consistently causes the viewer to doubt whether the human species is worthy of evolution or whether it should merely be allowed to go extinct. This final pair of texts provides an example of evolution in which interaction with the divine pushes humankind beyond the limits of the body and certainly beyond the limits of the human.

In this chapter, I shall primarily focus on the last two episodes of the *Evangelion* series and the final moments of the film *The End of Evangelion*, for Anno provides two alternate versions of the events that conclude his storyline.[16] *Evangelion* takes place 14 years after Second Impact, the discovery of the first Angel (Adam) that destroyed more than half of the world's population in the year 2000. The series opens *in medias res* with the attack of the third Angel, and the arrival of Shinji Ikari in Tokyo-III at the summons of his father, Commander Gendo Ikari. Gendo commands a covert military organization known as NERV whose sole mission is to defend against the return of the Angels and to forestall a possible Third Impact that would potentially destroy the remainder of human civilization. Drawing from Robert Browning's dramatic poem "Pippa Passes" (1841), NERV features the ironic motto "God's in His Heaven—All's right with the world," a motto that will prove completely untrue in every sense over the course of the story (Browning 177). To combat the Angels, NERV created the Evangelions, which appear to be giant robots (or mechs) but which are actually biological copies of the first Angel that include pieces of human minds and souls within them. Only children born within the first year after Second Impact can pilot the Evangelions, and Shinji quickly becomes NERV's star pilot in Evangelion Unit-01. Together with the other Evangelion pilots (Rei and Asuka), Shinji defeats the Angels throughout the series and protects the world from obliteration. But NERV has bigger plans than the destruction of the Angels, for their ultimate goal is to enact the Human Instrumentality Project, which will preserve humanity beyond apocalypse by melding the consciousnesses of all people together. Humankind's time as a species has run out, and they must seek new avenues of evolution if they are to survive into the future.

The narrative of *Evangelion* "is an essentially bifurcated one" that is split between NERV's battles with the beings known as the "Angels" and a "narrative strand [that] is far more complex and provocative as it becomes increasingly concerned with the problematic mental and emotional states of the main characters, all of whom carry deep psychic wounds and whose psychic turmoil is represented against an increasingly frenzied apocalyptic background" (Napier, "Machines" 425). The characters' deep psychological scars prove fundamental to the story's investigation of human desire and loneliness, and each character's traumas play significant roles in how certain parts of the story unfold. The teenage Evangelion pilots, who are labeled in order of their admittance into the program, each face emotionally crippling psychological struggles: Rei (the First Child) faces feelings of alienation and existential angst because she is merely a clone; Asuka's (the Second Child's) overly competitive spirit and lack of self-esteem stem from her mother's madness and suicide; and Shinji Ikari (the Third Child) copes with the death of his mother and subsequent abandonment by his father. The adults who run Evangelion are not immune to such traumas either: Misato (the commander of NERV combat operations) deals with the memories of her distant father who ultimately died saving her life, and Gendo (Shinji's father and the head of NERV) continues to build walls around himself that block out his own son in order to handle his deceased wife's absence. In *Evangelion*, the traumas of the past are constantly bubbling just below the surface—in Lacanian terms, the horrors of the real are always threatening to erupt and crush the characters.

The first 24 episodes of the series deal with the destruction of the third through the seventeenth Angels, which vary in form from giant monstrosities to geometrical shapes to nanobot computer viruses. Both the Angels and Evangelions feature AT (or anti-terror) Fields that function as a kind of force field that protects them and that can only be punctured with certain specialized forms of weaponry, such as the progressive knife that vibrates at almost supersonic frequencies, enabling the Evangelions to slice matter at an atomic level. The series later reveals that humans also have AT Fields, but in humans they serve as the force that surrounds the human soul and separates it from all other souls: "It is the light of my soul," as Kaoru (the seventeenth Angel who appears in the form of a 14-year-old boy) explains to Shinji (*E* 24).[17] The AT Fields are what inscribe lack in the human heart, and the Human Instrumentality Project's ultimate goal is to lower the AT Fields of all humankind so that all souls may join together in a state beyond lack.

The last 2 episodes occur after the Angels have been defeated and chronicle the transformation of Shinji's consciousness as NERV's Human Instrumentality Project takes effect. To escape the postapocalyptic world created by Second Impact, NERV seeks to create a form of collective consciousness, a melding of all the consciousnesses on Earth to preserve them eternally in a realm beyond the body. NERV's goal is to, in the words of Gendo Ikari, manufacture "a new genesis for mankind" (*E* 21).[18] NERV hopes to accomplish "another 'beginning,' in a truly apocalyptic turn," for "not only do the viewers witness the individual reborn into a world made new, but the entire human species is remade immortal, liberated from its biological and psychological constraints to embrace a return to Edenic bliss" (Broderick 8). The final pair of episodes in the series become entirely stream-of-consciousness as they depict the process of unification, or instrumentality, in Shinji Ikari's mind. The second half of the penultimate episode portrays Shinji's disembodiment, which he describes as his image blurs to blackness: "What is this sensation? I feel like I've experienced it before, as if the shape of my body is melting away. It feels so good. I feel like I'm growing, expanding outward... On and on..." (*E* 25). Then, a black screen appears with text on it, an event that reoccurs throughout the last two episodes and that acts as a sort of narrator/interlocutor. Although the series never reveals the identity or nature of this narrative voice, the characters respond to it as if it is a diegetic voice and not simply a narrative intertitle. After Shinji blurs out, the text screen explains, "That was the beginning of the instrumentality of people. What people are lacking, the loss in their hearts. In order to fill that void in their hearts, the instrumentality of hearts and souls begins, returning all things to nothingness. The instrumentality of people had begun" (*E* 25). Commander Ikari then responds to the text's description of Human Instrumentality: "No, it is not that we are returning to nothingness. We are restoring everything to its original state. We are only returning to our mother, who has been lost to this world. All souls will become one and find eternal peace. That is all there is to it" (*E* 25). Ikari views instrumentality as a return to "Edenic bliss," one that for him holds a reunion with his dead wife, Yui—Shinji's mother—who disappeared and became merged with Evangelion Unit-01 during its initial tests.

The text voice also explains that this lack in the human heart causes all human desire and fear: "That is what gives rise to the hunger in our hearts. That is what gives rise to fear and insecurity" (*E* 25). Indeed, throughout the series, desire plays a fundamental part in the lives of the characters, and Anno deals explicitly with the desires of each of the major characters and examines how they remain unsatisfied in the normal course of human life. Instrumentality finally provides the means of satiating human desire and of eradicating fear and insecurity, but, in order to achieve instrumentality in a fashion that renders the subject as happy as possible, the subject must first face his/her desires head-on and learn to accept them.

Shinji's primary desire is to be accepted and loved by other people, particularly the women around him (Misato, Rei, and Asuka) and his father, yet he also remains incapable of accepting love from others because of his mother's death and his father's abandonment of him at a young age. Consequently, Shinji persistently worries about other people's perceptions of him and usually concludes that everyone hates him. Psychoanalytically, Shinji desires for others to desire him, yet he remains incapable of realizing when they return his desire, when they bestow recognition and love upon him. Even when he gains a wide circle of friends after coming to live in Tokyo-III, he still never recognizes himself as the object of others' love. Instead, he views himself as an object of scorn and ridicule and therefore hates himself (or thinks he hates himself). Because of his father's desertion, which denied Shinji the recognition of fatherly love, we might argue that Shinji experiences his lack so profoundly that it precludes him from being able to achieve a functioning state of sublimation. Thus, after the Human Instrumentality Project has taken effect, Shinji's world initially remains a solipsistic one in which only he exists—he exists in a state of pure lack with no others present. *Evangelion* chronicles the mass migration of humanity from a sense of identity predicated upon lack to one comprised of pure immanence, of the literal body without organs. If organs are to exist, then the subject must shape them according to his/her own desire. At first, Shinji proves incapable of dealing with this world of pure freedom, which the series depicts by having a black and white Shinji falling through a stark whiteness that has no dimensions, not even the spatial coordinates of up and down. Initially, then, Shinji only exhibits a will to nothingness, for he must learn to shape his own reality and sense of truth and to realize that this world represents only one of many possibilities.

This leads Shinji to the parodic anime sequence in which the world of *Evangelion* is crafted anew in such a way that all of the characters' roles are altered to create the ultimate blissful experience for

Shinji: Asuka is Shinji's girlfriend, Rei is the spunky new girl at school, Misato is their supercool teacher, and his mother and father live together with him as a normal nuclear family. This scene features the upbeat and ludicrous slapstick humor of stereotypical anime in which erection jokes, upskirt shots, and constantly suggestive comments create a world in which all of life's cares are literally laughed away. This vision of one possible utopian world leads to Shinji's first true revelation: "I get it, this is also a possible world. One possibility that's in me. The me right now is not exactly who I am. All sorts of me's are possible. That's right. A me that's not an Eva pilot is possible too" (*E* 26). At this point, Shinji comes to a truly Deleuzian realization: his self is not unified but instead composed of a multiplicity of drives, none of which remains dominant for long, and hence his "self" changes from one moment to the next. Once Shinji realizes the nature of his being as a multiplicity, he finally manages to understand how to love himself and how to allow others to love him: "I hate myself. But maybe I can learn to love myself. Maybe it's okay for me to be here! That's right! I'm me, nothing more, nothing less! I'm me. I want to be me! I want to be here! And it's okay for me to be here!" (*E* 26). After making this declaration, the solipsistic world created by Shinji's "will to nothingness" dissipates, and all his friends come to tell him "Congratulations." Thus, through a melting of his physical form and a melding of his mind with all of humanity, Shinji overcomes the world of desire and fills the lack within his identity, allowing him to achieve a state of pure becoming in which he "coexist[s] with time, space, and other people" (*E* 26). By experiencing the stripping of his self down to a plane of immanence, Shinji realizes that his self is ultimately mutable and that he can sculpt it as a work of art, one that he can truly learn to respect and love.

While this creation of a new Eden seems somewhat optimistic at the end of the series, the film *The End of Evangelion* portrays a much darker vision of this "new genesis," which appropriately depicts a new Adam and Eve in a world "purged of original sin" but which also leaves the viewer with dark forebodings concerning humanity's future (*E* 12).[19] Anno created the film to retell the events of these episodes in a more straightforward manner. Instead of being a predominately internal, mental depiction of Human Instrumentality like the series' finale, *End of Evangelion* shows the viewer explicitly what happens in the external world while still diving into the mind of Shinji to portray his psychic deterioration. In the outside world, *End of Evangelion* chronicles the apocalypse and humankind's subsequent rebirth as a new form of life. Initially, the series leads the audience to believe that

NERV has been secretly hiding Adam, the first Angel, underneath their headquarters, but the final episodes of the series and the film reveal that this gigantic being is actually the second Angel, Lilith. Rei joins with the crucified Lilith and brings it back to life. As the gigantic figure of Lilith/Rei towers above the clouds and reaches for Shinji, he begins his series of primal screams that dominate the film's climax. The film then depicts the events that initiate the Human Instrumentality Project, namely the joining of Lilith and Adam.

The film reveals that Shinji's Evangelion was actually patterned after Adam, who led to the Second Impact when he was unearthed in Antarctica. Later, NERV also exhumes a monstrously oversized spear on the surface of the Moon. Called the Lance of Longinus, the gigantic spear receives its name from the spear that pierced the side of Christ. In the film, Anno depicts the penetration of EVA Unit-01 by the Lance, which consequently turns the Evangelion (with Shinji inside it) into a new Adam. As Adam and Lilith come into contact with one another and the Lance, they form a new Tree of Life, a gigantic phallic-shaped tree that towers into the heavens. As Fuyutski further explains,

> The fruit of life is held by the angels. The fruit of wisdom is held by man. EVA Unit-01 now possesses them both and therefore becomes God. Now, the source of all souls, the Tree of Life, has been formed again. Will it be an ark to save mankind from the vacuum of Third Impact or is it a demon that will destroy us all? The fate of mankind now lies in Shinji's hands. (*End* 9)[20]

And, indeed, these two options begin to play out in Shinji's fractured psyche as he descends past the imaginary and symbolic levels and into the very heart of the real.

The real is the space of anxiety, trauma, hallucinations, and the unknowable. Of the three primary psychic structures (the symbolic, the imaginary, and the real), the real is the structure in which the opposition between "externality and internality [...] makes no sense" because "the real is without fissure" (Lacan, *Seminar II* 97). Similarly, the action in the final moments of *End of Evangelion* collapses this distinction—the external world and the images of the psyche become indistinguishable. And whether we are watching memories, hal- lucinations, or divine visions remains ambiguous. Similarly, Lacan states, "we have no means of apprehending this real—on any level and not only on that of knowledge—except via the go-between of the symbolic" (Lacan, *Seminar II* 97). Despite the fact that the real "resists symbolization entirely," the characters in *Evangelion* directly experience it as the Human Instrumentality Project melts the walls that separate the different parts of the psyche (Lacan, *Seminar I* 66). The real resists symbolization because it "is distinguished [...] by its separation from the field of the pleasure principle, by its desexualization, by the fact that its economy, later, admits something new, which is precisely the impossible" (Lacan, *Seminar XI* 167). In *End of Evangelion*, Shinji experiences the impossible—he is pushed out of the realm of the symbolic into the incomprehensible space of the pure real. In Lacan's words, he experiences "the revelation of that which is least penetrable in the real, the real lacking any possible mediation, of the ultimate real, of the essential object which isn't an object any longer, but this something faced with which all words cease and all categories fail, the object of anxiety *par excellence*" (Lacan, *Seminar II* 164). The real holds sway in both the "real" world that is undergoing a new genesis, and the world of Shinji's mind where he finally comes face-to-face with the inexplicable source of his anxiety: desire and anxiety intertwine into an insolvable Gordian knot, an Ouroboros of lust and guilt that threatens to consume Shinji.

As the Tree of Life is forming in reality, the film dissolves to the internal struggle occurring within the mind of Shinji Ikari. A stream-of-consciousness section opens with a depiction of a childhood version of Shinji on a lonely playground where he stomps through a sandcastle in the shape of a perfect pyramid, the shape of NERV headquarters. Nondiegetic sound ceases during the montage as we listen to the child's grunts and then witness his tears as he numbly tries to rebuild the pyramid from its ruins. The film proceeds into a montage featuring the women in Shinji's life: Asuka in bed with Shinji and Shinji's witnessing of the primal scene of his surrogate mother Misato having sex. Subsequently, we watch as Asuka berates Shinji in the kitchen for not being able to understand her and for his "jerk-off fantasies" that feature her as the star. Shinji screams, as he so often does, at the three swirling faces of "his" women (Asuka, Misato, and Rei), "Liars! You're just hiding behind those smiles, but you intentionally keep things ambiguous" (*End* 9). Rei responds, "Because the truth causes everyone pain. Because the truth is very, very traumatic" (*End* 9). Somewhere between a masturbation fantasy and an existential nervous breakdown, the scene ends with Shinji standing with his back toward the three women.

The film then cuts to an imaginary scene in Misato's kitchen, where Shinji declares his devotion to Asuka. But she remains bent over the table in an almost catatonically depressed pose. She rises suddenly to accuse Shinji of fearing everyone except her—she believes that he is merely settling for her because he is too scared to approach Rei or Misato. She begins to physically bully him by pushing him around the kitchen. She knocks him to the floor, spilling piping hot coffee over him. Shinji begins to rise from his defeated, existentially prone position and states, "Somebody please help me" (*End* 9). As he stands up, he keeps his head bent with his eyes plastered on the floor as if he has succumbed to the horrors of the real. But then he begins to lash out because anger at least provides some proof of his being. Overturning the table, he yells, "Somebody help me. Leave me alone. Don't abandon me. Don't kill me" (*End* 9). Asuka looks at him as if he is little more than a pathetic worm. And suddenly, Shinji's hands shoot up around her neck. With his head still down, he begins strangling her as the film cuts to a series of morbid children's drawings in crayon: screaming demon faces, disemboweled dogs, a decapitated fish head with a hook in its mouth, etc. As he begins strangling her, the film returns to the first use of nondiegetic sound since the stream-of-consciousness sequence began. Over the series of drawings, a poignant yet upbeat pop ballad begins to lilt along with the images. The song continues to play as Shinji chokes Asuka and as Human Instrumentality takes effect in the real world. Of course, the distinction between reality and dream or psychic state proves entirely illusory by the film's conclusion. The film proceeds to flash-cut between images from the series, particularly images involving the women in Shinji's life. As images flicker past, Shinji and Rei's disembodied voices hold a discussion about Shinji's feelings toward humanity: "Nobody wants me, so they can all just die [. . .] It would be better if I never existed. I should just die, too" (*End* 9). The conversation ends abruptly as the Japanese character for "silence" appears on the screen to which Shinji responds with another sustained primal scream. The film cuts speed up to the point where the images blur beyond the ability to distinguish them, and a series of violent crayon squiggles appears across them as if an angry child has attempted to scratch them out of existence.

The Tree of Life signals the beginning of Human Instrumentality. As Lilith spreads her wings across the entire expanse of the Earth and lifts her egg aloft, an Anti-AT field spreads out from her. Once Human Instrumentality takes effect, the Anti-AT field neutralizes every individual's AT Field, and they literally burst open and metamorphose into a yellow liquid called LCL, an experience of *jouissance* that recalls the term's literal meaning of ejaculation. As Lilith stands above the Earth and the souls flow up to her from the sea of neon crosses rising above the planet, a giant vaginal slit appears in her fore-head, and the Tree of Life penetrates it, disappearing inside Lilith's head. Following this cosmic penetration, Shinji witnesses thousands of Reis swimming like schools of sperm as the souls of humanity flow together and become one. This cosmic coitus of Adam and Lilith cul-minates in humankind's metamorphosis into a primordial sea team-ing with the primordial life force—a sea of sentient jissom produced by this act of celestial copulation. Just as the intercourse between Adam and Eve provides the genesis of humankind's lineage in the Judeo-Christian story, so does this union of Adam and Lilith lead to a new genesis for humankind.

All of humanity's LCL flows together to form this giant sea, and Shinji must make a choice between living in the LCL sea that con-tains the gestalt consciousness of humanity or returning to a bodily form that will still suffer from the lack that NERV has worked so hard to fill. Shinji chooses the latter option as evidenced by the scene that depicts Rei literally joined at the hip with Shinji—they are both nude with her straddling Shinji, giving the impression that she is impaled upon his penis, and her arm is thrust into Shinji's chest as his arm dis-appears inside her leg. Amongst this confusion of bodies and psyches, Rei explains to Shinji the choice that lies before him:

> This place is a sea of LCL. The primordial soup of life. A place with no AT fields, where individual forms do not exist. An ambiguous world where you can't tell where you end and others begin. A world where you exist everywhere and yet you're nowhere, all at once [...] If you wish for others to exist, the walls of their hearts will separate them again. They will all feel fear once more. (*End* 11)

Shinji's love for other people causes him to decide to reinhabit his physical form, despite the fact that he will be returning to a world of pain and lack. Although Instrumentality extends the promise of a pain-free world, Shinji still craves the feelings and emotions attached to desire, the struggle for satiation and recognition that makes his being seem "real." Finally, Shinji proves incapable of giving up on "the human." Unlike Kusanagi from *Ghost in the Shell*, Shinji chooses a unified sense of identity over an existence as a pure multiplicity because he still remains incapable of freeing himself from the desire that society has inscribed in his psyche.

Shinji emerges from the LCL sea back into bodily form, and the film's last scene depicts him lying beside Asuka, the pilot of Evangelion Unit-02 and the object of much of his adolescent sexual angst. Indeed, the film's beginning features a rather disturbing scene in which Shinji visits a comatose Asuka, who was injured in an earlier battle with one of the angels, in the hospital. Shinji begins to violently shake her in an attempt to rouse her from her coma, and her hospital gown inadvertently falls open to reveal her breasts. In a fit of anger and tears, Shinji proceeds to masturbate while Asuka lies unconscious, and this scene succinctly summarizes the torturous nature of desire not only between Shinji and Asuka but also in *Evangelion* as a whole. In this final scene, the two lie on a deserted beach that abuts a sea of blood beneath a horizon filled with the decapitated head of Lilith, the crucified forms of the Evangelions, and a blood-streaked Moon. Climbing on top of her, Shinji slowly begins to choke Asuka, but she raises her hand to his face and he relents. As he still remains sitting astride her prostrate body and crying on her, Asuka moves her one unwounded eye and glances at his distraught form. Her response is merely the words "How disgusting," at which point the movie ends abruptly (*End* 12). At the end of the film, the human race has achieved virtual immortality, albeit in a liquefied and conjoined form. As Shinji's mother, Yui, states: "Humans can only exist on this earth, but the Evangelion can live forever along with the human soul that dwells within. Even 5 billion years from now, when the Earth, the Moon, and the Sun are gone, Eva will exist. It will be lonely, but as long as one person still lives" (*End* 12). Professor Fuyutski finishes her thought with the statement "it will be eternal proof that mankind ever existed" (*End* 12). The ending thus proves to be simultaneously pessimistic and optimistic, but, unlike the series, the dystopian aspects far outweigh the utopian ones.

Interestingly, Anno's two different endings respectively offer a schizoanalytical and a psychoanalytical angle on the storyline. While the series ends with the subject's ability to understand his/her own multiplicity and to shape his/her identity as a work of art, *End of Evangelion* ultimately argues that human identity must remain predicated upon lack if the status of the human is to be maintained. The series effectively refutes the film's argument by displaying how humans are capable of understanding their identity in a different fashion when they are no longer tied to the sociocultural system that inscribes lack in their hearts: humankind can generate its own system of ethics beyond the judgments of good and evil that society forces upon them. They can reshape their identity to a point where they no longer feel lack and no longer seek fulfillment through the petty fantasy of sublimation: they can achieve a state of constant becoming in which they can continually will themselves into new forms of identity. They eschew the stabilizing forces of identity and the body in favor of a multiplicitous existence in which the self remains in a perpetual state of flux. In essence, Anno leaves the viewer with a choice of interpretations of the "human": does transcending a formulation of desire based upon lack lead to a static state of existence in which future evolution becomes impossible, or does it free humankind to experience a boundless field of evolution in which constant change becomes possible?

CONCLUSION: AND MUST WE ALWAYS LACK?

So, in *End of Evangelion*, Shinji must choose between the body without organs and a being based upon lack, between a multiplicitous absence of hierarchies and a rigidly organized existence in which he knows he will never find true fulfillment. Indeed, Shinji's decision narrativizes the theoretical debate that resides at the heart of this chapter: does the human always necessitate an assemblage of desire predicated upon lack, or can the concept of the human be revised to include a new formulation of identity in which desire always represents a positive force and the basis for ethical development? In effect, each of the texts in this chapter depicts a further stage of evolution in which humans achieve a form of immortality—they portray an evolutionary passage in which the human passes beyond the confines of the body and into a realm generally reserved for deities. Deleuze and Guattari contend that "the work of art is itself a desiring machine," and each of these texts represents the manner in which science fiction texts also function as desiring machines; that is, they act as mirrors that reflect our desires back to us in a way that allows for their problematization and theorization (*Anti-Oedipus* 32). Through its construction of radically estranging spaces, science fiction acts as a means of projecting our most basic wishes either onto the page of novels and stories or onto the screen of the cinema. In many ways, anime proves especially adept at this projection because the image it creates is fantastic and estranging at its core: even the animation style represents a fantasy of the human that destabilizes the concept of the human form (the dramatically oversized eyes being the most readily apparent feature of the anime aesthetic), thus making anime a privileged medium for dealing with questions of the body and desire.

No doubt, the human subject never truly receives the choice between the body and the body without organs or between lack and multiplicity as Tetsuo, Kusanagi, and Shinji do, but these texts allow us to consider a fundamental theoretical question surrounding the concept of desire: can the individual learn to bring the multiplicitous into their lives, to recognize that lack is inscribed by society, and to achieve the status of a new ethical subject who remains untethered to various sociocultural institutions that force morality upon the populace? Such texts embody the desire to attain a liberatory state beyond the strictures of mortality, society, and a psychology built upon lack, but can the subject truly abandon stable concepts of identity in favor of an existence (un)structured by multiplicity? Of course, no text can provide a definitive answer to such inquiries, but science fiction can open up what Deleuze terms "lines of flight" through which the critic can explore different schematizations of desire and its relation to the human. Unless radical events, such as those depicted in these texts, occur, the subject will always remain tied to sociopolitical systems and hence will remain subject to lack according to Deleuze, yet these texts also indicate that perhaps the subject can learn to communicate with the body without organs, with rhizomes, and with lines of flight while still being subjected to lack, desire, and the organization of the body and society. As Deleuze and Guattari make clear, "You never reach the Body without Organs, you can't reach it, you are forever attaining it, it is a limit" (*Plateaus* 150). In effect, like desire itself, the body without organs represents a goal that can never be reached. Instead, through constant deterritorializations and movements toward the body without organs, the subject can increasingly liberate him/herself from the various systems that attempt to impose structure on his/her identity. What Deleuze and Guattari's work teaches us is that other systems always remain possible—other organizations of our thoughts, our bodies, and our societies exist as potentials. This does not mean that structure can be abandoned entirely, for to do so would mean either literal death or emptying one's self out to the point where existence becomes nothingness:

> And how necessary caution is, the art of dosages, since overdose is a danger. You don't do it with a sledgehammer, you use a very fine file. You invent self-destructions that have nothing to do with the death drive. Dismantling the organism has never meant killing yourself, but rather opening the body to connections that presuppose an entire assemblage, circuits, conjunctions, levels and thresholds, passages and distributions of intensity, and territories and deterritorializations measured with the craft of a surveyor. (Deleuze and Guattari, *Plateaus* 160)

To move beyond lack, then, individuals must slowly divest themselves of the various organizational strata that structure and hence pervert their desire: they must constantly deterritorialize in order to refashion themselves in liberatory ways. To live without lack might squash the basis of human desire that has driven the greatest (as well as the worst) endeavors of human civilization, but to forego considering the "schizo" side of things precludes the possibility of even more radical forms of human achievement. These texts demonstrate how our lives and identities can always be considered anew and how the potential for reshaping them according to our own guidelines remains possible even in the most oppressive, dystopian societies. Therefore, while Freud and Lacan foreclose the prospect of evolution beyond the neurotic, Deleuze and Guattari at least open us up to conceiving of our identities as our own, that is, as works of art.

PART II

Science Fictions of the Present

The Eversion of the Virtual: Postmodernity and Control Societies in William Gibson's Science Fictions of the Present

For the apparent realism, or representationality, of SF has concealed another, far more complex temporal structure: not to give us 'images' of the future...but rather to defamiliarize and restructure our experience of our present, and to do so in specific ways distinct from all other forms of defamiliarization.

—*Fredric Jameson* ("*Progress*" 286)

We barely have time to reach maturity before our pasts become history, our individual histories belong to history writ large [...] Nowadays the recent past—'the sixties,' 'the seventies,' now 'the eighties'—become history as soon as it has been lived. History is on our heels, following us like our shadows, like death.

—*Marc Augé* (Non-Places 26–7)

In an endnote to a recent article, Katherine Hayles comments upon how "it is interesting that science fiction writers, traditionally the ones who prognosticate possible futures, are increasingly setting their fictions in the present" ("Computing" 149, n.2). In this article, Hayles contends with the human desire to generate prognostications about the future, and she argues that such attempts (whether they are in scientific discourses or in the literary domain of science fiction) prove inherently problematic: "If the record of past predictions is any guide, the one thing we know for certain is that when the future arrives, it will be different from the future we expected" (131). Hayles argues that such speculations are important not for what they tell us about the future but for how they allow us "to explore the influence that such predictions have on our *present* concepts" (131). She proceeds to examine the ways in which speculations about the future of computers and robotics affect our views of such technologies in the present. Therefore, both scientific and science-fictional visions of the future prove to not be about the future at all but about the present in which we live.

This trend that Hayles notes in recent science fiction represents a significant transformation of the genre because, among other things, it problematizes the traditional sense of it as a mode of estrangement. In general, science fiction has been defined by a certain kind of futurity or alterity, but this recent shift forces us to reevaluate the basic tropes of the genre. The history of traditional science fiction writers who have abandoned the genre to pursue more realistic writing can be traced back at least as far as J. G. Ballard, who moved away from writing the apocalyptic science fiction of his early days (*The Wind from Nowhere* [1961], *The Drowned World* [1962], *The Burning World* [1964], and *The Crystal World* [1966]) and began writing more directly realistic works such as *The Atrocity Exhibition* (1969), *Crash* (1973), *Concrete Island* (1974), *High Rise* (1975), and *Running Wild* (1988), all of which examine science-fictional themes like the effects of technology upon the human body and psyche but in predominately realistic milieus. More recently, science fiction authors such as Neal Stephenson and William Gibson have turned away from their traditional cyberpunk fare in favor of crafting more realistic works set in the past or present instead of in a distant future.[1] What has changed in recent years to induce such a fundamental transformation of the genre's basic characteristics? By means of an examination of William Gibson's *Pattern Recognition* (2003) and *Spook Country* (2007), this chapter argues that the increasing ascendancy of postmodern culture—and the "society of control" that increasingly characterizes it—has generated the need for a new imagination of the present. In chapters 1 and 2, we began to delve into the nature of the control society but always in the context of futuristic science fictions of estrangement. Now, we will begin to explore how the control society has already become our world of today. Gibson's recent novels, *Pattern Recognition* and *Spook Country*, enable us to grasp the constituents, both formal and conceptual, of what I will call "science fictions of the present," sci-fi texts that privilege the realistic tendency over an aesthetic of estrangement. Indeed, Gibson's novels suggest that the present has become its own science fiction, or, what amounts to the same thing, that the present might be evaluated and understood on the basis of a genre traditionally reserved for the future. Moreover, because the novels examine the inextricable linkage between the hegemonic force of computerization and the rise of the society of control, they also demonstrate the manner in which the present has become dystopian (a social pattern that has generally been reserved for the future tense).

THE PRESENT AS SCIENCE FICTION: SEPTEMBER 11TH AND THE ASCENDANCY OF POSTMODERNITY

Generally speaking, Gibson has received credit for coining the term "cyberspace" in the early 1980s with his "Sprawl Trilogy" and for imagining the potential of the still gestating technology of the Internet. But insofar as the Internet has become a staple technology of our global society, Gibson has recalibrated his fiction according to a recognition that the future is *now*. In a 2003 interview, Andrew Leonard asked him, "Was it a challenge to keep writing about the future, as the Internet exploded and so much of what you imagined came closer?" (par. 22). Gibson responded,

> It just seemed to be happening—it was like the windshield kept getting closer and closer. The event horizon was getting closer [...] I have this conviction that the present is actually inexpressibly peculiar now, and that's the only thing that's worth dealing with [...] You learn how you go to a novel and how you relate to it. There's an extra set of moves in classic SF that you learn as a reader, and then if you want to write the stuff you have to have internalized those sufficiently. Once you do that you can be in a special relationship with your readers. I find that when I transfer that special relationship into a piece of mimetic fiction set in the present, I get interesting results—I get *Pattern Recognition* [...] The volume of technological weirdness was being turned up all the time, but the world felt increasingly familiar. (par. 23–5)

Gibson labels the border between the present and the future an event horizon, which refers to the slice of space-time surrounding a black hole. Events that occur or light that is emitted from inside an event horizon cannot reach an observer stationed outside the event horizon. For Gibson, the event horizon of the future has migrated so close to the present moment that it makes it impossible—and perhaps unnecessary—to envision anything beyond *this* moment.

In his earlier novels, Gibson used temporal estrangement to narrativize and interrogate the psychological, sociological, political, and philosophical issues surrounding computerization, but now these futuristic themes have become our daily concerns. Thus, in his most recent novels, Gibson completely eschews temporal estrangement and chooses to set them directly in our present reality—a reality that has become so estranging in itself that it has caused the real, contemporary world to become a kind of science fiction. In effect, *Pattern Recognition* suggests that we have already arrived in the future, for "many of us who live in technoculture have come to experience the present as a kind of future at which we've inadvertently arrived, one of the many futures imagined by science fiction" (Hollinger 452). *Pattern Recognition* actually explains its own aesthetic in the words of the protagonist's boss, Blue Ant CEO Hubertus Bigend:

> We have no idea, now, of who, or what the inhabitants of our future might be. In that sense, we have no future. Not in the sense that your grandparents had a future, or thought they did. Fully imagined futures were the luxury of another day, one in which "now" was of some greater duration. For us, of course, things can change so abruptly, so violently, so profoundly, that futures like our grandparents' have insufficient "now" to stand on. We have no future because our present is too volatile...We have only risk management. The spinning of the given moment's scenarios. Pattern recognition. (*PR* 58–9)[2]

Ours is a world in which the "now" constantly slips away, in which the future is already present and then gone before it can even be recognized. As Lee Konstantinou points out, Gibson's concept of pattern recognition derives from Marshall McLuhan, and Bigend acts in such moments as a mouthpiece who spouts McLuhanite philosophy. Konstantinou points to the moment in *The Medium is the Massage* in which McLuhan himself makes a similar statement, "Electric circuitry profoundly involves men with one another. Information pours upon us, instantaneously and continuously. As soon as information is acquired, it is very rapidly replaced by still newer information. Our electrically configured world has been forced to move from the habit of data classification to the mode of pattern recognition" (63). Since we live under a constant barrage of information that bombards us from all sides through computers, cell phones, televisions, GPS systems, etc., we never have the capacity to look beyond the present moment. We already live in the future, so the need to create fictional futures becomes pointless.

Konstantinou argues that Gibson's novel exemplifies what he terms "Socio-economic science fiction, part of a growing subgenre that not only critiques economic and marketing theories but also uses these theories as the basis for exercises in worldbuilding" (74). I prefer the term "science fictions of the present" because, as we shall see in chapter 4, it encompasses a larger category of texts than the purely socio-economic works such as Gibson's. Konstantinou further contends that such science fiction texts engage in the process of what Fredric Jameson terms "cognitive mapping." In *Postmodernism, or, the Cultural Logic of Late Capitalism*, Jameson explains that for art to maintain a political edge in the postmodern era, it must engage with the economic and cultural structure of the new world system on a fundamental level. Consequently, Jameson calls for "an aesthetic of cognitive mapping—a pedagogical political culture which seeks to endow the individual subject with some new heightened sense of its place in the global system" (*Postmodernism* 54). As Konstantinou points out, Jameson generally turned to conspiracy texts for his examinations of cognitive mapping: David Cronenberg's *Videodrome* (1983), Sydney Pollack's *Three Days of the Condor* (1975), Alan J. Pakula's conspiracy trilogy (*Klute* [1971], *The Parallax View* [1974], and *All the President's Men* [1976]), Michelangelo Antonioni's *Blow-Up* (1966), and Brian De Palma's *Blow Out* (1981) all figure prominently in *The Geopolitical Aesthetic*, Jameson's follow-up to *Postmodernism* that explores cinema's capacity for cognitive mapping.[3]

Konstantinou believes that such texts fail to truly depict the place of the subject in the postmodern global worldscape because they focus solely on the power structure of control instead of on the postmodern system of capital that is predicated upon brand-name recognition. Konstantinou insightfully explores the depiction of trademarks in *Pattern Recognition* and how these trademarks cognitively map the subject's position as a consumer caught between the multinational corporations of first-world countries and the exploited labor that produces these products in the third world. But he never connects the novel's portrayal of the capitalist system of advertising together with its paranoid conspiracy elements that concern the society of control and the September 11th attacks. To fully understand how *Pattern Recognition* cognitively maps postmodern globalization, we must consider both the novel's depiction of capital and its exploration of 9/11's significance.

In this sense, *Pattern Recognition* operates in the present because it concerns itself with the absolute ascendancy of the postmodern, which implies both the rise of the late-capitalist marketing machine and the power structure of control. The term "postmodern" implicitly suggests a kind of oxymoron, a paradoxical state of history in which the future already exists in the present: it denotes a condition that literally defines us as existing "after the modern." Of course, the term "postmodern" has accrued a slew of different connotations, and in this chapter I will deal with the epistemological, socio-historical, and aesthetic senses of postmodernism. In *Pattern Recognition*, the World Trade Center attacks serve as the watershed moment when the postmodern episteme that had been gestating for decades was finally revealed to have achieved absolute ascendancy over the older, modern, sociocultural paradigm. No doubt, it has become a standard cliché to argue that 9/11 fundamentally altered the world, but Gibson's point is much more subtle: *Pattern Recognition* and *Spook Country* depict 9/11 as only one distinctive moment in the history of postmodernization, a socio-cultural force that has slowly been evolving since the end of World War II. The novel's action occurs in August 2002, only a scant eleven months after the attacks, and the text deals explicitly with the attacks by means of the backstory of its protagonist, Cayce Pollard.

Still fresh at the novel's outset, "9/11" remains omnipresent throughout the text in a vague, hazy fashion like images seared on the retina, lingering long after they have already faded from actual existence. For example, the simple phrase "heaps of bone" in an email to Cayce provokes her into recalling the attacks: "That initial seventeen stories of twisted impacted girder. Funeral ash. That taste in the back of the throat" (*PR* 79). Such oblique references in the text eventually give way to the discovery that Cayce's father (Win Pollard, an employee of the CIA) inexplicably disappeared on the day of the attacks. In the year following the disaster, Cayce and her mother never discover whether he died in the Twin Towers' collapse or simply vanished from existence on that fateful day. The revelation about Win Pollard's disappearance occurs in a chapter entitled "Singularity," and the attacks function as not just a singularity in Cayce's life but also as *the* singular moment of our historical age.

In effect, *Pattern Recognition* operates after the end of history,[4] when, as Bigend claims, "we have no future" nor any connection to the past. In the novel, like in our own world, September 11, 2001 constitutes a historical rupture that is no less than the rupture of history itself: "*Pattern Recognition* can be read as a kind of post-singularity fiction of the present [...] Gibson's singularity may be more symbolic, finally, than material; nevertheless, it functions in much the same way as the technological singularity, as an apocalyptic event that cuts us off from the historical past, leaving us stranded in difference" (Hollinger 462–3). Thus, the 9/11 attacks replace the normally estranging elements of science fiction such as technological innovations that completely alter society or "apocalyptic event(s)" that shatter the traditional molds of civilization. As Slavoj Žižek points out, September 11th actually enacted the cataclysmic scenarios played out in so many disaster films:

> Not only were the media bombarding us all the time with talk about the terrorist threat; this threat was also obviously libidinally invested— just remember the series of movies from *Escape from New York* to *Independence Day*. That is the rationale of the often-mentioned association of the attacks with Hollywood disaster movies: the unthinkable which happened was the object of fantasy, so that, in a way, America got what it fantasized about, and that was the biggest surprise. (*Desert* 15–6)

As Žižek further suggests, the experience of watching the Twin Towers' collapse was *jouissance* in its purest form—we as society were placed in direct contact with the real. And Žižek plays on the definition of the real in both its Lacanian sense as the space of true trauma underlying the structures of the imaginary and the symbolic and in the sense of the real versus the false (or simulacral). While the 9/11 attacks reflected the images from Hollywood's seemingly neverending stream of disaster films, the attacks also highlighted the inherent fakeness of most television: "It was when we watched the WTC towers collapsing on the TV screen, that it became possible to experience the falsity of 'reality TV shows': even if these shows are 'for real,' people still act in them—they simply play themselves" (Žižek, *Desert* 12). Gibson's novel unfolds during a time period when the United States was still struggling to understand this intrusion of the real into our daily lives. The attacks represent a profoundly postmodern event because the real ruptures the American imaginary and symbolic—the social narratives of unity, coherence, and world dominance imploded along with the World Trade Center, and our society was forced to create new narratives to cope with this loss of meaning.

Notably, Gibson had already envisioned *Pattern Recognition*'s plot before the events of 9/11, but the attacks forced him to reevaluate his story. Gibson claims to have already been well into the novel's composition when the attacks occurred, and, as he has claimed in an interview, the events of September 11th fundamentally altered not just his view of the novel but also his outlook on history in general:

> I saw that my protagonist's back story, that I'd been sort of interrogating and looking for and starting to find, was taking place right then—her memories were of *that autumn* [...] I had a sense that the

back-story world my character had been tentatively inhabiting for me, as I tried to figure out what the hell was wrong with her, had clicked off—it had forked and diverged like Borges' "Garden of Forking Paths." [...] And there was this terrible irony in that. But that was completely swept aside by my recognition at that point that my world no longer existed and that the meaning of everything [...] ever that had gone before had to be reconsidered in the light of something that had happened. (Leonard par. 34)

For Gibson, September 11th represents what he once called a "nodal point"—a singularity that forever cuts the world off from what came before and fundamentally alters everything that occurs afterward.

The World Trade Center attacks constitute a point of rupture in which the faces of the twin processes of postmodernization and globalization were laid bare. *Pattern Recognition* examines 9/11 as the crystallizing moment of postmodernization: it serves as the ultimate event in a series of events (heretofore, the most important of which was probably the fall of the Berlin Wall) that signifies the passage from the modern regime of sovereignty to the postmodern order of control. In short, 9/11 corresponds with the end of Cold War ideologies. In the postmodern world, the disciplinary power of military-industrial complexes like the United States and their enforcement agencies begins to wane in the face of the onslaught of globalization. Because Cayce's father was a CIA operative,

he serves in the novel as one of a number of figures of the old cold war world, defined as it was by its struggles between the massive state disciplinary, security, and military apparatuses of the United Sates, the Soviet Union, and their allies [...] September 11, Gibson's novel suggests, is the sign that order has finally and definitely come to an end, clearing the space for the emergence of something new. (Wegner 196)

Like Cayce's father, the Cold War apparatus of power vanished along with the twin towers on 9/11. While the Cold War functioned according to the traditional, modern paradigm in which nation states struggled for dominance, September 11th signals the culmination of the postmodern process of globalization. The World Trade Center Attacks reveal the fully globalized body of the Earth by demonstrating how an attack on one location can strike at the heart of the entire global capitalist order. As Jean Baudrillard argues,

We must, then, assume that the collapse of the towers [...] prefigures a kind of dramatic ending and, all in all, disappearance of this form of architecture and of the world system it embodies. Shaped in the pure computer image of banking and finance, (ac)countable and digital, they in a sense are its brain, and in striking there the terrorists have struck at the brain, at the nerve-center of the system. (*Terrorism* 40–1)

Pattern Recognition acts as an index of this new topology of power, which has shifted from what Michel Foucault calls "disciplinary societies" to what Gilles Deleuze terms "controls societies."

Patterns of the Postmodern: The Computerization of Society and the Subject

Before examining how *Pattern Recognition* provides an index or cognitive map to our fully globalized and computerized society, we must first chart the trajectory of Gibson's writings because the course of his literary output parallels the growth of computerization in the past three decades. Only by placing *Pattern Recognition* within the overall framework of his oeuvre can we fully grasp the significance of the text in relation to the postmodern society of control. Gibson's body of work almost exclusively examines the potential effects of computer networks. Gibson initially envisioned the invention of cyberspace in a series of stories that appeared in *Omni* magazine during the early 1980s and first introduced readers to the world of "The Sprawl." But he attained true notoriety with the publication of his first "Sprawl" novel *Neuromancer* (1984) and its two sequels: *Count Zero* (1986) and *Mona Lisa Overdrive* (1988). This series played a fundamental role in giving birth to the science fiction subgenre of cyberpunk. As its name indicates, "The Sprawl Trilogy" depicts a seemingly bleak, noirish future in which cities have spread out and engulfed their surrounding environs and in which information is housed and transmitted through a global computer network known as the Matrix.

Gibson's "Sprawl" series spans the 1980s when the Internet was still in its gestation phase, but, once the Internet went public, Gibson's fiction underwent a foundational transformation in order to accommodate the new technological advances occurring around him. Gibson's next major series deals with a much less distant future, one in which the technological innovations seem to be just around the corner. Generally referred to as "The Bridge Trilogy," this series began in 1993 with the publication of *Virtual Light* and was followed by *Idoru* (1996) and *All Tomorrow's Parties* (1999). While the Bridge novels feature such technological advancements as virtual reality helmets and a computer-generated pop music icon with artificial intelligence, they still operate in a future barely removed from the contemporary world in which they were written—for example, *Virtual Light* is set in the year 2005, only a scant 12 years from its publication date. As Gibson states in his interview with Andrew Leonard, these works read almost like adventures in an "alternative present" reached along a different forking path, to follow Gibson's Borgesian metaphor (par. 23). With his next novel, *Pattern Recognition*, Gibson began to forego futurity and alterity altogether, and he continued this new narrative paradigm in the two later entries of his most recent trilogy: *Spook Country* (2007) and *Zero History* (2010). For the bulk of this chapter, I will focus on *Pattern Recognition* because it provides the most sophisticated investigation of the computerization of the postmodern worldscape, but, in the conclusion, I will transition into a brief discussion of *Spook Country* in order to provide some final thoughts on the topic of control.

Gibson's novels have often dealt with the implications of rampant globalization. In the two decades since *Neuromancer*, Gibson's interests have not altered, but his approach has changed. Gibson still writes about globalization, the effects of information upon the psyche, the cyborgization of the human, and international intrigues surrounding information, but now he writes about such anxieties in a realistic present or recent past milieu instead of in futuristic worldscapes. In this respect, *Pattern Recognition* represents the moment in Gibson's own body of work at which the distinction between the present and future vanishes. From *Neuromancer* to *Pattern Recognition*, Gibson's literary output charts the collapsing of the temporal event horizon that he discusses; that is, as linear time has progressed from past to present to future, Gibson's works have inverted this paradigm by migrating steadily from the future to the present or even the past. By means of this inversion, Gibson's texts schematize the manner in which the objects of speculative fiction have become the real world technologies of today, or, in other words, how *the future has become the present.* Furthermore, because Gibson's texts always deal with computer technology, they act as programmatic indexes of what Francois Lyotard terms "the hegemony of computers"; that is, each of his works acts as a response to the growth of computer and communication technology by tracing the effects of this computerization upon both the individual and sociopolitical levels. In short, we might say, Gibson's works concern nothing less than postmodernity itself.

In *The Postmodern Condition: A Report on Knowledge* (1979), Jean-Francois Lyotard explicitly links the postmodern era with the rise of computer and cybernetic technology. Lyotard remains most famous for his definition of the *"postmodern* as incredulity towards metanarratives," that is as a skepticism toward any schematic attempt to explain human identity, reality, or historical forces (xxiv). Any over-arching narrative that attempts to provide the key to understanding all of or some facet of human experience becomes a dubious object: psychoanalysis, Darwinian evolution, Marxism, scientific empiricism, etc. all become suspect under the auspices of postmodern epistemol-ogy. For Lyotard, the *"Modern* [...] designate[s] any science that legit-imates itself with reference to a metadiscourse of this kind making an explicit appeal to some grand narrative, such as the dialectics of the Spirit, the hermeneutics of meaning, the emancipation of the rational or working subject, or the creation of wealth" (xxiii). But knowledge undergoes a transformation "as societies enter what is known as the postindustrial age and cultures enter what is known as the postmodern age" (Lyotard 3). In the era of postindustrialism and postmodernism, the legitimation of knowledge ceases to depend upon metanarratives; instead, it is increasingly grounded in its exchange value—it under-goes a process of "mercantilization" (Lyotard 5).

With the advent of cybernetics, which concerns itself with flows of information and the ability of computers and robots to process and exhibit information, Lyotard argues that our definition of knowledge must undergo an alteration in order to accommodate the emergent concept of information:

> The nature of knowledge cannot survive unchanged within this con-text of general transformation. It can fit into the new channels, and become operational, only if learning is translated into quantities of information. We can predict that anything in the constituted body of knowledge that is not translatable in this way will be abandoned and that the direction of new research will be dictated by the possibility of its eventual results being translatable into computer language. (4)

Thus, the postmodern era gives rise to what Lyotard terms the "hegemony of computers," a hegemony in which, to be legitimated, all knowledge must be translatable into information, into a language that can be read and processed by computers. Because of this hegem-ony of computers, knowledge becomes exterior to the knower, and it "ceases to be an end in itself, it loses its 'use value'" (Lyotard 5). There is no use apart from information, no value apart from capital: "Knowledge is and will be produced in order to be sold, it is and will be consumed in order to be valorized in a new production" (Lyotard 4). For Lyotard, information and its exchange value achieve hegemony over knowledge—information becomes a commodity to be bought, sold, and housed by computers.

Pattern Recognition traces this transformation of knowledge by means of the novel's protagonist, Cayce Pollard, who inhabits an almost mystical position in the world of postmodern marketing, advertising, and computerization. She works as a "coolhunter," someone gifted with the intuitive ability to recognize the next hot trend.[5] She possesses this talent because she has internalized not just the commodity marketplace but also the hegemony of computers. This hegemony is established in the book's opening pages that describe Cayce's profession through her Google search results: "Google Cayce and you will find 'coolhunter,' and if you look closely you may see it suggested that she is a 'sensitive' of some kind, a dowser in the world of global marketing. Though the truth [...] is closer to an allergy, a morbid and sometimes violent reaction to the semiotics of the marketplace" (*PR* 2). Google and other such search engines have become indexes of society—they provide a basic structuring principle for the flow of capital and information in the postmodern economy.[6] The fact that "google" has become a verb officially recognized by the *Oxford English Dictionary* demonstrates again how the computer has become the primary organizing principle of the postmodern episteme.

As its title indicates, the novel explores the growing importance of pattern recognition in the newly computerized global market, and sites such as Google function by means of such pattern recognition. Similarly, as Cayce explains, her employment depends upon her pattern recognition skills: "It's about a group behavior pattern around a particular class of object. What I do is pattern recognition. I try to recognize a pattern before anyone else does" (*PR* 88). Her ability relies on the fact that social images, particularly those of company trademarks, have become so deeply embedded in her psyche that they elicit complex emotional responses. She has even developed an allergy to some of them, "A sometimes violent reactivity to the semiotics of the marketplace [...] a side effect of too much exposure to the reactor cores of fashion [...] She is, literally, allergic to fashion" (*PR* 2, 8). Because of this sensitivity, she only wears nondescript outfits with the trademarks removed. This practice allows her to avoid suffering violent reactions to the logos—in effect, she removes her body from the sphere of brand-named commodities. Her seemingly brandless outfits represent her attempt "to carve out an original identity in a world filled with 'simulacra of simulacra of simulacra'" (Konstantinou 69; *PR* 18). The proliferation of simulacra serves as another major characteristic generally associated with the postmodern era.[7] As Jean

Baudrillard argues, in the era of simulation and simulacra, "it is a question of substituting the signs of the real for the real itself"; hence, we are left with "the knowledge that truth, reference, objective cause have ceased to exist" (*Simulation* 2–3). The destruction of the World Trade Center seemed to reveal that the American dream of progress and world dominance was itself nothing more than a simulacrum. Therefore, like so many Americans in the aftermath of the attacks, Cayce struggles to find her own "trademark," to inscribe her own meaning upon the seemingly random and cruel nature of existence. But her quest ultimately proves to be in vain because the novel proceeds to examine the manner in which postindustrial capitalism commodifies even the most aberrant or benign lifestyle choices.

In "Fear and Loathing in Globalization," Jameson terms Cayce's condition "commodity bulimia" as if her consumption at the constant buffet of commodity trademarks forces her psyche to purge them by wearing generic attire and developing an allergic response:

> Indeed, within the brand name the whole contradictory dialectic of universality and particularity is played out as a tug of war between visual recognition and what we call the work of consumption (as Freud spoke of the work of mourning). And yet, to paraphrase Empson, the name remains, the name remains and kills; and the logo into which the brand name gradually hardens soaks up its toxicity and retains the poison. (390–1)[8]

Postmodern capitalism administers a lethal injection of commodities into each consumer, causing them to internalize the commodity system like an incurable virus. In essence, Cayce acts as a sort of commodity mystic, "a very specialized piece of human litmus paper" who can merely look at company logos and determine, without any kind of rational thought, whether they will function as lucrative product symbols (*PR* 13). Therefore, the novel demonstrates the manner in which the human becomes like a computer: by means of Cayce's internalization of the commodity system and its attendant system of advertising, Cayce becomes capable of *processing* trademarks, logos, and brand names—it is a "hermeneutic disposition" that allows her mind to intuitively perform the massive endeavors of real-world coolhunters who employ "focus groups, market research, consumer surveys, and statistical models as the basis for their predictions" (Konstantinou 72). Her brain has internalized the semiotics of the marketplace so deeply that it can instantly recognize patterns; it is no accident that her friend Damien jokingly refers to her bland outfits as CPUs (Cayce Pollard

Units, but, of course, also Central Processing Units). The pattern recognition protocols of computer programs have become the operational parameters of Cayce's own psyche. Similar to the manner in which various companies offer product suggestions based on previous consumption patterns without any need for additional details about a consumer's life, Cayce can identify logos that will prove profitable among the largest possible demographic. She achieves this without rational thought because she has internalized the commodity marketing system and the hegemony of computers to the point that they have become like deep psychic structures that operate akin to a reflex response.

The Digitized Aesthetic: The Façade of Freedom and the Web of Control

The effects of the postmodern hegemony of computers extend beyond epistemology and into the realm of aesthetics as well. As we have already seen, each of Gibson's texts functions as a response to computerization's steady growth toward hegemonic power, and the aesthetics of his works mark this progress as well. The "Sprawl" stories and novels feature a language that attempts to capture the epistemological processes of the texts' futuristic characters, who are completely enmeshed in the virtual/digital world. Filled with jargon that often never receives satisfactory explanations and featuring word choice that stresses how computer technology has become vitally linked to the human psyche, the "Sprawl" novels prove to be a dense web of intrigues unfolding against an almost unimaginable techno-landscape. One need only examine a sample passage from the opening pages of *Neuromancer* to see this digital aesthetic at work:

> A year here and he still dreamed of cyberspace, hope fading nightly. All the speed he took, all the turns he'd taken and the corners he'd cut in Night City, and still he'd see the matrix in his sleep, bright lattices of logic unfolding across that colorless void [...]The Sprawl was a long strange way home over the Pacific now, and he was no console man, no cyberspace cowboy. Just another hustler, trying to make it through. But the dreams came on in the Japanese night like livewire voodoo, and he'd cry for it, cry in his sleep, and wake alone in the dark, curled in his capsule in some coffin hotel, his hands clawed into the bedslab, temperfoam bunched between his fingers, trying to reach the console that wasn't there. (4)

In this passage, every line bristles with the electricity of the computer world it is describing to the reader—fantastical phrases like "cyberspace," "bright lattices of logic," and "livewire voodoo" convey the manner in which computerization can infiltrate not only the psyche but also aesthetic production.

As Scott Bukatman explains, Gibson built the techno-language of the Sprawl universe from a variety of sources: "Gibson coalesced an eclectic range of generic protocols, contemporary idiolects, and a pervasive technological eroticism combined with a future-shocking ambivalence. Aside from the old and new waves of science fiction, Gibson's prose and perspective owes much to the streetwise weariness of Chandler and the neologistic prowess of William Burroughs" (146). Bukatman's observation explains the manner in which the prose style of *Neuromancer* features a gestalt aesthetic that blends together the hard-boiled style of Raymond Chandler and Dashiell Hammett together with the fantastic and ambiguous science-fictional language of William S. Burroughs. But this writing style gives way in Gibson's later texts to a more quotidian, sparse style that plays well for audiences beyond the traditional science fiction fanbase. The language of these early works acts as an aesthetic attempt to textually embody the cognitive effects of the development of such technology, but just as Gibson's settings have moved from the future to the present so has the syntax of his novels migrated temporally as well: now his novels feature the vernacular of the contemporary moment, which is itself filled with its own cyber-language. While the hegemony of computers and the society of control still seemed like objects of speculation in "The Sprawl Trilogy," the form and content of *Pattern Recognition* display the manner in which both have become the norm of the day.

On the formal level, the novel includes numerous emails, which have displaced modernist epistolary communication. In fact, the final chapter, "Mail," consists almost entirely of emails to Cayce that provide the novel's closure. Thus, we can see how the shift in epistemology has infiltrated the literary realm on a basic, structural level. Indeed, one could imagine a postmodern epistolary novel in which the entirety of the text was comprised of emails or text messages complete with headers, Internet acronyms, images, and emoticons. In fact, David Foster Wallace's non-SF short story "The Suffering Channel" (2004) proceeds one step further than Gibson in this regard by incorporating the entirety of an email, including its attendant HTML tags, into the story's text.[9] *Pattern Recognition* further deals with the computerization of aesthetics at the level of its narrative that centers around a work of art that seems to participate fully in the "hegemony of computers" while remaining free from capitalist control: the Footage, a film (or series of films) that epitomizes the possibilities of art in the postmodern, computerized era. For Cayce Pollard, the Footage constitutes the one constant in her life—while she jetsets around the world meeting with corporate bigwigs, Cayce lives her real, passionate existence through the channels of the Internet. Cayce herself represents a form of *otaku*, or fanboy, because her *raison d'être* resides in cultishly following "the Footage," film clips of an unknown origin that appear sporadically on the Internet and which she and the other "Footageheads" debate *ad infinitum* on a web forum entitled "FETISH: FOOTAGE: FORUM" or "F: F: F." Cayce's main obsession in life only exists on the Internet: the "mystery of the Footage itself often feels closer to the core of her life than Bigend, Blue Ant, Dorotea, even her career" (*PR* 78). The Footage epitomizes the liberatory dream of the Internet, the dream that users across the world can convene in a virtual space to share knowledge free from national and corporate boundaries. And, indeed, the Footage Forum is a fully globalized entity that brings together users of diverse economic, national, and cultural backgrounds. For Cayce and the other Footageheads, the Footage signifies art free from commodification (no small feat in the postmodern era when art comes to be recognized as a commodity).

As Jameson states, "The Footage is an epoch of rest, an escape from the noisy commodities themselves, which turn out, as Marx always thought they would, to be living entities preying on the humans who have to coexist with them" ("Fear" 391). In a world in which everything has become "simulacra of simulacra of simulacra," the Footage offers freedom for its viewers from the endless procession of commodities, trademarks, and advertising gimmicks—it is an escape from the "logo-maze" (*PR* 18). For Cayce, it functions as a form of "psychological prophylaxis," a preventative measure against the further impregnation of her psyche by the virile and viral force of commodities (*PR* 51). The Footage segments that the Footage Forum labels with numbers based on the chronology of their dissemination, represent minimalist, nonnarrative filmic images that always feature the same couple in a variety of indeterminate settings. When Cayce receives an email with an attached Footage segment, the novel describes her watching it in almost ecstatically sublime terms:

It is as if she participates in the very birth of cinema, that Lumière moment, the steam locomotive about to emerge from the screen, sending the audience fleeing into the Parisian night. Light and shadow. Lovers' cheekbones in the prelude to embrace ... So long now, and they have not been seen to touch ... They are dressed as they have always been dressed, in clothing Cayce posted on extensively, fascinated by its timelessness, something she knows and understands [...] And here in Damien's flat, watching their lips meet, she knows that she knows nothing, but wants nothing more than to see the film of which this must be a part. Must be. (*PR* 23–4)

The Footage constitutes a pure aesthetic object, one that gives no clues as to its genre or even of its individual elements form a linear narrative: it is merely a series of images open to endless interpretation. In fact, the Footage segments hearken back to what Tom Gunning has termed the "cinema of attractions": the early, silent films of Auguste and Louis Lumière and George Méliès that create effects more directly through images than overarching narratives.[10] For the Footageheads, the Forum provides a public space of free discourse surrounding an aesthetic object that remains free from the ubiquitous commodification present in all other spheres of society.

On account of its viral dissemination through obscure Internet locations, the origins of the Footage remain shrouded in mystery. Throughout the majority of the novel, it remains unclear whether or not a narrative strand connects the individual segments, and hence the Footage appears to be a virginal artistic object, unsullied by the commodifying forces of the cinema industry. In *Pattern Recognition*, the Footage Forum acts as a microcosm of literary/film theory because it features various factions who dogmatically debate theories of interpretation. For example, whether the individual segments comprise pieces of "a work in progress" or "something completed years ago" proves to be an unsolvable antinomy for the Footageheads, giving rise to two competing camps known as the Progressives and the Completists (*PR* 22). Cayce's friend Parkaboy acts as the "de facto spokesperson" of the Progressives who believe "that the footage consists of fragments of a work in progress, something unfinished and still being generated by its maker" (*PR* 49). On the other side of the debate, the Completists "are convinced that the footage is comprised of snippets from a finished work, one whose maker chooses to expose it piecemeal and in non-sequential order" (49). In addition to theories concerning the Footage's narrative, the Footageheads also debate the number of people responsible for the Footage's creation. Parkaboy develops the theory of "the Garage Kubrick," the *auteur* theory of the critical universe that orbits the footage: "It is possible that this footage is generated single-handedly by some technologically empowered solo auteur, some guerilla creator out there alone in the night of the Internet" (50). Hence, the Footage Forum instantiates a true space of art: neither tied to commercial machinery nor even to the dominance of proper names, the Footage resides in anonymity as an object open to pure interpretation. But the Footage also epitomizes a certain sense of angst that comes with the Internet, a sense that the anonymity provided by the web harbors unknowable secrets in the black, semiotically unstable "night of the Internet."

Despite the hermeneutical inscrutability of the Footage, Cayce manages to track down its point of origin. By working through these communication channels, which we shall see are the same channels that allow the society of control to function, Cayce finally receives a Russian email address of one Stella Volkova, who claims that her mentally disabled sister Nora is the creator of the Footage. Cayce hops a plane to Moscow and discovers that Nora suffers from brain damage incurred during a bomb attack that killed her parents, driving home the novel's terrorism theme. Because of her mental impairment, *Pattern Recognition* reveals Nora as an artist free from the influence of commodities because her damaged mind cannot even function as part of the capitalist regime: "Their [the Footage's] production is not seeking an instant capital gain but rather the expansion of their trade, which has been manufactured in order to be shared visually with other users online" (Rapatzikou 160). Ultimately, the Footage merely represents one disordered mind's attempt to communicate. When Cayce asks if the film contains a linear narrative, Stella responds, "I do not know. One day, perhaps, she will start to edit as she edited her student film: to a single frame. Or perhaps one day they speak, the characters. Who knows? Nora? She does not say" (*PR* 312). Cayce watches as Nora creates a new segment, and she discovers that Nora crafts her film digitally from found footage, thus negating any of the Footagehead theories about the significance or potential narrative of the clips. Cayce discovers that the Footage is "only the wound speaking wordlessly in the dark" (*PR* 316). The Footage gives voice to the traumatized psyche of the world: "What matters here is the neutral and non-sequential make-up of the footage that seems to be echoing the sudden and inexplicable (for the characters in the novel) collapse of the Twin Towers" (Rapatzikou 159).

In effect, the Footage constitutes an enigmatic space to which its viewers attempt to ascribe meaning just as American citizens were still trying to understand the nature of the September 11th attacks: "Rather, in the light of 'events' like the bursting of the dot-com bubble and the attacks of September 11, we now desperately search for patterns in the fabric of history but find that 'now' changes too abruptly to map completely or meaningfully. We try to recognize patterns or employ coolhunters as a means of coping with what we cannot understand" (Konstantinou 80). Moreover, the Footageheads' devotion to the film clips demonstrates another means of inscribing meaning upon reality. If we think back to chapter 2, the Footage represents a form of sublimation—it provides a substitute object that can fill the lack of being that has become less deniable in the post-9/11 era. While the reality outside their windows may no longer make sense, the Footageheads find solace in attempting to sort out the meaning underlying the Footage. The Footage provides a worthy sanctuary from the post-9/11 geopolitical situation because it seems to exist in a space that has not yet been territorialized by capital and control. But Cayce points out that Nora's work has garnered too much attention to remain free from the strictures of capitalist control: "Any creation that attracts the attention of the world, on an ongoing basis, becomes valuable, if only in terms of potential" (317). And, once Cayce uncovers the Footage's source, Bigend promptly moves in to territorialize this seemingly liberatory aesthetic space.

VIRTUAL IDENTITIES: SELF-FASHIONING IN THE WEB OF CONTROL

While the Footage Forum functions as one example of the liberatory capacities of the Internet, the novel also examines the utopian potential of creating new identities whole cloth on the web. Indeed, such an act of virtual self-fashioning provides Cayce with the first steps on her quest for the Footage's author. Cayce's search for the Footage is initially conditioned by Parkaboy's discovery of a digital watermark steganographically concealed within one of the older segments of film, thus proving that the Footage is not an entirely anonymous work of art. As Parkaboy explains in an email to Cayce, steganography "is about concealing information by spreading it throughout other information" (*PR* 78). Steganography represents a pattern distributed throughout a digital object beyond the capabilities of the normal human eye to recognize. Parkaboy and his friend Darryl discover references to the watermarking while reading Japanese sites concerning the Footage. In order to find out more about the watermark, Parkaboy and Darryl undertake an act of self-fashioning that becomes possible only within the virtual sphere of anonymity created by the Internet: They "began to lovingly generate a Japanese persona, namely one Keiko, who began to post, in Japanese, on that same Osaka site" (*PR* 78). Parkaboy and Darryl's creation of Keiko exhibits how the Internet can function as a plane of immanence in which identity can be restructured anew and as a heterotopia, a non-place that is simultaneously connected to all places.

They craft this faux-personality in order to attract Footage otaku, for as Parkaboy says, "There's nothing like genderbait for the nerds" (*PR* 78). They sculpt her identity to resemble something out of a fanboy's wet dream and immediately catch someone with their "bait": "Very shortly, we had one Takayuchi eating out of our flowerlike palm. Taki, as he prefers we call him" (*PR* 78–9). The simulacral Keiko displays the manner in which subjects can craft their dream existences, even if only virtually—they can transform themselves into intelligent and sexy individuals with fascinating life stories. As Deleuze would say, the Internet grants the user the ability to truly create his/her self as a work of art. Thus, "the past," as Cayce explains, becomes "mutable too, as mutable as the future" (*PR* 121). Subjects can even generate fake pictures of themselves—as Parkaboy and Darryl do with Keiko—pictures that can represent themselves as they would like to be seen. In an email to Cayce, Parkaboy describes the creation of Keiko's photograph:

> What we did to up the wattage for Taki, aiming to maximize libidinal disturbance, we shot this long tall Judy then reduced her by at least a third, in Photoshop. Cut'n'pasted her into Musashi's kid's sister's dorm room at Cal. Darryl did the costuming himself, and then we decided to try enlarging the eyes a few clicks. That made all the difference. Judy's epicanthic folds are long gone, the way of the modest bust nature intended for her (actually we've got her wrapped in Ace bandage for the shot, but nothing too tight) and the resulting big round eyes are pure Anime Magic. (*PR* 132)

As Konstantinou points out, Keiko embodies the manner in which sexual fetishes function as yet another form of pattern because they "are part of the mind's 'culture module,' whose parameters get set in the particular cultural environment one happens to grow up in" (Konstantinou 77). Sexual fetishes, like brands, operate according to "cognitive maps."[11] By harnessing the power of these cognitive maps, Parkaboy and Darryl use Keiko to dupe an unsuspecting Japanese programmer. This incident simultaneously highlights the hermeneutic instability of human interactions in cyberspace, where self-fashioning becomes uniquely possible, but it also demonstrates how all manners of subject behavior can be read according to the protocol of pattern recognition.

As we saw with the technology in *Trouble on Triton*, the Internet opens up new types for the subject by means of technology. The non-place of the Internet allows the subject to experience forms of difference not available in normal reality. The subject (whether male or female) can thus live out a virtual existence as a sleek, sexy anime girl within the various communities of the Internet. The "otaku-coven" of which Taki is a part represents one of these subcommunities within the overall community of the Internet, and by means of such subcommunities the subject can find a space that grants the recognition s/he desires either for their real identity and life history or for the identity they have constructed for themselves. For Deleuze, such virtual identities could be just as "real" as one's quotidian, workaday identity: "A life contains only virtuals. It is made up of virtualities, events, singularities. What we call virtual is not something that lacks reality but something that is engaged in a process of actualization following the plane that gives it its particular reality" (*Immanence* 31). But do such practices and simulacral selves truly contain liberatory potential? Can the subject really experience a realm of freedom and becoming by means of the Internet, or does the Internet merely function as one more arm of control?

Hubertus Bigend provides the answers to these questions when he shatters Cayce's idea of the Footage as a pure aesthetic object while simultaneously revealing the nature of control societies. In Cayce's initial conversation with Bigend, he problematizes all of the Footage theories when he offers Cayce another potential reading of it: he proposes that the Footage may not have been "uploaded randomly" but "very carefully, intending to provide the illusion of randomness" (*PR* 66). Bigend conceives of the Footage's dissemination as "the single most effective piece of guerilla marketing ever": by spying on the Forum, he "saw attention focused daily on a product that may not even exist" (*PR* 67). Whereas the Footageheads view the Footage as an artistic text worthy of endless criticism and debate, Bigend sees it as nothing more than one more object to be commodified and exploited to increase his profit margins. But Bigend's conversation further reveals that the Internet's utopian sheen is merely a mask that hides the underlying machinery of the control grid. This conversation causes Cayce to undergo a cognitive shift from perceiving the Forum as a closed world to recognizing it, as Bigend points out, as "a matter of public record": "The site had come to feel like a second home, but she'd always known that it was also a fishbowl; it felt like a friend's living room, but it was a sort of text-based broadcast, available in its entirety to anyone who cared to access it" (*PR* 67). Bigend desires the Footage so that he can properly commodify it within the global system of information. For something to be so stimulating to the masses, *it cannot remain free*. Here one might think of examples of corporations buying sites like MySpace or YouTube in order to properly commodify them, to make them into productive sites instead of merely social ones. Most importantly, Bigend's words reveal that the Internet does not constitute a utopian space of free communication and that the anonymity offered by the web proves to be a mere façade.

Gibson's cyberpunk output holds a privileged place in the history of postmodern science fiction because it traces the collapse of modernity in the face of full-blown postmodernization, but it also examines the innate connection between the hegemony of computers and the rise of the control society. While Gibson's early novels depict how computerization will inevitably lead to a dystopian society of control, *Pattern Recognition* and *Spook Country* demonstrate the manner in which the hegemony of computers has already lead to the instantiation of control, albeit in a more subdued, quiet form than most science fiction authors had envisioned. In his essay on control societies, Gilles Deleuze argues, "It's easy to set up a correspondence between any society and some kind of machine, which isn't to say that their machines determine different kinds of society but that they express the social forms capable of producing them and making use of them" ("Postscript" 180).[12] Deleuze contends that whereas "sovereign societies worked with simple machines, levers, pulleys, clocks," disciplinary societies, which arose in the eighteenth century according to Michel Foucault, "were equipped with thermodynamic machines presenting the passive danger of entropy and the active danger of sabotage" ("Postscript" 180).[13] Based on Foucault's description of disciplinary societies, Deleuze posits that we have recently moved into a new social organization of power, "control" that "function[s] with a third generation of machines, with information technology and computers, where the passive danger is noise and the active, piracy and contamination" ("Postscript" 180). Whereas the disciplinary society "operat[es] by organizing major sites of confinement," control functions by establishing the illusion of freedom: "Control is not discipline. You do not confine people with a highway. But by making highways, you multiply the means of control. I am not saying this is the only aim of highways, but people can travel infinitely and 'freely' without being confined while being perfectly controlled" ("Creative" 322).

In effect, control societies rely upon the computerization of the individual—the hegemony of computers extends beyond the confines of the computer screen to include not just knowledge (which becomes information) but also the subject, who becomes a "dividual" instead of an individual, a code in a database:

> The key thing is no longer a signature or a number but a code [...] The digital language of control is made up of codes indicating whether access to some information should be allowed or denied. We're no longer dealing with a duality of mass and individual. Individuals becomes "*dividuals*," and masses become samples, data, markets, or "*banks*." ("Postscript" 180)

Individuals become little more than the sum of their data, and the paradigmatic image of the control society "is no longer a man confined but a man in debt" ("Postscript" 181). The control society is not equivalent to the hegemony of computers, but, since computers serve as the paradigm for control, the rise in computerization entails a consequent consolidation of control's power. In the age of control, power becomes decentralized—it moves out of the prisons, hospitals, schools, and other institutions of confinement and spreads across the entire terrain of the socius. Control signals a radical territorialization of all the various strata of everyday life: biopower stretches itself out globally to form and direct every aspect of our existence. Building upon the work of Michel Foucault, Giorgio Agamben, and others, Roberto Esposito makes a useful distinction between biopower and biopolitics, Foucaultian terms that are often collapsed into one another in critical discourse: "By the first is meant a politics in the name of life and by the second a life subjected to command of politics" (15). But Esposito makes it clear that biopolitics also has an affirmative side:

> Biopolitics does not limit or coerce [*violenta*] life but expands it in a manner proportional to its development [...] Moreover, if it wants to stimulate the action of subjects, power must not only presuppose but also produce the conditions of freedom of the subjects to whom it addresses itself [...] if we are free *for* power, we are also free *against* power. We are able to not only support power and increase it, but also to resist and oppose power. (37–8)

The era of control further expands the illusion of power and resistance as the biopolitical regime becomes fully hegemonic on a global level.[14] As Deleuze makes clear, the computer offers the façade of freedom, but it simultaneously organizes and manages the practice of everyday life, to return to Michel de Certeau, who, even before the consolidation of the hegemony of computers, recognized—along with Foucault—how power arranges space in order to manage even the most mundane of the subject's activities. Founded upon the advent of the computer, the society of control's establishment rests upon the protocols of pattern recognition, and Gibson's novel cognitively maps this new geopolitical terrain.

Bigend's quest to appropriate the Footage as a profitable commodity represents the manner in which the forces of control (whether they be governmental institutions or corporations) always monitor and keep records of even the most seemingly quotidian or marginal events. To this end, Bigend's company Blue Ant has been keeping tabs on the Footage Forum. Bigend's employee Dorotea Benedetti engages in her own form of self-fashioning when she creates an online persona named Mama Anarchia, a Footage fan drenched in critical theory, to covertly infiltrate the Forum's close-knit community. In order to legitimate her virtual performance, she employs a graduate student to translate her posts into theory-speak, always being careful to use words such as "hegemonic" and to namedrop French theorists like Baudrillard. Moreover, the faux-character of Mama Anarchia demonstrates how presumably liberatory acts of virtual self-fashioning can also be appropriated by the system of control in order to better exercise its power over individuals. Her pseudonym itself ("Anarchia") suggests the apparently anarchic, rhizomatic, deterritorialized space of the Internet; however, Dorotea's presence on the Forum indicates that the purely democratic space of the web remains permeated with agents of control.

No aspect of life remains outside the society of control's sphere of interest and influence—it extends the disciplinary society's panoptic gaze across the entire terrain of the socius but in a supple manner that is almost imperceptible to the masses. As Hubertus Bigend states in *Spook Country*, the pseudo-sequel to *Pattern Recognition*, "I've learned to value anomalous phenomena. Very peculiar things that people do, often secretly, interest me in a certain way. I spend a lot of money, often, trying to understand those things. From them, sometimes, emerge Blue Ant's most successful efforts. Trope Slope, for instance, our viral pitchman platform, was based on pieces of anonymous Footage being posted on the Net" (Gibson, *Spook* 105). Here, Bigend reveals the subsequent fate of the Footage after *Pattern Recognition*'s conclusion: its viral distribution pattern gets adopted in the form of Trope Slope, a viral advertising campaign that inserts ads into old films, turning people's love for historic cinema into an opportunity to, as Bigend says, "sell shoes" (Gibson, *Spook* 106). Bigend's actions expose how corporations appropriate the desires of the multitude and transform them into moneymaking venues, and his commodification of the Footage exemplifies how individuals cannot remain free from the strictures of control—he is the representative of both capital and control in the novel. Moreover, he is the face of what Horkheimer and Adorno term "the culture industry":

> All mass culture under monopoly is identical, and the contours of its skeleton, the conceptual armature fabricated by monopoly, are beginning to stand out. Those in charge no longer take much trouble to conceal the structure, the power of which increases the more bluntly its existence is admitted. Film and radio no longer need to represent themselves as art. The truth that they are nothing but business is used as an ideology to legitimize the trash they intentionally produce. (95)

While Hollywood continues to pump out complete trash on a weekly basis, technology has allowed Bigend to perfect the mass culture industry—he can reach out and infect even legitimate art with the toxin of commodification, to follow Jameson's metaphor from earlier. By means of Bigend's endeavors, the Footage and Nora become trapped within the intertwined webs of capitalist production and control. By turning their attention to the most mundane and seemingly inconsequential activities of users' daily lives, the forces of control open up an endless array of sites in which behavior can be monitored, catalogued, and consequently controlled.

The computer represents *the image of control* because it grants or restricts access based on information it maintains on its users with no need to refer to a higher power—the society of control becomes purely rhizomatic as every point in the network becomes a potential space for exercising control. Of course, the disciplinary society does not simply vanish overnight; instead, the transformation from a modern diagram to a postmodern one represents an ongoing process. For Gibson, September 11th marked a point of rupture in which it became apparent that the underlying diagram of society had shifted, that the postmodern era and its control society now firmly held sway over the diminishing, modern, disciplinary paradigm of power. The attacks highlighted the fully globalized nature of power, the fact that power no longer operated according to striated spaces but now functioned as a smooth space that extended across the entire expanse of the globe. Insofar as power had become a global force, a calculated strike on one location (or three if we count the Pentagon attack and the other attempted attack on DC using United Flight 93) represents an assault upon the entire, global terrain of power. In essence, then, *Pattern Recognition* stages September 11th as just such an event: an event that reveals the modular shift that has been going on somewhat silently for decades from the disciplinary society with its various sites of confinement to the control society in which the world is linked together by computer networks in a vast array that creates the circuits of power in a limitless number of locations. Against this background, *Pattern Recognition* demonstrates that the generation of these postmodern circuits of power has not been random or haphazard; instead, these circuits have coalesced into a system that serves as control's backbone.

Conclusion: Annotating the Global: The Eversion of Cyberspace in William Gibson's *Spook Country*

While *Pattern Recognition* depicts the manner in which the forces of control invest themselves in the digital realm and examines the intricate linkage between the hegemony of computers and the society of control, Gibson's most recent novel, *Spook Country* (2007), takes this train of inquiry one step further by portraying the manner in which the hegemony of computers extends beyond the confines of the virtual and spreads itself across the physical realm. The non-place of the Internet becomes a true heterotopia as it leaves behind its "unreality" and becomes connected to all places. *Spook Country* continues Gibson's foray into writing science fictions of the present and again features Blue Ant CEO Hubertus Bigend. Also set in our present world, *Spook Country* features technological advancements that do not exist just yet but that are only barely extrapolated from current technological capabilities. In the novel, the major new technology relies upon the recent strides in perfecting GPS (Global Positioning System) technology, which the United States military first began developing in the 1970s and which Ronald Reagan approved for civilian use in 1983. The GPS system became fully operational in 1995 and steadily began to infiltrate the consumer marketplace, but Gibson's novel imagines a new usage for GPS coordinates as well as for virtual reality (VR) helmets, a trend that enjoyed a brief commercial heyday in the video game and film industries during the 1990s before vanishing again into laboratories. Like *Pattern Recognition*, the novel focuses on a newly emergent realm of aesthetics by way of its depiction of "locative art," artworks or videos that can only be seen with VR helmets at particular GPS coordinate points. The novel revolves around Hollis Henry, a former pop musician who Bigend hires to write a piece on locative art for his start-up tech magazine named *Node*. She begins her research by interviewing Alberto Corrales (the creator behind the pieces of locative art), who explains the implications of this new usage of GPS technology to Hollis: "Bare-espace…it is everting" (Gibson, *Spook* 20). In other words, GPS technology has caused the epistemology of cyberspace to leak out into the physical world. The informational patterns that once governed virtual experiences have now migrated out of the computer and spread themselves across the physical globe—they have undergone a process of "eversion." The virtual has been turned inside out—it has everted—hence blurring its distinction from the actual.

At first, the locative art technology seems to harbor little more than insignificant entertainment value: the novel introduces the technology when River Phoenix stumbles up and dies in front of Hollis on the spot of his actual death in West Hollywood. The true benefits of this new technology become apparent when Hollis Henry visits a room that has been annotated using the locative system. As Hollis's friend Odile explains in her broken English, "Cartographic attributes of the invisible…Spatially tagged hypermedia…The artist annotating every centimeter of a place, of every physical thing" (Gibson, *Spook* 22). By means of locative art, the structure of the network begins to influence real space to an unprecedented degree: no longer purely virtual, networks become actualized in the physical realm. Thus, objects can become synonymous with hyperlinks that lead the user to a vast wealth of information pertaining to their history, use, symbolism, etc. The objects around us are suddenly imbued with an almost chaotic proliferation of signification. By means of GPS, the globe undergoes computerization in an astoundingly literal way, a process epitomized in the worldview of Bobby Chombo, the hacker who performs the technological grunt work that allows Alberto to generate his locative artworks. Alberto explains that the locative system and GPS technology have altered Bobby's view of the world: "Bobby divides his place up into smaller squares, within the grid. He sees everything in terms of GPS gridlines, the world divided up that way…He won't sleep in the same square twice. He crosses them off, never goes back to one where he's slept before" (Gibson,

Spook 40). Just as Cayce Pollard's psyche computerized itself until it could scan and process trademark logos, Bobby has internalized the GPS computer system while simultaneously developing an attendant paranoia about it. Although Bobby never explains the motivations for his compulsory behavior toward the gridlines, one can assume that he fears being found in the same place twice. By constantly moving from square to square, Bobby appears to behave unpredictably.

In effect, *Spook Country* depicts the full-blown consolidation of the hegemony of computers. In the novel (and in our real world), GPS coordinates effectively render the globe into data readable by a computer. The spread of the hegemony of computers to a fully spatialized dimension signals the triumph of control over discipline, the virtual over the actual, and the postmodern over the modern—the illusion of freedom is maintained while every space on the globe becomes accessible as a potential site for the exercise of control. Indeed, Deleuze's description of Guattari's vision from the end of "Postscript on Control Societies" becomes a viable reality in a world mapped by GPS systems:

> We don't have to stray into science fiction to find a control mechanism that can fix the position of any element at any given moment—an animal in a game reserve, a man in a business (electronic tagging). Félix Guattari has imagined a town where anyone can leave their flat, their street, their neighborhood, using their (dividual) electronic card that opens this or that barrier; but the card may also be rejected on a particular day, or between certain times of day; it doesn't depend on the barrier but on the computer that is making sure everyone is in a permissible place, and effecting a universal modulation. (181–2)

Communication technologies do not necessarily construct liberatory experiences for the subject, or, if they do, then these liberties merely mask a deeper structure of control. Since the channels of communication remain controlled by corporations and regulated by the government, an individual's right to use them can easily be denied. Once one is plugged into the system, which includes not just the Internet but also cell phones, tablet computers, and other devices, then one becomes a subject of control: "Every connection has its price; the one thing you can be sure of is that, sooner or later, you will have to pay" (3). As Shaviro succinctly sums it up in his discussion of K. W. Jeter's *Noir* (1998), "In short, if you're connected, you're fucked" (3).

But is it possible that the system of control can be turned against itself? In his 1990 interview with Gilles Deleuze, Antonio Negri poses precisely this question to Deleuze concerning his theory of control societies:

> You suggest we should look in more detail at three kinds of power: sovereign power, disciplinary power, and above all the control of "communication" that's on the way to becoming hegemonic. On the one hand this third scenario relates to the most perfect form of domination, extending even to speech and imagination, but on the other hand any man, any minority, any singularity, is more than ever before potentially able to speak out and thereby recover a greater degree of freedom. In the Marxist utopia of the *Grundrisse*, communism takes precisely the form of a transversal organization of free individuals built on a technology that makes it possible. Is communism still a viable option? Maybe in a communication society it's less utopian than it used to be? (Deleuze, "Becoming" 174)

In this question, no doubt, Negri anticipates the evocation of the global revolution of *Empire* (2000), *Multitude* (2004), and *Commonwealth* (2009),[15] but Deleuze promptly disavows any such positive reading of the control society in his response:

> The quest for "universals of communication" ought to make us shudder [...] You ask whether control or communication societies will lead to forms of resistance that might reopen the way for a communism understood as the "transversal organization of free individuals." Maybe, I don't know. But it would be nothing to do with minorities speaking out. Maybe speech and communication have been corrupted. They're thoroughly permeated by money—and not by accident but by their very nature. ("Becoming" 175)

As Deleuze makes clear, the utopian potential of communication will constantly be undercut by the fact that communication devices and services remain commodities in themselves, that they remain trapped in the systems of capitalism and control that will constantly negate their revolutionary potential. And, by using various communication services, users only insert themselves more firmly into the grid of control. *Pattern Recognition* makes this clear in the object of the Footage and the character of Nora, both of which seem to remain free from the strictures of capitalist society, but both of which ultimately end up as just two more sites upon which control and capital can exercise their power. Furthermore, *Spook Country* demonstrates the manner in which the society of control is "everting"; that is, the control society that had operated virtually by means of computers and other digital technologies is crafting itself a physical body that stretches across the entire length and breadth of the globe. In the control society, the concept of an outside vanishes as every specific point on the map becomes subject to the hegemony of computers and consequently subject to the influence of power, whether such power be that of nation states or of corporations. The eversion of cyberspace designates a singular moment in the march of globalization, a moment in which no site (no matter how remote) remains free from the influence of capitalism and control.

CHAPTER 4

The Spectacle of Memory: Realism, Narrative, and Time Travel Cinema

No one has lived in the past, and no one will live in the future. The present is the form of all life.

— *Jean Luc Godard* (Alphaville)[1]

The cinema may be best able to picture thought and to call for thinking because like thought its ideas are comprised of movements, both spatial and temporal, characterized by connections and conjunctions of particular kinds. Every instance of art is expressive of an idea which implies a concept, and what philosophy does with respect to art is to produce new constructions or assemblages that express or give form to the concepts implied in art's ideas.

— *D. N. Rodowick* (*"Elegy"* 32)

Henri Bergson once argued that "the *mechanism of our ordinary knowledge is of a cinematographical kind.*"[2] Bergson resorts to the cinematograph as a metaphor in his discussion of becoming and its relation to perception and knowledge: "We take snapshots, as it were, of the passing reality, and, as these are characteristic of reality, we have only to string them on a becoming, abstract, uniform, and invisible, situated at the back of the apparatus of knowledge, in order to imitate what there is that is characteristic of this becoming itself. Perception, intellection, language so proceed in general" (306). For Bergson, cinema mirrors our natural perceptual schema—from the initial images of reality, our intellects engage in an ongoing process of transforming these into linear narratives. This consistent ordering of reality constitutes the basis of becoming as we continually revise our own linear narrative in relation to the perceptions that our brain orders into coherence on a constant basis.

But Deleuze argues that Bergson's vision of cinema proves flawed because he was writing during the earliest stage of cinema (the days of the Lumières, Edison, and their peers). As Deleuze states in *Cinema 1*, "the essence of a thing never appears at the outset, but in the middle, in the course of its development, when its strength is assured [. . .] Is not cinema at the outset forced to imitate natural perception?" (3) For Deleuze, cinema violates the laws of natural perception through the specific linkages that exist between individual shots or photograms (frames): cinema can call upon a whole arsenal of transitional editing techniques (wipes, dissolves, fade-ins and fade-outs, match cuts, jump cuts) that allow for instantaneous spatial displacement; the film's plot can use an array of techniques (flashbacks, flashforwards, and memories) to violate the normal linear logic of time; and films can even employ an assortment of optical effects (filters, gels, canted angels, and the entire world of special effects) to create a skewed view of reality or depict an alternate state of consciousness. Cinema, hence, plays with our ideas about time and perception—it has the power to undermine our concepts of time and memory by revealing their inherently fragmentary nature. In this chapter, we will explore how cinema—time travel films, in particular—allows us to reimagine and retheorize our concepts of time, memory, and self.

Science fiction has always been a genre obsessed with time: it imagines potential futures and often uses these as a means of commenting upon the present moment;[3] it considers the implications of introducing radically new technologies into our contemporary world;[4] it features alien visitors or futuristic societies in order to comment upon current socio-cultural structures;[5] or it imagines alternate presents.[6] Beyond these basic plotlines of temporal estrangement, science fiction has also developed a self-conscious plot archetype that allows it to more fully reflect upon the nature of time—the time travel narrative. Of course, stories of time travel are not a recent occurrence. Such narratives became one of the major strands of science fiction as early as the nineteenth century, and these tales have proliferated far beyond the bounds of science fiction proper.[7] Cinema proves especially conducive to time travel narratives because the technology of film itself has often been compared to a time machine. As Paul Coates argues, "the emergence of time travel as a literary theme at the end of the nineteenth century is a phenomenon one may suspect to be linked to the simultaneous emergence of cinema, with its capacity to manipulate the illusion of time" (307). In many ways, "cinema itself has the properties of a time machine" because it can transport us to the past, whisk us away to unimaginable futures, or simply preserve slices of time (Penley 128). If time travel narratives have always harbored this connection to cinema, then it makes sense to ask what insights time travel films can offer about the filmic medium.

In *Theory of Film*, Siegfried Kracauer argues that cinema has always divided itself into two distinct tendencies: the realistic tendency and the formative tendency, or, to put it in other terms, films either follow in the lineage of the Lumière brothers or Georges Méliès.[8] As Kracauer explains, the realistic tendency expands upon the realism of photography through its incorporation of movement and staging. Initially, films of the realistic tendency only featured narratives if they occurred naturally and movement only if the objects within the frame moved. Of course, it became immensely popular to shoot films from moving trains, but this form of movement still originated in nature. This kind of "objective movement" differs from "subjective" movement in which the director uses camera movement (pans, tilts, tracking shots, etc.) as well as editing techniques to move the audience through "vast expanses of time and/or space" (Kracauer 34). By including these various kinds of movement, cinema became a more perfect recreation of reality than mere photography, but Kracauer maintains that it further built upon this realism by means of staging, which includes not just the choosing of locations but also the creation of artificial settings. Of course, staging should "convey the impression of actuality, so that the spectator feels he is watching events which might have occurred in real life and have been photographed on the spot" (Kracauer 34). The realistic tradition of filmmaking seeks to reproduce reality, to give the impression that these events have actually occurred. Certain directors, such as Werner Herzog, still adamantly adhere to this doctrine and insist on always filming on location. Herzog even went so far as to physically drag a boat over an Amazonian mountain to instill authenticity into *Fitzcarraldo* (1982). While the Lumière tradition strives for the illusion of reality, the formative tendency, which derives from Méliès, seeks "to penetrate the realms of history and fantasy" by harnessing the various formative powers that cinema opens up for the director (Kracauer 35). For Méliès, who was a magician by trade, the cinema provided new spaces for him to experiment with his illusions, allowing him to craft narrative films, such as his science fiction classic, *Le Voyage dans le lune* (1902) or "A Trip to the Moon." Méliès inaugurated the filmic tradition of science fiction by means of illusions and special effects— his films were built around their spectacles.

Contrary to Kracauer, Tom Gunning does not see a major distinction between the Lumière brothers and Méliès. Gunning argues that both the Lumières' realistic films and Méliès' fantastic films function according to the same underlying aesthetic, an aesthetic he labels as "the cinema of attractions." He defines the cinema of attractions in opposition to narrative cinema, which began to exert a hegemonic force over cinema between 1907 and 1913 with the rise of directors like D. W. Griffith.[9] In contrast to narrative cinema, Gunning explains that the cinema of attractions "envisioned cinema as a series of visual shocks" and that even the realistic filmmaking "was valued largely for its uncanny effects" ("Astonishment" 116). Initially, cinema remained inextricably linked to spectacle, either the spectacle of the cinematograph itself or the spectacles that filmmakers could create through the medium of film. Even the fantastic cinema of attractions films, such as those of Méliès, featured narrative only as a pretense: "the story simply provides a frame upon which to string a demonstration of the magical possibilities of the cinema" (Gunning, "Attractions" 58). For Méliès, narrative merely provided a structure to connect multiple "tricks" together into a unified whole. Of course, cinema's recreation of reality no longer stuns us as it did the audiences who attended the Lumière brothers' screenings—we do not generally flee into the night believing the images to be real, a story many, such as Gunning, consider apocryphal. But filmmakers still often strive to shock audiences in a variety of ways: comedies include increasingly raunchy subject matter; horror films incorporate gorier and more gruesome death scenes; blockbuster films strive for ever more impressive special effects; and directors such as Lars von Trier, Michael Haneke, Takashi Miike, and Park Chan Wook create shock effects through the use of frank, fetishistic, and even pornographic sex scenes as well as extreme violence.[10] In general, science fiction films operate according to the aesthetic of the cinema of attractions through their inclusion of estranging elements and storylines and their use of ever more complex forms of special effects. But is it possible to still create the other kind of shock that Gunning suggests? Can cinema still be used to render reality "uncanny" in the same fashion that the Lumières did? In this chapter, I will examine two films that function as what I will term "documentary science fiction"—the cinematic equivalent of science fictions of the present—that present reality to us in just such an uncanny fashion. These films demonstrate how cinema can serve as a heterotopian mirror, a real space that reflects an unreal version of reality back to us.

Whereas the majority of science fiction films participate in the tradition of Méliès, this chapter explores two films that feature traditional science fiction plots but that deviate from conventional sci-fi by privileging the realistic tendency. Because cinema itself has often been compared to a time machine, it seems fitting that time travel films would provide the ideal method for investigating this concept. This chapter examines two time travel films that eschew spectacle in favor of creating films that not only problematize the genre of science fiction but that comment upon the nature of cinematic expression itself. Chris Marker's *La Jetée* (1962) and Shane Carruth's *Primer* (2004) both exhibit a counter-spectacle aesthetic that deconstructs the relation between time and memory in a way that will allow us to reconsider the struggle between the modalities of spectacle and narrative in cinema. Documentary science fictions represent the cinematic equivalent of science fictions of the present: while they may feature estranging elements, they use a realistic aesthetic to comment upon our present world or to interrogate the manners in which we perceive reality. These two films participate in the Lumière tradition because they concern the cinema's ability to seemingly preserve time and depict reality, and hence the films simultaneously explore the implicit desire of cinema to relive the past or to reorder it according to our whims.

STILL-LIFES OF THE FUTURE: *LA JETÉE* AND SCIENCE FICTIONS OF REALISM

The rudiments of documentary science fiction can be found in the films of Jean-Luc Goddard and Andrei Tarkovsky. Godard's *Alphaville* (1965) features none of the normal science fiction visuals—it appears to be set directly in the present; only its storyline clues the reader into the fact that it is a science fiction film. Goddard forgoes special effects and elaborate futuristic settings partly due to his extremely limited budget but also to evoke a feeling in the audience that the future has already arrived. Likewise in his apocalyptic film *Weekend* (1967), Godard utilizes a counter-spectacle aesthetic to imagine a rather annoying traffic jam snowballing into the disintegration of bourgeois society. Similarly, in *Solaris* (1972), Tarkovsky's camera spends an inordinate amount of time dwelling upon wholly unfuturistic elements: the film's opening includes numerous images of nature on which Tarkovsky poignantly lingers during his trademark long takes. Despite the film's futuristic setting, Tarkovsky refuses to incorporate futuristic cars and opts instead for the common conveyances of his day, thus driving home the film's message that humankind has become so alienated from its natural environment that the present has become equivalent to the future. Based on Boris and

Arkady Strugatsky's *Roadside Picnic* (1972), Tarkovsky continues his experiments with documentary science fiction in the perplexing and beautiful *Stalker* (1979), a film that (like Thomas Pynchon's *Gravity's Rainbow* [1973]) explores a liminal space known simply as "The Zone," the site of an unknown alien landing or other disastrous/paranormal occurrence. Even more so than *Solaris*, *Stalker* features nothing outside of its narrative that would demarcate it as science fiction. The film sculpts its otherworldly atmosphere from natural locations and fully urbanized spaces, which again are juxtaposed against one another in a dichotomy. Indeed, whether the paranormal or extraterrestrial exists in *Stalker* or whether it is merely a hoax or hallucination remains an issue of debate long after its credits role. More recently, Darren Aronofsky's π (1998) and Wong Kar Wai's *2046* (2004) both, to one degree or another, continue to experiment with this aesthetic approach to the genre. But *La Jetée* and *Primer* provide a special example of this subgenre of science fiction because their stories of time travel reflect upon cinema as a means of capturing time and upon the medium's ability to render reality uncanny. Because time travel narratives inevitably play with and frustrate our general narrative expectations, these two documentary science fictions provide the perfect venue for exploring the gulf between the realistic and formative tendencies and between the cinema of pure spectacle and narrative cinema.

In the history of time travel narratives, there exists none quite as unique as Chris Marker's *La Jetée*. Now perhaps best known as the basis for Terry Gilliam's *12 Monkeys* (1995), Marker's film remains a critical text in the history of cinematic experimentation because it consists almost entirely of still images—it, in essence, devolves the filmic image back to its photographic forebears. *La Jetée* (in English, "The Jetty" or "The Pier") takes place in a dystopian future after global nuclear war has annihilated the majority of the Earth's population. Attempting to improve their present situation, a group of scientists begin conducting experiments in time travel. The main character, who is known simply as "the Man," repeatedly travels back in time and eventually even into the future, where he learns that humanity will rise from the ashes into a brighter tomorrow. Although the plot of Marker's film contains estranging elements, its use of still photography instead of moving images distinctly marks it as documentary science fiction. Because it forgoes the basic technology of film, Marker's *La Jetée* provides the ideal space for examining cinema as spectacle and considering film's ability to capture the human and reflect upon the relation between identity, memory, and time.

La Jetée opens with a shot of Orly Airport, just south of Paris, the setting that inaugurates and closes this brief circuit of a film. Sounds of planes and choral singing swell as the credits roll across the still image of the airport. Abruptly, Marker cuts to a black screen with white text that states, "*Ceci est l'histoire d'un homme marqué par une image d'enfance*" ("this is the history of a man marked by an image from his childhood"). (*LJ* 1).[11] An unseen narrator reads these words to the viewer, and the film never reveals the narrator's identity or purpose—he simply exists alongside the series of images to deliver the story, a job he undertakes in a monotonous and clinical tone of voice, almost as if he is reporting lab results. The film features no direct dialogue—the narrator renders all the characters' words in indirect discourse and only refers to himself (for it is a masculine voice) as "we." Moreover, the narrator only uses the past tense to describe the events, which makes the film feel like a series of snapshots that the narrator is displaying while recalling the story. This aesthetic further heightens the realism of the film because it gives the impression that the film's events have actually occurred and are being presented in this document for our inspection.

At the film's beginning, the Man's parents have brought him to the airport as a child to watch the planes arrive and depart. Thus, the film starts with an examination of the human fascination with motion, motion which is almost entirely absent from *La Jetée* since Marker's film denies the very technology that provides the basis of the cinematic medium—the illusion of movement created by the rapid succession of still images. *La Jetée* "reduc[es] film to its origin in a series of stills in black and white," and this "use of still photographs creates a sense that all that remains after the disaster of World War III are the fragments of a narrative" (Coates 312). Film has been devolved back even further than the Lumière shorts that feature little more narrative than a photograph: a train arriving at a station, people going swimming, people exiting a factory—the narrative of all of these could almost be conveyed in simple snapshots. But the narrative of *La Jetée* could not be so simply deduced from the procession of images without the narrative voice to connect them. Only narrative can piece together the fragmented images that compose the film, for as D. N. Rodowick argues, "Movement, drained from the image and divorced from representation and action, has relinquished its role as the measure of time" (4). If movement no longer serves as a measure of time, then we are plunged back into time as it exists in the Eleatic paradoxes of Zeno. Zeno of Elea remains famous (or infamous) for his paradoxes of motion, all of which involve subjects attempting to pass through an infinite number of points in a finite space of time, thus rendering Achilles incapable of ever catching the Tortoise.[12] From the film's outset, Marker's use of still images creates a cinematic space that deterritorializes the filmic medium, enabling the critic to perform a complete reevaluation of the relationship between the filmic spectacle of movement and its narrative content. In general, film reduces the multiplicity of time to an illusion, to a neat linear pattern of narrative. As Gregory Flaxman explains, "Perception constitutes the dark surface on which the ceaseless flow of images is momentarily captured and thereby transformed into a set," and film seems to replicate this ordering capacity of perception (94). Because Marker's film eschews the cinematic illusion of movement, it also denies an inherent narrative to the images because movement generally implies at least a basic narrative action. But without the narrative voice, the film's storyline would remain incomprehensible, for its images in isolation from the plot would persist in their ambiguity to the point of being aporetic. Furthermore, since the film foregoes any attempt to create spectacle through the use of special effects and instead features images that could just as easily be from our reality, the narrative voice provides the only evidence of this being science fiction cinema.

This particular visit to Orly proves auspicious for the young child because he witnesses a man dying on the pier, a memory that will haunt him for the remainder of his life. Just before the murder occurs, he witnesses something entirely different: the peaceful countenance of a woman's face. As the narrator explains,

> Nothing tells memories from ordinary moments. Only afterwards do they claim remembrance on account of their scars. That face which was to be a unique image of peace time to carry with him through the whole wartime. He often wondered if he had ever seen it or if he had dreamed a lovely moment to catch up with the crazy moment that came next. (*LJ* 1)

From the beginning, *La Jetée* interrogates the relation between memory and narrative as well as how particular instants in time are inscribed in the subject's mind as memories, much in the same way that cinema carves out slices of time. The image of the woman's face only becomes a memory when it is tied together in the Man's subsequent life narrative, that is, when a narrative bridge has been erected between the still images. But, as the narrative voice makes clear, these narrative bridges always harbor the potential of being mere fictions that the individual has generated in order to make sense of their chaotic existence. Indeed, as Elena del Rio points out, the still images recall Roland Barthes's argument about the relation of photography to the past: "The Photograph does not necessarily say *what is no* longer, but only and for certain *what has been*" (Barthes, *Camera* 85). It points toward "the inherent poignancy of the photograph, that sign of an absent presence" (Coates 312). The photograph represents our tortured relationship with the past, a relationship that time travel narratives interrogate at a fundamental level. Perhaps even more than the future, the past beckons to us to solve its riddles and mysteries or to remember those foggy moments that may hold keys to our identity while also instantiating the belief in us that altering the past could lead to a metamorphosis of the present.

Such is the case with the Man in *La Jetée* who still wonders about that pre-war day at Orly when the image of a woman's face was etched forever in his mind's eye—his memory focuses on this image as one worthy of remembrance, much in the way that cinema chooses discrete images from the chaotic manifold of space-time. In his later life, he ponders whether he actually witnessed the woman's face or whether it was merely a fiction created by his psyche to grapple with the image that followed it: the horrifying picture of a man being killed. As Frank Kermode argues, we use, whether consciously or unconsciously, fictions to "satisfy our needs," for they provide "models of the world [which] make tolerable one's moment between beginning and end" (4–5). Or as Constance Penley argues, "time travel stories are fantasies of origins," and "they are also fantasies of endings" (312). From the film's beginning, Marker forces the viewer to consider how we create notions of beginnings and endings, how we parse out certain slices of time as worthy of remembrance. Hence, all memories harbor the potential of remaining purely fictional, of having been sculpted into significance by our subsequent rewriting of them. As the narrator from Marker's pseudo-documentary *Sans Soleil* (1983) states, "I'll have spent my life trying to understand the function of remembering, which is not the opposite of forgetting, but rather its inner lining. We do not remember. We rewrite memory much as history is rewritten."[13] In one sense, *La Jetée* compels us to wonder whether all memory contains less of what was perceived and more of the narrative that the subject has generated to explain these remembered perceptions. But, as Kracauer suggests with regards to film, "It is entirely possible that a staged real-life event evokes a stronger illusion of reality on the screen than would the original event if it had been captured directly by the camera" (35). And *La Jetée* suggests that we perhaps stage reality in our minds in a manner akin to cinema.

After this initial setup regarding the woman's face, *La Jetée* proceeds to tell the Man's subsequent story. Shortly after the Man's visit to Orly Airport as a child, World War III erupts and decimates the surface of the earth, leaving Paris in ruins, a state evoked by photographs of Paris intercut with shots of ruins. The narrative voice explains, "Many died. Some fancied themselves to be victors. Others were made prisoners. The survivors settled beneath *Chaillot*. Above ground everything was rotten with radioactivity. The survivors stood guard over a kingdom of rats" (*LJ* 3). While they "guard" the radioactive surface of the Earth, their entire existence remains confined to a series of catacombs under the *Palais de Chaillot*, catacombs that both protect them from the fallout on the surface and that represent the past from which they have been forever sundered. Amongst the religious statuary that litters the catacombs, a small plaque reads "tête apôtre" or "mind apostle." And, in effect, the Man must learn to become a mind apostle in order to save the human race from extinction. To stave off humanity's annihilation, the survivors devise a series of time travel experiments: "This was the purpose of the experiments: to throw emissaries into time to call past and future to the rescue of the present. But the human mind balked. To wake up in another time meant to be born again as an adult. The shock would be too much" (*LJ* 4). For the traveler, the journey to a different time represents a form of rebirth, a journey back through a psychic birth canal and an arrival in a completely new set of narrative parameters. Like the Lumières' films, reality becomes uncanny for these pathetic travelers through time, for they have witnessed spatiotemporal transformations that seem fundamentally impossible. Insofar as time shapes human identity and perception, the possibility of awaking in a new time proves to be completely shattering for the psyche: it means the recreation of one's identity, a complete rewriting of one's personal narrative.

To circumvent this fault in the human mind, the experimenters seek out prisoners with strong mental connections to their pasts—individuals who harbor distinct memories of the past and of themselves within that time frame. They surreptitiously stumble upon the ideal test subject in the Man because of his continued obsession with that particular day at Orly. As the narrator explains, "The camp police spied even on dreams," and they are fully cognizant of the fact that the Man "was glued to an image of the past," an image that has developed so much significance for him that it will enable the Man to travel back in time without losing his sense of identity (*LJ* 4). Indeed, his whole identity remains inextricably linked to this image—the image has been "overemplotted," to use Hayden White's term, in his life narrative: he "has charged [it] with a meaning so intense that, whether real or merely imagined, [it] continue[s] to shape both his perceptions and his responses to the world long after [it] should have become 'past history'" ("Historical" 86–7). Because he has overemplotted this memory, the camp scientists believe that he harbors a better chance of successfully returning to the past.[14] The image of the Woman's face remains crystallized in his mind like the images that comprise *La Jetée*, and the Man desires to set time running again on that day at the pier, to reinsert motion and to salvage his meaningless, fragmented existence.

Like a research report, the narrator's statements record the results of these temporal experiments into the past: "At first nothing else but a stripping out of the present," a stripping out that leaves the Man awash in a sea of blackness and pain (*LJ* 4). But, then, on the tenth day, a change occurs—a procession of images appears to the Man: "Images begin to ooze like confessions. A peace time morning. A peace time bedroom. A *real* bedroom. *Real* children. *Real* birds. *Real* cats. *Real* graves" (*LJ* 5). The images that flow over the Man have no narrative connection—they "ooze" in a nonnarrative, nontemporal sequence like a dream. These static pictures highlight the imagistic quality of memory. These sights are obviously from before the war because they depict landscapes not yet scarred by nuclear blasts, but this provides the only connective theme between them. Yet this basic thread throughout the images coupled with the narrator's repeated use of the terms "peace time" and "real" implies that they are brief, static glimpses of the past. Indeed, the repetition of the word "real" suggests that the film's present world is, in some sense, "false," that it has somehow had reality stripped out of it. And, in effect, the diegetic present of the film functions as an island in time because it has ceased to be a part of a serial narrative—its connection with the past has been severed, and the survivors currently lack the ability to move forward into the future. Also, "The insistence on the reality of these things paradoxically draws attention to their status as *images*" (Coates 310). Like the still images of which the film is comprised, the Man's present is one that contains no linkage to a larger narrative.

Furthermore, the repetition of the word "real" recalls the constructed nature of memory, the potentially fictional character of our remembered images:

> The repeated use of the word 'real' in this sequence gives credence to the traveler's fantasies/memories, while deconstructing the metaphysical

binarism reality/fantasy in at least two important ways. The first one, of course, concerns the reality of psychic contents themselves. No less significantly, the unequivocal sense of reality conferred on these photographic images seems to challenge the Platonic indictment of representation as copy or forgery of an original truth. Photography and film are to be taken not as simple illusions in relation to a reality 'out there,' but as realities in their own right, with their own specific ontologies and epistemologies. (Del Rio 387)

In the images that appear to the Man, the film begins to blur the line between reality and fiction, between original and duplicated image. The "real" status of the images highlights the potentially false nature of this dystopian future version of Paris, and this future proves false precisely because the survivors no longer maintain any connection to the narrative thread of history. To reinsert themselves into narrative and, consequently, into history, the survivors must turn their attention toward time itself—they must force themselves back into the narrative schema from which they have been expelled and left floating in a timeless sea.

Finally, on the thirtieth day of the experiments, the Man perceives more than mere glimpses of the past: he travels back himself and meets the Woman from the earlier images: "Now he is sure she is the one. As a matter of fact, it is the one thing he may be sure of. In the middle of this *dateless* world, which first stuns him by its splendor" (*LJ* 6). Unable to focus because of the various shiny baubles that present themselves to him in a department store, the Man loses sight of the Woman and she disappears. But the experimenters immediately return him to the past: "Time rolls back again. The moment happens once more. They have no memories, no plans. Time builds itself painlessly around them. As *landmarks*, they have the very taste of this moment they live as scribblings on the walls" (*LJ* 6). Finally, in this second permutation, the Man actually meets the Woman (she also never receives a name), and they seem to genuinely enjoy one another's company. Here, we see the film imposing a spatial language upon temporality with the term "landmarks"—they are islands in time around which the normal river of linear temporality flows; however, as the film demonstrates, linear or serial conceptions of time provide only one narrative model of organizing human experience. The narrative voice emphasizes that the couple "have the very taste of this moment" almost as if their infatuation causes them to exist in an extratemporal space in which the past and the future have no bearing: only the present exists—they are devoid of "memories" (no past), and "they have no plans" (no future) (*LJ* 6). Toward the end of their first meeting, the Man and Woman stroll through a park, and "he remembers there were gardens" (*LJ* 6). In the park, Marker pays homage to Alfred Hitchcock's *Vertigo* (1958) when the Man leads the Woman to an exhibit featuring a cross section of a Sequoia tree with significant dates in history posted on its various rings.[15] He points beyond the edge of the tree and explains to the Woman that he comes from there. Interestingly, the tree represents a true *spatialization of time*—it is time crystallized into an image. Here, whether one conceives of time as a circle or a line, the visual metaphor still proves valid. In essence, the tree constitutes the manner in which time can be distilled or transmuted into an image. Cinema normally creates just such images of time through its depiction of movement, but Marker refuses this spectacle even as he creates a film about time and memory.

Suddenly, the experimenters recall the Man to his own time because they have reached the end of their first round of experiments. In the second round of experiments, the technicians attempt to stage a perfect moment between the Man and the Woman. They send the Man back repeatedly, and he meets the Woman in different places each time: "She always welcomes him in a simple way. She calls him her ghost" (*LJ* 7). Then, on one particular day, she acts frightened when he meets her. As she leans over him, the film cuts to images of the Woman laying in bed, giving the impression that the two have slept together and that perhaps her fright stemmed from her inexplicable desire for this strange man who appears and vanishes like a phantom. The series of still images depicting the Woman lying in bed are finally interrupted by one image that lingers and then reveals itself to be an actual moving image, the only one in the film. The motion in the scene is so subtle that it could be easily missed: the Woman simply opens her eyes. But it is a truly powerful second of cinema, for, as Coates comments, "it is like the mysterious birth of time itself" (312). Only in such moments can the two lovers feel that they are truly living in the present, that the present has not already slipped away into the past. Generally, once one has the chance to name a moment "the present," then it has already become the past. The movement in this image implies that this is *the real present* because the movement in the three spatial dimensions signifies a consequent movement in time. The film's usage of still images suggests that these images already exist in the past, for how else could we be watching them? This scene breaks the illusion of the film as a series of snapshots and highlights this moment as perhaps the only occurrence in the narrative worthy of future remembrance—it represents the only experience precious enough to be ensconced as a filmic memory (*not* a photographic one) in the mind's eye. The Man has recaptured the woman who haunted him, and he has transformed her frozen visage from the pier into a sensuously mobile look of love. The film implies that it is only the power of love that allows the individual to exist in a state of pure duration, a state that lets them be fully in tune with the present with no cares about the past or the future. The Man and the Woman seem to step outside the normal constraints of the present as their love begins to blossom, for their relationship is built upon narrative incongruities due to the Man's random disappearances. As Coates further comments, "The girl's eyes are, as it were, animated by love, her love for the man/child, the love that has transported him into the past. For it is this sense of the possibility of renewed movement, of the flame of life being rekindled out of universal ashes, that draws the protagonist backwards" (312). Thus, without the constraints of the past (since the two never exchange personal histories) nor concerns for the future (since the Man could disappear at any moment), the couple believe they can exist in a perpetual present in which the strictures of time no longer matter.

Shortly after making love, the pair meet in a natural history museum filled with the preserved remains of animals ranging from small birds to giraffes and giant whales. The museum proves profoundly significant, for it is a space built upon the all-too-human belief that the passage of time can be arrested and that the present can be preserved in perpetuity. In other words, the museum represents a space in which humankind believes it can carve out blocks of immortality. With the museum, the experimenters achieve their goal: "Thrown in the right moment, he may stay there and move without trouble" (*LJ* 8). In effect, the scientists have engineered the perfect situation, one in which the two are infinitely compatible with one another. Perhaps the museum setting taps into past time in a way more exact than any other since it constitutes a three-dimensional space demarcated for the sole purpose of preserving spatial objects against the onslaught of temporal progression—it is a space created to keep time from getting lost. In the context of the museum, "The girl seems also to have been tamed," as the narrator says, as if she is one of the wild animals that have been "tamed" through the art of taxidermy (*LJ* 8). The narrator further explains that she has come to accept the Man's strange arrivals and disappearances as naturally occurring phenomena, and thus the engineers have achieved their goal of successfully inserting the Man into past time. Hence, when he returns to the future, the Man realizes that this was his last meeting with the Woman, for now the question becomes whether or not the scientists can send him into the future.

The journey into the future proves more difficult, but the Man manages to travel into a future world in which Paris had been rebuilt with "ten thousand incomprehensible streets" (*LJ* 9). As Coates points out, the film depicts these 10,000 streets by using "a close-up of the grain of piece of wood," recalling the earlier scene with the sequoia and demonstrating how images from reality can be used in estranging ways (311). A panel of leaders from the future greets him, and he pleads with them to send aid to the survivors in the past: "Since humanity had survived, it could not refuse to its own past the means of its own survival. This sophism was taken for Fate in disguise" (*LJ* 9). He offers them this circular argument: if the human race had survived, then this futuristic welcome committee must have been the cause of it; therefore, to deny help to the past would destroy themselves in the present. Of course, the argument proves questionable, and it recalls one of the basic paradoxes of time travel narratives—the grandfather paradox, "which warns of the possibility of a wayward traveler mistakenly killing his own grandfather, thus erasing himself from existence" (Slusser and Chatelain 168). A variation of the grandfather paradox also exists in which the traveler's journeys into past time actually cause the gestation of certain aspects of his/her present: this is the case in works such as Robert Heinlein's "By His Bootstraps" (1941) and James Cameron's *The Terminator* (1984) as well as in *La Jetée* and *12 Monkeys* to a lesser degree.

Despite the sophistic nature of his plea, the Man convinces the panel from the future to give him plans for a power plant capable of generating enough energy to restart industry across the planet. Equipped with this knowledge, the Man returns to the past, but no triumph awaits him there. Instead, the scientists take the information from the Man and prepare to execute him since he has outlived his usefulness. But one hope presents itself to him—the panel from the future travels back in time to offer him the chance to escape into the future and avoid his fate, but he desires something else:

> Now he only waited to be executed with somewhere inside him the memory of a twice-lived fragment of time. And deep in these limbos, he got the message from the men of the world to come. They too traveled through time and more easily. Now they were there ready to accept him as one of their own. But he had a different request. Rather than this pacified future, he wanted the world of his childhood and this woman who perhaps was waiting for him. (*LJ* 10)

So the Man travels to the past one last time to that childhood moment on the pier at Orly, thus literalizing Nietzsche's eternal return of the same and Freud's return of the repressed—he races back toward his fate but not the fate he expects.[16] As he enters the pier, he realizes that his childhood self will be there as well. Ignoring this thought, he focuses on rushing toward the Woman whose face he has carried with him in his memory all these years. But, sadly, they are not meant to be together, for he has been followed by one of the camp guards: "And when he recognized the man that had trailed him since the camp, he knew that there was no way out of time. And he knew that this haunted moment he had been granted to see as a child was the moment of his own death" (*LJ* 10). *La Jetée* ends with a static image of the Man falling backwards with his arm reaching up toward a frozen sun. Finally, he understands that the only way out of time lies in death (the final ending to our personal narrative), but *La Jetée* problematizes this very notion by making the ending equivalent with the beginning.

The Man believes he can escape from the strictures of time, that he can rewrite his personal narrative and generate a utopian existence for himself, that he can create his own happy ending. But he has repressed one aspect of that day at Orly: his memory focuses upon the woman's face and neglects the person being killed next to his childhood self. While the Man overemplotted the woman's face, he underemplotted or even overwrote the assassination. *La Jetée*'s ending proves especially significant because the end and beginning of the film are one and the same; thus, the film depicts how every moment is essentially an insignificant point in the procession of linear time. Marker's film demonstrates the manner in which film makes moments special even without recourse to spectacle. By way of its counter-spectacle aesthetic, *La Jetée* illustrates how cinema can translate the quotidian into the spectacular, how it can render plain reality into an estranging experience. While it lacks the spectacle generally associated with the genre, *La Jetée* effectively highlights how cinema makes even the most mundane events into sites of potential marvel: a group of men photographed in catacombs can become a cadre of postapocalyptic survivors capable of sending people back in time. *La Jetée* foregoes the conventional spectacles that attend science fiction and, by doing so, displays the manner in which all narrative remains science fictional, a theme we will pursue by way of Shane Carruth's *Primer*.

The Forking Paths of Time: The Multiplicity of the Self in Shane Carruth's *Primer*

As Tom Gunning points out, "The system of attraction remains an essential part of popular filmmaking," and most films achieve "a synthesis of attractions and narrative" ("Attractions" 60). But films like *La Jetée* structure themselves in a manner that divorces narrative from image, allowing the critic to speculate upon the relation between the two cinematic tendencies. To more directly problematize the concepts of spectacle and narrative, we must now examine another documentary science fiction film that also follows in the realistic tradition of the Lumières and that similarly deals with time travel but in an unestranging, contemporary setting—Shane Carruth's *Primer*. *Primer*'s story concerns two entrepeneuring engineers with the distinctly Biblical names of Abe and Aaron who inadvertently create possibly the greatest invention in the history of the world: a time machine or temporal stasis chamber (the film never gives the device a name) that permits them to travel back to the recent past. *Primer*'s austere cinematography and lack of special effects create a startlingly realistic mise-en-scène, almost as if we are watching a documentary about entrepreneurs instead of a science fiction film. *Primer* heightens its *cinéma vérité* feel by constantly shooting the characters in static long shots that make it seem as if a secret camera is spying on them through their garage windows. For example, when they have built their first version of the machine, the pair sprinkle paper circles over it to test whether it is indeed emitting some sort of field. As they do so, the camera tracks left and begins shooting the machine through the video camera the two have set up to document the experiment. When the paper scraps stop in midair without succumbing to gravity, the audience feels as if they are actually watching a video lab report of the experiment.

In addition to such cinematographic and directorial choices, *Primer* also creates a realistic aesthetic by foregoing elaborate props or special effects. The machines (or boxes, as the characters often call them) are composed entirely of materials available at any hardware store. The film even depicts the characters scouring various everyday items from their environment, such as the palladium they harvest from the catalytic converter in Abe's car. As the film's narrative voice says, "They took from their surroundings what was needed and made of it something more"—this phrase becomes a sort of refrain throughout the film (*P* 1).[17] Following along with this statement, the film even stages a dichotomy between two types of engineering: the high-powered and hyper-funded engineer, who has endless materials and resources versus the ingenious, garage-based inventors who must be creative with what is available, the inventors who, we might say, engage in their profession through the practice of *bricolage*. The film highlights this difference during Abe and Aaron's discussion of how NASA's solution to writing in zero gravity differed from the Soviet one. Because of the lack of gravity, traditional pens will not function in space, so NASA spent inordinate amounts of money creating a new pen that would work in the absence of gravity. The Soviets solved the problem in a much simpler fashion: they used pencils instead of pens.

The narrative describes the quartet of engineers in words that also explain *Primer*'s aesthetic approach to the genre of science fiction:

> Meticulous, yes. Methodical. Educated. They were these things. Nothing extreme. Like anyone, they varied. There were days of mistakes and laziness and infighting. And then there were days, good days, when by anyone's judgment, they would have to be considered clever. No one would say that what they were doing was complicated. It wouldn't even be considered new. Except maybe in the geological sense. (*P* 1)

While this passage describes the characters, it also evokes *Primer*'s relation to the genre of science fiction. The film's story is nothing new: time travel narratives have remained a science fiction mainstay for over a century, and narratives about the creation of alternate timelines and selves have also become common plot archetypes. But *Primer* takes these plotlines and creates something new. Like this statement, the film follows its events in a meticulous fashion, almost as if it wants to put the audience in the role of a scientist judging the evidence from a series of experiments. In addition, *Primer* eschews elaborate sets, famous actors and actresses, and dazzling special effects and chooses instead to appropriate what it needs from its surroundings and to make of it something more. Because the characters view their surroundings with an eye that sees the manner in which they can be deconstructed and rebuilt, the film from its very beginning forces the audience to consider the possibility that their normally stable definitions of reality do not represent the only readings of their environment or of reality in general. As the film peals away the layers of reality, it simultaneously deconstructs science fiction in a manner that gestures toward the realization that all film (and perhaps even all narrative) proves to be science fiction. Like *La Jetée*, *Primer* reveals the estranging and spectacular nature of the objects that exist around us—it takes reality and reflects it back to us in a way that highlights its innate uncanniness.

Primer opens with blackness, which is quickly illuminated by lights coming on in a typical suburban American garage, a motif that runs throughout the film. From the camera's vantage point inside the garage, the shot depicts the door beginning to rise and four men entering the garage. Then, the nondiegetic sound of a phone's ringing cuts across the scene. Someone answers the phone and a voice speaks, "Here's what going to happen. I'm going to read this and you're going to listen, and you're going to stay on the line. You're not going to interrupt. You're not going to speak for any reason. Now, some of this you know. I'm going to start at the top of the page" (*P* 1). From its outset, like *La Jetée*, *Primer* splinters itself between the narrative voice on the phone and the images projected for the viewer, the two of which do not always explain one another. Because the interlocutor who is listening to the narrative voice never speaks, the film offers little clarification about the disjunctions that appear between the narrative produced by the flow of images and the one read by the voice on the phone. Furthermore, the massive gaps in the narrator's story never receive satisfactory explication. The film, like the statement that the voice reads, acts as a primer on the events that follow, but a primer that remains fundamentally incomplete. It functions like a beginner's handbook that is missing crucial sentences and paragraphs if not entire pages.

For the majority of the film, the identities of the narrating voice and his listener remain unclear to the audience, but later the voice reveals that he is an alternate version of Aaron created by the pair's travels through time, and the interlocutor (who is never identified) is presumably some version of Abe. In a sense, the narrator represents a voice from the future because Aaron has already experienced the present, thus illustrating the fact that the future already exists in the present or that the concept of the present is virtually meaningless. It is important here to note that *Primer*'s title functions as a double entendre. The film itself acts as a primer, an introductory text for the viewer and for the interlocutor on the phone. At the same time, the word "primer" also evokes the notion of priming a machine. We might also say that the film deals with the priming (in both senses of the word) of the individual for a new kind of existence in which one's life narrative can be revised on a constant basis, opening the subject up to radical experiences of becoming.

Along with two other inventors/engineers, Abe and Aaron operate a garage-based mail-order company that supplies computer parts to hackers. But Abe and Aaron grow tired of fashioning these low-grade inventions and decide to pursue other avenues of experimentation in hopes of attracting corporate attention. Although the film never clarifies it precisely, Aaron and Abe begin by attempting to build a low-cost form of superconductor. In fact, the film never explains itself at all, an important facet of its plot that I will trace throughout the remainder of this chapter. But their experiments ultimately produce something entirely new, something that can only be described as a time machine or temporal stasis chamber (again, the film never gives the device a name). Early on, the film's coherence begins to fragment through techniques such as blackouts, the first of which occurs after Aaron and Abe have turned on the machine for the first time. As they lift up the machine's cover to see the experiment's results, the film abruptly cuts to black and then to an image of Abe waking up on a floor beside a phone, leaving the viewer to question whether or not the machine caused some sort of blackout or whether it is merely a jump cut. Like the film's beginning, the blackness is broken by a phone ringing, and the sequence features multiple, jarring shots of Abe awakening, adding to the confused feeling of the image. When Abe answers the phone, Aaron asks if he is hungry, but Abe's brain apparently remains somewhat addled. To alleviate Abe's sense of confusion, Aaron explains, "Abe, it's 7:00. Abe, it's 7:00 at night" (P 5). Aaron's insistence on the time makes it seem as if Abe needs to have his place in the narrative structure of reality explained for him. The film never explicates such instances, thus forcing the audience to supply their own narrative fillers. As we shall see, these absences of information highlight the manner in which the film interrogates the nature of cinema itself.

A large portion of the film consists of repeated versions of the same day, almost as if it is a cerebralized version of Harold Ramis's comedy *Groundhog Day* (1993). The viewer's first experience of this day again opens with blackness, which is illuminated by a blinding light as Abe opens a rooftop door. As before, the relation between this scene and the previous one remains shadowy. On the first iteration of the day, which is already at least its second permutation, Abe promises to show Aaron "the most important thing any living organism has ever seen" (P 7). To comprehend what happens next, one must first understand the device that the duo has constructed. They built the device in their garage predominantly from common items such as copper tubing. The machine has two ends (an A end and a B end), which should be thought of as two points on opposite poles of an elongated oval. Whatever object enters the box at one end falls into a feedback loop and curves parabolically around to the other end, but it consequently becomes untethered from normal physics; it only pops out on the other end after a significant number of cycles. In effect, the object in the device experiences a longer period of time than objects outside the machine. For instance, every five days, Abe wipes an amount of protein buildup out of the box that would normally require five to six years to produce. *Primer* never delves into the minds of its characters, and neither Abe nor Aaron ever offers their hypotheses in a straightforward fashion.

After explaining the protein accumulation to Aaron, Abe invites him to put his watch inside the machine. Initially, the two believe the machine degrades gravity or blocks information, but they discover that they are actually blocking something more fundamental—time. As Abe states,

> Everything we're putting in that box becomes ungrounded. And I don't mean grounded to the earth, I mean not tethered. We're blocking whatever keeps it moving forward, so they flip-flop. But Aaron, the Weeble's stupid. It can't move. Even if we were to put the Weeble in at point B, it's still just going to bounce back and forth until it's kicked out at the B end. But if it were smart, it could enter at the B end and exit at the A end before it flips back. (*P* 8)

At this point, the device's significance still remains unclear, but nonetheless Abe surprises Aaron by revealing that he has already built a device large enough to accommodate a person.

He drives Aaron to a climate-controlled storage facility, where Aaron witnesses a double of Abe entering one of the storage units, revealing that Abe has already used the device to travel back in time and that this already constitutes the second permutation of the day. Before continuing, I should briefly explain how the larger machines function. To set the machine, the user powers it up at the point in time to which s/he wants to return. Then, after a certain length of time has passed, the person enters the box, remains in it for that determined period of time, and then exits the box at the moment when s/he switched on the box's power. A delay timer keeps the person from meeting another version of his/her self. The boxes are basically constructed from collapsible metal frames with plastic tarps strung between the beams—they are flooded with argon and then must be tightened up to secure any leaks, for, as Abe explains, "There's always leaks" (*P* 10). And, as the film will display, leaks always exist in narrative as well, particularly film narratives which must condense stories down to a reasonable sitting length—*Primer* achieves this feat beautifully with its lean 77-minute running time.

Instead of creating a hermetically sealed representation of reality, film acts like a sieve through which certain moments of time drip away. Film cannot depict every moment of a story, so it must choose which pieces of time to include (this is, of course, true of literature as well as film, but film must choose even more particularly which details it includes and omits). In general, films compact stories to allow the audience to easily piece together the missing moments. As David Bordwell explains,

> In watching a film, the spectator submits to a programmed temporal form. Under normal viewing circumstances, the film absolutely controls the order, frequency, and duration of the presentation of events. You cannot skip a dull spot or linger over a rich one, jump back to an earlier passage or start at the end of the film and work your way forward. Because of this, a narrative film works quite directly on the limits of the spectator's perceptual-cognitive abilities. A gap will be closed only when the syuzhet [the Russian Formalist term for how the story is revealed to the reader versus the fabula, or chronologically reconstructed series of events] wants it that way; retarding material, however annoying, must be suffered through; a gap may be hidden so cunningly that the spectator cannot recall how the trick was pulled. (Bordwell 74)[18]

Primer chooses to highlight its manipulation of time instead of attempting to hide the gaps as Bordwell discusses. It refuses one of the most basic conventions of mainstream narrative cinema: its syuzhet offers enough of the pieces to create a skeletal structure of the chronological story (or fabula), but then it purposefully leaves massive gaps in a manner that demonstrates how all film represents a science fictional experience because cinema in itself implicitly proposes the belief that reality can be captured and made sensible. Yet, as *Primer* demonstrates, the gaps in narrative perhaps harbor information that would fundamentally alter the meaning of the whole. As Bordwell argues with regards to Bernardo Bertolucci's *The Spider's Stratagem* (1970), "editing" can "ambiguate duration indefinitely. We can take the cuts as temporally continuous or as containing ellipses that last as long as we like" (97). *Primer* also effects just such an ambiguation of duration: the viewer is forced to either read the film as linear or, as I argue, to view it as a series of fractured temporalities that are (un)structured at their cores by the temporal ellipses the characters experience while waiting inside the machines. As *Primer* progresses, the tension between narrative and spectacle becomes palpable as the images and narrative voice conflict with one another, and ultimately the film's ambiguation depicts how our belief in stable visions will perhaps prove as illusory as the cinematic movement our perceptual apparatus believes we are witnessing. We actually spend a large portion of our time in a theater sitting in the dark between the flickering images, and hence film itself, like our life narratives, functions at its core through the usage of ellipsis.

In their first attempts, Abe and Aaron travel trough time in order to make modest sums of money by playing the stock market—a radical new version of "insider trading." After the two power up the machines, they isolate themselves in a hotel room away from all contact with the world. As Abe explains, "If we're dealing with causality, and I don't even know for sure [...] I just took myself out of the equation" (*P* 10). The two gather stock information and pick up two tanks of oxygen to allow them to breathe while inside the boxes. When they enter the boxes for the first time, the film cuts to black, which is again illuminated by a light coming on in the box. Then, Abe describes a particular moment he experiences inside the box, "I don't know, maybe it was the Dramamine kicking in, but I remember this moment in there, in the dark with the reverberation of the machine. It was maybe the most content I've ever been" (*P* 10). Here, it is almost as if absenting one's self from the flow of history and creating an existence outside of time provides a profoundly blissful experience, almost as if it is time that causes us to suffer. When Aaron exits, he gets sick because he leaves the box too soon—the return to time proves too traumatic. They have returned to six hours earlier in the day, and they later revisit the storage facility and witness a duplicate version of themselves entering it. Thus, Abe and Aaron seem to have achieved their goal: they have created a marketable device, one of the greatest inventions humankind has ever witnessed, a page directly out of science fiction that has been transmitted into the real world.

Of course, human nature kicks in, driving Abe and Aaron's curiosity to further contemplate the implications of the machine. During a conversation, they discuss what action they would perform if they had absolute impunity, and Aaron expresses his desire to punch his boss in the face. However, his desire remains unfulfilled because of one ethical caveat: "I'd only do it though if I knew that no one would find out or get hurt. Like I wish there was a way that I could do it and then go back and tell myself not to" (*P* 12). The two discuss the infeasibility of the idea and attempt to play it off, but as the narrative voice states, "The idea had been spoken and the words wouldn't go back after they had been uttered aloud...And with no need for it, no possible real-world application, no advantage at all to be gained from it, the idea stayed" (*P* 12). During their subsequent discussions of the idea's absurdity, the two begin to consider the relation between time and identity. As Aaron ponders,

> I'm not going to pretend like I know anything about paradoxes or what follows them, and honestly, I really don't believe in that crap. I mean kill your mom before you were born, whatever. It has to work itself out somehow...Look this is what I know for sure. About the worst thing in the world is to know that the moment you are experiencing has already been defined...and do you ever feel like... maybe things aren't right, like maybe your life is in disarray or just not what you would like and you start to wonder what caused this. But what if it wasn't something you had to wonder about? What if you knew for sure this is not the way things are supposed to be? (P 12)

Here, *Primer* questions the nature of the present, of the present as an illusion based on the human capacity to narrate and string one event together with the next, but—even more fundamentally—the film begins to explore the connection between memory and the self, between time and identity. Aaron finds himself discontented with the eternal return of the same—he desires to insert difference into his past, to not only create his life as a work of art in the present but to reshape his personal history and consequently revise his identity. In effect, by splintering its narrative, *Primer* argues that our identities are never actually unified because they constantly fluctuate with the continually floating signifier of the present. Since the present can never be pinned down because it is always already past, identity remains fundamentally nonunifiable as well. But what if this was not the case? This is the question that Aaron decides to pursue.

Soon enough, the two begin traveling back more frequently to trade stocks and for other ambiguous reasons. Whether or not Aaron punches his boss is never depicted, but the film suggests he did, for Aaron has been traveling back without Abe's knowledge. Soon, after one of their stock-trading trips, Abe notices that Aaron has blood pouring out of his ear, an occurrence that never receives a full explanation. Instead, the viewer must presume that he has incurred some sort of physical trauma from the machine. At this point, what happens and does not happen becomes murky as the film increasingly splinters into a mosaic of different timelines. The film jump cuts across divergent places and times with few clear narrative connections, creating a disorienting effect that makes it impossible to distinguish the original versions of Abe and Aaron from the doppelgangers created by their travels. But whether the distinction between copy and original even matters becomes a question with no real answer in the film. Again, the film invites us to impose our own narrative upon the storyline in order to make sense of the fragments presented to us.

This intensification of the film's narrative confusion begins when Abe and Aaron witness a strange incident: they see their friend Rachel's father, Mr. Granger, inexplicably sitting in a car outside Aaron's house in the wee hours of the morning. They call him at home only to discover that he is there as well. They instantly realize that Granger has used the device and created a duplicate version of himself. The pair accost Granger, who flees and inexplicably falls into a vegetative state, and they remain incapable of determining when or how Granger entered one of the boxes. As the voice on the phone explains, "The permutations were endless" (*P* 16). How Granger even discovered the machine, much less ascertained how to use it, remains a mystery that the film never resolves. The two travel back in a desperate attempt to reset the situation before Granger entered the box, yet Granger's double still exists and cannot get near Abe without falling into a vegetative state. As the narrative voice explains, "From this they deduced that the problem was recursive, but beyond that, found themselves admitting, against their own nature, and once again, that the answer was unknowable" (*P* 15). While this statement applies to the situation with Mr. Granger, the narrator's statement could just as easily apply to the film itself: the film seems to repeatedly offer new realizations that will resolve its enigma but these realizations inevitably slip away into the chaotic vacuum of time that unfolds onscreen.

After the debacle with Granger, Abe decides that the experiments have gone too far and that he must reset the situation. At this point, the film divulges the existence of the failsafe machine, a secret machine Abe had built and left running since day one in case the consequences began to spin out of their control, in case causality slapped them in the face. He enters the failsafe machine, returns to the first day, and approaches Aaron in a manner that duplicates the earlier scene. But this iteration plays out differently when Aaron shockingly discloses that his earpiece actually contains a recording of the day's events which plays in his ear, giving him a three-second lead on the actions occurring around him—the earpiece appears in the first permutation of the day, but initially Aaron is simply listening to basketball. Abe cannot fathom such an improbable revelation, so Aaron explains how he had already discovered the failsafe machine and used it to return to the first day. Aaron describes how the modular design of the boxes allows them to be folded up and taken back in time. After taking one of the machines back with him, Aaron drugged that day's version of himself so that he could keep reliving the same day over and over again: "Aaron would describe how simple things become when you know precisely what someone will have for breakfast even in a world of tamper-proof lids" (*P* 16). On most variations of the day, Aaron stashes his double's body in the attic; however, on one particular version of the day, his double struggles with him. At this point, the narrative voice reveals himself to be this double of Aaron who refused to be imprisoned in the attic: "And that's where I would have entered the story. Or exited, depending upon your reference" (*P* 16). When the double realizes that Aaron has recorded the day's conversations, he leaves—he takes himself out of the equation as Abe says in an earlier scene. Consequently, Aaron achieves a state in which he already knows the narrative of not only his own life but of those lives around him. He becomes capable of truly experiencing the present because it is known in advance and hence can be fully lived before it slips away into the past. The present exists before him like an actuality film, such as those of Lumière, which allows him to control time and determine the shape of reality in a way that had previously only existed for filmmakers. He frames himself and directs the characters using his foreknowledge of the events that will unfold around him.

But why has Aaron chosen to relive this particular day? At the end of that fateful day, the two attend a birthday party only to witness their friend Rachel's ex-boyfriend entering the party with a shotgun. Deciding to use the device for ostensibly noble purposes, Aaron attempts to program the birthday party in such a way that he can act as the hero and stop Rachel's ex-boyfriend from threatening or even harming the other partygoers. While Abe offers viable alternatives to prevent the encounter, Aaron persists in his conviction that he must confront the irate ex-boyfriend: "This way, we know exactly what happens. We have complete control over it" (*P* 17). During this conversation, Abe interrupts Aaron and reveals that the machine has had other adverse side effects: "What's wrong with our hands?...Why can't we write like normal people?" Aaron responds, "I don't know. I can see the letters. I know what they should look like. I just can't get my hand to make them easily" (*P* 17). Again, the film never explains this strange side effect, but we can speculate as to its implications. Because the two have created an existence for themselves outside of time, they begin to lose their ability to communicate through written language. Like film, language unfolds according to a linear temporal scheme, and the pair of time travelers have violated such neat and tidy concepts of time and history to the point where they have become incapable of using language, incapable—in other words—of interacting with the normal flow of time. Instead of time being a line or even a circle as in *La Jetée*, *Primer* shatters such coherent and unified visions of time and replaces them with a dizzyingly chaotic shape. Instead of a simple shape like the line or the loop, *Primer* creates a chaotic pattern that can only be compared to Borges's "The Garden of Forking Paths" (1941). As Borges's character Stephen Albert explains about his translation of Ts'ui Pên's *The Garden of Forking Paths* (a fictional work in Borges's story),

> Your ancestor did not believe in a uniform, absolute time. He believed in an infinite series of times, in a growing, dizzying net of divergent, convergent, and parallel times. This network of times which approached one another, forked, broke off, or were unaware of one another for centuries, embraces *all* possibilities of time. (28)

This vision of the universe is one in which all possible scenarios are played out, in which every action we take has the potential to splinter time and create alternate timelines. We cannot know whether the universe functioned that way before Abe and Aaron took their first trip back to the past, but once they have, then time begins to splinter: each path or timeline creates infinite new paths. The hedge maze of time becomes ever denser, more chaotic, and difficult to navigate. While certain fans on the Internet have attempted to plot out the film's storyline, I maintain that the film's use of ellipsis and doubles creates a cinematic experience that makes it impossible to determine precisely who the original Abe and Aaron are or even what exactly happens at certain moments in the film.

It becomes impossible to tell how many alternate timelines and doubles of himself Aaron has created in his attempt to perfectly engineer that evening at Rachel's party. As the voiceover Aaron explains, the presumably original version of Aaron has replayed the scene numerous times before the audience actually sees it:

> So how many times did it take Aaron as he cycled through the same conversations lip-synching trivia over and over? How many times would it take before he got it right? Three? Four? Twenty? [...] Slowly and methodically, he reverse-engineered a perfect moment. He took from his surroundings what was needed and made of it something more. And once the details had been successfully navigated, there would be nothing left to do but wait for the conflict. Maybe the obligatory last-minute moral debate until the noise of the room escalates into panic and background screams as the gunman walks in. And eventually he must have got it perfect and it must have been beautiful with all the praise and adoration he had coming. (*P* 17)

Not surprisingly, the film does not depict the interaction between Aaron and the shotgun-wielding boyfriend, for the shot ends with Aaron walking over to accost him. Again, the audience is left to their own devices to supply the narrative that ensued. All we know is that Aaron was able to program a perfect moment by replaying the scene numerous times. As it does so often, *Primer* denies us the spectacle that we expect. Whereas such a violent confrontation would normally be included in the scene, *Primer* cuts the scene short without giving us the payoff. Examples such as this abound throughout the film, and they exemplify its counter-spectacle aesthetic. *Primer* forecloses meaning by never depicting the most crucial elements of the story and by never fully explaining the incidents it does choose to depict.

The film's penultimate scene depicts Abe and Aaron conversing in an airport terminal. During their discussion, the film splices in images of the drugged versions of Abe and Aaron waking up and breaking out of the rooms in which they have been locked. Abe plans to stay and sabotage the machine's development, but Aaron implies that he is staying because he secretly loves Aaron's wife, Kara: "I guess that it just won't go back far enough, will it? Tell you what, why don't you take Kara and Lauren [Aaron's daughter] and put them in the box and then you and Aaron can each keep a set and you can stop feeding off it" (*P* 18). Aaron makes this comment in bitterness, but his words gesture toward the machine's capacity to duplicate reality. Like cinema, the machines have the power to copy people and project them back to themselves. Cinema makes us uncanny to ourselves and enables us to exist in new narratives—we can recast ourselves as new characters. By using a purely realistic aesthetic, cinema allows us to reorder reality in a manner that highlights the fundamentally illusory nature of our concepts of existence.

The film's final shot reveals Aaron in an obviously foreign country with a group of French-speaking workmen that he is instructing on building a room-sized version of the box. Over this final shot, the voice ends its primer with these comments:

> Now I have repaid any debt I may have owed you. You know all that I know. My voice is the only proof that you will have of the truth of any of this. I might have written a letter with my signature, but my handwriting is not what it used to be. Maybe you've had the presence of mind to record this. That's your prerogative. You will not be contacted by me again. And if you look, you will not find me. (*P* 19)

The film then abruptly cuts to black again before the credits begin to roll across a gray screen. Aaron has wholeheartedly accepted the new powers that the machine has granted him: he is now capable of revising the narrative of history; of inserting, subtracting, or changing his role in stories; and of restarting narratives from their beginning almost like one would push the reset button on a videogame console. Aaron becomes like a director of what William S. Burroughs would term the "reality film"—he can stage scenes, replay scenes, alter the script, or even take himself out of scenes altogether.

In the final analysis, then, *Primer* highlights how the medium of film proves science fictional at its core because cinema uses technology to force unity upon the experience of reality; it creates the illusion of worlds in which life falls into neat narrative storylines. By foregoing traditional sci-fi spectacle and generating a documentary-style aesthetic of realism, *Primer* demonstrates how the reality projected by cinema is always science fictional—it is reality distilled into a framed image, lives reduced to fragments of a story, the universe slowed down to 24 frames per second. *Primer* brings the science fictional nature of cinema into sharp relief through its use of realism, jump cuts, plot holes, and other alienating effects, which turn it into a puzzle that may or may not have a solution. Like Granger's trip back in time, the permutations of the answer to the logical problem that is *Primer* remain endless. *Primer* fractures itself in order to reveal to the viewer that existence is fundamentally chaotic, that if there is unity then it has been forced upon existence by the human drive to narrate events into coherence. Ultimately, *Primer* highlights how science fiction serves as a form of critical theory by deconstructing our most fundamental notions not just of narrative and cinema but also of order, coherence, and unity.

Conclusion: The World as Spectacle...

From the spectacle of the cinematograph to the trick cinema of Méliès to the modern-day blockbuster, cinema has increasingly strived to sculpt ever more elaborate spectacles to capture the attention of ever-larger, more desensitized audiences. In fact, the blockbusters of today could be considered regressions back to the cinema of attractions because they increasingly privilege spectacle and visual shocks over plot, characterization, and style. Today, films are no longer even required to have connections to the real world—they can fashion their mise-en-scène entirely through green screens, motion-capture suits, and computer graphics. Films like James Cameron's *Avatar* (2009) break all connections to our reality and partake fully in the formative tradition—they even eschew staging, in its traditional sense at least, by digitally sculpting the environment in which their characters interact.

Indeed, despite its rather corny political allegory and its derivative plot, *Avatar* epitomizes the aesthetic aspirations of most science fiction cinema: it takes us on mind-boggling rides through completely alien worlds and introduces us to estranging forms of subjectivity. But the clever use of computer graphics in such films still make it appear as if they are comprised of real-life images; despite being fantastic, they still effect the cinema's impression of depicting, as Andre Bazin states, "the object itself, the object freed from the conditions of time and space that govern it" (Bazin 14). But, simultaneously, we know such films have no basis in the real; as Garrett Stewart argues, "the whole ontology of the photograph, in Bazin's sense, is dismantled, however, for the image is itself an orphaned signifier with no source or backing in the real, its icon of a wound bearing no index or scar on the present body" (89). But *La Jetée* and *Primer* use their counter-spectacle aesthetic to blur the line between realistic and fantastic cinema in a manner that makes us wonder whether cinema has ever truly been able to capture the real or whether it merely projects utopian dreams of reality.

Increasingly, we can find other examples of documentary science fiction as the reality around us becomes ever more estranging. For the most part, Alfonso Cuarón's *Children of Men* (2006) participates in a similar documentary-style aesthetic: its images of a world in which women can no longer get pregnant never differ drastically from our own world. Indeed, the footage of urban warfare could just as easily have come from a news report on Iraq or any other war-torn nation. Furthermore, Cuarón's long takes using handheld cameras give the impression that the film is actually being shot by a battlefield correspondent or documentary filmmaker. Even more recently, Neill Blomkamp's *District 9* (2009) staged itself as a documentary following the arrival, segregation, and attempted removal of a group of aliens who lands in South Africa. Despite the computer-generated alien creatures, the slums of District 9 (the section of Johannesburg reserved for these interplanetary refugees) already exist in any number of countries across the globe where people have been displaced by genocide or other geopolitical forces—*District 9* is, of course, based on the infamous District 6 from Apartheid-era Cape Town.

Proceeding a step beyond the gritty realism of *Children of Men* or the mockumentary aesthetic of *District 9* are the steady stream of found-footage (or mockumentary) genre films that have appeared over the two decades since the release of Daniel Myrick and Eduardo Sánchez's *The Blair Witch Project* (1999). For the most part, the found-footage aesthetic constitutes a profoundly independent genre of horror films that was inaugurated by Ruggero Deodato's infamous Italian exploitation classic *Cannibal Holocaust* (1980). *Cannibal Holocaust* took verisimilitude to an extreme with its inclusion of real animal cruelty staged and executed for the film, scenes that scar most viewers to the point that they have often been edited out of many editions of the film. Furthermore, the realistic deaths of the human characters so resonated with audiences that Deodato was forced to produce the actors and actresses in court to prove that it was not a snuff film. *The Blair Witch Project* brought the genre into its modern form with its cheaply made, improvised story about a group of college students who set out to film a documentary about a local legend and fall prey to seemingly supernatural forces. Recent years have seen an exponential increase in the number of found-footage films, particularly since the release of Oren Peli's *Paranormal Activity* (2007). While found-footage films predominately reside in the horror genre, a small contingent of sci-fi films have adopted the aesthetic as well: Matt Reeves's *Cloverfield* (2008), Olatunde Osunsanmi's *The Fourth Kind* (2009), and Gonzalo López-Gallego's *Apollo 18* (2011).

These three films still adhere to a horror or thriller formula, but they also feature typical sci-fi plots. Certainly the least impressive of the three, *Apollo 18* uses the found-footage genre to capitalize on the various conspiracy theories surrounding the Moon landing and the eventual abandonment of the U.S. missions to the Moon. In the film, the scrapped Apollo 18 Moon mission went ahead as a covert operation. Purportedly pieced together from surveillance cameras on the interior and exterior of the shuttle and the lunar module as well as video shot by the astronauts on the surface of the moon, *Apollo 18* follows a series of disturbing encounters with bizarre alien creatures. Ultimately, *Apollo 18* proves disappointing as both science fiction and horror, but it provides an interesting commentary on the rise of reality television from the 1960s to the present. The advent of television immediately opened up the potential for reality television even before the term was coined in the 1990s and became ubiquitous in the 2000s. Initially, reality television was confined to major events like the Moon landing or presidential inaugurations—John F. Kennedy's assassination provides one of the more gruesome examples (and its capture on film has made it the subject of countless conspiracy theories similar to the Moon landing). However, as the decades passed and film equipment became increasingly cheaper and more available to the masses, reality television became an ever more easily accessible medium.

The Fourth Kind similarly combines the found-footage format with conspiracy theories involving alien abduction. The title of the film refers to ufologist J. Allen Hyneck's categorization of different "kinds" of "close encounters." A close encounter of the fourth kind involves abduction by alien entities.[19] *The Fourth Kind* features an odd aesthetic that bends the found-footage format in bizarre ways. Instead of simply being a typical found-footage film featuring unknown actors and actresses and shots derived from "reality," *The Fourth Kind* mixes supposedly "real footage" together with "reenactments" starring sci-fi mainstay Milla Jovovich. This disjunction in the aesthetic hampers the film, and the found-footage scenes outshines the polished ones featuring Jovovich and the other "famous" talent. However, the film proves interesting as it draws on various theories about alien visitations during ancient history and uses the found-footage genre to explore the obsession with paranormal encounters and our society's desire for video proof of them. *The Fourth Kind* conjures associations with the legendary photos or films of aliens, cryptids, and other legendary creatures: Bigfoot, the Loch Ness Monster, and all the various images purporting to capture flying saucers.

Finally, *Cloverfield* takes the *daikaijū* (the giant monster movie) in new directions: the film features a story familiar to anyone who has seen the original *Gojira* or any of its countless sequels, spin-offs, and copies. But now we witness the action from an essentially first-person perspective (a perennially problematic claim for any film to make). A party being filmed by one of its guests is interrupted by an unknown attack on New York City. For the bulk of the film, the characters and the audience remain unsure of who or what is destroying the city until the beast finally appears on camera for only brief snippets of the movie. *Gojira* used sci-fi/horror as a means of exploring the traumas of the atomic decimation of Hiroshima and Nagasaki. Similarly, *Cloverfield* appropriates the *daikaijū* genre and the found-footage format to comment upon the traumas of 9/11 and the fears that arose from the subsequent "War on Terror." As the audience witnesses New York City being devastated firsthand by a seemingly irrational beast, *Cloverfield* places the viewer in the situation of those who experienced 9/11 firsthand. The whole world watched 9/11 through similar "found footage" shot by individuals on the scene. The film deliberately stages certain scenes to evoke particular videos released in the aftermath of 9/11: the image of smoke, dust, and ash filling the entire street between the towering skyscrapers; the shots taken from inside a convenience store as a cloud of destruction rolls down the street outside; and the images of buildings collapsing. *Cloverfield* also references the attacks through the desecration of the Statue of Liberty, a New York landmark even more iconic than the

Twin Towers. In the film, crowds run in terror as the statue's severed head lands in the street as an explosive fireball. Not since *The Planet of the Apes* (1968) has the Statue of Liberty been used to such powerful effect in sci-fi cinema. Films like *Cloverfield* demonstrate how cinema and video have become integral to any understanding of ourselves and our postmodern landscape. Film increasingly structures, defines, and captures our lives. Reality television and found-footage cinema exhibit how we increasingly expect our lives to be edited and organized like the films and television programs we see unspool on screen. Cinema is no longer a medium we experience sitting in a darkened theater or living room—it has become the mundane stuff of our minute-by-minute existence.

Found-footage films examine our society's obsession with video and film footage, our *Youtube* society's need to document even the most trivial of events with the dim, perhaps subconscious hope, that something abnormal or traumatic will occur. Hence, while films like *Avatar* may push the boundaries of cinematic technology and gesture toward the future of the filmic medium, *La Jetée, Primer, Children of Men, District 9*, and the found-footage genre provide a much more profound insight: they show us that our world is already science fiction, that the dystopianism of these futuristic worldscapes are the problems of our own global civilization, that the imaginary disasters of science fiction films stretching back to the 1950s are the possible events of seemingly normal days, and that the fractured or nightmarish realities that wind off the reels and onto the screen are nothing less than the lives we lead every day.

Beyond the Human: Ontogenesis, Technology, and the Posthuman in Kubrick and Clarke's *2001*

Alas, the time is coming when man will no longer shoot the arrow of his longing beyond man, and the string of his bow will have forgotten how to whir! I say unto you: one must still have chaos in oneself to be able to give birth to a dancing star. I say unto you: you still have chaos in yourselves. Alas, the time is coming when man will no longer give birth to a star. Alas, the time of the most despicable man is coming, he that is no longer able to despise himself. Behold, I show you the last man.

—Nietzsche (Zarathustra *Prologue* §5)

Perhaps in all honesty, in all sincerity, we've prevented human evolution because we don't want to meet the supermen.

—Isaac Asimov (Eternity *221*)

Like the term "postmodern," the more recent critical neologism "posthuman" has already accrued a series of meanings that differ from one theorist to another: theories that draw upon science and cybernetics, epistemology and ontology, ecocriticism, animal studies, feminism, etc. have all found the "posthuman" to be a concept that opens up new avenues of thought about humanity and identity as well as how human individuals fit into an environment that is determined both by natural and technological forces. Without delving too deeply into theorists like Donna Haraway, N. Katherine Hayles, and Cary Wolfe or the Transhumanist movement that champions avenues of transforming the human, a few basic points about the posthuman remain fairly true from one conceptualization to the next.[1]

The posthuman subject is a multiple subject, not a unified one, and she or he (a distinction that also gets blurred in posthumanism) is not separate from his/her environment. Technologies become extensions of the self, and humans become only one type of individual in a vast ecosystem that includes digital as well as natural environmental forces. In other words, posthumanism is partly about leaving behind the old notions of liberal humanism. As Katherine Hayles notes in a recent interview, the posthuman—at least partly—refers to "twentieth-century developments in which an Enlightenment inheritance that emphasized autonomy, rationality, individuality, and so forth, was being systematically challenged and disassembled" (Hayles, "Interview" 321). But it also begins to gesture toward a much more radical state, a state beyond the current human form. In many ways, science fiction has always been about the posthuman, and critical theory has only recently caught up with science fiction's investigations into such attempts to rethink the human and the socio-technological forms that determine it.

In this final section, I will turn to one last text that exemplifies science fiction's investigations into the limits of the human. As we have seen, science fiction and critical theory both represent inquiries into the human, and, in essence, I contend that it is partly these explorations that link the two discursive spaces. So far, we have explored several distinct variables of the human: gender and identity, desire and lack, the postmodern subject and the society of control, and the connections between time, memory, and identity. In this final section, I will bring all of these elements together to imagine how both critical theory and science fiction harbor the same implicit desire: to conceptualize and understand the human and/or to determine ways of advancing, perfecting, or even transcending the current human form and the structures or variables that define and control identity. However, while critical theory maintains the utopian hope that such conceptualizations remain possible, science fiction uses its heterotopian form to deconstruct such theorizations—science fiction allows us to weigh the possible positive and negative consequences of the posthuman condition that we increasingly (dis)embody on a daily basis. To explore this topic, I will be turning to a more classic science fiction text than those I have hitherto examined: Arthur C. Clarke's novel *2001: A Spacy Odyssey* (1968) and Stanley Kubrick's eponymous 1968 film provide the ideal spaces for bringing these seemingly disparate topics into convergence with one another because they concern the ontogenesis and evolution of the human itself from its prehuman to its posthuman formulations.

Evolution serves as the underlying, connective theme of the movie's four segments (or movements we might say, since the film's structure operates like a symphony): "These image patterns and visual metaphors document the true meaning of the word 'Odyssey' in the title—an evolutionary journey from beast, to technology, to a stage of evolution transcending the physical realm—and also underscore a central theme of the film: the limits of technology and the nature of humanity" (Fry 333). The film *2001* charts the evolutionary progress of humanity from the prehuman stage through the birth and growth of technology and into the posthuman era when human consciousness becomes capable of evolving beyond its present social and physical constraints. The film *2001* represents a filmic odyssey that takes the viewer through the evolution of consciousness—Kubrick crafts images that visualize and dramatize the place of the evolutionary subject, of the animal becoming human and the human metamorphosing into an almost divine posthuman existence. The film depicts how the human remains tied to technology and how the growth of technology leads inevitably to the society of control and simultaneously to the posthuman. In essence, *2001* concerns the dichotomy between being and becoming—the fundamental human choice—and it asks whether technology acts as an impetus for transformation or whether it ends up robbing the human of its innate potential.

THE PREHUMAN: THE BIRTH OF TECHNOLOGY AND THE WILL TO POWER

The origins of the film *2001: A Space Odyssey* lie 20 years prior to its release with Arthur C. Clarke's short story entitled "The Sentinel" (1951), which concerns the discovery of a strange pyramid stationed on a mountainside plateau on the Moon.[2] Eventually, the narrator speculates that the device was placed there by an ancient and advanced alien civilization who combed the young universe in search of planets that seemed poised to produce intelligent life. In many ways, this is the same narrative that Kubrick and Clarke tell in the film and novel; however, it has been expanded and tied into the evolutionary drama of humankind. Clarke's novelization still adheres mostly to this basic story, but Kubrick's film never offers such definite interpretations of the monolith's origins or purpose. Of course, to call Clarke's novel a "novelization" proves somewhat reductive since he and Kubrick developed the story together over the course of several years. But, as Suparno Banerjee explains, many critics to this day view "Clarke's novel as an explanation of the film," yet as he maintains, "A close comparative examination of the novel and the film clearly shows that Clarke's novel is neither an explanation nor a novelization of the film but a work existing independently. While Clarke's novel is rooted in the tradition of hardcore science fiction, Kubrick's film subverts all the norms of traditional films to create something unique" (39).

In many ways, the film *2001* not only tells a story about the human evolving into the posthuman but also attempts to use surrealistic imagery and special effects to visually express the change in consciousness that the main character, Dave Bowman, undergoes in the final section of the film. Although I will make references to Clarke's novel over the course of my argument, I will focus predominately upon Kubrick's film because it depicts the events in a more ambiguous manner that creates a more profoundly experimental narrative space than the novel. Since the novel explores the same or similar themes as the film, it acts as a useful companion piece due to its more discursive nature, but Banerjee correctly draws a sharp distinction between the two because Kubrick's film ultimately revels in discontinuity, ambiguity, and perhaps even aporia while Clarke's novel remains tied to linear narrative and explicit exposition in a way that squashes some of the power and critical potential inherent in the cinematic version.

Kubrick's *2001* bathes the viewer in estranging images of radical otherness, and, like *Primer*, it forces the audience to ascribe their own meaning to the series of images. The film begins with an overture and blackness after which it cuts to a shot of space as the opening of Richard Strauss's *Also sprach Zarathustra* (1896) immediately baptizes the viewer into the universe according to *2001*. Simultaneously, the music inaugurates the Nietzschean themes of the film: "Strauss's musical interpretation of Friedrich Nietzsche's philosophical poem begins with a glorious evocation of sunrise, which Kubrick visually reworks into Earthrise" (Rasmussen 53). The opening shot of the film initiates from behind the Moon and slowly tilts up to reveal the Earth and Sun in alignment with it. Shots of such alignments and the "Dawn" section of Strauss's *Zarathustra* function as refrains throughout the film, which tie together its seemingly disconnected sections. After this initial introduction, the film consists of four major sections: "The Dawn of Man," an unnamed second section, "The Jupiter Mission," and "Jupiter and Beyond the Infinite." The opening section follows a group of apelike creatures, which Clarke refers to as "man apes," who have yet to develop the use of tools and hence exist in a purely animalistic state. Clarke's novel remains tied to a traditional characterization scheme, for it "focuses on a main character in every part: Moon-Watcher in 'Primeval Night,' Heywood Floyd in

'TMA-1,' and Dave Bowman in the rest of the sections" (Banerjee 41). While Clarke focalizes his story of the man apes around the character of Moon-Watcher, the film's "Dawn of Man" segment provides no such center of focalization and instead functions more like wildlife documentary footage that follows the quotidian existence of these pre-Neolithic creatures.

The man apes live in a desert-like terrain that offers little in the way of sustenance.[3] Because they have not developed the capacity to hunt, they pick through the slim selection of vegetation available, and their access to water remains limited because another group of similar hominids also claims the same small, muddy water hole. Clarke's novel opens with a description of the man apes' precarious evolutionary situation: "In this barren and desiccated land, only the small or the swift could flourish, or even hope to survive. The man apes of the veldt were none of these things, and they were not flourishing; indeed, they were already far down the road to racial extinction" (3). The man apes stand poised on the precipice of extinction because they remain poorly adapted to the environment around them. They stay trapped in a state of being that will lead to their annihilation— for them, *stasis equals death*. They must learn to move from a state of being to one of becoming if they are to survive amidst their inhospitable surroundings. Whereas Deleuze talks about becoming-animal, the man apes must learn to enter a stage of becoming-human.

Initially, the film follows a day in the life of the man apes: the frustrating search for food, an attack by a leopard, and a showdown with a rival gang of man apes at the water hole that ends in retreat. The film depicts this typical day in juxtaposition to the transformation the man apes will soon undergo. On one auspicious morning, the man apes awake to discover that a giant, black, rectangular object, known as the monolith, has appeared in the middle of their rocky alcove.[4] The scene that ensues remains one of the most iconic moments in cinematic history. Choral voices, which may or may not be diegetic, imbue the scene with a creepy, otherworldly aura and instantiate the monolith's ambiguous symbolic status: "The monolith acts as the central symbol of the movie—the symbol of a higher intelligence and perhaps a higher order of existence. This symbolism is always reinforced by musical accompaniment" (Banerjee 42).[5] The monolith's symbolism (or its refusal of symbolism perhaps) will not become apparent until later in the film, but Kubrick already stages it in these early scenes to suggest a higher intelligence, whether it be divine or extraterrestrial. As the monolith calls out to them, the man apes devolve into a frenzy of anxiety and curiosity, taking turns approaching it before retreating again in terror. Eventually, one of them summons enough courage to touch it and soon others follow suit: they sniff, caress, and inspect the monolith's black surface. As the choral voices swell to a crescendo, Kubrick cuts to a low-angle shot of the monolith in which it seemingly towers upwards into the heavens. Its inky blackness engulfs the bottom two-thirds of the frame as the rising sun converges with the crescent moon above it against a background of blood-red clouds. This shot hearkens back to the opening shot of the Earthrise and gives the impression that the scene coincides with a cosmic alignment.

In the subsequent scene, the man apes forage among rocks and discarded bones for sustenance. Then, one particular man ape begins to cock his head in a mannerism that implies rational thought. This man ape, who would be Moon-Watcher in Clarke's novel, picks up a piece of this biological detritus and begins considering it as the first notes of Richard Strauss's *Also sprach Zarathustra* (1896) begin to waft gently into the scene. As the music builds with its blaring drums and trumpets, we watch as the man ape picks up a bone and begins to smash the remains of an animal skull. When we next see the man apes encountering the rival clan at the water hole, their adversaries crouch and jump like apes, but Moon-Watcher's clan stands upright in a more humanoid posture. When one of the rival man apes crosses the water, he is promptly beaten to death by the now bipedal tribe while his cohorts escape back into the desert.

The rousing introduction of Strauss's tone poem *Also sprach Zarathustra* already gestures toward a Nietzschean reading of the film, and, by turning to Nietzsche's conceptualization of becoming, we will bring the various aspects of the human we have discussed so far together into one final examination of the relation between science fiction and critical theory. In essence, *2001* allows us to conceive of science fiction and critical theory as two different discursive forms for theorizing the human both in its current state of being and in its potential for becoming. Jerold Abrams devotes an entire chapter to the representation of Nietzsche's concept of the *Übermensch* (the "Superman" or "Overman") in *2001*:

> In moving images—and almost no dialogue—Kubrick captures the entire evolutionary epic of Friedrich Nietzsche's magnum opus *Thus Spoke Zarathustra*. From worms to apes to humans, Nietzsche tracks the movement of life as will-to-power—ultimately claiming that it is not yet finished. We have only one stage left, the overman, a being who will look upon humanity as humanity now looks upon the apes. It is well

known that Nietzsche tells us little about what the overman will look like, except that he or she will emerge as a new kind of "child." (247)

The Overman represents the same kind of evolutionary leap as Akira—the human becomes like the ape or even the amoeba from the viewpoint of the Overman. But the coming of the Overman, which Zarathustra preaches, does not necessarily entail an evolution of the physical form. Instead, it is an evolution of ethics and identity, an evolution that moves the individual from a state of being to becoming, from a state of slavish morality to an ethos predicated upon freedom and self-definition. As Philip Kuberski notes in his essay on Kubrick's film, "There is an evolutionary drama implicit" in Nietzsche's *Thus Spoke Zarathustra* which

> can be concisely sketched with reference to the parable of "the three metamorphoses" from Nietzsche's introduction. The camel, like traditional human cultures, bends down to take on the load of transmitted values and demands. The lion, like enlightened technologists, confronts the dragon of tradition whose scales each bear the instruction: Thou Shalt. The final metamorphosis is that of the child acting out of its own impulse, free of tradition and free of resentment. (64)

While the opening segment of *2001* can and has been read as a depiction of Darwinian evolution in action, Abrams and Kuberski correctly note that the film actually concerns a Nietzschean form of evolution that takes the human through several cycles of becoming or metamorphoses as Zarathustra characterizes them. In the end, *2001* traces the subject's movement beyond the camel and the lion to the child that enacts its own will free from slavish constraints. A Nietzschean evolution, thus, leads back to the plane of immanence and involves a complete rebuilding of identity predicated upon the "revaluation of values" that Nietzsche calls for in *On the Genealogy of Morals*.

At first glance, the film may seem like it reads according to the most banal interpretation of Nietzsche as a sort of Darwinian philosopher who preaches a doctrine of overcoming the weak with one's strength of mind and purpose. This is Nietzsche boiled down to "that which does not kill him makes him stronger."[6] But, as Deleuze points out, while Nietzsche and Darwin both shook the foundations of traditional, Western, Christian thought in the nineteenth century, Nietzsche actually had little use for Darwin: "Nietzsche criticizes Darwin for interpreting evolution and chance within evolution in an entirely reactive way" (*Nietzsche* 42). Nietzsche himself explains how the instinct toward self-preservation can never in itself lead toward becoming, for its purpose lies in maintaining the stasis of being:

> To wish to preserve oneself is a sign of distress, of a limitation of the truly basic life instinct, which aims at *the expansion of power* and in so doing often enough risks and sacrifices self-preservation [...] and in nature, it is not distress which *rules*, but rather abundance, squandering—even to the point of absurdity. The struggle for survival is only an exception, a temporary restriction of the will to life; the great and small struggle revolves everywhere around preponderance, around growth and expansion, around power and in accordance the will to power, which is simply the will to life. (*Science* §349)

Darwinian evolution represents the mere preservation of the status quo, which for Nietzsche is the biological equivalent of slavish moral systems like Christianity: instead, "He admires Lamarck because Lamarck foretold the existence of a truly active *plastic force*, primary in relations of adaptations: a force of metamorphosis [...] The power of transformation, the Dionysian power, is the primary definition of activity" (Deleuze, *Nietzsche* 42). Nietzsche's vision of becoming—or evolution—remains tied to an innate potential within the human: the human has the ability to rise above its desire to simply defend a safe form of existence and to embrace the path of drastic metamorphosis. To truly grasp how the film ties together the various strands of this project, we must first examine precisely what Nietzsche means by becoming and the will to power.

To understand the concept of becoming, one must first banish the Platonic and Cartesian ideas of the unified self, of the doer who preexists the deed. Pierre Klossowski explains that for Nietzsche "The body is the *Self*...the *Self* resides in the midst of the body and expresses itself through the body" (32). As Nietzsche proposes, the idea of the subject or agent represents a grammatical illusion: "there is no 'being' behind doing, effecting, becoming; 'the doer' is merely a fiction added to the deed—the deed is everything...our entire science still lies under the misleading influence of language and has not disposed of that little changeling, the 'subject'" (*Genealogy* §13). By banishing Cartesian dualism, Nietzsche sought instead to "establish a new cohesion, beyond the agent, between the body and chaos—a state of tension between the fortuitous cohesion of the agent and the incoherence of Chaos" (Klossowski 50). The film *2001* is about embracing chaos, about putting oneself in contact with multiplicities and endless lines of flight, about rolling the dice of chance on a plane of pure immanence. But if the self equals nothing more than the body, then what precisely does Nietzsche mean by "the body"?

Deleuze explains, "There are nothing but quantities of force in mutual 'relations of tension' [...] Every force is related to other forces and it either obeys or commands. What defines a body is this relation between dominant and dominated forces" (*Nietzsche* 40).[7] Because the body is nothing more than a relation between conflicting forces, one can never speak of a unified self: "Being composed of a plurality of irreducible forces, the body is a multiple phenomenon, its unity is that of a multiple phenomenon, 'a unity of domination.' In a body, the superior or dominant forces are known as *active* and the inferior or dominated forces are known as *reactive*" (Deleuze, *Nietzsche* 40). We must, therefore, view the body, like society, as an interplay of forces, forces that either command or obey, for "every relationship of forces constitutes a body—whether it is chemical, biological, social, or political" (Deleuze, *Nietzsche* 40). Thus, according to Nietzsche, all of reality consists of bodies that emerge out chaos because of forces struggling with one another.

At the heart of Nietzsche's concept of force relations resides his theory of the will to power. Deleuze explains that the will to power is "the principle of the synthesis of forces" (Deleuze, *Nietzsche* 50). The will to power motivates one force to dominate another; it is the principle that determines the relation between active and reactive forces. As Nietzsche states,

> The victorious concept of "force," by means of which physicists have created God and the world, still needs to be completed: an inner will must be ascribed to it, which I designate as 'will to power,' i.e., as an insatiable desire to manifest power; or as the employment and exercise of power, as a creative drive, etc. [...] In the case of an animal, it is possible to trace all its drives to the will to power; likewise all the functions of organic life to this one source. (*Will* §619)

As Deleuze explains, by "victorious," Nietzsche means that "the relation of force to force, understood conceptually, is one of domination: when two forces are related one is dominant and the other is dominated" (Deleuze, *Nietzsche* 51). The will to power serves as the *primum mobile* for the struggle of forces, and it is the birth of this will to power that Kubrick depicts so powerfully when the man apes rise above their slavish heritage as the dominated in order to become masters of their world.

As Deleuze argues, it is the Nietzschean struggle of forces that demarcates "the diagram" that determines the particular organization of power in a given period of time. Sovereignty, discipline, and control each have their unique diagrams of power inscribed by the struggle of forces:

> In brief, forces are in a constant state of evolution; *there is an emergence of forces which doubles history,* or rather envelopes it, according to the Nietzschean conception. This means that the diagram, in so far as it exposes a set of relations between forces, is not a place but rather 'a non-place': it is the place only of mutation. Suddenly, things are no longer perceived or propositions articulated in the same way. (*Foucault* 80)

The struggle of forces takes place in a non-place, but they serve as structural parameters for the organization of power. But this struggle also takes place on the individual as well as the social level. While Deleuze does not directly draw the comparison, the *Übermensch* itself can be conceived of as a "non-place," a nonexistent being that nevertheless can profoundly impact the individual's desire and will to power. As Deleuze explains,

> There is no need to uphold man in order to resist. The superman has never meant anything but that: it is in man himself that we must liberate life, since man himself is a form of imprisonment for man. Life becomes resistance to power when power takes life as its object [...] When power becomes bio-power resistance becomes the power of life, a vital power that cannot be confined within species, environment or the paths of a particular diagram. (*Foucault* 92)

Hence, in the society of control, biopower seeks to control life, so we must attempt to tap into the instinctual vitality that resides at the heart of the human. As Nietzsche, Foucault, and Deleuze contend, humankind must turn inwards in order to find the means of resisting control. Like the non-place of science fiction, the *Übermensch* provides the paradigm for evolution and resistance—it is the utopian limit toward which humanity must strive. But, first, humanity must learn to embrace affirmation and becoming and leave behind reactive being.

While the will to power retains the possibility of being either active or reactive, it also has two possible "primordial qualities" of its own—it is either affirmative or negative (Deleuze, *Nietzsche* 54). There is always a will present, even if it is a will that denies, that is guilt-ridden by *ressentiment* and the bad conscience, or that is purely reactive based on either God/morality or on Nihilism. However, as Deleuze states, "Affirmation and negation extend beyond action and reaction because they are the immediate qualities of becoming itself. Affirmation is not action but the power of becoming active, *becoming active* personified. Negation is not simple reaction but a *becoming reactive*" (*Nietzsche* 54). Therefore, the affirmative or negative qualities of the will are directly linked to the process of becoming. To become the Overman, Nietzsche argues that you must learn to affirm becoming active, to embrace chance and chaos, to be willing to risk everything for the sake of transformation. The desire for becoming has driven the progress of the human species: it allowed us to rise from the prehuman into the human and it is steadily moving us beyond the limits of the human and into a posthuman existence.

In essence, the monolith instantiates this desire for becoming in the man apes, which is more apparent in the novel because the monolith presents Moon-Watcher with a nocturnal vision. In this vision, Moon-Watcher sees himself and his tribe in a better condition of life: no longer emaciated, they appear plump, well-groomed, and more highly civilized. The monolith teases Moon-Watcher with this image until he finally begins to feel the first faint stirrings of desire, of something more than the mere instinctual urges that normally govern his behavior. The monolith inscribes a notion of lack in the man apes' brains. While the man apes cannot exhibit the actual *manqué-à-être* that can only truly arise along with the signifier, they begin to experience the first gnawing of lack—they have become dissatisfied with being and seek the transformative power of becoming. In this first segment of the film, which features no dialogue (the absence of the signifier), we witness these creatures move from a state of being (a state of reactive self-preservation) into a transformative, active state of becoming. The man apes embrace chance and the roll of the dice; they are willing to take hold of their tools (or hammers if we want to use another of Nietzsche's favorite metaphors) to embrace the forces of chaos and smash themselves into a new form. The monolith actuates their desire for becoming, and we consequently see the birth of the element that will give rise to humanity—technology. Simultaneously, this simple piece of technology also heralds the birth of weaponry and property, for the man apes use the weapon to claim the water hole. But, above all else, it signifies the birth of the will to power.

The monolith functions as an evolutionary catalyst that enables species to leap across evolutionary chasms that might have hindered evolutionary progress. In "The Dawn of Man" segment, the monolith facilitates the apelike species in crossing an evolutionary gap to become tool-users, a gap that could conceivably have never been traversed without the appropriate cerebral modifications made possible by the presence of the monolith. Hence, "The Dawn of Man" segment depicts the sowing of the seeds of the human—the monolith introduces perhaps the most important variable of the human: desire. Even in this first instance of desire, it always strives toward utopian ideals, and the methods for attaining these utopian desires rely upon technological innovation.

THE HUMAN: DESIRE, TECHNOLOGY, CONTROL

At the end of Part one, Clarke's novel charts the progression of human tools and weapons from the man apes to the present while exhibiting a typical Cold War sensibility that these weapons inevitably will lead to the extinction of humanity: "The spear, the bow, the gun, and finally the guided missile had given him [humankind] weapons of infinite range and all but infinite power [...] But now, as long as they existed, he was living on borrowed time" (36–7). While technology leads to ever higher levels of civilization and to presumably ever more utopian experiences for the citizenry, it also inevitably generates new methods of global destruction—it instantiates the classic Promethean dilemma. In Clarke's novel, humankind must evolve because it has reached a self-destructive stalemate, but Kubrick foregoes such narrative connections, and the second section of his film jumps three million years in time to depict the exponential growth that has occurred between the era of the man apes and the age of space exploration. The film 2001's second segment depicts the utopian nature of technology and the new states of being that it opens up for humankind, but it also gestures toward the controlling aspects of technology that arise alongside its utopian aspirations.

The film's second part receives no title because Kubrick uses a match cut to link together the technological elements of the first two sections. In one of the most famous match cuts in cinematic history, Kubrick cuts from a shot of the man ape throwing his bone into the air to a shot of a similarly shaped space vehicle floating through the cosmos between the Earth and the Moon. This match provides a profound connection between the two scenes because it not only serves as an editing technique but also as a symbol that embodies the thematic link between the two sections: the discovery of this simple tool or weapon provided the impetus for a historical progression that led to space travel. Without the bone club, there could be no space odysseys. This section opens with images of the Earth, Sun, and Moon and the various space craft floating in the space between the Earth and the Moon. The spaceships, satellites, and space stations gently drift in this liminal space between planetary bodies. As Johann Strauss's *An der schönen blauen Donau* (1866; "On the Beautiful Blue Danube") languidly plays across this montage, the vehicles all seem to have been cut adrift and to be floating with no real sense of propulsion. As Mario Falsetto notes, in such scenes, "*2001* offer[s] up a kind of cinematic ballet" in which "the narrative momentum seems secondary" to the depiction of movement itself (44). Of course, the film concerns movement on numerous levels: not just the movement in zero-gravity or the propulsion systems of spacecraft but also the movement of evolution. The scene creates a sort of cognitive disjunction with the previous scenes of the man apes because the technological leap from bone to space station seems almost inconceivable, especially since "the harmony of space technology is, at first glance, free of the destructive violence evident in 'The Dawn of Man'" (Rasmussen 61). Indeed, this section depicts technology as a force that seems to have lost its violent character in favor of its utopian possibilities that make new modes of existence available to the subject by means of space travel.

From this "*valse méchanique*," as Kuberski terms it, the film cuts to interior shots of the spacecraft carrying Dr. Heywood Floyd to the space station that serves as a kind of cosmic rest stop between the Earth and the Moon (Kuberski 66). The space station's circular shape is further accentuated by Kubrick's use of an extremely wide-angle lens that gives the images a slightly skewed or bent perspective at the corners. The décor of the space station is distinctly Kubrickian and portends the milk bar from *A Clockwork Orange* (1971) and the bathroom of the Overlook Hotel in *The Shining* (1980): stark white walls and bizarrely shaped furniture in vivid shades of red. Kubrick depicts a variety of technological advancements: grip shoes that allow one to walk in zero gravity, video phones, voice-print identification systems, drinkable meals, zero-gravity toilets, and a space station that rotates in order to generate its own low-level gravity. Even in these smaller instances, Kubrick keeps the film's emphasis on the progress of technology, but this seemingly bright technological future constitutes a utopia in which humans are reduced to the state of what Nietzsche terms "the last men," people whose existence has ceased to be predicated upon struggle and who have succumbed to the allures of so-called "happiness."

Floyd stops at the space station just long enough to share a drink with some acquaintances and hear gossip about the strange occurrences on the Moon: communication has been lost with the Clavius base.

The scenes aboard the space station gesture toward the fact that the seemingly utopian façade of the future still remains mired in corporate control: Pan-Am owns and operates the space shuttles, and the space station features a Hilton hotel. As we see on a daily basis, Capital always keeps tabs on and appropriates the latest technological advancements in order to not cede that market to newer corporations—the "logo-maze" of Gibson's *Pattern Recognition* persists even in space. Such instances actually highlight the fact that space travel has been privatized to some degree in *2001*—the forces of postindustrial capitalism persist even into the film's seemingly utopian world.

The *Blue Danube's* waltz rhythm returns as Floyd progresses on from the space station to the Moon's surface. Dr. Floyd has been summoned to the Clavius base because another monolith has been exhumed on the Moon. During a roundtable meeting between Dr. Floyd and the Clavius scientists, the film reveals that a cover story has been issued to keep the public from learning about the monolith's existence. To avoid cultural shock, the United States government has issued a statement claiming that Clavius has been quarantined due to an epidemic. After noticing an electromagnetic field of untold magnitude emanating from the crater known as Tycho, the researchers on Clavius unearthed what they term "TMA-1" or "Tycho Magnetic Anomaly 1" (a monolith exactly like the one from the film's opening). Evidence points to its having been deliberately buried on the moon four million years ago, making it the first hard evidence of extraterrestrial life that apparently exceeded the current technological capacities of the human race before the species had even begun to evolve.

After listening to the scientists' gripes about the cover story, Dr. Floyd flies out to Tycho to perform an inspection of the monolith. He and the scientists gather in front of the monolith to take a picture, and it begins emitting an ear-piercing screech. As Dr. Floyd flails about from the pain of this sonic emission, he looks up to catch sight of the Sun and the Moon converging over the monolith, a shot that replicates the alignment during the man ape segment. Then, Kubrick abruptly cuts to a shot of empty space that features the logo "Jupiter Mission Eighteen Months Later." Again, Kubrick provides no narrative links between the segments—he forces the audience to draw their own connections as the film progresses. This second, unnamed segment of the film acts as a narrative bridge between the man ape segment and the larger narrative of the film that concerns the voyage of *Discovery One*. It further serves to highlight the banal aspects of the *2001* universe and to inaugurate the themes of control and computerization that will play out in the film's third part.

Philip Kuberski argues that the scenes with Dr. Floyd provide glimpses of a world in which the prosaic has triumphed over the creative or, as we might say, in which reactive being has triumphed over active becoming:

> Kubrick dramatizes the shift in human culture by leaving the earth behind; from this point on, all action is confined to artificial and space environments [...] Space, now inhabited and comfortably imprinted with corporate logos, has become an adjunct of the earth [...] We see people devoid of spontaneity performing rather than experiencing humor, collegiality, duty, curiosity. (66–7)

While the world has progressed infinitely in terms of civilization and technology, it has also regressed in terms of reality—it has become a world of simulacra. Like the postmodern landscape of *Pattern Recognition*, the world (or worlds) of *2001* are populated by trademarks and peopled by individuals incapable of genuine interactions with their environment. Their needs have all been satisfied, so their everyday existence forecloses the possibility of struggle or becoming. They exist in a state of reactive being because their lives become the performance of roles—they become characters aping the behaviors they are expected to exhibit. In Clarke's novel, the Earth remains torn apart by warring factions and Cold War ideological stalemates, but this geopolitical friction is completely absent from Kubrick's film. Indeed, Earth in Kubrick's film more closely resembles the version of the world in Clarke's *Childhood's End* (1953) in which a race of alien Overlords, who just happen to have the physical appearance of Satan, take charge of Earth and forcefully spread peace across the globe. While the world enters a so-called "Golden Age," this utopian existence simultaneously destroys much of what had been beautiful and majestic about the human condition: "The world's now passive, featureless, and culturally dead: nothing really new has been created since the Overlords came. The reason's obvious. There's nothing left to struggle for and there are too many distractions and entertainments" (135). In Kubrick's *2001*, humankind has similarly been stripped of the need for struggle—it has settled into a contentment that is predicated upon its technological innovations, but these innovations simultaneously reduce individuals to a simulacral existence in which the fundamentals of the human have vanished.

Kuberski points to the scene at the Tycho crater as an example of humankind's simulacral identities and their lack of contact with reality: "When they assemble before the excavated monolith in its flood-lit trench, one is reminded of a movie set. When Dr. Floyd sees and touches the monolith, it is through the insulation of his space helmet and glove. There is no ecstatic mystical participation, as there was with the ape-men. Like tourists, the scientists gather round the monument for a group photograph" (68). Humankind has achieved technological marvels, but they no longer engage in real connections with their environment—they experience everything through mediating technologies and hence they become trapped in a state of being like the man apes before the monolith's arrival. A new evolution is required if humankind is to reclaim the potential that has been lost in the synthetic textures of the postmodern world, and TMA-1 directs the way to this evolution—it lies around Jupiter.[8]

The "Jupiter Mission" segment follows the odd events aboard the *Discovery One* as it nears Jupiter. The sounds emitted by TMA-1 actually serve as a celestial beacon pointing toward Jupiter, and Earth sends *Discovery One* to explore the endpoint of this transmission. The *Discovery* crew consists of seven members: Dave Bowman, Frank Poole, the three hibernating members of the survey team, and the HAL-9000 computer, a computer capable of reproducing human thought and overseeing the entire ship. The HAL-9000 ("HAL" stands for "Heuristic Algorithm") prefers to be called "Hal," and he seems to exhibit independent thought and perhaps even emotions at various points in the film. Hal watches the events on the ship through a system of fish-eyed cameras that feature a bright red light in the center, giving them the appearance of eyes. Kubrick even cuts frequently to shots from Hal's perspective—he uses a fish-eyed lens to illustrate how Hal sees the world from a slightly skewed, mechanistic perspective. Hal seems like a normal (albeit bodiless) member of the crew: he engages in conversations with Dave and Frank, wishes Frank a "Happy Birthday," and plays chess with Dave, always with his soothing, affectless tone of voice.

Hal's complete control of the mission seems benevolent and flawless until he engages in a rather strange conversation with Dave about the bizarre circumstances surrounding their trip to Jupiter. Hal wonders if Dave "might be having second thoughts about the mission," but the computer admits that he might be "projecting" his "own concern about it" (*Odyssey* 16).[9] Hal proceeds to explain his consternation regarding the mission: "Well, certainly no one could have been unaware of the very strange stories floating around before we left. Rumors about something being dug up on the Moon. I never gave these stories much credence, but particularly in view of some of the other things that have happened I find them difficult to put out of my mind" (*Odyssey* 16). This exchange exhibits the manner in which Hal represents far more than a computer capable of voice interaction—he harbors a genuine intellect capable of forming his own opinions, questions, and forebodings about data, events, and even rumors. As the conversation progresses, a slow sense of unease develops over the scene until Hal suddenly begins repeating "Just a moment" like a stuck record, as if he is experiencing some sort of glitch or is processing a complex piece of information (16). Suddenly, he explains to Dave that he has found a fault in one of the communication dishes on the outside of the ship. From this point forward, Hal begins to transform from the friendly, omniscient ship's computer into a malevolent force of control that (or perhaps "who") manipulates the human element of the ship according to his own ideas about what is best for the mission.

In the sequence that follows, Dave ventures outside the ship in a space pod used for extravehicular maneuvers and retrieves the malfunctioning device. No sound occurs in this scene except for Dave's deep breathing inside his suit. The sound of his respiration generates a claustrophobic feeling and begins to demonstrate the fragility of the voyage's human element. Incapable of finding any faults in the device, a bewildered Dave and Frank contact Earth to discuss the situation. But they also caution that the twin HAL-9000 unit on Earth has determined that the device is indeed intact and that the error lies with Hal on the *Discovery*. When Dave asks if Hal can explain this discrepancy, the computer responds "Well, I don't think there's any question about it. It can only be attributable to human error. This sort of thing has cropped up before, and it has always been due to human error" (*Odyssey* 18). Outside of the computer's hearing, in one of the space pods, Dave and Frank have a secret conversation about disconnecting Hal if he proves to be malfunctioning, but a shot through Hal's fish-eyed lens reveals that the computer can read their lips, at which point the film abruptly cuts to black, signaling the intermission's beginning.

After the intermission, the film returns with an exterior shot of Discovery moving through space, and Kubrick plunges us back into the claustrophobia of extravehicular space maneuvers as Frank replaces the satellite component—again the scene features no sound other than his breathing. While he is refitting the part, the pod begins rotating all by itself and lowering its arms in an attack position. A series of rapid, jarring cuts highlight Hal's eye on the outside of the pod. Meanwhile, aboard *Discovery*, Dave watches as Frank flies off into space with the line to his oxygen tank cut while the unmanned pod spins wildly off into the void. Again, as with the scientists on the moon, Dave remains disconnected from his environment: he only experiences these tragic events secondhand through a monitor. When Dave exits the ship to recover Frank's body, Hal turns off the life support systems for the three hibernating crewmembers, making Dave the only surviving "human" element on the mission. When Dave returns, Hal refuses to open the pod bay doors for him, and he explains, "This mission is too important for me to allow you to jeopardize it" (*Odyssey* 24). The film never reveals why Hal began to malfunction—we only witness his actions, but his motives can be presumed from his statements.[10] After witnessing Frank and Dave's discussion in the space pod, Hal begins to fear that the mission might fail, so he decides to erase the human variables from the equation to prevent human error from interfering with his calculations.

Dave manages to save himself by blowing himself out of his space pod and into *Discovery*'s airlock. Then, the film cuts to a grimly determined Dave who begins the process of shutting down Hal, and, like any human facing execution, Hal tries to reason with Dave in a manner that at least mimics the intonations of fear. Ultimately, Hal even resorts to confessing his fear, "I'm afraid, Dave. My mind is going. I can feel it" (*Odyssey* 26). Inside a glowing red room, Dave methodically turns off the various databanks that represent Hal's memory and cognitive centers. As Hal's voice slowly degrades, we witness a mind slowly dying, until Hal devolves back to reciting his initial introduction speech, culminating in his heart-wrenching rendition of the song "Daisy" during which his voice slowly loses coherence and then ceases altogether. Few human death scenes so dramatically epitomize Hamlet's last words, "The rest is silence" (Shakespeare V.2.359). In his final moments, Hal's pleading seems to indicate that he indeed has feelings and hence represents a true artificial life-form. In Delany's *Triton*, computers became capable of controlling subject behavior to a certain degree and of reprogramming an individual's human variables to create new identities. In the universe of *2001*, humans actually can program the human variables into a machine so precisely that it can begin to function just like a human. As Rodney Brooks explains, "We are machines, and from that I conclude that there is no reason, in principle, that it is not possible to build a machine from silicon and steel that has genuine emotions and consciousness" (180). Brooks proceeds to argue that what frightens humankind about robots and artificial intelligence is not their potential to develop autonomous consciousness but the fact that they reveal humans to be nothing more than machines themselves. In essence, then, Hal reveals this essentially mechanistic nature of the human—his ability to perfectly mimic and perhaps experience human emotions demonstrates the manner in which humanity truly becomes programmable by the society of control. But while computers begin to act like humans, humans begin to operate like machines. As we saw earlier, humans have devolved in this vision of the future because of the mediating technologies that separate them from their environments. Indeed, Hal represents the most sympathetic being in the film because the human characters seldom (if ever) exhibit anything approximating genuine emotion—they have been programmed by the society of control to respond logically like machines without recourse to desire, fear, love, or any other emotion. They remain trapped at the level of being because, like a computer, they remain incapable of breaking the programming that orders their existence.

In essence, the "Jupiter Mission" segment reveals that the world of *2001* functions according to the diagram of control, similar to systems of power we have already seen depicted in *Ghost in the Shell*, *Trouble on Triton*, *Pattern Recognition*, and *Spook Country*. Examples of control abound in the scenes concerning Heywood Floyd: voice print identification systems and government cover-ups, to name only the two most explicit ones. But Hal's ever-watchful eye and virtually omnipotent control of *Discovery* exemplifies Deleuze's vision of the control society. Undoubtedly, Hal recalls Michel Foucault's discussions of Jeremy Bentham's panopticon, which acts as the paradigmatic structure of disciplinary societies, but control societies perfect the panoptic gaze by decentering it and spreading it throughout society. Like our current world, which is increasingly monitored by cameras on every corner and in the hands of every citizen, *Discovery* represents a space in which one's actions are never free from the all-seeing eye of control.

Furthermore, Hal not only oversees the crewmembers but also controls what information they receive, "As the segment unfolds, HAL's surveillance capabilities (d)evolve towards totality [...] HAL knows best, and he sees with the greatest clarity. HAL not only sees/oversees Bowman and Poole, but he also controls what *they* see" (Rhodes 98). Rhodes points out that HAL always controls the images and information that Dave and Frank receive even to the point of barring Dave from witnessing the space pod attack Frank. Rhodes further demonstrates that this control extends beyond HAL because

> Disconnecting HAL does not remove oversight; it simply transfers the power of surveillance to another. Initially, it comes in the form of a pre-recorded message from Dr. Heywood Floyd, who stares into the camera as he announces the real reason for the Jupiter Mission. His eyes lock on Bowman to announce that another force has been monitoring

earth. Keep watching the skies, Bowman, because the skies have been watching us since the very beginning. (Rhodes 99)

Of course, Rhodes's words echo the final lines of Christian Nyby's *The Thing from Another World* (1951): "Keep watching the skies."[11] The film *2001* is not as paranoid a film as this comparison or Rhodes's comments might suggest, but surveillance remains a subtle undertone throughout. But the society of *2001* does not rely upon the feeble eighteenth- and nineteenth-century disciplinary modalities of power but instead operates according to the paradigm of control. As Foucault explains, the panopticon is "a form of architecture that makes possible a mind-over-mind-type of power; a sort of institution that serves equally well, it would seem, for schools, hospitals, prisons, reformatories, poorhouses, and factories [...] The panopticon is the utopia of a society and a type of power that is basically the society we are familiar with at present, a utopia that was actually realized" ("Truth" 58). And we could say that the panopticon provides a perfect paradigm for organizing power aboard a spaceship as well. Like the panopticon, *Discovery* represents a utopian space, a space that features a computer capable of attending to one's every need. But this utopianism comes at a price, and, as we saw in chapter 3, computers perfect the disciplinary/panoptic society and transform it into the society of control. Hal does not hold the position of warden but instead acts like a friend and fellow crewmember that supposedly has the crew's best interests at heart. But *Discovery*'s apparent freedom and Hal's outwardly friendly demeanor mask the manner in which Hal controls subject behavior on the *Discovery*. Whereas Deleuze's essay on control foresees a society in which one's access to various spaces can be granted or forbidden by computer systems, *2001* takes this a step further by depicting a computer that not only restricts and manipulates information or blocks off particular spaces (the pod bay doors, for example) but that also becomes capable of simply shutting down life-support systems (Deleuze, "Postscript" 181–2). Hence, Dave encounters pure, unvarnished control, and he finds no alternative for further existence except through a transcendence of the bodily form, a transcendence that the monolith proves happy to grant him.

The Posthuman: Ontogenesis and Infinite Becoming

After Dave disconnects Hal, a video appears of Heywood Floyd explaining the secret reason for the *Discovery* mission. After this video ends, Kubrick abruptly cuts to the final section of the film, "Jupiter and Beyond the Infinite," which forecloses linear narrative logic to become a flow of spectacular and surrealistic images. Kubrick opens this last segment with a shot of Jupiter—the sun appears tiny and insignificant as the scene depicts *Discovery* hovering above the nightside of Jupiter with a giant monolith twisting in space above it. A lone space pod exits *Discovery*, and then the film cuts to a shot of the planets aligned with Jupiter, replicating the earlier alignments of the film. As the monolith floats across this line of planets, a series of lights and stars begin rushing toward the camera as Dave enters what is known as "the star gate."[12] As with most aspects of the film, this series of images never receives an explanation, and the film never refers to it as a "the star gate"; indeed, this final section of the film features no dialogue. But Clarke gives it this name in the novel, and critics of the film generally maintain this term. Whereas Clarke's novel explicates the occurrences in the final part of his story, Kubrick's film provides such an iconic cinematic experience because it is structured in a manner that actually belies structure: it revels in disjunction and ambiguity. These images that resist strict interpretation fit well with the film's overall purpose because they are depicting the human as it moves into a posthuman state that borders on divinity. It is a moment of ontogenesis, the birth of a new kind of being no longer hampered by the limits of the human. In *2001*'s final moments, the viewer becomes like an amoeba trying to see through the eyes of God.

As Dave travels through the star gate, Kubrick alternates shots of stars, lights, and other galactic wonders with still images of Dave's face contorted into various expressions of disbelief, horror, and wonder. These still images of Dave's face give way to extreme close-ups of his eye as he witnesses various space phenomena never before witnessed by the naked human eye. What Dave experiences is more than an acid-freak's dream come true—it is nebulas giving birth to universes, black holes sucking light out of the cosmos, supernovas spewing out the entire contents of the periodic table, fields of stars beyond human comprehension, and a general closeness to the universe with which humankind's brain was not meant to deal, and thus Dave must be pushed beyond the limits of the human.

Eventually, Dave begins to encounter phenomena that perhaps point to some higher intelligence. For example, at one point, he witnesses a plane of lights spread out against the stars with a series of glowing and pulsing polyhedrons floating across the surface. Of course, in the film, Dave never encounters aliens per se, yet he no doubt finds evidence of a more complex life-form or entity, an intelligence of which he becomes a constituent part at the film's end. Clarke's series of novels explains that the monoliths represent technology from an alien civilization that has scoured the universe for millions of years in search of life-forms that have the capacity to develop intelligence: "And because, in all the galaxy, they had found nothing more precious than Mind, they encouraged its dawning everywhere. They became farmers in the fields of stars; they sowed, and sometimes they reaped. And sometimes, dispassionately, they had to weed" (Clarke, *2010* 328).[13] But, in many ways, Kubrick's film remains more provocative because it leaves us wondering whether Dave has encountered aliens or whether he has possibly made contact with some sort of deity that drives evolution. As Carolyn Geduld points out, "The easiest sensible interpretation of the slab [the monolith], disregarding Clarke's is to call it a religious symbol. Kubrick, however, has pointed out that alien technology would probably look strange enough to appear godlike to humans on Earth" (41). In essence, the film leaves open the possibility that Dave attains oneness with God and that these images represent his mind evolving into a divine state of consciousness.

As Deleuze argues in *Cinema 2: The Time-Image*, "Kubrick is renewing the theme of the initiatory journey because every journey in the world is an exploration of the brain" (206). In effect, then, *2001* proves to be a sort of strange, cosmic bildungsroman that traces Dave's progression toward a state of psychic maturity through the evolution of his consciousness and his consequent communal interaction with the entirety of the cosmos. Dave journeys not just to Jupiter but also into the depths of his cerebral makeup which the monolith adjusts in order to allow him to become one with the universe. Lambert and Flaxman explain, "If the brain is a plane of immanence or consistency, then we might understand its function through networks of images themselves. The brain is a screen, Deleuze says, but the screen, the cinema, is also a brain, an organization of images and memories whose connections (regular or irrational) comprise an 'image of thought'" (par. 5). What is the "image of thought" projected onto the screen at the end of *2001*? It is literally the evolution of Dave Bowman's brain, a "mental image," in Deleuzian terms, of how the monolith alters not only Dave's brain but his entire state of being—he is reduced to the body without organs, a plane of pure immanence from which he can restructure (or perhaps deconstruct) himself into a new cosmic (or perhaps even divine) form of existence.

Finally, Dave arrives—if one can use such a word because Dave has most likely moved beyond places in any concrete sense of the term—in a strange white room decorated in a Louis XVI style where he witnesses himself at various stages of life. Here, Dave escapes from time and his body: he watches himself wasting away through various stages of old age, each of which he becomes. At the verge of death, the monolith returns to beckon him onwards to a new life, a life beyond the reach of decay, beyond the limits of knowledge, and certainly "beyond the infinite." Dave is reborn in the form of the Starchild, a child because he is no longer subject to temporal constraints but also because he has become like the child in Nietzsche's three metamorphoses—he has cast off the constraints of society and slavish morality and been born anew into a state of pure becoming. In the film's finale, the Starchild returns to Earth, and we see it floating in space above the Earth. As Deleuze explains, the sphere of the child coincides with the globe of the Earth to point the way for the new evolution of humankind: "At the end of *Space Odyssey*, it is in consequence of a fourth dimension that the sphere of the foetus and the sphere of the earth have a chance of entering into a new, incommensurable, unknown relation, which could convert death into a new life" (*Cinema 2* 206). Thus, Dave's "initiatory journey" is complete; he has reached out "beyond the infinite" and matured into a new realm of knowledge and consciousness. As Arthur C. Clarke's sequel (*2010: Odyssey Two*) makes clear, Dave can now interact with the Earth (and all of the universe) at a very basic—yet infinitely complex level— that is direct and without interferences such as language or the ego. He can literally beam his presence or voice between points almost instantaneously. As the embodiment of cosmic awareness, the monolith aids Dave Bowman in achieving a state that humankind never dreamed of: oneness with the stars. For, in the novel, when Dave states "The thing's hollow—it goes on forever—and—oh my God— *it's full of stars!*," he means not just the monolith but himself as well (254).[14] For at the film's end, Dave's Lacanian "lack" has been filled permanently; it has been filled with "stars," with the cosmos itself. He has moved beyond the realm of the body and into a potentially blissful realm of cosmic beauty, total communication, and limitless knowledge.

Dave embraces the chaos of the universe over the rigid organization of the human form to become a body without organs. Or, he might be said to embrace a higher structure since, of course, chaos theory posits that chaos represents an order too complex for the human mind to comprehend. But is *2001*'s image of human evolution truly libratory? Andrei Tarkovsky "disliked it [*2001*] as cold and sterile," and hence tried to create a science fiction film that truly depicted human emotion: the result, of course, was his classic adaptation of

Stanislaw Lem's *Solaris* (Lopate par. 3). While *2001* does remain cold in the sense that the viewer cannot glean any real sense of Dave's desires, it nonetheless explores how desire and identity might change as the subject approaches the body without organs. As Deleuze explains, organs are not the enemies of the organless body: "The organs themselves, however, are not the real enemy of the organless body. Organism is the enemy, in other words, any organization that imposes on the organs a regime of totalization, collaboration, synergy, integration, inhibition and disjunction" ("Schizophrenia" 20). Dave moves beyond the regime of organism to become pure consciousness. Generally, to achieve the state of the body without organs entails reaching a state of stasis or death, but for Dave who has moved entirely beyond the realm of bodies, it means an ascendance to a condition of pure self beyond the constraints of any physical limitations. Indeed, the monolith acts as a perfect symbolic representation of the body without organs, for, as Deleuze and Guattari explain, "In order to resist organ-machines, the body without organs presents its smooth, slippery, opaque, taut surface as a barrier [...] In order to resist using words composed of articulated phonetic units, it utters only gasps and cries that are sheer unarticulated blocks of sound" (*Anti-Oedipus* 9). The shiny, black, geometrically perfect surface of the monolith presents just such an undifferentiated, unknowable mass, and its utterances manifest themselves only in dissonant sounds or creepy choral arrangements. Like Tarkovsky, one can read *2001* as a cold depiction of Darwinian evolution, or one can read it as an attempt to imagine something beyond the organization of the human form, beyond the lack that language, hierarchical organizations, and repressive social systems force upon the individual. Its black exterior demarcates the limits of the human and points to the possibilities that lie beyond them if one proves willing to embrace chaos and becoming. In *Anti-Oedipus*, Deleuze and Guattari pose a fundamental question: "Is it really necessary or desirable to submit to such repression?" (3). The organization of desiring-machines inflicts pain upon the body, for "Desiring-machines make us an organism; but at the very heart of this production, within the very production of this production, the body suffers from being organized in this way, from not having some other sort of organization or no organization at all" (*Anti-Oedipus* 8). The monolith represents this other form of organization, a completely free-flowing, horizontal (not vertical and hierarchical) organization that allows rhizomatic lines of flight to form at any given point. The monolith inducts Dave into a similar existence as he casts off his desiring machines to become a full body without organs, an empty slate (or *tabula rasa*, to use John Locke's term) upon which his new existence as the star child can be inscribed without reference to repressive systems.[15]

Ultimately, *2001* provides a paradigmatic example of what Gilles Deleuze terms a "cinema of the brain" in which "The world itself is a brain, there is an identity of brain and world, as in the great circular and luminous table in *Doctor Strangelove*, the giant computer in *2001: A Space Odyssey*, the Overlook hotel in *The Shining*" (*Cinema 2* 205). While Hal may provide the initial example of the "world as brain" in the film, the entire filmic image becomes a depiction of Dave Bowman's brain in the last section. The final sequence achieves what Lambert and Flaxman call "the full cerebralization of the cinema," a cerebralization that allows the audience to directly experience the evolutionary changes in Dave Bowman's consciousness (par. 5). While discussing the concept of the "world-brain" in Kubrick's films, Deleuze explains the limit that is posited by such a cinema:

> The identity of world and brain, the automaton, does not form a whole, but rather a limit, a membrane which puts an outside and an inside in contact, makes them present to each other, confronts them or makes them clash. The inside is psychology, the past, involution, a whole psychology of depths which excavate the brain. The outside is the cosmology of galaxies, the future, evolution, a whole supernatural which makes the world explode. (*Cinema 2* 206)

The end of *2001* depicts Dave Bowman's movement from the inside to the outside—we watch as the heterotopian space of the film causes our paltry visions of the universe to "explode." No longer is Dave to be governed by bodily limitations, temporal demarcations, and a psychology that ends at the borders of the ego. Instead, Dave "enter[s] a world devoid of logic" because his "trip [is] one beyond logic, where no human mind can understand what is happening," and the Starchild represents "the possibility of a new human being possessing a new intelligence that can understand the new illogicality of space and time because they are perceived as changeable, rather than as coherent or immutable parameters" (Mainar 130). Kubrick's film breaks logical narrative connections in a manner akin to *La Jetée* and *Primer* in order to visualize this state beyond logic. While *2001* remains tied to spectacle in the tradition of Méliès, it still breaks with traditional structures in order to imagine a state beyond narrative and temporal strictures. Dave manages to attain a state usually accorded only to deities: an extemporal, omnipresent existence that allows communication not only with other humans but with the cosmos itself. The monolith embodies this experience as a black void of screeching dissonance. When the monolith appears for the second time and subjects Dr. Floyd and the other scientists to a piercing burst of sound, it seems to not lead to direct evolution, yet it paves the way for evolution by pointing toward Jupiter using its sonic assault. This audio burst represents the seething chaos that communion with the monolith and the cosmos holds. By pointing the way to Jupiter, the monolith incites humankind's desire for knowledge and meaning, but, as we saw in chapter 2, desire remains predicated upon lack as long as one remains subject to the society of control. But Dave transcends the bodily form and becomes the body without organs in order to transmute his desire into the will to power, a motor for infinite becoming instead of an Oedipal lack that impedes his progression.

Conclusion: Beyond the Infinite . . .

In Nietzsche's prologue to *Thus Spoke Zarathustra*, Zarathustra decries the coming of the last men, men who have achieved a utopian level of happiness based on the eradication of struggle. They strive neither for too much nor too little, but instead have "invented happiness" by always dwelling in the mean between two extremes ("Prologue" §17). When Zarathustra attempts to warn the townspeople about the coming of this "despicable" race of humans, the townspeople misunderstand him and ask him to teach them how to become these last men ("Prologue" §17). Indeed, to many people, the world of the last men might seem idyllic, yet Zarathustra (or Nietzsche) argues that this world robs us of essential aspects of the human: struggle, desire, and becoming. As Nietzsche's example suggests, utopias learn to manipulate the variables of the human into a social equation that provides the greatest possible contentment to the largest demographic of individuals.

Arthur C. Clarke's other evolutionary epic, *Childhood's End*, features just such a utopian transformation of humankind, a transformation in which humankind literally becomes "the last men." As stated previously, the novel concerns a race of aliens known as the Overlords who appear above the major cities of Earth and eventually reveal the paltry role that humankind plays in the universe's affairs. As Clarke's novel elucidates, utopia leads toward peace and plenty but also toward the death of the human. When the Overlords bring global peace to Earth in *Childhood's End*, humankind loses its sense of struggle: "I fear that the human race has lost its *initiative*. It has peace, it has plenty—but it has no *horizons*" (155). When humankind achieves peace and is provided with endless distractions, then it loses its desire for becoming, for reaching beyond the present and into the future. This leads to the creation of a colony called "New Athens" where artists and scientists try to reignite the human impulse for advancement and culture. But soon the humans learn that the Overlords are merely servants of an even more powerful entity known as the Overmind, which seeks out worlds and then spurs the evolution of their children into a new form of being. Initially, the children of Earth develop psychic powers and begin taking mental journeys through the universe, but soon they evolve further and leave their bodies behind. After shedding their physical forms, the children become united into one consciousness (*Childhood's End* was one of Hideaki Anno's inspirations for *Neon Genesis Evangelion*). The children's parents are left behind with no future, and they soon destroy themselves with nuclear weapons. Like Nietzsche's discussion of the last men, *Childhood's End* demonstrates how humanity must rid itself of utopian orderliness and embrace the chaos of the heterotopian if it is to achieve new states of becoming.

Of course, such forms of evolution do not come without a risk; as Kevin Stoehr argues, "*2001* is not necessarily a celebration of the idea of any evolution or advancement toward such a form of existence, since the dangers inherent in this type of transcendence (i.e., the surpassing of the need for physical embodiment) are also evoked in the film" (122). For instance, as Stoehr elaborates, the idea of existing beyond the body destroys our sense of being because it robs us of the context within which we define ourselves: "Those who pretend to locate themselves somehow beyond the borders of their present life-situation are left only with nothing in particular—an absence of meaning and value" (130). Stoehr makes a valid point, but he also misunderstands the critical apparatus of science fiction. While works such as Kubrick's definitely attempt to imagine alternative forms of existence, they more directly comment upon our present systems of thought—they are texts that allow us to make first contact with spaces of radical otherness in a way that incites us to question our most basic concepts of reality and the self. Kubrick's *2001* exemplifies this critical function of science fiction because it depicts the transcendence of a utopian space in order to attain communication with a heterotopian space in which radical difference can reactivate struggle and becoming. The heterotopian exposes our traditional, stable images of the universe to the chaos of multiplicity—it opens the realms of chance in which becoming can thrive. In Kubrick's film and in Clarke's novel, society has progressed to the point where further development remains impossible while the individual remains tied to corporeal limitations. Dave's disembodiment exposes him directly to chaos in a manner at which the human mind would balk—the heterotopian represents a sublime moment, as Kant defines it in *Critique of the Power of Judgment*, in which reason fails because it cannot fathom the complexity of chaos.[16] Hence, whereas the traditional fictional narrative might expose us to the beautiful, to the orderliness and structure of the utopian, science fiction brings us into contact with the heterotopian, a sublime space that shreds our concepts and decimates our attempts to impose structure and coherence. By doing so, science fiction allows us to not simply conceive of other states of being but to use our contact with the heterotopian to engage in a critique of our traditional theoretical discourses and to generate new theoretical concepts that can displace or advance existing critical strands. In essence, science fiction allows critical theory to move beyond its state of reactive being and to embrace a state of radical becoming in which thought can struggle past its conventional restrictions and thrive upon a new plane of immanence.

Notes

Introduction: The Genre of the Non-Place: Science Fiction as Critical Theory

1. For Plato's "Allegory of the Cave," see *The Republic* Book VII.
2. For a thorough analysis of science fiction's origins, see Brian W. Aldiss and David Wingrove's *Trillion Year Spree: The History of Science Fiction* (1986).
3. See William S. Burroughs's *Naked Lunch* (1959), the Nova (Or Cut-Up) Trilogy (*The Soft Machine* [1961], *The Ticket that Exploded* [1962], and *Nova Express* [1964]), *The Wild Boys* (1971), and the "Red Night" Trilogy (*Cities of the Red Night* [1981], *The Place of Dead Roads* [1983], and *The Western Lands* [1987]; Thomas Pynchon's *V* (1963), *Mason & Dixon* (1997), and *Against the Day* (2006); John Barth's *Giles Goat-Boy; or, The Revised New Syllabus* (1966); Don DeLillo's *White Noise* (1985); Kathy Acker's *Don Quixote: Which Was a Dream* (1986) and *Empire of the Senseless* (1988); Italo Calvino's *Cosmicomics* (1965) or *Invisible Cities* (1972); David Foster Wallace's *Infinite Jest* (1996); Mark Z. Danielewski's *House of Leaves* (2000); and Jonathan Lethem's *The Fortress of Solitude* (2003).
4. McHale derives this concept of "projecting worlds" from Thomas Pynchon's *The Crying of Lot 49* (1965). As Oedipa Maas begins to explore the potential existence of a secret mail system known as Tristero, she writes underneath the Tristero horn that she has copied off of a bathroom wall, "*Shall I project a world?*" (65). Here, Oedipa is contemplating the possible existence of an entire other pattern of reality of which she (and most of the world) remains unaware.
5. For Ferdinand de Saussure's original theorization of the sign, the signified, and the signifier, see *Course in General Linguistics*. For Lacan's earliest discussion of the bar (*barre*) that divides the signified and signifier, see his essay "The Instance of the Letter in the Unconscious, or Reason since Freud." In subsequent seminars, Lacan further develops his concept of the bar, and it becomes a part of his "algebra." The bar is used to strike out the subject and the Other in order to designate the presence of lack that is instilled by language.
6. For the texts that influence Michel de Certeau, see Foucault's *Discipline and Punish* and *The Order of Things* and Pierre Bourdieu's *Outline of a Theory of Practice*.

7. For Nietzsche's concept of the revaluation (or "transvaluation," as it is sometimes translated) of values, see the second essay in *On the Genealogy of Morals*.

8. For just a few examples of such antinarrative cinema, see such avant-garde classics as Fernand Léger and Dudley Murphy's *Ballet Mécanique* (1924), Luis Buñuel and Salvador Dali's *Un chien Andalou* (1929) and *L'Âge d'Or* (1930), or Kenneth Anger's *The Inauguration of the Pleasure Dome* (1954). Surrealism often intersects with science fiction in a variety of ways, and surrealist works undoubtedly create their own heterotopian spaces as they twist and reimagine our reality, often bringing the internal out into the open and creating fantastic vistas that often feel like the stuff of sci-fi novels.

9. Estrangement" was also theorized by Russian Formalist critic Viktor Shklovsky. See his essay entitled "Art as Device" (1917)—sometimes translated as "Art as Technique," which was later collected in *Theory of Prose* (1929).

10. In his essay entitled "The Uncanny," Freud develops his concept of *unheimlich*. Usually translated as "uncanny," *unheimlich* more precisely means "unhomely." The uncanny occurs when one experiences an event that is both familiar yet profoundly strange and unsettling— Freud cites examples like the *Doppelganger* (or "the double"). The uncanny is an example of the return of the repressed and is usually connected to childhood traumas and anxieties.

11. Kant initially reflects upon the nature of space and time in *On the Form and Principles of the Sensible and Intelligible World [Inaugural Dissertation]* in which he argues that time and space are pure intuitions necessary for coordinating sensory perceptions. Kant expands upon his conceptualization of space and time in *Critique of Pure Reason*: space and time are pure *a priori* intuitions that must exist before the understanding can become capable of making judgments: "Time is the *a priori* formal condition of all appearances in general. Space, as the pure form of all outer intuitions, is limited as an *a priori* condition merely to outer intuitions" (A 34). Therefore, time is the immediate condition of our inner senses and space is the immediate condition of our outer senses, but time remains more fundamental because space must also pass through the inner senses, so time is the mediate condition for space as well. Hence, time functions as the ordering principle for all perceptions. I am indebted in this note to Howard Caygill's *A Kant Dictionary* for helping me to easily assemble these references.

12. For René Descartes's famous discussion of the statement "*Cogito ergo sum*" or "I think; therefore, I am," see *Meditations on First Philosophy*. The famous phrase actually appears in the "Objections and Replies" section.

13. In *Problems in General Linguistics*, Emile Benveniste points out that "there are languages, like Hopi, in which the verb implies absolutely

no temporal modality, and others, like Tübatulabal (of the same Uto-Aztec group as Hopi), in which the clearest expression of the past belongs not to the verb but to the noun" (133). But any language provides the means of conveying narratives that involve temporality.

14. I take the term "manifold" from the philosophy of Immanuel Kant. As Kant explains, "Now space and time contain a manifold of pure *a priori* intuitions, but belong nevertheless among the conditions of the receptivity of our mind, under which alone it can receive representations of objects, and thus they must also affect the concept of these objects. Only the spontaneity of our thought requires that this manifold first be gone through, taken up, and combined in a certain way in order for a cognition to be made out of it. I call this action synthesis. By synthesis in the most general sense, however, I understand the action of putting different representations together with each other and comprehending their manifoldness in one cognition" (*Reason* A 77).

1   Variables of the Human: Gender and the Programmable Subject in Samuel R. Delany's *Triton*

1. The novel was entitled simply *Triton* when it was first published in 1976. The novel's subtitle is a reference to Ursula K. Le Guin's novel *The Dispossessed* (1974), which features "an ambiguous utopia." Douglas Barbour mentions this connection and explains that Delany, in his titles especially, "is inclined to be ironic in his allusion to traditional genre sf" (121). Le Guin's novel deals with two different planets: Annares, which was settled by anarchist utopians from the capitalist system on the planet Urras. Which planet represents the actual utopia becomes the source of the ambiguity throughout this novel.

2. *Equinox* was originally published under the name *The Tides of Lust*.

3. Even though their plots are unrelated, Delany describes *Trouble on Triton* as the prelude to his "Return to Nevèrÿon" tales, a series of 11 "sword and sorcery" short stories, novels, and novellas that again function on the very limits of their genre. The "Return to Nevèrÿon" series is published in four volumes: *Tales of Nevèrÿon* (1979), *Neveryóna* (1983), *Flight from Nevèrÿon* (1985), and *Return to Nevèrÿon* (1987). *Triton* is related to "Nevèrÿon" in two distinct ways. First, it contains the first two parts of a larger five-part, unclassifiable work entitled "Some Informal Remarks Towards the Modular Calculus," a work that continues in various parts of the "Nevèrÿon" tales. The "Informal Remarks," which Delany terms "a critical fiction," consists of five parts, which span different genres: the first part is the novel *Triton*; the second part is *Triton*'s second appendix entitled "Ashima Slade and the Harbin-Y Lectures"; the third part is the first appendix to *Tales of Nevèrÿon*; the fourth part consists of the novel *Neveryóna*; and the final part is Delany's story about AIDS entitled "The Tale of

Plagues and Carnivals" in *Flight from* Nevèrÿon. Secondly, as Delany explains in his afterword to *Stars in My Pockets Like Grains of Sand*, *Triton* has a thematic link to his other works: Delany claims that his work from *Dhalgren* through the "Return to Nevèrÿon" series deals with "the fragmented subject as a 'natural' condition" (356). Across these works, Delany examines various, socially-constructed identificatory schemas and the ways in which fragmented subjects interact with them and grapple with their loss of unity.

4. For further biographical information on Delany, see Sandra Y. Govan's "Samuel R. Delany"; Peter S. Alterman's "Samuel R. Delany"; and the entry "Samuel R. Delany" in *Contemporary Authors Online*.

5. Delany, *Triton* 1. Hereafter, the abbreviation "*T*" will refer to the text of Samuel Delany's *Trouble on Triton*.

6. See Sonya Andermahr, Terry Lovell, and Carol Wolkowitz's "Gender," in *A Glossary of Feminist Theory*. The authors take this information partly from Ann Oakley's *Sex, Gender, and Society* (1972).

7. Such topics also crop up throughout many of Butler's other works, including *The Psychic Life of Power: Theories in Subjection* (1997), *Excitable Speech: A Politics of the Performative* (1997), *Giving an Account of Oneself* (2005), and even her early book on Hegel entitled *Subjects of Desire: Hegelian Reflections in Twentieth-Century France* (1987).

8. The epigraph appears at the beginning of Appendix B, which is entitled "Ashima Slade and the Harbin-Y Lectures."

9. Hegel argues that recognition serves as the basis of our identities and desires as well as our interactions with others. For Hegel, in the *Phenomenology of Spirit*, a subject cannot become self-conscious (or even become a subject) until s/he has been recognized (or acknowledged) by an other: "self-consciousness exists in and for itself, and by the fact, it so exists for another; that is, it exists only in being acknowledged" (§178). To become an individual, one must first engage with an other who recognizes him/her as an entity separate from all other entities and as an entity with its own consciousness and desires. As Kojève explains, for Hegel, recognition provides the foundation for the movement from being a mere biological entity to being a full-fledged person: "It is only Desire of such a *Recognition* (*Anerkennung*), it is only Action that flows from such a Desire, that creates, realizes, and reveals a *human*, non-biological I" (40). To become fully human then requires recognition, a satiation of the subject's desire through his/her recognition of another subject's desire.

10. Jeffrey Allen Tucker makes a similar point when he argues that "the novel depicts an ideal society, but not one characterized by unity, totality, or singularity, but by the enormous multiplicity of subject positions available to be occupied" (43).

11. I will continue to refer to Bron using the masculine pronouns for the sole purpose of avoiding confusion.

12. Robert Elliot Fox makes a similar claim when he argues that Bron "behaves as if things were merely black and white" or "male/female" instead of opening himself up to "a more concrete and demanding freedom" (50).

13. Lacan uses "encore" here according to its general meaning of "again," but he later puns on it as well by using the word "*en-corps*," which is a homonym in French that means "in-body."

14. For the most basic formulation of the existential doctrine of "existence precedes essence," see Jean-Paul Sartre's essay "Existentialism is a Humanism." He also explores such themes in his existential magnum opus *Being and Nothingness: A Phenomenological Essay on Ontology*.

2 The Human as Desiring Machine: Anime Explorations of Disembodiment and Evolution

1. Lacan develops his concept of "lack" from the Hegelian dialectic and particularly the process of recognition (*anerkennung*). In *The Phenomenology of Spirit*, Hegel explains recognition as the basis of self-consciousness: "Self-consciousness exists in and for itself when, and by the fact that, it exists for another; that is, it exists only in being acknowledged" (Part IV, A, §178). Alexandre Kojève, whose lectures on Hegel profoundly influenced Lacan's theories, explains that the origin of self-awareness lies in the subject's desire which must be complemented by the desire of the other: "When man first experiences desire, when he is hungry...and wants to eat, and when he becomes aware of it, he necessarily becomes aware of *himself*. Desire is always revealed as *my* desire, and to reveal desire, one must use the word 'I'" (Kojève 37). However, at this point the subject still operates at the level of "animal desire," for "to be *human*, man must act not for the sake of subjugating a *thing*, but for the sake of subjugating another *Desire* (for the thing). The man who desires a thing humanly acts not so much to possess the *thing* as to make another *recognize* his *right*...to that thing, to make another recognize him as the *owner* of the thing (Kojève 39–40). To become truly human thus means engaging in the conflict of desires, in the dialectical struggle between master and slave. Becoming human then means the recognition of the things one desires as being external to ones self coupled with the recognition of the other's desire for the same things. As Kojève explains "the I of Desire [is nothing] but an *emptiness* greedy for content," or, that is, "an *absence* of Being" (38, 40). Because of this absence, humans enter the Master/Slave dialectic in which they struggle for mastery, which forms the basis of history as well as individual self-consciousness.

2. I am indebted to Daniel Smith's "Deleuze and the Question of Desire: Toward an Immanent Theory of Ethics" for helping me to

articulate the conceptualization of desire that Deleuze and Guattari develop in the two volumes of *Capitalism and Schizophrenia*.

3. For a full discussion of the base and superstructure, see Marx's preface to *A Contribution to the Critique of Political Economy* (1859). Gramsci famously divides the superstructure into political society and civil society, both of which contribute to cultural hegemony. See the section entitled "Stave and Civil Society" in *Selections from the Prison Notebooks of Antonio Gramsci*.

4. Related to Marxist theories of ideology and commodity fetishism, the concept of false consciousness is not really developed by Marx himself but by later Marxist theorists. For a full discussion of the idea, see Georg Lukács's *History and Class Consciousness: Studies in Marxist Dialectics*.

5. For other important cyberpunk novels, see Bruce Sterling's *Schismatrix* (1985) and *Islands in the Net* (1989); Pat Cadigan's *Synners* (1991), *Tea from an Empty Cup* (1998), and *The Dervish is Digital* (2000); John Shirley's *A Song Called Youth* trilogy (*Eclipse* [1985], *Eclipse Penumbra* [1988], and *Eclipse Corona* [1990]); and Rudy Rucker's *The Ware Tetralogy* (*Software* [1982], *Wetware* [1988], *Freeware* [1997], and *Realware* [2000]).

6. In the United States, the manga series has been collected in a six-volume translation by Dark Horse Comics. In many respects, the anime of *Akira* proves more mysterious and ambiguous than the manga. The anime keeps the viewer wondering about the nature of Akira until the film's last segment when Akira actually appears for a few brief seconds. However, Akira appears early in the manga and continues to be a presence throughout it.

7. Hereafter, the abbreviation "*A*" will refer to the anime film *Akira*, and the attending numbers will refer to the scene numbers on the Special Edition DVD of the film. All quotes come from the English language subtitles on this DVD.

8. William S. Burroughs's novels provide the first sustained body of work dedicated to explorations of body horror, but the genre can no doubt be traced back to horror authors such as H. P. Lovecraft and absurdist works like Franz Kafka's "In the Penal Colony" (1919) and *The Metamorphosis* (1915). The genre began to truly blossom in the late 1970s and early 1980s with directors such as Ridley Scott, David Cronenberg, and John Carpenter. See Ridley Scott's *Alien* (1979); David Cronenberg's *Shivers* (1975), *Rabid* (1976), *The Brood* (1979), *Scanners* (1981), *Videodrome* (1983), and *The Fly* (1986); and John Carpenter's *The Thing* (1982).

9. In *Seminar III*, Lacan explains that the psychotic's psychic structure engages in the act of *Verwerfung*, or foreclosure as Lacan himself translates it: it relies on something being "refused in the symbolic order," but whatever constitutes this repressed element "reappears in

the real" in the form of delusions and hallucinations (13). Ultimately, such subjects rewrite the world in order to create hermetically sealed systems of meaning in which there is no lack and in which meaning is always stable.

10. For a discussion of *Ghost in the Shell*'s cityscape, its basis in the real-life urban landscape of Hong Kong, and its similarities to Ridley Scott's *Blade Runner*, see Wong Kin Yuen's "On the Edge of Spaces: *Blade Runner*, *Ghost in the Shell*, and Hong Kong's Cityscape."

11. In this passage, Haraway is making reference to Zoe Sofia's "Exterminating Fetuses: Abortion, Disarmament, and the Sexo-Semiotics of Extra-Terrestrialism."

12. See Philip K. Dick's *Do Androids Dream of Electric Sheep?* (1968), the novel that served as the basis for Ridley Scott's *Blade Runner*.

13. Hereafter, the abbreviation "G" will designate the anime film *Ghost in the Shell*, and the numbers following the abbreviation will refer to chapter numbers on the DVD. Unless otherwise noted, quotes derive from the English-language subtitles on the DVD.

14. This famous quote comes from Paul's first epistle to Corinth: "When I was a child, I spake as a child, I understood as a child, I thought as a child: but when I became a man, I put away childish things./ For now we see through a glass darkly; but then face to face: now I know in part; but then I shall know even as also I am known" (1 Cor. 13:11–12).

15. Numerous classic works of science fiction have imagined gestalt forms of consciousness. For one example, see my discussion of Arthur C. Clarke's *Childhood's End* in the introduction and conclusion of this study. Greg Bear's *Blood Music* (1985) follows a cellular biologist who turns each of his cells into sentient beings that subsequently refashion his body and soon the entire world into a collective lifeform. In a slightly different vein, Octavia Butler's "Patternist Series" details the millennia-long development of psychic powers that mentally link all individuals together. The series features five novels: *Patternmaster* (1976), *Mind of My Mind* (1977), *Survivor* (1978), *Wild Seed* (1980), and *Clay's Ark* (1984).

16. Anno has recently reimagined the entire story from beginning to end, and Gainax Studios has begun releasing a quadrilogy of films entitled *Evangerion Shin Gekijōban* (or *Rebuild of Evangelion* as the series has been dubbed in English). So far, two films have been released to the Japanese theatrical market and Western home video market: *Evangerion Shin Gekijōban: Jō* (2007) and *Evangerion Shin Gekijōban: Ha* (2009) or *Evangelion 1.0: You Are (Not) Alone* and *Evangelion 2.0: You Can (Not) Advance* as they were translated for English-speaking audiences. Since the remainder of this new series has yet to be released, this chapter will leave them aside for future critics.

17. Hereafter, the abbreviation "*E*" will refer to the anime series *Neon Genesis Evangelion*, and the number after it will reference the episode number from which the quote is derived. Unless otherwise noted, quotes are from the English dub of the series.
18. In the subtitled version, Commander Ikari calls it "a new era in human history" instead of a "new genesis."
19. There are actually two original *Evangelion* films: *Evangelion: Death and Rebirth* (1997) and *The End of Evangelion*. I will disregard *Death and Rebirth* because the first half features an impressionistic retelling of the series' events and the second half became the first part of *The End of Evangelion*.
20. Hereafter, the abbreviation "*End*" will refer to Hideaki Anno's The *End of Evangelion*. The numbers following the abbreviation will refer to the scene numbers on the DVD version of the film, and quotes come from this DVD's English dub.

3 THE EVERSION OF THE VIRTUAL: POSTMODERNITY AND CONTROL SOCIETIES IN WILLIAM GIBSON'S SCIENCE FICTIONS OF THE PRESENT

1. See Neal Stephenson's early cyberpunk fare like *Snow Crash* (1992) and *The Diamond Age or, A Young Lady's Illustrated Primer* (1995) versus his later realistic works: *Cryptonomicon* (1999), the "Baroque Trilogy" (*Quicksilver* [2003], *The Confusion* [2004], and *The System of the World* [2004]), and *Reamde* (2011).
2. Hereafter, the abbreviation "*PR*" will refer to the text of *Pattern Recognition*.
3. For Jameson's readings of these texts, see Part One, "Totality as Conspiracy," in *The Geopolitical Aesthetic: Cinema and Space in the World System*.
4. Of course, the concept of the "end of history" has a rich genealogy in the history of philosophy and critical theory. Originally, the concept derives from the dialectical philosophy of Hegel who conceived of the French Revolution and his simultaneous writing of the *Phenomenology of Spirit* as the end of history. Various philosophers since Hegel have posited different moments as "the end of history." For Marx, who adopts Hegel's dialectical conceptualization of history, the end of history would arrive when capitalism was overthrown because the need for struggle would cease and hence the dialectical wheel would stop spinning. Francis Fukuyama's *The End of History and the Last Man* attempts to refute Marx by arguing that the triumph of liberal democracy over communism signaled the end of history. Walter Benn Michaels adopts a similar stance in *The Shape of the Signifier: 1967 to the End of History*. Jacques Derrida famously criticizes Fukuyama for attempting to bury Marx and proselytize in favor of a so-called liberal democracy that still carries out one war after another and keeps

a large portion of the world's population in abject poverty with few human rights. For Derrida's criticism of Fukuyama and other similar theorists, see his book *Specters of Marx: The State of the Debt, the Work of Mourning, and the New International*. More recently, in *Empire*, Michael Hardt and Antonio Negri argue that the arrival of the global order of Empire signifies the end of history because it exists as *the* world order, one that regulates all international struggles within its own matrix. Hardt and Negri believe that the advent of Empire signals the exhaustion of the dialectical wheel's spinning because capitalism has finally become a totalizing, global structure.

5. For a fuller exploration of the "cool hunting" in both the real world and Gibson's novel, see Lee Konstantinou's "The Brand as Cognitive Map in William Gibson's *Pattern Recognition*."

6. The Internet has only taken over this role as the predominate index or cognitive map of our globalized society in recent times. This role was previously held by television. Park Chan Wook's recent film *Oldboy* (2003) explores this capacity of television. In *Oldboy*, the main character Oh Dae-Su is locked for 15 years in a hotel room that functions as a space in which rich clients can pay to have people imprisoned for prescribed lengths of time. Despite his absence from the outside world, Oh Dae-Su continues to learn and follow the history of civilization by means of the television in the room. Oh Dae-Su's narration during his 15-year imprisonment in *Oldboy* provides an insightful reading of both the television and the Internet: "If you stand outside a phone booth on a rainy day and meet a man whose face is hidden by a violet umbrella, my advice is that you make friends with television. The television is both clock and calendar. It is your school, home, church, friend, and lover. But my lover's song is too short" (Scene 2). Oh Dae-Su makes this last statement as he is masturbating and watching a female pop singer, whose song climaxes prematurely before he manages to achieve a similar feat. Oh Dae-Su's complaint about his "lover's song" being overly brief depicts the one flaw of television that the Internet does not share: temporal constraint. His situation is similar to the one Paul Virilio discusses in *The Vision Machine* involving inmates' watching television in prison during his discussion of the private space's loss of autonomy: "The private sphere thus continues to lose its relative autonomy. The recent installation of TV sets in prisoners' cells rather than just in recreation rooms ought to have alerted us ... From now on, the inmates can *monitor actuality*, can observe television events—unless we turn around and point out that, as soon as viewers switch on their sets, it is they, prisoners or otherwise, who are in the field of television, a field in which they are obviously powerless to intervene" (64–5). Virilio here recognizes the power of the image and its ability to control the subject, for Virilio quotes the prisoner who states that watching television makes prison more difficult because the prisoners are allowed to witness

all the aspects of the world in which they are not allowed to take part. Virilio's concept of "imprisonment in the cathode-ray tube" almost directly evokes David Cronenberg's *Videodrome* (1983), and indeed the television controls our perceptions of reality through its portrayal of everything from politics to sexuality to its definition of "fun." As *Pattern Recognition* explains, the Internet operates in the same sphere as television because certain places, such as Brazil in the novel, make no real distinction between TV and Net culture (90). The Internet is thus the logical successor of the television. Virilio's discussion of the private sphere hearkens back to Jürgen Habermas's theorization of the public and the private sphere and their place in modernity versus postmodernity in *The Structural Transformation of the Public Sphere: An Inquiry into a Category of Bourgeois Society*.

7. The simulacrum, or the copy without an original, has remained an issue of philosophical angst and discussion since Plato's *Sophist*, but the term has taken on new significance with theorists of postmodern society and its various artforms.

8. Jameson is purposefully misquoting the final line of William Empson's poem "Missing Dates" (1940): "The waste remains, the waste remains and kills" (19).

9. Interestingly, "The Suffering Channel" also concerns the September 11th attacks. Unlike Gibson's novel, Jonathan Safran Foer's *Extremely Loud and Incredibly Close* (2005), or Don DeLillo's *Falling Man* (2007), the attacks function as an absence in the text. Instead of directly depicting the attacks or examining their aftermath, "The Suffering Channel" revolves around the lives of writers at a magazine company in the World Trade Center a month before the attacks take place. While the attacks are never mentioned explicitly, Wallace does make passing references to who will live or die on the day of the Towers' collapse. Furthermore, like *Pattern Recognition*, "The Suffering Channel" examines the place of art and its commodification in the global, postmodern marketplace. Wallace problematizes the status of postmodern art by means of Brint Moltke's ability to excrete works of art: part of the text centers around the debate over whether his feces represent true art (found art, moreover, for he does not craft them in any way) or if they are in actuality just "shit."

10. For Gunning's discussion of the cinema of attractions, see "An Aesthetic of Astonishment: Early Film and (In)Credulous Spectator" and "The Cinema of Attractions: Early Film, its Spectator, and the Avant-Garde." Also, see my discussion of Gunning and the cinema of attractions in chapter 4.

11. See Konstantinou's argument in the "Brand as Cognitive Map."

12. In *Technics and Civilization*, Lewis Mumford makes a similar claim about technology and its effects upon the social episteme when he states, "Behind all the great material inventions of the last century

and a half was not merely a long internal development of technics: there was also a change of mind. Before the new industrial processes could take hold on a great scale, a reorientation of wishes, habits, ideas, goals was necessary" (3). Mumford proceeds to display how the mechanization of human civilization changed the way human beings thought and acted: how the clock changed the way in which people ordered their day and their relation to time, how increased speed of transportation altered the way in which distance was perceived, etc. Mumford thus portrays how technological advancement requires fundamental changes in the functioning and perceptions of the subject and the ordering principles of society.

13. Deleuze takes the term "control" from William S. Burroughs's novels and essays. Indeed, control remained Burroughs's overriding theme of investigation throughout his body of work.

14. Giorgio Agamben makes some insightful observations about how power and politics change once biopolitical regimes have developed. For instance, as with Nazi Germany (the nightmarish extreme of biopolitics), biopolitics signals "the integration of medicine and politics" (143). Furthermore, biopolitics the fusion of police and politics—it implies the disappearance of the difference between two terms: "The *police* now becomes *politics*" (147).

15. With the publication of *Empire*, Antonio Negri and Michael Hardt believed they were rewriting Marx's *Grundrisse* for the postmodern age. The *Grundrisse* marks a turning point in Marx's writings from earlier works co-authored with Engels like *The German Ideology* and *Manifesto for the Communist Party,* to later works like *Das Kapital,* and many critics regard the *Grundrisse* as the notebooks or outline of *Kapital*. In *Empire*, *Multitude*, and *Commonwealth*, Hardt and Negri contend that global communication simultaneously leads to the instantiation of the control society and the inscription of a space in which a utopian democratic revolution can be enacted by means of the multitude created by such circuits of communication.

4 The Spectacle of Memory: Realism, Narrative, and Time Travel Cinema

1. This line is spoken by Alpha 60, the computer that runs the city in Jean-Luc Goddard's *Alphaville.*

2. See Henri Bergson's *Creative Evolution* 306. In this section, I am indebted to Gregory Flaxman's article "Cinema Year Zero" for help with explicating the connection between Deleuze and Bergson.

3. For such usages of the genre, see dystopian fiction and cinema like Aldous Huxley's *Brave New World* (1932); George Orwell's *Animal Farm* (1946) and *Nineteen Eighty-Four* (1949); Ray Bradbury's *Fahrenheit 451*(1953); Anthony Burgess's *A Clockwork Orange*

(1962) and *The Wanting Seed* (1962); Robert Heinlein's *Starship Troopers* (1959); William F. Nolan and George Clayton Johnson's *Logan's Run* (1967); George Lucas's *THX-1138* (1971); and Terry Gilliam's *Brazil* (1985).

4. The history of science fiction is replete with such examples beginning with one of the earliest sci-fi novels—Mary Shelley's *Frankenstein* (1818). The nineteenth century lays the groundwork for this plot archetype in the genre with the writings of Jules Verne and H. G. Wells. In particular, see H. G. Wells's *The Time Machine* (1895), *The Island of Dr. Moreau* (1896), and *The First Men in the Moon* (1901); and Jules Verne's *A Journey to the Center of the Earth* (1864), *From the Earth to the Moon* (1865), and *Twenty Thousand Leagues under the Sea* (1870).

5. For older examples of science fiction's reflections on the present, see the slew of 1950s and 1960s American and Japanese science fiction films that dealt with lingering fears from World War II and the ensuing Cold War: Robert Wise's *The Day the Earth Stood Still* (1951); Don Siegel's *The Invasion of the Body Snatchers* (1956); Gordon Douglas's *Them!* (1954); Ishirō Honda's *Gojira* (1954), more commonly known in the United States as *Godzilla*; William Cameron Menzies's *Invaders from Mars* (1953); Ray Milland's *Panic in Year Zero!* (1962); and Harry Horner's *Red Planet Mars* (1952). Other SF works explore the nature of political systems in general. See Isaac Asimov's *Foundation* (1951); Frank Herbert's *Dune* (1965); Robert Heinlein's *The Moon is a Harsh Mistress* (1966); and Kim Stanley Robinson's more recent "Mars Trilogy": *Red Mars* (1992), *Green Mars* (1993), and *Blue Mars* (1996).

6. The most classic example of the alternative present is no doubt Philip K. Dick's *The Man in the High Castle* (1962), which depicts an alternate Earth in which the Axis defeated the Allies in World War II and in which North America was consequently partitioned into Japanese and German zones. Such alternative histories have also increasingly proliferated in the works of non-SF authors. For examples, see Vladimir Nabokov's *Ada or Ardor: A Family Chronicle* (1969) and Philip Roth's *The Plot Against America* (2004).

7. Literature in general over the last two centuries is filled with fantastic tales of individuals experiencing temporal displacement. For early examples, see Washington Irving's "Rip Van Winkle" (1819); Mark Twain's *A Connecticut Yankee in King Arthur's Court* (1889); Charles Dickens' *A Christmas Carol* (1843); Edward Bellamy's *Looking Backward: 2000–1887* (1888); and H. G. Wells's *The Time Machine* (1895). For twentieth-century examples, see Robert Heinlein's "By His Bootstraps" (1941); Ray Bradbury's "A Sound of Thunder" (1952); Isaac Asimov's *The End of Eternity* (1955); Kurt Vonnegut's *Slaughterhouse-Five* (1969); and Octavia Butler's *Kindred* (1979) to

name only a few in the world of fiction. For a full study of the various scientific theories and literary depictions of time travel, see Paul J. Nahin's *Time Machines: Time Travel in Physics, Metaphysics, and Science Fiction.* Gary Westfahl, George Slusser, and David Leiby's *Worlds Enough and Time: Explorations of Time in Science Fiction and Fantasy* is also a useful anthology of articles on different depictions of time travel.

8. For a Méliès retrospective, see the DVD collection entitled *Georges Méliès: The First Wizard of Cinema (1896–1913).* For the Lumière brothers' films, see the DVD collection entitled *Landmarks of Early Cinema, Vol. 1.*

9. Despite the problematically racist content of *The Birth of the Nation*, Griffith remains one of the first great master craftsmen of narrative cinema. In particular, see his epic masterpieces: *The Birth of the Nation* (1915) and *Intolerance* (1916).

10. See von Trier's *Breaking the Waves* (1996), *The Idiots* (1998), *Dogville* (2003) and *Antichrist* (2009). Also, see von Trier's films that operate on the boundaries between science fiction, horror, and traditional realistic cinema: *The Element of Crime* (1984), *Epidemic* (1987), and *Europa* (1991). In addition, see Michael Haneke's *Benny's Video* (1992), *Funny Games* (1997), and *The Piano Teacher* (2001); Takashi Miike's *Audition* (1999), *Ichi the Killer* (2001), *Visitor Q* (2001), and *Gozu* (2003); and Park Chan Wook's "Revenge Trilogy": *Sympathy for Mr. Vengeance* (2002), *Oldboy* (2003), and *Lady Vengeance* (2005).

11. Hereafter, the abbreviation "*LJ*" will refer to the Criterion Collection DVD of Chris Marker's *La Jetée.* The subsequent numbers refer to the scene numbers on the DVD. Unless otherwise noted, the quotes from *La Jetée* are derived from the English dub of the film.

12. Zeno's paradoxes rest upon a fundamental illusion about infinity, for, as set theory teaches us, there are many levels of infinity, some of which can be traversed by Achilles and others that cannot be. As Aristotle responds to Zeno's paradox of Achilles and the tortoise in his *Physics*, "So when someone asks the question whether it is possible to traverse infinite things—either in time or in distance—we must reply that in a way it is but in a way it is not. For if they exist actually, it is not possible, but if potentially, it is; for someone in continuous movement has traversed infinite things incidentally, not without qualification; for it is incidental to the line to be infinitely many halves, but its essence and being are different" (§321). Again, as set theory teaches us, there are different orders of infinity, and Zeno's paradoxes represent a fundamental misconstruing of the nature of space and time. In *Matter and Memory*, trans. N. M. Paul and W. S. Palmer, Bergson refutes Zeno by explaining how time is not ultimately divisible into instants because motion is indivisible, and "this indivisibility of motion implies, then, the impossibility of real instants [...] The Arguments of

Zeno of Elea have no other origin than this illusion. They all consist in making time and movement coincide with the line which underlies them, in attributing to them the same subdivisions as to the line, in short, in treating them like the line" (190–1). This translation of Aristotle derives from G. S. Kirk, J. E. Raven, and M. Schofield's *The Presocractic Philosophers: A Critical History with a Selection of Texts*, which also collects all of the extant fragments and ancient discussions of Zeno. For the complete texts of Aristotle's *Physics*, see *The Complete Works of Aristotle: The Revised Oxford Translation*.

13. See scene 4 on the Criterion Collection DVD of the film.

14. When White discusses overemplotment, he is using the term to discuss the manner in which analysands overemplot certain moments from their past. Indeed, the analysand's experience of dream analysis during psychoanalysis provides a useful corollary here that will help to demonstrate the manner in which narrative functions as a synthesis of the chaotic manifold of sensory perceptions. In *The Interpretation of Dreams*, Freud explains that "to complete a dream-analysis" requires the act of a "dream-synthesis" (345). In other words, as Freud proceeds to explain, "When the whole mass of dream-thoughts is brought under the pressure of the dream-work, and its elements are turned about, broken into fragments and jammed together—almost like pack-ice— the question arises of what happens to the logical connections which have hitherto formed its framework [...] The restoration of the connections which the dream-work has destroyed is a task which has to be performed by the interpretive process" (Freud, *Dreams* 347). Thus, only through the interpretative process can a patient's dream achieve a state of narrative coherence. Of course, it would be a fallacy to directly equate the illogical nature of the dream experience to perceptions of everyday life, but a similar narrative act must constantly attend an individual's sensory impressions—only through the cohesive capacity of narrative can a person force unity upon the chaotic manifold. And memories of the distant past often take on the aura of dreams.

15. *Vertigo*'s scene takes place in a sequoia forest and features similar dialogue to the Man and Woman's interaction. Like *La Jetée*, *Vertigo* concerns the power that images from the past can continue to hold over an individual's life. The connections between *Vertigo* and *La Jetée* do not end with just these two films, for this scene in the Sequoia forest recurs in two subsequent films: Marker's own *Sans Soleil* and Terry Gilliam's *12 Monkeys*, which was inspired by *La Jetée*.

16. For Nietzsche's most profound statement of the eternal return of the same (or eternal recurrence), see §341 of *The Gay Science*. For some of Freud's theorization of the return of the repressed, a concept that crops up throughout his body of works, see the essays "Repression" and "The Unconscious," both of which are collected in *General Psychological Theory*.

17. Hereafter, the abbreviation "*P*" will refer to the film *Primer*, and the attending numbers will refer to scene numbers on the DVD.

18. For the original Russian Formalist usage of the terms, see Vladimir Propp's *Morphology of the Folktale* and Viktor Shklovsky's "The Relationship between Devices of Plot Construction and General Devices of Style" (1919) in *Theory of Prose*.

19. For a full discussion of ufology and alien encounters, see J. Allen Hynek's classic work of pseudo-science *The UFO Experience: A Scientific Inquiry* (1972).

CONCLUSION: BEYOND THE HUMAN: ONTOGENESIS, TECHNOLOGY, AND THE POSTHUMAN IN KUBRICK AND CLARKE'S *2001*

1. For some of the major conceptualizations of posthumanism, see Donna Haraway's *Simians, Cyborgs, and Women: The Reinvention of Nature* and *When Species Meet*; N. Katherine Hayles's *How We Became Posthuman: Virtual Bodies in Cybernetics, Literature, and Informatics* and *My Mother was a Computer: Digital Subjects and Literary Texts*; and Cary Wolfe's *What is Posthumanism?*

2. "The Sentinel" was written for a 1948 BBC competition in which it failed to place. Arthur C. Clarke wrote the screenplay of *2001: A Space Odyssey* together with Stanley Kubrick and simultaneously penned the full-length novel. He later wrote three sequels in his "Space Odyssey" series: *2010: Odyssey Two* (1982), *2061: Odyssey Three* (1987), and *3001: The Final Odyssey* (1997).

3. Clarke's novel places the man apes in Africa, and *3001: The Final Odyssey* reveals that Earth scientists ultimately unearthed a monolith in Africa.

4. The "Primeval Night" section of the novel only refers to it as "the slab," but the mysterious entity appears in a different form in Clarke's rendition. In the opening section of the novel, the monolith is transparent and even generates patterns of light that foreshadow the intergalactic journey through the Star Gate later in the novel/film.

5. As Carol Geduld points out, the choral music is actually the "unworldly music" of Gyorgy Ligeti (40). However, if one proves unfamiliar with the work of Ligeti, then the music could also easily represent sounds being emitted by the monolith. In fact, in the novel, the monolith makes screeching sounds and drumming noises that presage the later encounter with the monolith on the Moon.

6. See Friedrich Nietzsche's *Ecce Homo* "Why I am So Wise" §2.

7. Deleuze takes the phrase "relations of tension" from Nietzsche's collection of notebooks entitled *The Will to Power* §635. The ellipsis in this quote represents the citations in the original text.

8. In Clarke's novel, the monolith actually points toward Saturn, and *Discovery* merely uses the gravitational pull of Jupiter to slingshot itself and increase its velocity in order to reach Saturn more quickly.

9. In this chapter, the citation "*Odyssey*" refers to the film *2001: A Space Odyssey* and the numbers refer to the scenes on the DVD of the film.

10. *2010: Odyssey Two* (1982) and Peter Hyam's adaptation of the novel entitled *2010: The Year We Make Contact* (1984) both explain that Hal begins malfunctioning because his devotion to the crewmembers and his prime directive to provide them with knowledge conflicts with his mission directive that requires him to conceal the mission's true purpose from Dave and Frank. Because of this conflict, Hal becomes capable of harming a human, thus violating one of the Asimov's famous three rules. For Asimov's three laws of robotics, see his story collection *I, Robot* (1950) and the subsequent series of novels in the Robot universe, a universe that Asimov combines with his "Foundation Series" that began with *Foundation* (1951).

11. See Scene 24 on the DVD of *The Thing from Another World*.

12. While Kubrick's film never explains the nature of the star gate, Clarke's novel depicts it as a hyperspace gateway that transports Dave to points around the universe at almost instantaneous speeds.

13. Clarke's three sequels to *2001* actually depict the aliens' cultivation of life on Europa, one of the moons of Jupiter.

14. Kubrick's film does not feature the classic line, although the less-than-stellar sequel, *2010: The Year We Make Contact*, which of course was not a Kubrick film, makes copious use of the quote as the last transmission from Dave Bowman. Kubrick's film, unlike the novel, includes no dialogue after Hal's shutdown.

15. For Locke's discussion of the human mind as a *tabula rasa* or "blank slate," see his *An Essay Concerning Human Understanding*.

16. Kant defines the sublime in contradistinction to the beautiful: "The beautiful in nature concerns the form of the object, which consists in limitation; the sublime, by contrast, is to be found in a formless object insofar as limitlessness is represented in it" (*Judgment* §23).

BIBLIOGRAPHY

Abbott, H. Porter. *The Cambridge Companion to Narrative*. Cambridge: Cambridge UP, 2002. Print.

Abrams, Jerold J. *The Philosophy of Stanley Kubrick*. Lexington: UP of Kentucky, 2007. Print.

Acker, Kathy. *Don Quixote: Which Was a Dream*. New York: Grove, 1986. Print.

———. *Empire of the Senseless*. New York: Grove, 1988. Print.

Agamben, Giorgio. *Homo Sacer: Sovereign Power and Bare Life*. 1995. Trans. Daniel Heller-Roazen. Stanford: Stanford UP, 1998. Print.

Aldiss, Brian W. and David Wingrove. *Trillion Year Spree: The History of Science Fiction*. New York: Antheneum, 1986. Print.

Alterman, Peter S. "Samuel R. Delany." *Dictionary of Literary Biography* 8 (1981): 119–28. The Gale Group. Web. Mar 25, 2012.

Althusser, Louis. "Ideology and Ideological State Apparatuses." 1970. *Lenin and Philosophy and Other Essays*. New York: Monthly Review, 2001. 85–126. Print.

Andermahr, Sonya, Terry Lovell, and Carol Wolkowitz, eds. "Gender." *A Glossary of Feminist Theory*. London: Arnold, 2000. 102–4. Print.

Anger, Kenneth. *Inauguration of the Pleasure Dome*. 1954. *The Films of Kenneth Anger I*. Fantoma, 2006. DVD.

Anno, Hideaki, dir. *The End of Evangelion*. 1997. Manga Entertainment, 2002. DVD.

———. *Evangelion 1.11: You Are (Not) Alone*. 2007. Funimation, 2011. DVD.

———. *Evangelion 2.22: You Can (Not) Advance*. 2009. Funimation, 2011. DVD.

———. *Evangelion: Death and Rebirth*. 1997. Manga Entertainment, 2002. DVD.

———. *Neon Genesis Evangelion*. 26 episodes. 1995. *The Perfect Collection*. A. D. Vision, 2002. DVD.

Antonioni, Michelangelo, dir. *Blow-Up*. 1966. Turner, 2004. DVD.

Aristotle. *Physics. The Complete Works of Aristotle: The Revised Oxford Translation*. Ed. Jonathan Barnes. Vol. 1. Princeton, NJ: Princeton UP, 1984. 315–446. Print.

Aronofsky, Darren, dir. *π*. Artisan, 1998. DVD.

Asimov, Isaac. *The End of Eternity.* New York: Tor, 1955. Print.

———. *Foundation.* New York: Bantam, 1951. Print.

———. *I, Robot.* 1950. New York: Bantam, 1991. Print.

Atwood, Margaret. *The Handmaid's Tale.* New York: Anchor Books, 1985. Print.

Augé, Marc. *Non-Places: Introduction to an Anthropology of Supermodernity.* 1992. Trans. John Howe. London: Verso, 1995. Print.

Austin, J. L. *How to Do Things with Words.* 2nd Ed. Eds. J. O. Urmson and Marina Sbisà. Cambridge: Harvard UP, 1962. Print.

Ballard, J. G. *The Atrocity Exhibition.* 1969. Expanded and Annotated Edition. London: Harper Perennial, 1990. Print.

———. *The Burning World.* New York: Berkeley, 1964. Print.

———. *Crash.* New York: Picador, 1973. Print.

———. *Concrete Island.* New York: Picador, 1974. Print.

———. *The Crystal World.* New York: Farrar, Straus, & Giroux, 1966. Print.

———. *The Drowned World and the Wind from Nowhere.* Garden City: Doubleday, 1965. Print.

———. *High Rise.* London: Harper Perennial, 1975. Print.

———. *Running Wild.* New York: Farrar, Straus, & Giroux, 1988. Print.

Banerjee, Suparno. "*2001: A Space Odyssey*: A Transcendental Trans-locution." *Journal of the Fantastic in the Arts* 19.1 (2008): 39–50. Print.

Barbour, Douglas. *Worlds out of Words: The SF Novels of Samuel R. Delany.* Frome: Hunting Raven, 1979. Print.

Barth, John. *Giles Goat-Boy; or, The Revised New Syllabus.* Garden City: Doubleday, 1966. Print.

Barthes, Roland. *Camera Lucida: Reflections on Photography.* 1980. Trans. Richard Howard. New York: Hill and Wang, 1981. Print.

———. "Introduction to the Structural Analysis of Narratives." *Image—Music—Text.* Trans. Stephen Heath. New York: Hill and Wang, 1977. 79–124. Print.

Baudrillard, Jean. *Simulacra and Simulation.* 1981. Trans. Sheila Faria Glaser. Ann Arbor: U of Michigan P, 1994. Print.

———. *The Spirit of Terrorism and Other Essays.* Trans. Chris Turner. London: Verso, 2002. Print.

Bazin, André. "The Ontology of the Photographic Image." *What is Cinema? Vol. 1.* Trans. Hugh Gray. Berkeley: U of California P, 1967. 9–16. Print.

Bear, Greg. *Blood Music.* New York: Ace Books, 1985. Print.

De Beauvoir, Simone. *The Second Sex.* 1952. Trans. and ed. H. M. Parshley. New York: Vintage, 1989. Print.

Bellamy, Edward. *Looking Backward: 2000–1887.* 1888. Ed. Daniel H. Borus. Boston: Bedford Books, 1995. Print.

Benveniste, Emile. *Problems in General Linguistics.* Trans. Mary Elizabeth Meek. Coral Gables: U of Miami P, 1971. Print.

Bergson, Henri. *Creative Evolution.* 1911. Trans. Arthur Mitchell. Mineola: Dover, 1998. Print.

———. *Matter and Memory.* 1908. Trans. N. M. Paul and W. S. Palmer. New York: Zone Books, 1991. Print.

Bertolucci, Bernardo, dir. *The Spider's Stratagem.* 1970. New Yorker Video, 1998. VHS.

Blackford, Russell. "Jewels in Junk City: To Read *Triton.*" *Review of Contemporary Fiction* 16.3 (1996): 142–7. Print.

Blake, William. *The Marriage of Heaven and Hell.* 1790. *The Complete Poetry and Prose of William Blake.* Newly Revised Edition. Ed. David V. Erdman. New York: Anchor, 1988. Print.

Blomkamp, Neill, dir. *District 9.* Sony Pictures, 2009. DVD.

Bordwell, David. *Narration in the Fiction Film.* London: Routledge, 1985. Print.

Borges, Jorge Luis. "The Garden of Forking Paths." 1941. *Labyrinths: Selected Stories and Other Writings.* New York: New Directions, 1962. 19–29. Print.

Bourdieu, Pierre. *Outline of a Theory of Practice.* 1972. Trans. Richard Nice. Cambridge: Cambridge UP, 1977. Print.

Bradbury, Ray. *Fahrenheit 451.* 1953. New York: Random House, 2003. Print.

———. "A Sound of Thunder." *The Stories of Ray Bradbury.* 1952. New York: Everyman's Library, 2010. 231–40. Print.

Braunstein, Néstor. "Desire and Jouissance in the Teachings of Lacan." *The Cambridge Companion to Lacan.* Ed. Jean-Michel Rabaté. Cambridge: Cambridge UP, 2003. 102–15. Print.

Brecht, Bertold. *Brecht on Theatre: The Development of an Aesthetic.* Ed. and trans. John Willett. New York: Hill and Wang, 1957. Print.

Broderick, Mick. "Anime's Apocalypse: *Neon Genesis Evangelion* as Millenarian Mecha." *Intersections 7* (2002): 1–11. Print.

Brooks, Rodney A. *Flesh and Machines: How Robots Will Change Us.* New York: Vintage, 2002. Print.

Browning, Robert. "Pippa Passes." 1841. *Victorian Poetry and Poetics.* 2nd ed. Eds. Walter E. Houghton and G. Robert Stange. Boston: Houghton Mifflin, 1968. 171–93. Print.

Buchanan, Ian. "Space in the Age of Non-Place." *Deleuze and Space.* Eds. Ian Buchanan and Gregg Lambert. Toronto: U of Toronto P, 2005: 16–35. Print.

Bukatman, Scott. *Terminal Identity: The Virtual Subject in Postmodern Science Fiction.* Durham: Duke UP, 1993. Print.

Buñuel, Luis, dir. *L'Âge d'Or.* 1930. Screenplay by Salvador Dali and Luis Buñuel. Kino, 2004. DVD.

———. *Un chien Andalou.* 1929. Screenplay by Salvador Dali and Luis Buñuel. Transflux, 2004. DVD.

Burgess, Anthony. *A Clockwork Orange.* New York: Norton, 1962. Print.

———. *The Wanting Seed.* New York: Norton, 1962. Print.

Burroughs, William S. *Cities of the Red Night.* New York: Henry Holt, 1981. Print.

———. *Naked Lunch.* New York: Grove, 1959. Print.
———. *Nova Express.* New York: Grove, 1964. Print.
———. *The Place of Dead Roads.* New York: Henry Holt, 1983. Print.
———. *The Soft Machine.* New York: Grove, 1961. Print.
———. *The Ticket that Exploded.* New York: Grove, 1962. Print.
———. *The Western Lands.* New York: Penguin, 1987. Print.
———. *The Wild Boys: A Book of the Dead.* New York: Grove Press, 1971. Print.
Butler, Judith. *Bodies that Matter: On the Discursive Limits of "Sex."* New York: Routledge, 1993. Print.
———. *Excitable Speech: A Politics of the Performative.* New York: Routledge, 1997. Print.
———. *Gender Trouble: Feminism and the Subversion of Identity.* 1990. Tenth Anniversary Edition. New York: Routledge, 1999. Print.
———. *Giving an Account of Oneself.* New York: Fordham UP, 2005. Print.
———. *The Psychic Life of Power: Theories in Subjection.* Stanford: Stanford UP, 1997. Print.
———. *Subjects of Desire: Hegelian Reflections in Twentieth-Century France.* New York: Columbia UP, 1987. Print.
———. *Undoing Gender.* New York: Routledge, 2004. Print.
Butler, Octavia E. *Clay's Ark.* New York: Warner Books, 1984. Print.
———. *Kindred.* 1979. Boston: Beacon P, 2003. Print.
———. *Mind of My Mind.* New York: Warner Books, 1977. Print.
———. *Patternmaster.* New York: Warner Books, 1976. Print.
———. *Survivor.* New York: Signet, 1978. Print.
———. *Wild Seed.* New York: Warner Books, 1980. Print.
Butler, Samuel. *Erewhon: Or, Over the Range.* 1872. Eds. Hans-Peter Breuer and Daniel F. Howard. Newark: U of Delaware P, 1980. Print.
Cadigan, Pat. *Dervish is Digital.* New York: Tor, 2000. Print.
———. *Synners.* New York: Four Walls Eight Windows, 1991. Print.
———. *Tea from an Empty Cup.* New York: Tor, 1998. Print.
Calvino, Italo. *Cosmicomics.* 1965. Trans. William Weaver. New York: Harcourt Brace Jovanovich, 1976. Print.
———. *Invisible Cities.* 1972. Trans. William Weaver. New York: Harcourt Brace Jovanovich, 1974. Print.
Cameron, James, dir. *Avatar.* 20th Century Fox, 2009. DVD.
———. *The Terminator.* 1984. MGM, 2001. DVD.
Cantin, Lucie. "The Trauma of Language." *After Lacan: Clinical Practice and the Subject of the Unconscious.* Eds. Robert Hughes and Kareen Ror Malone. Albany: SUNY Press, 2002. 35–48. Print.
Carpenter, John, dir. *Escape from New York.* 1981. Special Edition. MGM, 2003. DVD.
———. *The Thing.* 1982. Universal, 2005. DVD.
Carruth, Shane, dir. *Primer.* 2004. New Line, 2005. DVD.
Caygill, Howard. *A Kant Dictionary.* Malden: Blackwell, 1995. Print.

De Certeau, Michel. *The Practice of Everyday Life*. Trans. Steven Rendall. Berkeley: U of California P, 1984. Print.

Chan, Edward. "(Vulgar) Identity Politics in Outer Space: Delany's *Triton* and the Heterotopian Narrative." *The Journal of Narrative Theory* 31.2 (Summer 2001): 180–213. Print.

Clarke, Arthur C. *2001: A Space Odyssey*. 1968. New York: ROC, 2000. Print.

———. *2010: Odyssey Two*. New York: Del Rey, 1982. Print.

———. *2061: Odyssey Three*. New York: Del Rey, 1987. Print.

———. *3001: The Final Odyssey*. New York: Del Rey, 1997. Print.

———. *Childhood's End*. New York: Del Rey, 1953. Print.

———. "The Sentinel." 1951. *The Collected Stories*. London: Victor Gollancz, 2000. 301–8. Print.

Coates, Paul. "Chris Marker and the Cinema as Time Machine." *Science Fiction Studies* 14.3 (1987): 307–15. Print.

Cronenberg, David, dir. *The Brood*. 1979. MGM, 2003. DVD.

———. *The Fly*. 1986. 20th Century Fox, 2005. DVD.

———. *Rabid*. Somerville House Releasing, 1976. DVD.

———. *Scanners*. 1981. MGM, 2001. DVD.

———. *Shivers*. 1975. Image Entertainment, 1998. DVD.

———. *Videodrome*. 1983. Universal Studios/The Criterion Collection, 2004. DVD.

Cuarón, Alfonso, dir. *Children of Men*. 2006. Universal, 2007. DVD.

Danielewski, Mark Z. *House of Leaves*. New York: Pantheon Books, 2000. Print.

Davidson, Guy. "Sexuality and the Statistical Imaginary in Samuel R. Delany's *Trouble on Triton*." *Queer Universes: Sexualities in Science Fiction*. Eds. Wendy Gay Pearson, Veronica Hollinger, and Joan Gordon. Liverpool: Liverpool UP, 2008. 101–20. Print.

Delany, Samuel R. "Afterword." 1990. *Stars in My Pockets Like Grains of Sand*. 1984. Twentieth Anniversary Edition. Middletown: Wesleyan UP, 2004. 349–56. Print.

———. "Aye, and Gomorrah." 1967. *Aye, and Gomorrah and Other Stories*. New York: Vintage, 2003. 91–101. Print.

———. *Dhalgren*. New York: Vintage, 1974. Print.

———. *Flight from Nevèrÿon*. Hanover: Wesleyan UP, 1985. Print.

———. *Neveryóna, or: The Tales of Signs and Cities*. Hanover: Wesleyan UP, 1983. Print.

———. *Nova*. New York: Vintage, 1968. Print.

———. *Return to Nevèrÿon*. Hanover: Wesleyan UP, 1987. Print.

———. "Science Fiction and Criticism: The *Diacritics* Interview." *Silent Interviews: On Language, Race, Sex, Science Fiction, and Some Comics*. Hanover: Wesleyan UP, 1994. 186–215. Print.

———. "The Second *Science Fiction Studies* Interview: Of *Trouble on Triton* and Other Matters." *Shorter Views: Queer Thoughts & the Politics of the Paraliterary*. Hanover: Wesleyan UP, 1999. 315–49. Print.

————. *Tales of Nevèrÿon*. Hanover: Wesleyan UP, 1979. Print.

————. *The Tides of Lust*. New York: Lancer Books, 1973. Print.

————. *Trouble on Triton: An Ambiguous Heterotopia*. Middletown: Wesleyan UP, 1976. Print.

Deleuze, Gilles. *Cinema 1: The Movement-Image*. 1983. Trans. Hugh Tomlinson and Barbara Habberjam. Minneapolis: U of Minnesota P, 1986. Print.

————. *Cinema 2: The Time-Image*. 1985. Trans. Hugh Tomlinson and Robert Galeta. Minneapolis: U of Minnesota P, 1989. Print.

————. "Control and Becoming." Interview with Antonio Negri. 1990. *Negotiations 1972–1990*. Trans. Martin Joughin. New York: Columbia UP, 1995. 169–176. Print.

————. *Difference and Repetition*. 1968. Trans. Paul Patton. New York: Columbia UP, 1994. Print.

————. *Foucault*. 1986. Trans. Seán Hand. Minneapolis: U of Minnesota P, 1988. Print.

————. "Immanence: A Life." 1995. *Pure Immanence: Essays on a Life*. Trans. Anne Boyman. New York: Zone, 2002. Print. 25–33.

————. *Nietzsche and Philosophy*. 1962. Trans. Hugh Tomlinson. New York: Columbia UP, 1983. Print.

————. "Postscript on Control Societies." 1990. *Negotiations, 1972–1990*. Trans. Martin Joughin. New York: Columbia UP, 1995. 177–82. Print.

————. "Schizophrenia and Society." 1975. *Two Regimes of Madness: Texts and Interviews 1975–1995*. Ed. David Lapoujade. Trans. Ames Hodges and Mike Taormina. New York: Semiotext(e), 2006. 17–29. Print.

————. "What is the Creative Act?" 1987. *Two Regimes of Madness: Texts and Interviews 1975–1995*. Ed. David Lapoujade. Trans. Ames Hodges and Mike Taormina. New York: Semiotext(e), 2006. 312–24. Print.

Deleuze, Gilles and Félix Guattari. *Anti-Oedipus: Capitalism and Schizophrenia*. 1972. Trans. Robert Hurley, Mark Seem, and Helen R. Lane. Minneapolis: U of Minnesota P, 1983. Print.

————. *A Thousand Plateaus: Capitalism and Schizophrenia*. 1980. Trans. Brian Massumi. Minneapolis: U of Minnesota P, 1987. Print.

————. *What is Philosophy?* 1991. Trans. Hugh Tomlinson and Graham Burchell. New York: Columbia UP, 1994. Print.

DeLillo, Don. *Falling Man*. New York: Scribner, 2007.

————. *White Noise: Text and Criticism*. 1985. New York: Penguin, 1998. Print.

Deodato, Ruggero, dir. *Cannibal Holocaust*. 1980. Deluxe Collector's Edition. VIP Media and Grindhouse Releasing, 2006. DVD.

Derrida, Jacques. "Signature, Event, Context." 1972. *Limited Inc.* Ed. Gerald Graff. Evanston: Northwestern UP, 1988. 1–23. Print.

————. *Specters of Marx: The State of the Debt, the Work of Mourning, and the New International*. 1993. Trans. Peggy Kamuf. New York: Routledge, 1994. Print.

Descartes, René. *Meditations on First Philosophy*. 1641, 1644. *Meditations and Other Metaphysical Writings*. Trans. Desmond M. Clarke. New York: Penguin, 1998. 3–104. Print.

Dick, Philip K. *Do Androids Dream of Electric Sheep?* New York: Del Rey, 1968. Print.

———. *The Man in the High Castle*. New York: Vintage, 1962. Print.

Dickens, Charles. *A Christmas Carol*. 1843. *A Christmas Carol and Other Christmas Writings*. Ed. Michael Slater. New York: Penguin, 2003. 27–118. Print.

Docherty, Thomas. "The Ethics of Alterity." 1996. *Postmodern Literary Theory: An Anthology*. Ed. Niall Lucy. Oxford: Blackwell, 2000. 140–8. Print.

Douglas, Gordon, dir. *Them!* 1954. Warner Home Video, 2002. DVD.

Emmerich, Roland, dir. *Independence Day*. 1996. 20th Century Fox, 2003. DVD.

Empson, William. "Missing Dates." 1940. *The Norton Anthology of Modern Poetry*. 2nd ed. Eds. Richard Ellmann and Robert O'Clair. New York: Norton, 1988. 731–2. Print.

Esposito, Roberto. *Bíos: Biopolitics and Philosophy*. 2004. Trans. Timothy Campbell. Minneapolis: U of Minnesota P, 2008. Print.

Evans, Dylan. *An Introductory Dictionary of Lacanian Psychoanalysis*. New York: Routledge, 1996. Print.

Falsetto, Mario. *Stanley Kubrick: A Narrative and Stylistic Analysis*. 2nd ed. Westport: Praeger, 2001. Print.

Fisher, William. "Of Living Machines and Living-Machines: *Blade Runner* and the Terminal Genre." *New Literary History* 20.1 (1988): 187–98. Print.

Flaxman, Gregory. "Cinema Year Zero." *The Brain and the Screen: Deleuze and the Philosophy of Cinema*. Ed. Gregory Flaxman. Minneapolis: U of Minnesota P, 2000. 87–108. Print.

Foer, Jonathan Safran. *Extremely Loud and Incredibly Close*. New York: Mariner, 2005.

Foucault, Michel. "Different Spaces." 1966. *Essential Writings of Foucault 1954–1984 Volume 2: Aesthetics, Method, and Epistemology*. Ed. James D. Faubion. Series ed. Paul Rabinow. Trans. Robert Hurley and others. New York: New P, 2000. 175–86. Print.

———. *Discipline and Punish: The Birth of the Prison*. 1975. Trans. Alan Sheridan. New York: Vintage, 1977. Print.

———. *The History of Sexuality Volume I: An Introduction*. 1978. Trans. Robert Hurley. New York: Vintage, 1990. Print.

———. *The Order of Things: An Archaeology of the Human Sciences*. 1966. New York: Vintage, 1970. Print.

———. "Truth and Juridical Forms." 1973. *Essential Writings of Foucault 1954–1984 Volume 3: Power*. Ed. James D. Faubion. Series ed. Paul Rabinow. Trans. Robert Hurley and others. New York: New P, 2000. 1–89. Print.

Fox, Robert Elliot. "The Politics of Desire in Delany's *Triton* and *The Tides of Lust.*" *Black American Literature Forum* 18.2 (1984): 49–56. Print.

Freedman, Carl. *Critical Theory and Science Fiction.* Hanover: Wesleyan UP, 2000. Print.

Freud, Sigmund. *Beyond the Pleasure Principle.* 1920. Trans. and ed. James Strachey. New York: Norton, 1961. Print.

———. *Civilization and its Discontents.* 1930. Trans. and ed. James Strachey. New York: Norton, 1961. Print.

———. *The Interpretation of Dreams.* 1899. Trans. and ed. James Strachey. New York: Avon, 1965. Print.

———. "Repression." 1915. *General Psychological Theory.* Ed. Philip Rieff. New York: Touchstone, 1963. 104–15. Print.

———. *The Uncanny.* 1919. Trans. David McLintock. New York: Penguin, 2003.

———. "The Unconscious." 1915. *General Psychological Theory.* Ed. Philip Rieff. New York: Touchstone, 1963. 116–50. Print.

Fry, Carrol L. "From Technology to Transcendence: Humanity's Evolutionary Journey in *2001: A Space Odyssey,*" *Extrapolation* 44.3 (Fall 2003): 331–43. Print.

Fukuyama, Francis. *The End of History and the Last Man.* New York: Avon, 1992.

Geduld, Carolyn. *Filmguide to 2001: A Space Odyssey.* Bloomington: Indiana UP, 1973. Print.

Gibson, William. *All Tomorrow's Parties.* New York: Ace Books, 1999. Print.

———. *Count Zero.* New York: Ace Books, 1986. Print.

———. *Idoru.* New York: Berkley Books, 1996. Print.

———. *Mona Lisa Overdrive.* New York: Bantam Books, 1988. Print.

———. *Neuromancer.* New York: Ace Books, 1984. Print.

———. *Pattern Recognition.* New York: Berkeley Books, 2003. Print.

———. *Spook Country.* New York: G. P. Putnam's Sons, 2007. Print.

———. *Virtual Light.* New York: Bantam Books, 1993. Print.

———. *Zero History.* New York: G. P. Putnam's Sons, 2010. Print.

Gilliam, Terry, dir. *12 Monkeys.* 1995. Universal, 2005. DVD.

———. *Brazil.* 1985. The Criterion Collection Box Set Edition. Universal Pictures/The Criterion Collection, 1999. DVD.

Godard, Jean-Luc, dir. *Alphaville.* 1965. Janus Films/Home Vision Cinema/The Criterion Collection, 1998. DVD.

———. *Weekend.* 1967. New Yorker Video, 2005. DVD.

Govan, Sandra Y. "Samuel R. Delany." *Dictionary of Literary Biography* 33 (1984). The Gale Group, 1984. 52–9. Web. Mar 3, 2012.

Gramsci, Antonio. *Selections from the Prison Notebooks.* Ed. and trans. Quintin Hoare and Geoffrey Nowell Smith. New York: International, 1971. Print.

Griffith, D. W. *The Birth of a Nation.* 1915. Image Entertainment, 1998. DVD.

———. *Intolerance.* 1916. Kino, 2002. DVD.

BIBLIOGRAPHY ❖ 215

Gunning, Tom. "An Aesthetic of Astonishment: Early Film and (In) Credulous Spectators." *Viewing Positions: Ways of Seeing Film.* Ed. Linda Williams. New Brunswick: Rutgers UP, 1997. 114–33. Print.

———. "The Cinema of Attractions: Early Film, its Spectator, and the Avant-Garde." *Early Cinema: Space, Frame, Narrative.* Eds. Thomas Elsaesser and Adam Barker. London: BFI Publishing, 1990. 56–62. Print.

Habermas, Jürgen. *The Structural Transformation of the Public Sphere: An Inquiry into a Category of Bourgeois Society.* 1962. Trans. Thomas Burger and Frederick Lawrence. Cambridge: MIT P, 1989. Print.

Haneke, Michael, dir. *Benny's Video.* 1992. Kino, 2006. DVD.

———. *Funny Games.* 1997. Kino, 2006. DVD.

———. *The Piano Teacher.* 2001. Kino, 2002. DVD.

Haraway, Donna J. *Simians, Cyborgs, and Women: The Reinvention of Nature.* New York: Routledge, 1991. Print.

———. *When Species Meet.* Minneapolis: U of Minnesota P, 2007. Print.

Hardt, Michael and Antonio Negri. *Commonwealth.* Cambridge: Belknap Press, 2009. Print.

———. *Empire.* Cambridge: Harvard UP, 2000. Print.

———. *Multitude: War and Democracy in the Age of Empire.* New York: Penguin, 2004. Print.

Hayles, N. Katherine. "Computing the Human." *Theory, Culture & Society* 22 (2005): 131–51. Print.

———. "*How We Became Posthuman*: Ten Years on an Interview with N. Katherine Hayles." By Arthur Piper. *Paragraph* 33.3 (2010): 318–330. Print.

———. *How We Became Posthuman: Virtual Bodies in Cybernetics, Literature, and Informatics.* Chicago: U of Chicago P, 1999. Print.

———. *My Mother Was a Computer: Digital Subjects and Literary Texts.* Chicago: U of Chicago P, 2005. Print.

Heath, Stephen. "Translator's Note." *Image—Music—Text.* By Roland Barthes. New York: Hill and Wang, 1977. 7–11. Print.

Hegel, Georg Wilhelm Friedrich. *Phenomenology of Spirit.* 1807. Trans. A. V. Miller. Oxford: Oxford UP, 1977. Print.

Heinlein, Robert. "By His Bootstraps." 1941. *The Menace from Earth.* 1959. New York: Baen Books, 1987. Print.

———. *The Moon is a Harsh Mistress.* New York: Orb, 1966. Print.

———. *Starship Troopers.* New York: Ace, 1959. Print.

Herbert, Frank. *Dune.* 1965. New York: Berkeley Publishing, 1977. Print.

Herzog, Werner, dir. *Fitzcarraldo.* 1982. Anchor Bay, 2002. DVD.

Hitchcock, Alfred, dir. *Vertigo.* 1958. Universal, 1999. DVD.

Holliday, Valerie. "Delany Dispossessed." *Extrapolation* 44.4 (2003): 425–36. Print.

Hollinger, Veronica. "Stories About the Future: From Patterns to Expectations in *Pattern Recognition*." *Science Fiction Studies* 33.3 (Fall 2006): 452–72. Print.

The Holy Bible: King James Version. The New Open Bible Study Edition. Nashville: Thomas Nelson Publishers, 1990. Print.

Honda, Ishirō, dir. *Gojira*. 1954. Master Collection Edition. Toho, 2004. DVD.

Horkheimer, Max and Theodor W. Adorno. *Dialectic of Enlightment: Philosophical Fragments*. Ed. Gunzelin Schmid Noerr. Tran. Edmund Jephcott. Stanford: Stanford UP, 2002. Print.

Horner, Harry, dir. *Red Planet Mars*. 1952. DVD. Unite States: Cheezy Flicks, 2006.

Hurley, Kelly. "Reading Like an Alien: Posthuman Identity in Ridley Scott's *Alien* and David Cronenberg's *Rabid*." *Posthuman Bodies*. Eds. Judith Halberstram and Ira Livingston. Bloomington: Indiana UP, 1995. 203–24. Print.

Huxley, Aldous. *Brave New World*. New York: HarperPerennial, 1932. Print.

Hyams, Peter, dir. *2010: The Year We Make Contact*. 1984. Warner, 2000. DVD.

Hyneck, J. Allen. *The UFO Experience: A Scientific Inquiry*. New York: Marlow, 1972. Print.

Irving, Washington. "Rip Van Winkle." 1819. *The Complete Tales of Washington Irving*. New York: Da Capo P, 1998. 1–16. Print.

Jameson, Fredric. *Archaeologies of the Future: The Desire Called Utopia and Other Science Fictions*. London: Verso, 2005. Print.

———. "Fear and Loathing in Globalization." *New Left Review* 23 (2003): 105–14. Rpt. in *Archaeologies of the Future: The Desire Called Utopia and Other Science Fictions*. London: Verso, 2005. 384–92. Print.

———. *The Geopolitical Aesthetic: Cinema and Space in the World System*. Bloomington: Indiana UP, 1992. Print.

———. *Postmodernism, or, the Cultural Logic of Late Capitalism*. Durham: Duke UP, 1991. Print.

———. "Progress versus Utopia, or, Can We Imagine the Future?" *Science Fiction Studies* 27 (1982): 147–58. Rpt. in *Archaeologies of the Future: The Desire Called Utopia and Other Science Fictions*. London: Verso, 2005. 281–95. Print.

Jeter, K. W. *Noir*. New York: Bantam, 1998. Print.

Kafka, Franz. "In the Penal Colony." 1919. *The Complete Stories*. Ed. Nahum N. Glazer. Trans. Willa and Edwin Muir. New York: Shocken, 1971. 140–67. Print.

———. *The Metamorphosis*. 1915. *The Complete Stories*. Ed. Nahum N. Glazer. Trans. Willa and Edwin Muir. New York: Shocken, 1971. 89–139. Print.

Kamiyama, Kenji, dir. *Ghost in the Shell: Stand Alone Complex*. 26 episodes. Production I. G., 2003–4. DVD.

Kant, Immanuel. *Critique of the Power of Judgment*. 1790, 1793. Ed. Paul Guyer. Trans. Paul Guyer and Eric Matthews. Cambridge: Cambridge UP, 2000. Print.

———. *Critique of Pure Reason.* 1781, 1787. Trans. and ed. Paul Guyer and Allen W. Wood. Cambridge: Cambridge UP, 1998. Print.

———. *On the Form and Principles of the Sensible and Intelligible World [Inaugural Dissertation].* 1770. *Theoretical Philosophy 1755–1770.* Trans. and ed. David Walford. Cambridge: Cambridge UP, 1992. 373–416. Print.

Kermode, Frank. The *Sense of an Ending: Studies in the Theory of Fiction with a New Epilogue.* 1966. Oxford: Oxford UP, 2000. Print.

Kirk, G. S., J. E. Raven, and M. Schofield. *The Presocratic Philosophers: A Critical History with a Selection of Texts.* 2nd ed. Cambridge, UK: Cambridge UP, 1983.

Klossowski, Pierre. *Nietzsche and the Vicious Circle.* 1969. Trans. Daniel W. Smith. Chicago: Chicago UP, 1997. Print.

Kojève, Alexandre. *Introduction to the Reading of Hegel: Lectures on the Phenomenology of Spirit.* Ed. Allan Bloom. Trans. James H. Nichols, Jr. Ithaca: Cornell UP, 1969. Print.

Konstantinou, Lee. "The Brand as Cognitive Map in William Gibson's *Pattern Recognition.*" *Boundary 2* 36.2 (2009): 67–97. Print.

Kracauer, Siegfried. *Theory of Film: The Redemption of Physical Reality.* Princeton: Princeton UP, 1960. Print.

Kristeva, Julia. *Power of Horror: An Essay on Abjection.* Trans. Leion S. Roudiez. New York: Columbia UP, 1982. Print.

Kuberski, Phillip. "Kubrick's *Odyssey*: Myth, Technology, Gnosis." *The Arizona Quarterly* 64.3 (2008): 51–73. Print.

Kubrick, Stanley, dir. *2001: A Space Odyssey.* 1968. Turner, 2001. DVD.

———. *A Clockwork Orange.* 1971. Warner, 1999. DVD.

———. *Dr. Strangelove or, How I Learned to Stop Worrying and Love the Bomb.* 1963. Columbia Tristar, 1999. DVD.

———. *The Shining.* 1980. Warner, 1999. DVD.

Lacan, Jacques. "The Instance of the Letter in the Unconscious, Or Reason Since Freud." *Écrits: The First Complete Edition in English.* 1970. Trans. Bruce Fink. New York: Norton, 2006. 412–41. Print.

———. *The Seminar of Jacques Lacan Book I: Freud's Papers on Technique 1953–1954.* 1975. Ed. Jacques-Alain Miller. Trans. John Forrester. New York: Norton, 1988. Print.

———. *The Seminar of Jacques Lacan Book II: The Ego in Freud's Theory and in the Technique of Psychoanalysis, 1954–1955.* Ed. Jacques-Alain Miller. Trans. Sylvania Tomaselli. New York: Norton, 1988. Print.

———. *The Seminar of Jacques Lacan Book III: The Psychoses 1955–1956.* 1981. Ed. Jacques-Alain Miller. Trans. Russell Grigg. New York: Norton, 1993. Print.

———. *The Seminar of Jacques Lacan Book VII: The Ethics of Psychoanalysis.* 1986. Ed. Jacques-Alain Miller. Trans. Dennis Porter. New York: Norton, 1992. Print.

———. *The Seminar of Jacques Lacan Book XI: The Four Fundamental Concepts of Psychoanalysis.* Ed. Jacques-Alain Miller. Trans. Alan Sheridan. New York: Norton, 1977. Print.

————. *The Seminar of Jacques Lacan Book XX Encore 1972–1973: On Feminine Sexuality, The Limits of Love and Knowledge.* 1975. Ed. Jacques-Alain Miller. Trans. Bruce Fink. New York: Norton, 1998. Print.

————. "The Signification of the Phallus." *Écrits: The First Complete Edition in English.* Trans. Bruce Fink. New York: Norton, 2006. 575–84. Print.

Lambert, Gregg and Gregory Flaxman. "Five Propositions on the Brain." *Journal of Neuro-Aesthetic Theory* 2.2 (2000–2002). Web. Mar 25, 2012.

De Lauretis, Teresa. *Technologies of Gender: Essays on Theory, Film, and Fiction.* Bloomington: Indiana UP, 1987. Print.

Léger, Fernand and Dudley Murphy, dirs. *Ballet Mécanique.* 1924. *Avant-garde: Experimental Cinema 1920s and '30s.* Kino, 2005. DVD.

Le Guin, Ursula K. *The Dispossessed.* New York : HarperPerennial, 1974. Print.

————. *The Left Hand of Darkness.* New York: Ace Books, 1969. Print.

————. "The Ones Who Walk Away from Omelas." 1973. *The Wind's Twelve Quarters.* New York: Perennial, 1975. 275–84. Print.

Lem, Stanislaw. *Solaris.* 1961. Trans. Joanna Kilmartin and Steve Cox. San Diego: Harcourt, 1970. Print.

Leonard, Andrew. "Nodal Point: Interview with William Gibson." *Salon. com.* Feb 13, 2003. Web. Mar 25, 2012.

Lethem, Jonathan. *The Fortress of Solitude.* New York: Doubleday, 2003. Print.

Livingston, Jennie, dir. *Paris is Burning.* Buena Vista, 1990. DVD.

Locke, John. *An Essay Concerning Human Understanding.* 1689. Cambridge: Oxford UP, 1979. Print.

Lopate, Philip. "*Solaris* Liner Notes." 1992. *Solaris.* The Criterion Collection, 2002. DVD.

López-Gallego, Gonzalo, dir. *Apollo 18.* Weinstein Company and Anchor Bay, 2011. DVD.

Lucas, George, dir. *THX 1138: The George Lucas Director's Cut.* 1971. Warner, 2004. DVD.

Lukács, Georg. *History and Class Consciousness: Studies in Marxist Dialectics.* 1968. Trans. Rodney Livingstone. Cambridge: MIT P, 1971. Print.

Lumière, August, Louis Lumière, Thomas Edison, et al., dir. *Landmarks of Early Cinema, Vol. 1.* Image Entertainment, 1997. DVD.

Lyotard, Jean-Francois. *The Postmodern Condition: A Report on Knowledge.* 1979. Trans. Geoff Bennington and Brian Massumi. Minneapolis: U of Minnesota P, 1984. Print.

Takayama, Hideki, dir. *Urotsukidōji: Legend of the Overfiend.* 1989. Anime 18, 1992. DVD.

Mainar, Luis M. García. *Narrative and Stylistic Patterns in the Films of Stanley Kubrick.* Rochester: Camden House, 1999. Print.

Marker, Chris, dir. *La Jetée.* 1962. *La Jetée and Sans Soleil: Two Films by Chris Marker.* Janus Films/The Criterion Collection, 2007. DVD.

————. *Sans Soleil.* 1983. *La Jetée and Sans Soleil: Two Films by Chris Marker.* Janus Films/The Criterion Collection, 2007. DVD.

Marx, Karl. *Capital: A Critique of Political Economy Volume I.* Trans. Ben Fowkes. New York: Penguin, 1976. Print.

———. *A Contribution to a Critique of Political Economy.* 1859. Trans. Rodney Livingstone and Gregor Benton. New York: Penguin, 1974. 424–9. Print.

———. *Grundrisse: Foundations of the Critique of Political Economy.* New York: Penguin, 1993. Print.

Marx, Karl and Friedrich Engels. "Manifesto of the Communist Party." 1848. *The Marx-Engels Reader.* 2nd ed. Ed. Robert C. Tucker. New York and London: Norton, 1978. 469–500. Print.

———. *The German Ideology.* Eastford: Martino Fine Books, 2011. Print.

McHale, Brian. *Postmodernist Fiction.* London: Routledge, 1987. Print.

McKeon, Michael. *The Origins of the English Novel 1600–1740.* Fifteenth Anniversary Edition. Baltimore: Johns Hopkins UP, 2002. Print.

McLuhan, Marshall and Quentin Fiore. *The Medium is the Massage: An Inventory of Effects.* Produced by Jerome Agel. Corte Madera: Gingko P, 1967. Print.

Méliès, Georges, dir. *A Trip to the Moon.* 1902. *Georges Méliès: The First Wizard of Cinema (1896–1913).* Flicker Alley, 2008. DVD.

Menzies, William Cameron, dir. *Invaders from Mars.* 1953. Fiftieth Anniversary Special Edition. Image Entertainment, 2002. DVD.

Michaels, Walter Benn. *The Shape of the Signifier: 1967 to the End of History.* Princeton: Princeton UP, 2004. Print.

Miike, Takashi, dir. *Audition.* 1999. Lion's Gate, 2005. DVD.

———. *Gozu.* 2003. Pathfinder Home Entertainment, 2004. DVD.

———. *Ichi the Killer.* 2001. Media Blasters, 2003. DVD.

———. *Visitor Q.* 2001. Tokyo Shock, 2002. DVD.

Milland, Ray, dir. *Panic in Year Zero.* 1962. *Midnight Movies Double Feature: Panic in Year Zero and The Last Man on Earth.* DVD. Santa Monica, CA: MGM Home Entertainment, 2005: Disc 1.

Miller, George, dir. *Mad Max.* 1979. MGM, 2002. DVD.

———. *The Road Warrior.* 1982. Warner, 1997. DVD.

More, Sir Thomas. *Utopia.* 1516. New York: Norton, 1991. Print.

Moylan, Tom. "Beyond Negation: The Critical Utopias of Ursula K. Le Guin and Samuel R. Delany." *Extrapolation* 21.3 (1980): 236–53. Print.

———. *Demand the Impossible: Science Fiction and the Utopian Imagination.* New York: Methuen, 1986. Print.

Mumford, Lewis. *Technics and Civilization.* San Diego: Harcourt Brace, 1934. Print.

Myrick, Daniel and Eduardo Sánchez, dirs. *The Blair Witch Project.* Lionsgate, 1999. DVD.

Nabokov, Vladimir. *Ada, or Ardor: A Family Chronicle.* New York: Vintage, 1969. Print.

Nahin, Paul J. *Time Machines: Time Travel in Physics, Metaphysics, and Science Fiction.* New York: American Institute of Physics, 1993. Print.

Napier, Susan J. *Anime from Akira to Princess Mononoke: Experiencing Contemporary Japanese Animation.* New York: Palgrave, 2001. Print.

——. "When the Machines Stop: Fantasy, Reality, and Terminal Identity in *Neon Genesis Evangelion* and *Serial Experiments Lain.*" *Science Fiction Studies* 29 (2002): 418–35. Print.

Newitz, Annalee. "Magical Girls and Atomic Bomb Sperm: Japanese Animation in America." *Film Quarterly* 4.1 (1995): 2–15. Print.

Nietzsche, Friedrich. *Ecce Homo.* 1908. *On the Genealogy of Morals and Ecce Homo.* Trans. Walter Kaufmann and R. J. Hollingdale. New York: Vintage, 1967. 199–344. Print.

——. *The Gay Science: With a Prelude in German Rhymes and an Appendix of Songs.* 1882, 1887. Ed. Bernard Williams. Trans. Josefine Nauckhoff and Adrian Del Caro. Cambridge: Cambridge UP, 2001. Print.

——. *On the Genealogy of Morals.* 1887. *On the Genealogy of Morals and Ecce Homo.* Trans. Walter Kaufmann and R. J. Hollingdale. New York: Vintage, 1967. 1–198. Print.

——. *Thus Spoke Zarathustra: A Book for None and All.* 1883–92. Trans. Walter Kaufmann. New York: Penguin, 1954. Print.

——. *The Will to Power.* Trans. Walter Kaufmann and R. J. Hollingdale. Ed. Walter Kaufmann. New York: Vintage, 1967. Print.

Nolan, William F. and George Clayton Johnson. *Logan's Run.* New York: Bantam, 1976.

Nyby, Christian, dir. *The Thing from Another World.* 1951. Turner, 2003. DVD.

Oakley, Ann. *Sex, Gender, and Society.* London: Temple-Smith, 1972. Print.

Orbaugh, Sharalyn. "Sex and the Single Cyborg: Japanese Popular Culture Experiments in Subjectivity." *Science Fiction Studies* 29 (2002): 436–52. Print.

Orwell, George. *Animal Farm.* New York: Signet, 1946. Print.

——. *Nineteen Eighty-Four.* 1949. Centennial Edition. New York: Plume/ Harcourt Brace, 2003. Print.

Oshii, Mamoru, dir. *Ghost in the Shell.* 1995. Manga Entertainment, 1996. DVD.

——. *Ghost in the Shell 2: Innocence.* Dreamworks Video, 2004. DVD.

Osunsanmi, Olatunde, dir. *The Fourth Kind.* 2009. Universal, 2010. DVD.

Otomo, Katsuhiro. *Akira.* 1985–6. 6 vols. Trans. Yoko Umezawa and Jo Duffy. Milwaukie: Dark Horse Comics, 2001. Print.

Otomo, Katsuhiro, dir. *Akira.* 1988. Special Edition. Pioneer, 2000. DVD.

Pakula, Alan J, dir. *All the President's Men.* 1976. Warner, 1997. DVD.

——. *Klute.* 1971. Turner, 2002. DVD.

——. *The Parallax View.* 1974. Paramount, 1999. DVD.

De Palma, Brian, dir. *Blow Out.* 1981. MGM, 2001. DVD.

Peli, Oren, dir. *Paranormal Activity.* 2007. Paramount, 2009. DVD.

Penley, Constance. "Time Travel, Primal Scene, and the Critical Dystopia." *Close Encounters: Film, Feminism, and Science Fiction.* Ed. Constance Penley. Minneapolis: U of Minnesota P, 1991. 63–80. Rpt. in *Liquid Metal: The Science Fiction Film Reader.* Ed. Sean Redmond. London: Wallflower P, 2004. 126–35. Print.

Perry, Elizabeth M. and Rosemary A. Joyce. "Past Performance: The Archaeology of Gender Influenced by the Work of Judith Butler." *Butler Matters: Judith Butler's Impact on Feminist and Queer Studies.* Eds. Margaret Sönser Breen and Warren J. Blumenfeld. Hampshire: Ashgate, 2005. 113–26. Print.

Piercy, Marge. *Woman on the Edge of Time.* New York: Fawcett Books, 1976. Print.

Plato. *The Republic.* Trans. Allan Bloom. United States: Basic Books, 1968. Print.

———. *Sophist. The Collected Dialogues.* Trans. F. M. Cornford. Eds. Edith Hamilton and Huntington Cairnes. Princeton: Princeton UP, 1961. 957–1017. Print.

Poe, Edgar Allan. "The Black Cat." 1843. *The Fall of the House of Usher and Other Writings.* New York: Penguin, 2003. Print.

Pollack, Sydney, dir. *Three Days of the Condor.* 1975. Paramount, 1999. DVD.

Propp, Vladimir. *Morphology of the Folktale.* 1928. 2nd ed. Ed. Louis A. Wagner. Trans. Laurence Scott. Austin: U of Texas P, 1968. Print.

Pynchon, Thomas. *Against the Day.* New York: Penguin, 2006. Print.

———. *The Crying of Lot 49.* New York: HarperPerennial, 1965. Print.

———. *Gravity's Rainbow.* New York: Penguin, 1973. Print.

———. *Mason & Dixon.* New York: Henry Holt, 1997. Print.

———. *V.* New York: Harper and Row, 1961. Print.

Rabelais, Francois. *Gargantua and Pantagruel.* Trans. Burton Raffel. New York and London: Norton, 1990. Print.

Ramis, Harold, dir. *Groundhog Day.* 1993. Sony, 2002. DVD.

Rapatzikou, Tatiani G. "Authorial Identity in the Era of Electronic Technologies." *Authorship in Context: From the Theoretical to the Material.* Eds. Kyriaki Hadjiafxendi and Polina Mackay. New York: Palgrave Macmillan, 2007. 145–62. Print.

Rasmussen, Randy. *Stanley Kubrick: Seven Films Analyzed.* Jefferson: McFarland, 2001. Print.

Reeves, Matt, dir. *Cloverfield.* Paramount, 2008. DVD.

Rhodes, Gary D. "Believing is Seeing: Surveillance and *2001: A Space Odyssey.*" *Stanley Kubrick: Essays on His Films and Legacy.* Jefferson: McFarland, 2008. 94–104. Print.

Ricoeur, Paul. "Narrated Time." *Philosophy Today* 29.4 (Winter 1985): 259–72. Print.

———. *Oneself as Another.* 1990. Trans. Kathleen Blamey. Chicago: U of Chicago P, 1992. Print.

———. *Time and Narrative*. 3 vols. 1983–5. Trans Kathleen McLaughlin and David Pellauer. Chicago: U of Chicago P, 1984–8. Print.

Del Rio, Elena. "The Remaking of 'La Jetée's' Time-Travel Narrative: 'Twelve Monkeys' and the Rhetoric of Absolute Visibility." *Science Fiction Studies* 28.3 (2001): 383–98. Print.

Robinson, Kim Stanley. *Blue Mars*. New York: Bantam, 1996. Print.

———. *Green Mars*. New York: Bantam, 1994. Print.

———. *Red Mars*. New York: Bantam, 1993. Print.

Rodowick, D. N. *Gilles Deleuze's Time Machine*. Durham: Duke UP, 1997. Print.

———. "An Elegy for Theory." *October* 122 (Fall 2007): 91–109. Rpt. in *The Film Theory Reader: Debates and Arguments*. Ed. Marc Furstenau. London: Routledge, 2010. 23–37. Print.

Rogan, Alcena Madeline Davis. "Alien Sex Acts in Feminist Science Fiction: Heuristic Models for Thinking a Feminist Future of Desire." *PMLA* 119.3 (2004): 442–56. Print.

Ross, Andrew. *Strange Weather: Culture, Science, and Technology in the Age of Limits*. London: Verso, 1991. Print.

Roth, Philip. *The Plot Against America*. New York: Vintage, 2004. Print.

Rucker, Rudy. *The Ware Tetralogy*. Gaithersburg: Prime Books, 2010. Print.

Russ, Joanna. *The Female Man*. Boston: Beacon, 1975. Print.

"Samuel R. Delany." *Contemporary Authors Online*. Thomas Gale, 2006. Web. Mar 25, 2012.

Sartre, Jean-Paul. *Being and Nothingness: A Phenomenological Essay on Ontology*. 1943. Trans. Hazel E. Barnes. New York: Washington Square P, 1956. Print.

———. *Existentialism Is a Humanism*. 1945. Trans. Carol Macomber. New Haven: Yale UP, 2007. Print.

De Saussure, Ferdinand. *Course in General Linguistics*. Eds. Charles Bally and Albert Sechehaye. Trans. Wade Baskin. New York: McGraw-Hill, 1959. Print.

Schaffner, Franlkin, dir. *The Planet of the Apes*. 1968. The Legacy Collection. 20th Century Fox, 2006. DVD.

Scott, Ridley, dir. *Alien*. 1979. *Alien Quadrilogy*. 20th Century Fox, 2003. Discs 1–2. DVD.

———. *Blade Runner: The Director's Cut*. 1982. Warner, 1999. DVD.

Seerin, Declan. *Deleuze and Ricoeur: Disavowed Affinities and the Narrative Self*. London: Continuum, 2009. Print.

Shakespeare, William. *The Tragedy of Hamlet Prince of Denmark*. Ed. Edward Hubler. New York: Signet, 1963. Print.

Shaviro, Steven. *Connected, or, What It Means to Live in the Network Society*. Minneapolis: U of Minnesota P, 2003. Print.

Shelley, Mary. *Frankenstein; or, The Modern Prometheus*. 1818. New York: Penguin, 2003. Print.

Shirley, John. *A Song Called Youth*. Gaithersburg: Prime Books, 2012. Print.

Shirow, Masamune. *Ghost in the Shell*. 1991. Trans. Frederick Schodt and Toren Smith. Milwaukie: Dark Horse Comics, 1995. Print.

Shklovsky, Viktor.."Art as Device." 1917. *Theory of Prose*. 1929. Trans. Benjamin Sher. Normal: Dalkey Archive P, 1990. 1–14. Print.

———. "The Relationship between Devices of Plot Construction and General Devices of Style." 1919. *Theory of Prose*. 1929. Trans. Benjamin Sher. Normal: Dalkey Archive P, 1990. 15–51. Print.

Siegel, Don, dir. *Invasion of the Body Snatchers*. 1956. Republic Pictures, 1998. DVD.

Silvio, Carl. "Refiguring the Radical Cyborg in Mamoru Oshii's *Ghost in the Shell*." *Science Fiction Studies* 26 (1999): 54–72. Print.

Slusser, George and Daniele Chatelain. "Spacetime Geometries: Time Travel and the Modern Geometrical Narrative." *Science Fiction Studies* 22.2 (July 1995): 161–86. Print.

Smith, Daniel. "Deleuze and the Question of Desire: Toward an Immanent Theory of Ethics." *Parrhesia* 2 (2007): 66–78. Web. May 1, 2012.

Sofia, Zoe. "Exterminating Fetuses: Abortion, Disarmament, and the Sexo-Semiotics of Extra-Terrestrialism." *Diacritics* 14 (2) (1984): 47–59. Print.

Standish, Isolde. "*Akira*, Postmodernism, and Resistance." *Liquid Metal: The Science Fiction Film Reader*. Ed. Sean Redmond. London: Wallflower, 2004. 249–59. Print.

Stephenson, Neal. *The Confusion*. New York: William Morrow, 2004. Print.

———. *Cryptonomicon*. New York: Harper Perennial, 1999. Print.

———. *The Diamond Age or, A Young Lady's Illustrated Primer*. New York: Dell, 1995. Print.

———. *Quicksilver*. New York: HarperCollins, 2003. Print.

———. *Reamde*. New York: William Morrow, 2011. Print.

———. *Snow Crash*. New York: Bantam Books, 1992. Print.

———. *The System of the World*. New York: William Morrow, 2004. Print.

Sterling, Bruce. *Islands in the Net*. New York: Ace Books, 1989. Print.

———. "Preface." *Burning Chrome*. New York: HarperCollins, 1986. xi–xiv. Print.

———. *Schismatrix Plus*. 1985. New York: Ace Books, 1996. Print.

Stewart, Garrett. *Framed Time: Toward a Postfilmic Cinema*. Chicago: U of Chicago P, 2007. Print.

Stoehr, Kevin L. "*2001*: A Philosophical Odyssey." *The Philosophy of Science Fiction*. Ed. Steven M. Sanders. Lexington: UP of Kentucky, 2008. 199–33. Print.

Stoller, Robert J. *Sex and Gender: On Masculinity and Femininity*. New York: Science House, 1968. Print.

Strauss, Johann. *An der schönen blauen Donau*, Op. 314. 1866. *Best of Waltzes and Polkas*. Perm. Vienna Philharmonic. Deutsche Grammophon, 1999. Disc 1. CD.

Strauss, Richard. *Also Sprach Zarathustra*, Op. 30. 1896. *Richard Strauss: Orchestral Works*. Perm. The Berlin Philharmonic. Decca, 2011. Disc 1. CD.

Strugatsky, Boris and Arkady Strugatsky. *Roadside Picnic*. London: Victor Gollancz, 1972. Print.

Suvin, Darko. *Metamorphoses of Science Fiction: On the Poetics and History of a Literary Genre*. New Haven: Yale UP, 1979. Print.

Swift, Jonathan. *Gulliver's Travels*. 1726, 1735. New York: Penguin, 2003. Print.

Tarkovsky, Andrei, dir. *Solaris*. 1972. The Criterion Collection, 2002. DVD.

———. *Stalker*. 1979. Kino, 2006. DVD.

Todorov, Tzvetan. *The Fantastic: A Structural Approach to a Literary Genre*. 1970. Trans. Richard Howard. Ithaca: Cornell UP, 1973. Print.

Von Trier, Lars, dir. *Antichrist*. Denmark: Zentropa, 2009. DVD.

———. *Breaking the Waves*. 1996. Artisan, 2000. DVD.

———. *Dogville*. 2003. Lions Gate, 2004. DVD.

———. *The Element of Crime*. 1984. Nordisk Film/Criterion Collection, 2000. DVD.

———. *Epidemic*. 1987. Home Vision/Zentropa, 2004. DVD.

———. *Europa*. 1991. Zentropa/Criterion Collection, 2008. DVD.

———. *The Idiots*. 1998. Tartan, 1999. DVD.

Tucker, Jeffrey Allen. *A Sense of Wonder: Samuel R. Delany, Race, Identity, and Difference*. Middletown: Wesleyan UP, 2004. Print.

Twain, Mark. *A Connecticut Yankee in King Arthur's Court*. 1889. New York: Penguin, 1972. Print.

Verne, Jules. *From the Earth to the Moon*. 1865. United States: CreateSpace, 2011. Print.

———. *Journey to the Center of the Earth*. 1864. New York: Signet, 2003. Print.

———. *Twenty Thousand Leagues Under the Sea*. 1870. New York: Vintage, 2011. Print.

Virilio, Paul. *The Vision Machine*. 1988. Trans. Julie Rose. Bloomington and Indianapolis: Indiana UP, 1994.

Vonnegut, Kurt. *Slaughterhouse-Five, or, The Children's Crusade: A Dance with Death*. 1968. New York: Dell, 1988. Print.

Wackowski, Andy and Lana Wachowski, dir. *The Matrix*. Warner, 1999. DVD.

Wai, Wong Kar, dir. *2046*. 2004. Sony Picture Classics, 2006. DVD.

Wallace, David Foster. *Infinite Jest*. Boston: Little Brown and Co., 1996. Print.

———. "The Suffering Channel." *Oblivion*. New York: Back Bay, 2004. 238–329. Print.

Watt, Ian. *The Rise of the Novel*. Berkeley: U of California P, 1957. Print.

Wegner, Leonard. "Recognizing the Patterns." *New Literary History: A Journal of Theory and Interpretation* 38.1 (Winter 2007): 183–200. Print.

Welles, Orson, dir. *The Lady from Shanghai*. 1947. United States: Sony, 2000. DVD.

Wells, H. G. *The First Men in the Moon*. 1901. New York: Penguin, 2005. Print.

———. *The Island of Dr. Moreau*. 1896. New York: Penguin, 2005. Print.

———. *The Time Machine*. 1895. New York: Penguin, 2005. Print.

Westfahl, Gary, George Slusser, and David Leiby, eds. *Worlds Enough and Time: Explorations of Time in Science Fiction and Fantasy*. Westport: Greenwood Press, 2002. Print.

Wheat, Leonard F. *Kubrick's 2001: A Triple Allegory*. Lanham: Scarecrow P, 2000. Print.

White, Hayden. "The Historical Text as Literary Artifact." *Tropics of Discourse: Essays in Cultural Criticism*. Baltimore: Johns Hopkins UP, 1978. 81–100. Print.

———. "The Value of Narrative in the Representation of Reality." *The Content of the Form: Narrative Discourse and Historical Representation*. Baltimore: Johns Hopkins UP, 1987. 1–25. Print.

Wise, Robert. *The Day the Earth Stood Still*. 1951. 20th Century Fox, 2002. DVD.

Wolfe, Cary. *What is Posthumanism?* Minneapolis: U of Minnesota P, 2010. Print.

Wook, Park Chan. *Lady Vengeance*. 2005. Tartan Video, 2006. DVD.

———. *Oldboy*. 2003. Ultimate Collector's Edition. Tartan Video, 2006. DVD.

———. *Sympathy for Mr. Vengeance*. 2002. Tartan Video, 2005. DVD.

Yuen, Wong Kin. "On the Edge of Spaces: *Blade Runner, Ghost in the Shell*, and the Hong Kong Cityscape." *Science Fictions Studies* 27.1 (2000): 1–21. Rpt. in *Liquid Metal: The Science Fiction Film Reader*. Ed. Sean Redmond. New York: Wallflower P, 2004. 98–111. Print.

Zamyatin, Yevgeny. *We*. 1932. Trans. Clarence Brown. New York: Penguin, 1993. Print.

Žižek, Slavoj. *Looking Awry: An Introduction to Jacques Lacan Through Popular Culture*. Cambridge: MIT P, 1991. Print.

———. *Welcome to the Desert of the Real!: Five Essays on September 11 and Related Dates*. London: Verso, 2002. Print.

———. "You May!" *The London Review of Books* 21.6 (18 Mar 1999): 3–6. Web. Mar 25, 2012.

INDEX

Bad Conscience 172
Ballard, J.G 100
Barth, John 6, 191n3
Barthes, Roland 22, 73, 137
Base and Superstructure 21, 67, 196n3
Baudrillard, Jean 106–7, 111, 122
Bazin, Andre 158
Bear, Greg 197n15
De Beauvoir, Simone 38
Becoming 11, 44, 74, 88, 93, 119, 129, 147, 165, 167–73, 177, 182, 185–6, 188–90, 195n1
Being vs. Doing 38–40, 61–2, 170
Belief 2, 10–11, 13, 17–18, 48, 60, 66–7, 137, 142, 150–1
Bellamy, Edward 202
Benny's Video 203n10
Bentham, Jeremy 181
Benveniste, Emile 192n13
Bergson, Henri 129–30, 201n2, 203n12
Berlin Wall 106
Bertolluci, Bernardo 150
Bigfoot 160
Binarisms 34–6, 38–9, 42–6, 48, 56–8, 62, 140
Biology 26, 34–5, 38, 46–7, 86, 171, 194n9, 197n15
Biopolitics 121–2, 201n14
Biopower 121, 172
"Black Cat, The" 6
Blade Runner 68–9, 77, 197n10, 197n12
The Blair Witch Project 158–9
Blake, William 75–6
Blood Music 197n15
Blow-Out 103
Blow-Up 103
Blue Mars 202n5
Body, The 28, 33, 35, 39, 49, 53, 60, 68–84, 86–8, 91, 93–5, 100, 110, 170–1, 184–6, 188–9, 195n13, 197n15
Body Horror 71–2, 196n8

Body Without Organs 74, 76, 80, 82, 87, 94–5, 184–6, 188
Bordwell, David 150
Bourdieu, Pierre 191n6
Bradbury, Ray 201n3, 202n7
Brand Names 103, 110–11
Brave New World 17, 201n3
Brazil 201n3
Breaking the Waves 203n10
Brecht, Bertold 14–15, 17
Bricolage 145
Brood, The 196n8
Brooks, Rodney 180
Brown, Charles Brockden 6
Browning, Robert 84
Buchanan, Ian 11
Bukatman, Scott 113
Buñuel, Luis 192n8
Burgess, Anthony 201n3
Burning World, The 100
Burroughs, William S. vii–viii, 113, 157, 191n3, 196n8, 201n13
Butler, Judith 26, 33, 38–44, 49, 52–3, 59–60, 63, 194n7
Butler, Octavia 197n15, 202n7
Butler, Samuel 17
"By His Bootstraps" 143

Cadigan, Pat 196n5
Calculus 25, 57
Calvino, Italo 6, 191n3
Cameron, James 143, 157
Cannibal Holocaust 159
Capitalism 17–18, 67, 70, 103, 106, 109–11, 114, 116–17, 123, 127–8, 176, 193n1, 198n4
Carpenter, John 196n8
Cartesian Dualism 170
Castration 65
Causality 23, 151, 153
Cell Phones 102, 126
Central Intelligence Agency (C.I.A.) 104, 106
De Certeau, Michel 7–8, 62, 122, 191n6

Printed in the United States of America